HE WILL KILL YOU

An absolutely gripping crime thriller with a massive twist

CHARLIE GALLAGHER

Published 2019 by Joffe Books, London.

www.joffebooks.com

ISBN-13: 978-1-78931-086-3

Author's Note

There is a strong theme of domestic violence throughout this book. Some scenes describe actions that are brutal, inexcusable and shocking, and may be harrowing or traumatic to read.

They are based on unequivocal fact. Two out of three murder victims in the UK are killed by an intimate partner. Most victims of domestic violence take years to seek help, if at all.

This book carries a message: if you recognise even a small part of your situation or yourself in these pages, any part of it, then know that you don't have to suffer it; you don't have to live it. You're worth so much more.

Tell someone. Tell the police or a mate or one of the many excellent domestic violence charities that can easily be found on the internet or whoever you can.

Get yourself safe.

I am inspired by what I do and see in my day job as a front-line police detective, though my books are entirely fictional. I am aware that the police officers in my novels are not always shown positively. They are human and they make mistakes. This is sometimes the case in real life too, but the vast majority of officers are honest and do a good job in trying circumstances. From what I see on a daily basis, the men and women who wear the uniform are among the very finest, and I am proud to be part of one of the best police forces in the world.

Charlie Gallagher

Chapter 1

Noon Monday

Christine Lang stepped out of the house, gripping her young son tightly. Her husband, Scott, followed her out, still yelling, despite them moving beyond the confines of their home.

'Why can't we talk about this?' he bawled. 'Whenever we try and talk, you just run away! Just like now!'

Christine tugged open the rear door of their hatchback. It bumped off her shoulder as she slid Ethan into his baby seat. Ethan wriggled and scowled at his new surroundings. He was usually good in the car and they had used a car ride to settle him down more times than she could remember over the previous six months. Today, it was her husband who was doing the wailing and she was running late.

'Look, Scott, I'm out of time. I'll drop Ethan at my mum's for the afternoon so you can get on with some work. I need to get going. I'm not running away from anything.'

'But you acted like I was being unreasonable! I just need some time to work. I've been running around all morning doing your chores and now I need to work!'

'Yes, Scott. And so do I. And I'm going to be late. If you'd told me your schedule a little earlier I might have been able to plan something. As it is, I've upset my mum's day as well as my own. But you have your peace and quiet.' She pushed the rear door shut and moved around to the driver's side.

'Fine! I *will* have Ethan for the afternoon! I wouldn't want to upset your precious mother!' Scott tore the door back open. He dipped his head into the back. Christine stood in her open door, sighed and folded her arms. She was so tired. All they seemed to do these days was fight. It was always the same outcome, too.

They were both tired. All they had been told throughout her pregnancy was how much of a blessing it was, how it was going to make their little family complete. He truly was a blessing too, she loved him to his very bones, but complete their family? Right now she felt she was holding it together at the seams. She watched Scott bending over Ethan, cooing at him. Scott didn't hide stress well and she could see the colour running to his face. He was a tall man and he had stooped to get into the back of the car. The clasp on the seat was fiddly; you had to have the knack. Scott had never been able to do it since they had bought the thing. She watched Ethan's tiny hand reach up and push into Scott's mouth. She stifled a laugh. She was almost past being stressed now. What was the point? It didn't get them anywhere.

Scott was still struggling with the clasp. He was starting to get very angry. 'Stupid thing! Stupid THING!'

Ethan made the noise he did just before he cried.

'Shouting in his face won't help the situation, Scott. You need to be calm to undo that seat. Just pulling on it won't do it. Press the red button.'

'I . . .' He stopped himself. She saw him take a deep breath. He backed out of the car and straightened to stare at her over the top of the car. 'I am *pressing* the red button.'

Christine rubbed her eyes and sighed. 'Look, Scott, what are we doing? We're yelling at each other on the drive. Let's just not be those people. I'm not upset at you — I know you have a lot to do right now. We should have planned out how this week looked. Now I'm back to work, it's going to be a bit more difficult, but we'll sort it. I'll take him to my mum's. She's expecting him now and it's no big deal. You have four hours. Make the most of it!' She tried a grin.

Scott's whole body was tensed; he looked like he was ready for a fight, certainly like he was expecting one. He relaxed. His shoulders slunk forward in unison. He smiled back. It looked weak and tired. Last night had been worse than usual for sleep. Poor Ethan was teething. They knew he was in pain, it had to be horrible for the little fella — but it was hell for them too. In truth it had been nearly two weeks since their last reasonable sleep. Something had to give and right now it was their combined patience.

'I can't get him out of the damned seat anyway!' His grin got wider.

'Outwitted by a child seat!' She chuckled.

Scott pushed the rear door shut. 'Right, then. Go away. I've only got three hours, fifty-nine minutes now.' He walked round the car to peck her on the lips. When he trudged back towards the house she could almost see the relief ebbing off him. He was in battered old slippers, board shorts and a cosy hoody. If he had any sense he would nap first. Hell, he would nap for the whole four hours. She felt more than just a pang of jealousy as she pulled off the drive.

Christine worked the late shift in a care home — permanent lates for now. Between them they had decided that this was the best way to work childcare. Scott was a self-employed architect. He worked from home. He hadn't been self-employed for long. Had they known what a baby would mean, he would probably have stayed with his old firm, where he was paid a regular pay cheque for regular hours.

Christine checked her mirror — angled so that she could see Ethan in the back. He hadn't cried. He seemed to settle down with the movement of the car. Soon he would be asleep.

She turned right, joining one of the main roads out of the seaside town of Langthorne. She was in a stream of traffic and chose the lane to head for the motorway. Her mother lived in Dover and her place of work was on the outskirts of the same town. It was a fifteen-minute deviation and she was due to start work in ten. She was beyond caring about that too.

As she moved onto the motorway, her vision blurred a little with a yawn. She heard Ethan giggle. She had no idea what he might find amusing lying on his back staring at the roof. Her heavy eyes flicked to the mirror again and she felt herself smile; there was surely no better sound. The Roundhill Tunnels approached. The motorway was on stilts at this point, suspended high over the North Downs area of outstanding natural beauty. She could see long-haired cattle grazing on the wild grasses far below. In front of her was a huge, grass-topped mound of earth, shaped like a giant dome. The tunnels were cut crudely through it. Her tyres thumped on a grate as she entered its darkness. Immediately she could see brake lights trailing off in front of her. She applied her own brakes. The car slowed. The tunnels weren't long, maybe two hundred metres. They weren't quite straight either, she could see daylight framed in the oval exit ahead and off to the right. Orange strip lights ran along the ceiling and on the curved walls. She had to bring the car to a complete stop. The road was down to two lanes at this point, and both were at a standstill. She checked her side mirror; the traffic was already backed up behind her as far as she could see. She was about halfway through. She sighed and pulled out her phone to check for any traffic updates.

'Ah, dammit!' Her phone was dead. She remembered taking it off charge at 2 a.m. to play some soothing noises for Ethan. Sometimes that worked. It hadn't last night. She must have forgotten to charge it back up. She looked ahead. There was still a row of brake lights. Movement caught her eye. A figure was walking down the middle of the two lanes. The walk looked masculine, albeit with a slight limp. He wore a dark, hooded top and the hood was pulled up. His head was fixed, as if all his attention was straight ahead. His feet followed the central lines. *Why would someone be walking back along a motorway?* He had come from further ahead and he must have seen what was causing the blockage. She whirred her window down. She would ask him what was going on. He was getting closer. He seemed to slow his pace and was around ten cars in front of her, walking past a red car, his head twisted towards it. He stopped near the rear and he stooped down. He seemed to be feeling around under the boot area. Then he stood up and walked away, his pace noticeably quicker, his limp more pronounced as a result. He was on her quickly. Her window was still open — he was going to walk right past.

'Excuse me!' she said.

His face was slightly turned away. She could just make out a nose and lips protruding out from the hood. He didn't acknowledge her. He strode right past.

She leant out. She considered shouting after him, but he obviously wasn't in a mood to answer. She shrugged. She checked his progress in the mirror. His head moved; it turned to the right as if he was looking through her rear window. Then he stopped close to the rear of their car. He turned side on and then he was gone. She thought maybe he had walked behind her car. She turned to look through the back window and saw movement again. The man appeared like he had got up from crouching behind her boot. He stepped back into the middle of the road, his hand pushed into his hip, his limp worse still. She looked back in her side mirror where she could see he was walking away, his pace still hurried. Suddenly he broke into a clumsy run. Her attention was snatched towards a roll of thunder that seemed to be coming from some distance in front. It was close enough for her to feel the vibrations through the road beneath her. She saw car doors pushing open in front. Some people stood in them, their arms hooked over the metal. Others pushed the doors shut and stepped away from their cars. All of them were staring forwards, towards the oval shaped glimpse of daylight.

Christine's eyes dropped to the armrest. Sometimes there was a cable in there, where she could charge her phone. There was no time to search, her attention snatched back to a huge noise, just like the first but closer. Only this time she knew it wasn't thunder.

The explosion ripped through the tunnel with a mighty roar. Her car rocked on its suspension and bits of something thudded and pinged all around her. Through her open window she could hear the sound of glass bursting and falling over the floor. She ducked down instinctively, her ears suddenly flashed with pain and the noise that had been deafening was suddenly muffled, as if it was being filtered through a stack of pillows. When her car's front window shattered suddenly, it happened in near silence. The red car that was ten ahead was now engulfed in flame and thick black smoke rolled upwards and outwards as it caught under the concrete arch. It swept back towards her like an incessant wave. The cars that had been around it all seemed to be a little further away and turned at angles, as if the red car had pushed out for a bit of room. She could see more doors opening. A man fell out onto his knees from the car in front of her. He clutched at his face then started stumbling back towards her before the dust cloud consumed him. Her mind cleared. There had been two explosions: one much further up and then a car much closer — the red one, where she had seen the man kneeling down. Her eyes flared open. She spun in her seat. Ethan's hands were straight up, his fists clenched as if he was crying. *The man had knelt down next to her car too!*

They had to get out.

She unclipped her belt and pushed the door. The dust and smoke was already piling in through the window but now it surrounded her like a thick, grey blanket. Instantly she couldn't breathe. She sucked in a deep breath so she could hold it in, but all she got was a lungful of black, putrid smoke and she coughed immediately. She made it to the back door, yanked it open and leant in. The car was filling quickly with smoke and Ethan's face was scrunched up in a cry — she could just about hear it. She told him it was going to be okay. She could hear her own voice louder than anything else. Her hands stumbled over the red button on his belt. There was a knack, she knew it; you had to do it one-handed and you had to be calm. Her hand was shaking so hard she could barely find the button. She forced herself to pause and rubbed Ethan's cheek with her free hand as a way of soothing them both. They needed to get out. It needed to be now.

She steadied her fingers and felt the central button push in. The straps should have snapped out either side. She tugged them; one side came free, the other didn't. She was tugging it at an angle; she knew you needed to pull it out straight. She focused. She couldn't hold her breath much longer. She coughed and it boomed inside her head. Ethan was still crying. Then the belt came away and she pushed her arm underneath him, scooped him out and pulled him close to her. She felt the door bang into her back. She was aware of people running past her car, away from the one that was burning. She started to run in the same direction but collided with someone and was struck in the side — hard enough to send her sprawling to the ground. She used one arm to cushion her fall, the other to hold Ethan tightly to her chest, managing to keep him from touching the ground. She looked across, under her own car. There were fewer people on the other side. She could cut across and out. Her eye was drawn to a brick-sized package towards the rear wheel. It had a smiley face drawn on it. Underneath was the word: *Boom!* Christine froze for just an instant then she scrambled to her feet. They had to go!

She ran towards the entrance with her head down. She needed air but it was still thick with smoke. Breathing it in was agony. She heard another roar that felt like it was just behind her. She kept running until she felt something strike her between her shoulder blades — hard enough to force the breath out of her in a coarse moan. Her right arm was stinging too, and her legs felt like they might give out. Her head wouldn't lift but she strained to see the curved roof where smoke was being sucked out into the daylight. It wasn't far now. She set her sights on it and kept moving. She knew she was slowing up; her legs were getting heavier as if she was wading through water.

She made it to the entrance and the light came all at once. She was now surrounded by people: some bent double, choking and spluttering; others laid out flat on their backs. Someone stepped towards her through the light. They reached out for Ethan. She let them take him. She could feel her strength seeping away and she needed him to be safe. A voice broke through the cloth over her ears.

'Oh, my God!' it said, 'Are you okay?'

Then the bright light was gone.

Chapter 2

Chief Inspector Julian Lowe collapsed into his chair. The radio was busy, officers cutting in over each other. He ignored his mobile phone: a major incident had been declared and they didn't know what they were facing right now. It had the potential to be anything from a vehicle fire to a terrorist attack. Multiple reports were coming in, many of them contradictory. He needed to get away from his desk and out onto the ground — that was the only way he was going to make sense of it all. There was a knock at the door, something he couldn't ignore.

'Come in!'

Jane Long stepped in. She was the uniform inspector covering the response teams for the division, a tall, slim woman who seemed to hang awkwardly on her frame. Her cheeks were flushed. She had a reputation for flapping at the littlest thing. Today was not the littlest thing.

'Julian! What's all this about then?' She perched on the chair opposite. 'I'm like a blue-arse fly out there!'

'We all are. We have everyone either at the scene or directed towards it. I've put the word out. We've declared a major incident so we'll get all the resources we need, including the Counter Terrorism response.'

'Are CT going to run with it?' She rocked forward, seemingly enthused by the idea. That would mean someone other than her making decisions. CT was funded separately from local policing and had its own leadership team who would certainly trump them both in a situation such as this.

'It looks that way. I think they'll have to. They're on their way here.'

'Nothing's confirmed, though.' Jane's tone was a little desperate. 'It's just an explosion in a tunnel on the surface of it.'

'I think it's a little more than that. One of the victims reckons she saw someone put something under a car just before it exploded.'

'I've got everyone who is wearing a uniform tucked up with this job somehow . . . scene preservation . . . out at the hospitals . . . witness statements — you name it.'

'There's nothing more you can do, then. You've responded, as is your role, and now you need to let those with the resources take up the slack.'

'You're right.' She stood up. She seemed to have a little more spring as she did so. 'I assume your people are all involved too?' While Jane managed the patrol teams, Julian was responsible for the investigatory side of the business.

'We've released everyone who is available.'

Jane made it to the door. She seemed like she had ticked off whatever reason she had for coming in there in the first place. 'Oh, I do still have one officer working elsewhere . . . Vince Arnold. He was out doing some work with one of your CID lot. I could call him back in?'

Julian considered this for a second. 'I know about that. They're working a specific operation. I think we're covered. We need to start taking people away rather than pushing more at this job. You know what it's like . . . the

CT lot will just turn up and start using whoever is there. It might make sense to hold back what we can. I'd leave that job running.'

Jane nodded. 'Okay, that makes sense. I'll do as you said.' She stepped out.

'Of course you will,' he said to the closed door. He looked down at his phone. It had barely stopped ringing the whole time. He sighed. It was time to start talking to people again.

* * *

The bell above his shop door thumped rather than rang these days. It had been a ring once — a cheerful noise, announcing an opportunity walking in off the street. Barry would stand to greet it, his hand proffered to shake or his arms open wide to the wares of his store, his voice practically singing: *How can I help you?*

Now he was a larger man and standing for any reason was an effort. His waistband had increased as his enthusiasm and ambitions had shrunk. There had seemed such an opportunity at the beginning. He had seen the seaside town of Langthorne as a place to set up a growing business: second-hand goods, antiques, collectables. There was money coming into the town, movement in from London. The people were changing and he thought he could, too.

It was three years since he had opened his door for the first time, but he hadn't been the only one to recognise the growth potential in the town. The movers from London hadn't just moved their homes; they had also moved their businesses. Barry couldn't compete with their eclectic displays, their big-city reputations and their blasé attitude towards the business rates that were squeezing him tighter and tighter, choking his profit margin until it was all but gone. He should fix that bell, but it was the least of his worries.

He brushed the crumbs from his lap and wrapped up what was left of his takeaway meatball-and-tomato-sauce roll with extra cheese. He moved his cookie so it was out of sight and out of reach. The sort of clientele he was attracting these days wouldn't think twice. He clambered to his feet, pushing down with his arms as well as his legs. Far from proffering his hand to the figure that strutted towards him, he took one look and damn near slumped straight back into his seat.

'All right, mate, yeah? How you doin'?' It was a slim woman, her long, dark hair unkempt, her fringe pushed across her forehead and held in place by a coating of grease. She wore baggy grey tracksuit bottoms that hung low enough to show the tops of yellowed underwear. Her top half was a white vest top with a hooded jacket unzipped and open. She wore fingerless gloves, allowing her to drum on the counter with dirty nails. She sniffed. She raised her hood then trapped it tightly against her head by pushing her soiled hands firmly into her jacket pockets. Her eyes flicked around the shop to the shelves beyond where Barry stood, then down to see what was stacked on the floor. She finished by looking up into the corners. Her eyes rested for a second on the CCTV camera. It was fake. She might have realised it but gave no reaction.

'Can I help you?' Barry dropped the *how*, giving the question a totally different meaning. The people in the town *were* changing, but his shop seemed immune. He hadn't seen this woman's face in here before, but he had seen a thousand just like her. While the eclectic shops took the real money and attracted the well-heeled collectors, he was left to deal in second-hand mobile phones on tick to those clinging to the town's underbelly.

'Yeah, I'm looking for some medals, yeah? On ribbons they are.' She sniffed again. She shuffled from one foot to the other. Her eyes darted around at the items behind him.

'I don't have any medals in,' he said.

'Not any?'

'Not any.'

'I heard you did.'

Barry ran his hand over his lips. More crumbs tumbled down his front. 'I can't say what you heard, or why. I haven't got any medals.'

'I heard they came in with some other stuff. Maybe some gold coins.'

Barry expelled air in a sort of laugh through his nostrils. 'What do you think this is, a pirate ship? I got phones, games consoles, used games, satnavs. I got some watches and bits of jewellery, but you need to make an appointment to see them and I would need to see the colour of your money. I don't have gold coins.'

'Krugerrand,' she persisted.

'Very good, yeah. Krugerrand is a gold coin. Probably the most famous. Anybody with Google on their phone could come in here and talk to me about Krugerrand. Doesn't mean I have any. I wish I did!'

The woman licked her lips. She turned towards the door. Barry looked over at it too. His attention had been on the girl. Now he could see someone stood outside with his back to the door. It was definitely a man, in a black jacket pulled tight over broad shoulders. A youth tried to walk around him to get to the door and the man moved to block him. The youth took one look and left without arguing.

'If you came in here to rob me, do what you like. The CCTV stores straight to a cloud. You can't delete it. You'd be wasting your time anyway. I don't have cash and there's nothing here worth your time. There definitely ain't no gold coins. I suggest you and your mate fuck off now.' Barry's eyes dropped to the stubby bat that leant against the desk beside his feet. He hadn't dreamed he might need a weapon when he first opened the store. But since he had needed to move into second-hand electronics provided by more dubious suppliers, he had realised that he might need something.

The woman's eyes met with his, having also risen from the floor. She smiled. It was a knowing smile, as if she was reading his mind, as if she knew he had glanced to where his weapon was.

'The way I see it, you got a choice. We ain't here to rob you. I'm here to buy, yeah? I got cash. I want to buy some medals. You show me what you got or I get him in to start looking for them. And he ain't in the mood to pay, know what I mean?'

Barry leant forward. The palms of his hands took his weight on the counter. 'I told you. I don't have any medals.'

She leaned forward too, stopping barely six inches from his face. Her smile was a tainted yellow. 'Those medals don't belong to you. They didn't belong to the sticky fingered little runt who brought them in here either. They belong to his granddad.' She jabbed her thumb towards the door for the second time. 'I managed to convince him I should come in here first. I can't have him going back to jail. I told him I would come in and get the medals. I told him you mustn't know who he is and you didn't know they belonged to him. Because if you did, you woulda turned them away in the first place, maybe with words of advice on taking them back. Them gold coins got robbed too.' She pushed off the counter and stepped back. She made a show of looking around. Her expression remained a sneer. 'But I believe you. I know you ain't got them in here. I bet he offered 'em to you though, didn't he? And I know you woulda wanted them. But they were too rich for ya right? What did he want? A grand a coin? Maybe he was in a hurry to get shot, maybe he said you could have two for a grand? I'm close, right? But you didn't have nothing to give him 'cause you're a sad old fat fucker with no pot to piss in.'

'You done?' Barry said. But his eyes flickered past her. They were drawn to the man stood at the door. He was facing in now. He had a beany hat pulled low over his eyes and was blowing into his hands. It was well below freezing outside. He stared in and needed to stoop to manage it.

'I want to buy them medals. I've got a twenty-pound note. Trust me yeah? That's a good deal.' Barry didn't see where the money came from but she slapped it firmly on the table and leaned forward. The note was trapped under her right hand. She stared straight at him. He looked back at her and then beyond to the man at the door. He didn't need this. He couldn't get rid of medals anyway. He'd known they were nicked from the start. He was going to shift them to a collector overseas, but that meant putting them on eBay. It meant the hassle of using an account that he hoped couldn't be traced to possibly, eventually, getting sixty quid a medal. He could get shot of the damned things for twenty quid in his hand. And this way his shop didn't get smashed up or worse.

'I need shot of the things anyway. I took them as a favour. That's all. In good faith. I didn't send no one out to get them. They came to me.'

'Spare me, yeah? I've already been in here too long. You're lucky the big man ain't come in here seeing what the holdup is. Take your money.' She stepped back. The money stayed on the counter. He snatched it up and pushed it into his back pocket. The medals were in a drawer down to his right. He kept his eyes on her as he pulled it open. They were still in their display box, pressed into felt with a plaque underneath. He slid the box across the counter. It stopped near the edge. She didn't take her eyes off him. She was leaning on her palms again.

'You got what you wanted,' he said.

Her head dipped, her bottom lip flinched. 'Who brought them in?'

'What?'

'Who robbed 'em?'

'I didn't know they were stolen.'

She smiled. 'I'm sure you didn't. Now, who brought them in?'

'I thought you knew. You were talking like you knew who brought them in. It's got nothing to do with me. I don't ask the questions. I'm a business man.'

'You're no better than a thief. How old was he, eh? Did he look the sort that might have got World War medals? Like he might keep them in a presentation box? You tell me that.'

'I don't ask no questions.'

'Tell me a name and I go. I know this thief comes in here a bit. So you know who he is. Or I'll get my mate in here from where he's cold outside. He *does* ask questions.'

'You know who brought them in. Now you have them back.'

'Say his name. I WANT YOU . . . to say his name.' The sudden volume and power in her voice caught him out. She had little flecks of spit in the corners of her mouth. He didn't need this shit.

'Toby. I know him as Toby.'

'Second name.'

'Toby. That's all I know!'

She spun and gestured. The door pushed open immediately. It banged off the wall. He took one step in.

'Routledge!' Barry flapped. 'I think that's it. It's something like that.' The big man stopped in the doorway.

'We cool?' he said. Even in two words his voice carried menace as it boomed among the dusty consoles and trinkets.

She looked Barry up and down and then sniffed again. 'Yeah. We're cool.' She scooped up the medals, turned and moved to the door. The man in the beanie hat had to turn sideways to let her past. He stared over at Barry the whole time. The woman turned left and moved away. The man held his gaze for another second. He seemed to be considering his next move. It turned out to be back out through the door, which he slammed shut. The bell crashed to the floor.

* * *

Detective Sergeant Maddie Ives strode along the pavement in the High Street, then took a right into a cul-de-sac with double yellows all along it and a churchyard at the end. Just one car was pulled over with its hazard lights flashing: a battered-looking hatchback with a trim missing from one of the back wheels. Maddie yanked open the grimy passenger door and Detective Constable Rhiannon Davies nodded at her from the driver's seat.

'You took your time!' Rhiannon said.

They pulled away. Rhiannon spun the car around and they drove along the back of a row of shops before turning left at a roundabout and down a steep hill. The sea was visible between the trees on their right. It was the long way back to Langthorne police station. Rhiannon would take a few more deviations. There was no suggestion they were being followed, but Maddie had taught her to get into the habit. And she was a fast learner.

Maddie lifted a phone to her ear. PC Vince Arnold picked up on the first ring and Maddie could hear traffic noises in the background.

'You get away clean?' she said.

'Of course I did! You ain't working with no amateur, Maddie. I keep telling you that.'

'So you do. Thanks for your help.'

'I didn't do nothing really. Just stood there in a beanie hat looking good! I reckon you should have let me smash the place up a bit till he gave you your twenty back.'

'Like I said at the briefing, Vince . . . we needed to fly a little more under the radar. He thinks we let him off so we didn't attract police attention, not because we *are* the police attention. It's job done.'

'He wouldn't think the police would slap him around the face a bit until he gave it back either!' He roared with laughter.

Maddie couldn't help but smile. He was nothing if not infectious. 'That is true. But we have rules to play by.'

'And I reckon you just broke every one of them!' Vince scoffed. 'You're my kind of bird, Maddie Ives. You know you're gonna give in one day. It might as well be tonight. Come on, let's go out and celebrate.'

'Wow! Thanks for the offer, Vince. I mean I am very flattered, but it seems I need to be out nicking me a little Burglar Bill tonight. But if I get that done in time, I can assure you I'll be washing my hair.'

'I bet you will. Right little prick tease ain't ya, Maddie!'

'Only in your world, Vince. Thanks for your help.'

'Ain't no need to thank me, love. All that was foreplay. You know that, right?'

'I didn't even notice. Which doesn't bode well, now, does it?'

Maddie cut the call. The views of the sea were gone. The town of Langthorne was now a blur of grey out of every window. She looked down at the medals in her lap.

'So you got a name?' Rhiannon said.

'Yeah. Toby Routledge. The same one we already had.'

'Well, at least we know for sure.'

'We do.'

'The CCTV still fake in there?'

'I'd put my mortgage on it. The last thing he needs is a record of what goes on in there.'

'How are you going to explain that we have stolen property back but no one in custody for handling?'

'I wasn't going to. If anyone asks I'll tell them someone got a sudden urge to do the right thing on the back of the media appeal and they were left on the steps back there.' It was plausible and Maddie knew it. She'd made sure their real victim, the war veteran pensioner, was front and centre of the local paper. Time was when even the most hardened thief wouldn't have even dreamed of touching something like that. But then there really was no honour left among thieves.

'We know Barry Lyle is taking all the stolen goods from the local burglars. Why don't we target him? Get him in for handling and shut him down?'

'Now you're starting to sound like management! It's short-sighted, Rhiannon. He's an easy collar. Right now we know where all the stolen stuff ends up. And with our friend opposite in the chemist's telling us who's coming and going we're getting a good idea who's out committing the break-ins in the first place. The burglars are the ones we want. We shut Barry down and they still need to take their stuff somewhere. We just won't know where and we won't know who.'

'So you reckon we go get Toby Routledge in now?'

'Yeah. Why not? We show him the medals. We tell him someone told us he nicked them and see if we can shake him down a bit. See what falls out.'

'He knows the game. He also has a solicitor. He always swaggers around like he owns the block, then says nothing in interview and walks. We've got no one actually naming him that we can mention, no forensics, no nothing. When are we going to get a job that sticks?'

'It's a long game, Rhiannon. We get to upset him. We'll do what we can to make sure he stays in for the full twenty-four hours and the residents of Langthorne can sleep easier in their beds for one night at least. He gets a reminder that we know what he's up to and maybe it forces him into a mistake, or someone around him bubbles him up. It's about disruption. We just need to keep the pressure up until he messes up. And he will. He's a seventeen-year-old kid. He only *thinks* he knows the game.'

Maddie was back to looking out the window. Rhiannon sighed. Maddie picked up on it. 'They've got every advantage, Rhiannon. There's no way we were getting this job home. There's no motivation for Barry Fat-boy back there to rat on Toby, to bite the hand that feeds him — not as part of official evidence. This way we get the medals back, we get a burglar off the street for twenty-four hours and I get to—'

'Dress up like a skank!' Rhiannon cut in with a chuckle.

'Dress up like a skank! Exactly. Speaking of which, are you ever going to head back towards the station? I need to peel this stuff off my teeth and then have a long shower.'

Maddie ran her fingers over the display box that carried the medals. Today was a good day. A small victory, but in policing you have to take those. Maybe they wouldn't get a charge out of Toby Routledge, but they would be able to reunite a war veteran with the irreplaceable. Just as soon as she had washed the grease out of her hair and changed into something more presentable.

Chapter 3

Patrol Sergeant Tim Betts thumped the front door. All was quiet; the only sound was the steady rain that beat out a rhythm on a nearby plastic bin. It was nothing like the description of the call they had been given. There were reports of an aggressive-sounding male, shouting loud enough to be heard down the street. A female had been heard screaming, too. The informant was a close neighbour who had called before; they said that they often heard a man's voice but this was the first time they had heard the girl. They said it sounded like she was fighting for her life.

Tim looked at his colleague, PC Vince Arnold, a brick shithouse of a man, who'd spent much of his career answering calls just like this one. "Another shitty domestic," he had said as the radio operator had given the details, just like he did every time. But he had still been the first one out of the car and Tim knew that men who beat on women were his pet hate.

Vince was scowling now. He was stood back enough to be able to look up at the top window from over the angular porch. His shoulders were dusted with rain and the rim of his hat held droplets that glinted from the street lighting. Vince sighed. He turned to look into a car that was left at an angle on the drive as if it had been parked in a hurry. It was a silver estate car, a Volkswagen. Vince ran his torch through the window. He huffed again. Tim had been able to release him earlier in their shift for some plain-clothes work with CID. He knew Vince liked that sort of work; it was something different at least.

Tim hit the door again, keeping up a steady rhythm that got louder. He stopped when his knuckles complained. There were lights on. It looked like they were at the back of the house. Vince moved to Tim's right to look into the windows. There were neat-looking blinds turned at an angle. Tim didn't think you would get much of a view and, sure enough, Vince didn't linger. He stepped back just as the light in the porch came on above them.

'Yeah?' A man with a large build opened the door. He looked pissed off. He was wearing a black vest that was tight over a slightly protruding gut. He had a thick neck and limbs and a tribal tattoo that ran up his arm, across his chest and neck and out of sight. Tim noticed that he was breathing a little heavier than he might expect. He was trying to disguise it too. Beads of sweat clung to his forehead where it met with his cropped hair.

'We got a call. Someone was concerned for the occupants here. We're just here to make sure everyone's okay.'

'Well, ain't that nice. We're fine, thanks.' The door pushed to close. Tim stuck his boot out. He caught it just in time. The man looked down at the boot in his door. He took his time to look back up again. His breathing had increased a little more.

'You wanna get that boot out of my door?' It was a growl, a man trying to contain anger.

'Yeah. Once I've checked everyone's okay. I just need a minute or so of your time and then I'm sure we can be on our way.'

'I told you. I said I'm fine.'

'No, you didn't. You said *we're* fine. Who else is here with you?'

'That ain't none of your business.'

'Like I said, I'm here to make sure everyone's okay. So yeah, it's my business. How about you ask her to come to the door so I can say hello at least. We've been here before. Her name is Grace, right? And you should be Craig?'

'I don't know you.'

'Not me, personally. The police. My colleagues have been here before.'

'We don't need you. No one called you here.'

'We don't just turn up, Craig. Someone called us. We are coming in and we are checking on Grace, I'm telling you that now. So you can let us in and we can have a conversation or we will push you out of the way and come in anyway. And that probably involves handcuffs.' Tim stepped forward. He felt Vince step in closer behind him. The man stood in the door had almost a foot in height on him, even before the step up into the house, and the same again in width. Tim was glad that Vince was here. The man stood firm. He was looking over the top of Tim.

'THE FEDS ARE HERE, GRACE!' His shout was sudden. Tim was close enough to smell his breath. It was tinged with alcohol. 'THEY'RE COMING IN.' He still blocked the door. A few more seconds passed. Tim shuffled forward to make it more uncomfortable. He heard a noise in the house. Then he saw movement. A young woman appeared. She hung back, skulking in the hall behind. Tim couldn't see her well, but she looked a lot younger than the man at the door. She was maybe twenty-five; he had the man at ten years older at least.

'Why do they need to come in?' she said. Her voice was low. She was looking to the floor. Tim answered her.

'We had reports of some loud shouting from this address. We just wanted to be sure that everyone's okay.'

'We're fine,' she said.

'Can we just come in and take some details. Then we'll get out of your hair.'

'You can see we're fine now.' The man cut back in and edged forward. The rim of Tim's cap bumped into his chest.

'And you can see we're getting wet.' Tim replied. 'We've got some paperwork to do before we can go and I'm not happy yet. We don't go until I'm happy. We are coming in and we will speak to you both separately and we don't leave here until that happens.' Tim angled his head to stare straight at the man blocking their way. He needed to get in that house. Something had happened; he was sure of it now. He needed to see if there were any signs of disturbance and to get the girl on her own. She wasn't going to talk freely while he was around. Tim wouldn't leave until he had done as much as he could.

The man took another few seconds but he did step back. Just far enough so that Tim could move into the hallway. He glared at Tim and Tim glared right back. Vince stepped in behind him. Grace slipped further back into the shadows of the hallway.

All the internal doors hung open. Tim could see the living room off to the right side. The kitchen was straight on.

'How about you come with me into the living room there?' Vince spoke to the man who was now stood awkwardly in the hallway.

The man snatched his glare from Tim to Vince. 'You fancy yourself then, big man?'

'Sorry, fancy myself at what?' Vince's voice was faux cheery — his goading voice. Tim had heard it enough times.

'You reckon you can take me, is that it?'

Vince still had his arms crossed. 'Well, sure. But I was just gonna take down your name. It's up to you what we do after that.'

The man sneered back. 'You'd need a lot more of you to take me down.'

'You're starting to bore me now, mate. How about we stop all this posturing bollocks so we can get this done, yeah? This doesn't need to take long.'

'I'll speak with Grace here in the kitchen.' Tim said. Vince nodded at him then gave a thumbs-up gesture confirming he was going to be okay.

'Nah,' said the man. 'I don't want to be split up from my missus. I don't trust you lot.'

'Worried what she'll say?' Tim snapped.

'I got no worries, mate. Nothing happened here but some telly and a bit o' dinner. Ain't that right, love?'

Grace kept her head bent. Her head jerked towards his voice but she didn't raise her eyes.

'Let's just get this fucking done!' He stepped across the hall and pushed past Tim on his way into the living room.

'Shout if you need me.' Tim said.

Vince rolled his eyes. 'Hopefully he kicks off!' he whispered.

The kitchen was typical of a new-build property: square, with a modern fitted kitchen and high stools under a raised island. The house was detached but still sat close to its neighbour. Tim could see out into the garden. It was small and surrounded by high fencing and punctured by white lights that looked to be dug into the ground. The kitchen overall was poorly lit; the garden was noticeably brighter. Soft downlighters under the units were the only light source inside. Grace's head still hung. She had long, dark hair that fell forward over half her face, enough to cover all of it in shadow. Tim could see from her outline that she had a tiny frame. She was backed into the sink.

'How long have you lived here then, Grace?'

'A year.'

'Okay. So you must have been the first in?' Tim referenced the estate the house was part of. Houses were still being finished around it. They were in the village of Hawkinge, which was on the outskirts of Langthorne.

'Yeah.'

Tim took out his notebook. 'And I assume that is Craig in there, is it? We got some information on the way up.'

'Yeah.'

'And he's your partner?'

'Boyfriend, yeah.'

'How long have you guys been together?'

'A while. Look, I'm fine, okay?'

'This won't take long. Do you mind if I just . . .' Tim flicked the main light switch on the wall right next to him and the room was instantly a harsh white. Grace jerked her head up to the source. Her hair shifted. Tim could see the redness around her eyes that stood out from her pale skin. She had been crying. No doubt.

'What happened, Grace?'

Grace finally met his eyes. She looked terrified. 'Nothing. We had dinner and watched some telly. Then you turned up.' Tim closed his pocket book to put it away. His experience taught him that it could be a barrier.

'I know what he said. And maybe you think that you have to stick to his story — that you can't tell me what happened. But you can. We can help you out, Grace, but we can't do it until you help us a little bit. You need to tell me what happened.'

'I told you what happened.'

Tim sighed. He took the time to look round the kitchen. It was immaculate. He realised that everywhere he had seen in the house so far had been too. 'Who made dinner?'

'I did.'

'What did you have?'

Grace hesitated. 'Lasagne.'

'Leftovers?'

'Some. In the fridge. You hungry?'

Tim smiled. 'Show me.'

The fridge was to Grace's left. She turned to it, shuffling her position so she could open the door with her right hand. It looked cumbersome; it would have been easier if she had led with her left. She pulled the door and stepped away, her left arm hanging awkwardly across her stomach.

'There. You happy?'

'Did you hurt your arm, Grace?' Tim said. He wasn't interested in the fridge's contents anymore.

'No.'

'Show me. Can you pull your sleeve up so I—'

'No! I don't need to be pulling my sleeve up or doing anything else. I've answered your questions. I've told you what happened!'

Tim held his palms out to let her know he was stepping down. 'Okay, okay. So you had dinner, then you cleaned every trace of it up. That's possible. So what made you cry?'

Grace's head fell forward again. Her hair fell over her face.

'We were watching something sad.'

'What was it?'

'The telly!' she snapped. It was anger of a different sort: one part irritation, two parts fear.

Tim also recognised the signs of someone who was lying to him. It wasn't difficult to spot. But knowing didn't help much, not in this situation. She wasn't making any accusations. There was no sign of disturbance and nothing other than watery eyes to give a clue that anything had happened at all. But Tim had been to enough violent domestic incidents to know how she might be a victim: the spotless house; the aggressive partner coaching her, reminding her of the story she needed to give while stood in front of them; the meek and terrified younger victim. He might have got her to the point where her biggest fear was the police, the very people sent to protect her. That's how far abusers could get inside someone's head. If Tim raised his voice she would burst into tears. He was sure to be soft with his tone for one last try.

'We're here now, Grace. Me and my mate in there. You say the word and we will take Craig down the station. You get some breathing space and you can tell us what happened. We will charge him and we will prosecute him. We can keep you safe. We can put conditions to keep him away, maybe even remand him in—'

'NO!' Tim saw a flash of strength. It was gone just as quick. She took a moment before she continued. 'We had dinner. Then we watched telly. I'm sorry you got called out to here and wasted your time. Maybe it was one of the other houses.'

Tim nodded. 'Maybe it was.' He expelled a long breath and took a moment to consider. 'Look, Grace. We've got a CID team. They work in plain clothes. A skipper I know has been doing some work with women . . . like you. She's making a real difference. She can meet you. Away from the home, somewhere safe. It's off the books. An informal conversation about how we can keep you safe. That's it. Would you consider it?'

'Maddie. Maddie Ives, right?' Grace muttered. She was back trying to hide behind her hair.

'That's right. Have you met her?'

'A couple of times.'

'Okay. So you know how it all works and you know she can be trusted. Did you see her recently?'

'A while ago. A few months maybe.'

'Would you see her again? If you felt like you needed to?'

'I told her I would get in touch if I needed to.'

'Right . . . So, will you be seeing her again? After what happened tonight?'

'I told you, nothing happened tonight.'

'Okay, Grace. As long as you know where you can go for help.' He longed to say what he was thinking — *Only I'd hate to see you turn up as the next statistic. Domestic violence can really get out of hand. I reckon you might know that. Victims can end up seriously hurt — or worse. Don't be that person, Grace.* But he knew it could just end up frightening her off. 'Please . . . speak with Maddie again at least.'

'I said I would. If I needed to.'

'I guess that will have to do.' He chanced a smile. His eyes ran back over her fragile frame. Her arms were wrapped across her front as if she was consoling herself. She was fooling no one. He walked into the hall and took a left into the living room. Again it was tidy. The only thing even remotely out of place was a thin duvet that was folded up on the arm of a single seat sofa. Craig was sitting down on a longer sofa against the same wall, facing the window with the angled blinds. He was leaning right back, doing his best impression of boredom. His head snapped up when Tim walked in.

'You fucking off then, boys?' Craig's whole face was a grin. This was the hardest bit. Tim knew they were leaving. And when they did, he knew that Grace would be in the gravest danger yet. Behind that grin, Tim could see the menace. They had only served to wind him up.

'We get reports of even the slightest noise from this address, Craig, and we will be back to start making arrests. You understand? Don't give us an excuse.'

Craig practically sprung to his feet. He stepped forward, his right hand fell to his crotch and he grabbed it firmly. Tim was aware of Vince tensing up next to him. Craig stepped in closer. Tim stood his ground. Craig's face was just a few inches from his.

'I make a lot of noise when I shag, though . . . *officer*. You know what I mean? And it's been a few hours now. I like to be nice and regular. Grace here knows how to do it, too. I'll get her to show me later, but she does like it rough!' He stepped back with his eyes bulging wide. His arms fell to his sides and swung in a sort of swagger. He licked his lips. His grin was still there — more of a sneer.

'There's a line, Craig. When rough is too rough. I'll be seeing you again soon.'

'No, you fucking won't, mate!'

They stepped back out onto the pavement. Tim hadn't seen Grace again. The front door was closed firmly behind them.

'What a cock!' Vince spoke first.

'He was at that.'

'I was trying to find something, anything. When I ran him through I was praying that he was wanted for something. No such luck.'

'Is he known for anything?'

'Yeah. Domestic assault, would you believe it! Not with her, though. He was nicked seven or eight times a few years back, once every couple of months at least — some serious. The last couple of years there's been nothing.'

They were back at their car and Tim slid into the driver's seat. He turned the ignition and lowered the window. The rain was lighter and it was turning to sleet. He could just see it against the porch light as he stared back over at the house.

'He didn't stop, though, did he?'

Vince had sat next to him. 'No. Grace in there just doesn't report him. The previous stuff was with two other women. The only time we've met her is when someone else has called it in.'

'Like tonight.' Tim said.

'Just like tonight,' Vince agreed.

Tim turned to face the front; it was time to leave. He turned the blue lights on to flicker in the quickly darkening night. He liked to make a show of wife-beaters, especially when he couldn't do anything about it. Nothing made neighbours' curtains twitch like a flashing blue light and maybe they would get the message that there was a woman in there who might need their help — even if she was refusing it now.

'She said she knows where she can get help,' Tim said.

* * *

Grace was standing in the living room, looking over at Craig's back. He was still at the front window and hadn't said a word since the police left. He tipped the blinds slightly, just enough to be able to see out. From her vantage point she could see beyond him. She saw the blue lights come on, flashing and flickering through the slats. Their intensity dimmed as the car moved away. Then they were gone.

Craig turned to her immediately. 'Where were we?' he said.

'Please, Craig. Please let me go to bed. Just let me go to bed! I'm tired, okay? I'm not going anywhere.' She kept her voice low and soothing. It was deliberate. She knew he couldn't take it if she raised her voice when she was scared. He called it *whiny*.

Craig was shaking his head. She had seen it too many times. It wasn't a normal shake, as if he was simply denying her request; it was faster, as if he was trying to shake the bad thoughts from his mind. He needed his head testing. He wasn't right. She didn't recognise him anymore.

'You sit in your seat.' He stopped to look down through eyes that didn't blink. His words were suddenly very deliberate, his feet were shoulder width apart and his strong arms hung wide as if his broad chest was tensed. His hands were bunched into fists. His voice was so low she would have missed it if she hadn't heard it so many times before.

'Please, Craig . . .'

'You sit in your seat.'

'I just—'

'SIT IN YOUR FUCKING SEAT!' He raised his head to the ceiling and his eyes bulged as if they might burst from their sockets.

Her whole body flinched and she inhaled with a shocked whimper. She knew she wasn't going to win. When she opened her eyes he was half turned back towards the window.

His head turned back slowly to face her. 'I swear . . . if you make me shout again . . . if someone calls them mugs back . . . if they get to stand in my house, taking the piss out of me again . . . You will answer for it, Grace. And it will be your own doing. Now, I am going out, and you sit in your seat when you're told. You *know* this.'

Grace swallowed hard. She knew she was going to have to move but her feet wouldn't. It was like she was frozen to the spot. She focused. She tried to console herself. If she did as he asked, he would go out. She would have some time on her own at least. Just her. She managed the few paces to the single seat sofa, the same sofa where she had bunched up the duvet when the police had knocked at the door so she could cover up what was underneath. Craig whipped the duvet off. Her stomach always fluttered when she saw it. The solid, black steel of the bench vice where the left arm of the sofa should be. She tried not to linger on it, as if by ignoring it, it wasn't real. But it *was* real. Two twelve-inch steel plates, each with a nobbled surface, faced each other to form a crushing pair of jaws. It was designed to grip solid metal to the point where it wouldn't move, no matter what was done to it. It worked well on flesh, too, and could cause catastrophic damage.

She sat in the chair. She was still trying not to look at the vice directly. Her left arm stayed by her side but she made sure to lift it before he did. It was agony if he lifted it up for her. It still hurt enough doing it herself. She felt a flash of pain and then a dull ache where blood tried to move through the damaged part. Her left arm didn't quite lie straight anymore when she rested it on the solid base. The steel felt so unforgiving, even just through her elbow.

Craig pulled the blinds tightly shut then walked back to her. He tugged back the sleeve of her top. She bit her lip. He reached for the handle of the vice, which turned on a buttress thread. It was designed so that when it was screwed shut it was impossible to part unless the thread turned in the other direction. The handle was on the side and lower down, designed specifically so that she couldn't reach it without snapping her arm.

She closed her eyes. She couldn't watch this part. She felt the ragged steel plates push into both sides of her arm at the same time. They stopped for an instant where he adjusted his grip to turn it again. Some days were tighter than others. Tonight he was angry, she could tell. She bit down again, harder this time to stop from crying out as the jaws clamped tighter. She knew if she made a noise it would make him twist it even more. She could feel the pinch; the blood being pushed out until it felt like it was pushing directly on the bone. She exhaled loudly, almost a groan. She couldn't help it.

She opened her eyes to see him stepping back. She fought to get her breath. She had to really concentrate to be still, she felt every movement through the damaged bone. She considered begging him to loosen it. Sometimes the pain was bearable. Not tonight. She had begged him before when he was angry. He had only tightened it more. That was how the bone in her arm had been broken in the first place. He liked to teach her a lesson. He rubbed at his mouth. His eyes were still wide and he looked agitated.

'You make me do this, Grace — you know that, right? I don't want to hurt you. I don't want to have to, but you make me do this.'

She couldn't speak. The pain was too much. Her breathing was long and laboured as she tried to cope. He was pulling on a jacket. He was sweating more and wiped at his brow.

'You make me do this!' he said again.
And then he was gone.

Chapter 4

Grace's diary

Monday 4 February

I'm writing this back in the chair. It is now six evenings in a row. I checked back through the pages of this diary to be sure. All of the days seem to blur into one now. It's getting worse. The pain is so bad.

I could tell I was going to get hurt the moment he came home from work. I heard his car pull up. Just the way he closed his door.

Tonight I upset him. I knew it was going to happen. I was trying not to give him an excuse to start. I made him dinner and then I was just trying to keep out of his way. He was watching TV. I dropped some pans when I was clearing up. It was nothing really but he went mad. Shouting at me, saying that I was hurting his head, that he had been at work all day. He was screaming at me. I kept quiet. I was waiting for it to end. I put my head down, he spits when he shouts. But I don't think he liked that. He grabbed my bad arm and it caught me by surprise. It hurt so bad, I screamed. I didn't mean to. I knew straight away that he would be angry. He just stopped. He stopped shouting and he let me go and he looked all surprised. Straight away he was at the window. It was like he knew they were coming.

Two police officers came. Two men. I didn't want to talk to them. I know he doesn't like me talking to them and I could tell I was going to pay for it when they left. The short one spoke to me in the kitchen. I think he was a sergeant. He said his name was Tim. He seemed nice. He said he wanted to help. He said he knew what was going on.

But he doesn't.

He told me about you, Maddie. I said we had met already and that I would talk to you if I needed to. I do need to. I have needed to for a long time. This is how I do it. I talk to you every day. In here. But soon, when the time is right, I will have the strength to show it to you.

He's getting worse. I know it will need to be soon or it will be too late. This diary gives me hope. You told me to write it down when I could and you were right. This is how you will know what was happening at 17 Campbell Road. This is how you will believe me.

Whether I get to give it to you in person or not.

Right now the chair is as tight as it has been since the night my arm changed shape. It has to be broken. It is even more misshapen now, it is getting worse. I need to go to hospital. I need something for the pain. I know he won't let me.

I shouldn't have screamed. I should be more controlled. I can't talk to the police. Not yet. Craig tells me they won't listen to me anyway. They won't believe me. He says I'm useless.

But I know you'll listen to me, Maddie. And I know you will help me.

I have taken photos. They are dated. I need to hide it all now.

If he knew, he would kill me, Maddie. I know that. I know you'll help me.

I know you will.

Grace xxx

Chapter 5

Maddie Ives turned into Southwall Street, Langthorne, and killed the engine. They were in the same beaten-up car they had used earlier. It was a good choice for blending in. Southwall Street was in the Epping Hill Estate, a two-mile square of concrete with a reputation as the most depraved and crime-riddled in the county. Toby Routledge lived among the tightly packed buildings; his was a top floor flat that they could just make out from their position. His girlfriend was registered as living there too with their eighteen-month-old son, but intelligence had her spending most of her time at her mother's address nearby. Any risk assessment, however, would have to include the assumption that the baby was there tonight, certainly if they got to the point where they were looking to force entry. Maddie was hoping that wouldn't be necessary. She was just off the phone to Vince Arnold who had agreed to assist — which made the door going in on the end of someone's foot far more likely.

'Vince is coming. He's out with his skipper. They're going to do our arrest and we'll stay for the search.'

'Of course he is!' Rhiannon giggled in the seat beside her.

'And what is that supposed to mean?'

'What do you think? There was never any doubt he was going to come running to your call!'

'He's far from subtle is our Vince. One of the good guys though. I'd much rather have him on my team.'

'Is he wearing you down? He always tells me he is!'

Maddie laughed harder. 'Maybe he is!'

'Just a few days ago you said it would be a cold day in hell before you stepped out on a date with that man.'

Maddie's attention was drawn to the top floor window. A light had come on in the furthest window. 'Well, I haven't checked the forecast recently.'

'That's his kitchen, right?' Rhiannon said. She must have been looking up at the flat too. They had both been in there a few times before. Toby Routledge was a well-known local burglar. He was the worst type — the 'creeper'. He liked to break into homes in the dead of night, usually while occupants were asleep upstairs. He got off on the thrill of it. He preferred small electrical items such as mobile phones and tablets, but he would take jewellery and cash if he came across it — anything that was on show. And his first port of call with stolen goods was always Barry Lyle's filthy little shop in Langthorne's High Street.

The light in the top window clicked back off again, just as Maddie was aware of headlights in her mirror. A marked police car slid past. She pushed her door open.

'Time to rock and roll,' she said.

The night air carried a chill that nipped at her neck. The rain had stopped at least. She zipped up her jacket and pulled it tighter as she walked to the pavement to greet the two officers. She could see the only entrance to the flats from her position and her attention moved away from it only briefly to greet the two men.

'You cold, Detective Sergeant Ives?' Vince's wide grin reflected the street lighting.

'There is a chill in the air, Vince. Not that you seem to be feeling it. That uniform suits you.' Maddie referenced his return to uniform after his plain-clothes assist earlier in the shift. Now he was stood in a black, short-sleeved, POLICE-marked T-shirt. It gripped tightly around his biceps. She reckoned he ordered them a size too small. His stab vest also looked like it was made with a smaller officer in mind.

'I don't feel the cold so much. If you ever need warming up, you let me know!'

'I'll bear that in mind.' Maddie moved the conversation on. 'I've seen a light go on and off since we've been here. It was literally a minute, so we know someone's in. No one's come out.'

Tim Betts's breath was visible as he spoke. 'We'll go give him a knock then.' He shifted from one foot to another as if he might be the one in need of Vince's radiant warmth.

The communal door to the building was wide open. There was some trampled mail on the floor and more of it pushed over to one side or stuffed on a shelf off to the left. Maddie and Rhiannon hung back a few paces. Maddie scanned the envelopes quickly and noted a lot of them were addressed to Mr T. Routledge, distinctive as bill reminders and demands. He was bailed to this address from a previous burglary offence but police hadn't been here for a few months. She hoped the build-up of mail wasn't a sign that he had moved out.

The carpet on the wooden staircase was thin and cheap. There would be no silent approach. Each step either boomed or creaked. Toby's flat was on the top floor. Vince's knock sounded more like an attempt to smash the door down than to attract the attention of the occupant. He waited just a couple of seconds before he made his second attempt.

'WHO IS IT!' It was a male voice from the other side.

'That's him,' Maddie said.

Vince nodded. 'Police!' he said.

'The fuck do you want?'

Vince's nostrils flared. There was a short landing, not enough room for two officers to be on it at the same time. Vince turned so he was fully facing the door. Tim Betts had to move down a couple of steps to make room. Vince's frustration was tangible.

'I ain't talking to you about it through a door, Toby. Open it up or I will.'

'You gonna smash my door in? You got a warrant?'

'Yeah. Open up and I'll show you.'

'You ain't got nothing!' Toby shouted back. 'I open that door and you're gonna nick me. I ain't even done nothing.'

'If you don't open the door I'm gonna nick you for wasting my time. You got five seconds before I come in.'

'What you nicking me for?'

'FOUR!' Vince bellowed back.

Maddie could hear mumbling from the other side of the door but could no longer make out words.

'THREE!'

'All right, yeah! But I ain't done nothing. You better not be here to nick me.'

'TWO!' Vince started banging the door again. This time it was with the bottom of his fist. It got progressively louder.

'ALRIGHT!' Toby screamed from the other side. Vince stopped. There was a moment's complete silence, then a scraping sound. The door pulled open.

Vince stepped in immediately. Tim followed him. Maddie could hear Toby protesting about how they couldn't just come in like that. By the time she walked through the door Toby was stood in handcuffs and nicked for burglary. His arms hung down his front. His pigeon-chest was bare, on his bottom half his dirty tracksuit bottoms were unzipped to make flares. The flat was stifling hot and stank of cannabis. The untidy living room was just about all there was to the flat. A clothes hanger stood against the window with a few items of baby clothes clinging to it. More littered the floor around it. There was an open pizza box with some bits of chewed crust. It looked like it had been yesterday's dinner. She could see two mobile phones next to it on the table.

'CID in da house!' Toby flicked his gaze from Maddie to Rhiannon, who moved in behind her. They'd met a few times, enough for him to recognise them instantly.

'How have you been, Toby?' Maddie said.

'I've been arrested! I suppose this is your doing, is it?'

'No, this is your doing, Toby. You just can't help yourself, can you?'

'I ain't done nothing. Burglary? I swear, every time something out there gets chored you come knocking on my door. You lot are just lazy, ain't nothing more to it. Something gets chored so you come after the last bloke you nicked for choring stuff. I know people. I see them out there, getting away with all kinds of shit because you lot are banging on my door every time. You need to get out there and do some detecting, yeah? The people you really want are out there now, laughing.'

'I'm sure they are. I seem to remember you giving me the same speech a couple of months ago. Just before I charged you with three burglaries at a care home for the elderly. These people that are *actually* doing all the stealing, they're using your fingerprints, too, are they? As much as I appreciate your advice, you won't mind if I ignore it completely, will you?'

'You ain't got no prints!'

'You upgraded to gloves now then, have you?' Vince chipped in.

Toby jerked his head to Vince as if he had something to say. He seemed to change his mind quickly. 'The care home thing was ages ago,' he said to Maddie. 'I been nicked two times maybe since then and you got nothing.'

'Third time lucky!' Maddie grinned. She picked up the more modern-looking phone from the table. 'What's the code for this then, Toby?'

'Dunno.'

'Of course you don't. I'll have to try and track down the owner for that then, won't I?'

'That's my phone! My mum got that for me. She's got a receipt. Two, five, eight, zero, okay? So you can check it here. You can see it ain't got nothing on it and you don't need to be taking it away. I still ain't had my last phone back.'

Maddie pulled an evidence bag from her pocket. She wrote the code on the front and dropped the phone in. 'We'll see,' she said.

'You lot just do what you want. I swear, one day . . .'

'One day what?' Maddie rounded on him. 'What's doing what you want if it isn't crawling through someone's window to steal their belongings just because you're out of drugs? One day maybe you'll realise that you *can* have whatever you want, you just need to go out and work for it.'

'Are we going, or what? I got a life to get back to.'

'I don't see much evidence of it here, Toby.' She looked to Vince while Toby was mumbling into the floor. 'Take this winner to get dressed will ya. It's freezing cold out there. Can't have him crying about that, can we? We'll get the search done.'

The search didn't take long at all. Toby knew the game well enough not to have any stolen property at his home address. He usually got rid of it pretty quick and stuff he couldn't get rid of he would farm out to a number of associates who would hold it for him. The irony was that he wasn't stupid and sometimes he could be out late at night and for long hours waiting for his opportunity. These were the attributes that might stand him in good stead in the world of employment. But the rewards for working a legit job were slow burning. Toby Routledge was part of the generation of kids that wanted everything immediately — so why not just go out and take it?

The night air felt colder still when Maddie stepped back out from Toby's torrid flat. Vince led him to the back seat of their marked car and pushed the door shut. A figure appeared in the middle of the road where the street lights formed the brightest patch.

'Oh, yeah, another man taken away! In this country you don't care. You don't care who he is, what he is.'

Maddie looked over. The voice was slurred and in an accent that sounded like it was from Eastern Europe. She walked towards it.

'You are police?' He looked unsteady on his feet. His outline was portly. He was leant on a single crutch and didn't look to be dressed for the weather in his polo shirt and jeans. She heard a car door clunk shut to her right. She looked over at Vince who was walking towards her.

'Yeah, sure. I'm police. Are you alright? You look like you might be cold?'

'Not alright! You are police. You are scum! You are taking people away for nothing!'

'Do you know who that is over there or why we are taking him away?'

The man seemed to consider this; it only took a second. 'He has done nothing. I do not know him, but I do know this.'

'I think you're a little drunk,' Vince said. 'Maybe you should go home.' He strode in front of Maddie and pushed himself right up close to the man, who seemed a little startled. He had to crick his neck to look up at Vince's face. 'I'll say it once more . . . you should go home.'

'The big man is the bully. Is this how it is? You here to bully me? Maybe you should take me in? Maybe I am bad man?' He pushed out and caught Vince in the chest, but rather than moving him, the man on the crutch had to adjust his feet quickly to stop himself from falling over.

'You get one more chance to piss off, mate.' Vince's tone carried enough menace. 'Or you're coming in.'

'Piss off! You swear at me! It is okay then? Piss! PISS! FUCKING PISS!' Vince's patience snapped. His hand reached out. The man swatted it away but stumbled backwards. The instant he got himself onto a firmer base he swung a kick towards Vince. It was never going to bother him. Vince grabbed the man by his right shoulder and his arm snapped back. The man folded forward and crashed onto the road. Vince almost looked surprised, like he hadn't meant to put him down so hard. He didn't know his own strength. Maddie rolled her eyes as Vince snapped handcuffs onto the man's wrists. She could see a graze on the bottom of his chin.

Vince shrugged. 'He just went down.'

'I reckon he's too drunk to feel it anyway. He might regret it in the morning, mind.'

'Oh, he'll regret it alright.'

'I'll do you a statement covering the assault.' Maddie sighed.

'Assault?'

'That's what you're nicking him for, right? The push in the chest and a kick?'

'No way! I ain't admitting to that! He can come in for drunk-and-disorderly. He can have a ticket when he sobers up and be thankful for it. I ain't wasting no one's time interviewing him and going through that rigmarole.'

Maddie smiled. It was a lot easier to deal with him for D-and-D, but she suspected that wasn't the only reason for his decision. 'That male pride of yours, Vince. You're letting the man off for the sake of it!'

'I don't let people off. That weren't an assault. I've been assaulted.' Maddie thought he actually looked a little hurt. He moved on quickly, 'I'll get a van out. You don't want a drunk in your car. What do you need from us before we go off tonight?'

'Just Toby in the bin, Vince. The arrest statements can wait. We won't be interviewing him until the morning, and even then I can't see us charging him.'

'You're not expecting a confession, then? The lad putting his hands up to the horrible things he's done and asking for a chance to apologise to his victims?' Vince's grin was back.

'No. I'm expecting the normal Toby Routledge. He'll strut around our custody block with his hand constantly down his trousers, moaning loads and then he'll give us a *no comment* with his middle finger in the air. The best I can hope for is to keep him in for as close to the twenty-four hours as I can.'

'And that starts with bedding him down and talking to him in the morning?'

'Yup.'

'So, you'll be going off-duty soon? I finish at eleven. It's been a long shift, what with me coming in on overs to help you out earlier. Maybe we should find somewhere open for a drink, you know — just one.'

'Washing my hair, Vince. You remember?' She turned to where Rhiannon was approaching. 'Thanks for your help today, though.'

'That's it? See ya later and thanks for the help? I was seriously assaulted today! What about my welfare?'

Maddie was still chuckling when she got to Rhiannon and their car.

'He does make you laugh,' Rhiannon said. 'Vince, I mean. That's a start surely?'

Maddie moved into the car without looking back. 'I'm laughing *at* him. That's not really the basis for anything more now, is it? Let's get back shall we so I can go home. I really do need to wash my hair.'

* * *

Tim Betts walked through an area of Canterbury Police Station with the nickname the range. The name had stuck, a hangover from its previous use. Beneath the scattered photocopiers, files and cluttered desks, you could still see the origins of the long, slim, open-plan building that would once have housed targets down one end and trainee firearms officers at the other. Now it was the home of CID — the Criminal Investigation Department, the team that dealt with creeper burglars like Toby Routledge. But Toby was already asleep in his cell. Tim wasn't here about him.

'Hey, Maddie. I hoped you would still be here.'

Maddie Ives was leant over her desk. The range was dimly lit as a whole. The only detective Tim had seen had been typing under a desk lamp. None of the main lights were on. Maddie looked up from under her own lamp.

'Always here, Tim. That's what it feels like at least. I think there are a lot of people working long days today. This bomb incident is still headlines, we got lucky being left alone today.'

'The CT lot have turned up with a lot of resources. It seems they all come out of the woodwork for the juicy jobs, where were they when we had four immediate calls outstanding earlier though, eh?'

'Not quite so keen to assist I would imagine.'

'They didn't seem so keen, no. It's one of those calls I was coming over to speak to you about. I won't take up your time. I just wanted to let you know that I saw Grace Hughes today. Early evening. A disturbance call from a neighbour.'

Maddie had started pushing items into her top drawer. Her computer was shutting down. She stopped her packing now. She sat back in her chair and gave him her full attention.

'And when you got there, there was no sign of any disturbance. Right?'

'Right.'

'And Grace . . . Did she speak to you?'

'She did. But only because I forced it. I made sure we got them separated so her fella was nowhere near. She didn't tell me anything, though. Suggested we were at the wrong house.'

'And you don't think you were?'

'I know we weren't. I told her about how you went out to meet people sometimes — women like her — who didn't think they could talk to us — off the record, like. I know it's one of your things. She said you've already met.'

'If you mean one of the *things* I'm passionate about, then I'll agree with you. These women need our protection and the old methods aren't working. I take it you met Craig, too?'

'Yeah. Bit of a lump.'

'He's a bit of a something, alright. His last partner is still in hiding. The police moved her to a refuge somewhere out of the area — somewhere he should never find her. I've spoken to the officer who sorted that move. She's pretty convinced they saved her life, not that she appreciates it.'

'You see it a lot. They go as far as getting them arrested but don't support a prosecution and then get the hump when we have to let the offender go.'

'Well, it takes a lot of guts to speak out. You can times that by ten to do it again in a courtroom. I'm working on Grace. She is getting there. We might start getting something from her soon. The only time he's been arrested since he's been with Grace was when he had a go at her in a supermarket and a member of the public made a call. I dread to think what happens to her behind closed doors.'

'She said she would speak to you again, if she needed to. I'm not convinced she will. I'm worried about her — we both were. There was a lot of bad feeling in that house, you know what I mean?'

'I do. You pick up on it.'

'I think she was hurt too. She had definitely been crying.'

'Hurt?'

'Her arm. She was holding it funny and it didn't look like she had full movement in it. I asked to see it and she quickly backed away. I didn't push it. Maybe I should have.'

Maddie closed her drawer. She now switched off her monitor completely and picked up her bag. She stretched as she stood. 'It's been a long day, Tim. I'll have a think about our Grace. I was looking for an excuse to approach her again and maybe this is it. Last I heard, Craig was out all day with his work. He's a delivery driver. One of these self-employed types for Amazon and the rest.' She rubbed her face. She looked tired all of a sudden. 'It would need a bit of planning, though. I couldn't risk him coming back. I would have to put someone outside to give a heads up if he came near.'

'Let me know if you need some support. I'll jump in a plain car and do the lookout bit. There's only one way in and out of that estate. It would be easy to sit up on.'

'Yeah, okay. You know what? I will go see her.'

'We're back on tomorrow — two o'clock start. But we would do a few hours early on overs if you have a budget. Let me know what you need. We'd appreciate an excuse not to get tucked up with this bomb investigation too. I never mind helping out but they've got us locals stood on scene preservation or picking up CCTV. The dirty work.'

Maddie nodded. 'Tomorrow it is then. Assuming we can stay free too and nothing else comes in. Thanks Tim. Keep your job mobile on and I'll confirm.'

'No problem. Vince will come in too. I'm sure he wouldn't mind helping you out.' Tim couldn't help but smirk. Maddie must have picked up on it because she had a smile of her own.

'I'm sure he wouldn't!'

Chapter 6

Tuesday

Maddie stood at the custody desk watching the clock on the wall click over to 10 a.m. The custody staff had been on the phone to her first thing, asking what the plan was for Toby Routledge. She had delayed coming down for as long as she could. Rhiannon was leading the interview. She had gone to get their prisoner, leaving Maddie doing her best not to make eye contact with the scruffy-looking man who had been led in by the detention officer and was now stood opposite her. You couldn't interview someone in custody aged under eighteen without someone present who was deemed an 'appropriate adult'. Toby's mother had refused, as she generally did, so the only option left was to consult with the Appropriate Adult Scheme, who could provide willing volunteers to stand next to the 'child' in question. They varied in quality and today the scruffy man was their provision. He was a thirty-something male with smudged lenses in his glasses and hair tied back around a bald spot. He was painfully thin and looked like he was resisting being physically dragged to the floor by the plastic visitor pass hanging round his neck.

A movement to Maddie's left caught her eye. She turned to where two of her uniform colleagues stood at the desk further along. They were looking to get rid of the drunk-and-disorderly that had come in at the same time as Toby after upsetting Vince. The man himself looked a little steadier on his feet than he had the night before, despite not having his crutch. The custody sergeant handed it back to him over the desk.

'The woman last night!' The man pointed to where Maddie stood before turning to the custody sergeant then to each of his accompanying officers. 'She will tell you! She was there! She will tell you that I was not — what you say? Drunk and disorderly! I was not this! The officer! He pushed and he swore. This is not how you do this!'

'Alright, Viktor,' the custody sergeant cut in, 'you've got your ticket, okay? So now you have two options. You can pay your fine, as it says on there, or you can have your day in court. We're not going to stand and discuss the circumstances here, okay?'

'I will discuss! I want to discuss. And, ah, look! The innocent boy! He saw them too. You saw this, right?' Toby appeared with Rhiannon. His hands hung by his side. His usual swagger was missing, he almost looked unsure of himself. He looked over at the gesticulating man for a brief second, then his eyes snatched away as the man continued to shout towards him. 'He knows what happen! He see it! I would like for his details. Can I take your name, boy? I would like for you to say what happened in the court?'

'Viktor!' The desk sergeant's voice cut in loud and firm. 'You have to deal with me first. I'm trying to get you out of here. If you decide to go to court later, all the relevant people will be contacted and asked to attend to give their evidence. That's how it works. You cannot do this here.'

'This is how you do it, is it? In England? This is how you run things? What about my human rights? I am citizen

— EU citizen! You know this. You are Brexit people! Racist people!'

'Viktor, calm yourself down.'

Viktor still stared over at Toby. 'You, innocent boy. You say nothing! You do yourself a favour and you say nothing to these people! These are not good people, these are not people that are interested in you!'

'Maddie . . .' She turned her attention to the custody sergeant who had addressed her. 'Do you mind sitting him in the holding cell while I deal with Viktor here? I don't think he needs any more distraction.'

'Sure.' Maddie smiled knowingly, and signalled for Rhiannon to follow her. Toby walked dutifully alongside. The appropriate adult moved over too, but he hung just outside the door like he was unsure where to stand. The holding cell was out of sight of the desk but not quite out of earshot. They could still hear Viktor shouting.

'YOU TELL THEM NOTHING, INNOCENT BOY! THEY BRING YOU HERE . . . YOU SAY NOTHING! THEY DO NOT WANT TRUTH. THEY JUST WANT ARREST AND THEN YOUR SILENCE!'

'Friend of yours?' Maddie jerked her thumb back towards the desk.

'Nah. Seems crazy to me.' Toby was now hunched on a wooden bench, his back pushed against a painted brick wall. He played with his hands. Maddie had seen him in custody more times than she could remember. Today was different.

'You okay today, Toby?' she probed.

'Yeah. I just wanna get this done.'

'You got something better to be doing?'

'Anything's better, right?'

'I guess so.'

'I don't want no solicitor, yeah? I just want the chat and then you can do what you need to do. I don't want to hold this all up.'

Maddie scowled. 'You sure? The skipper will ask you again anyway.'

'Yeah, I'm sure. I just want to get it done.'

'Your choice. This is your appropriate adult. Do you want to speak with him before we make a start?'

Toby leaned forward to see beyond her, to where the man still lingered outside of the holding cell.

'Fuck, no! Let's just get this done, yeah? I don't need no one.'

In other circumstances Maddie might have needed to hide a smirk, but she was concerned. Toby had seemed to enjoy the custody process on previous visits, like it was all some big game. He would strut around, giving the jailers a hard time and generally doing what he could to frustrate the process. He *always* had a solicitor; always the same one and they would take as long as possible in their consultation. Toby would then emerge to answer every question with a succinct *no comment*. He would treat every part of the process with utter contempt. Today was different. Maddie had no idea why.

Viktor was finally gone and some decorum returned to the custody block. Toby walked back to the desk so the skipper could ask him if he was healthy and happy to be interviewed. He typed that he had asked the question and then noted the answer. Another paperwork exercise. The police service was drowning in them. Toby still declined a solicitor. He looked a little more at ease, but his swagger was still missing as he walked the corridor to the interview room. He asked for water. Maddie got it for him while Rhiannon readied the recording device. She got herself a tea.

Toby found his seat without being asked. He still seemed furtive. His eyes flicked round the room, his head jerked to the door when a detention officer knocked to ask a question. It wasn't just nerves. He was scared. Maddie was desperate to know why. He hadn't seemed scared last night, even if getting through his front door had been easier than it could have been.

The door was closed and the tapes started. Rhiannon rattled through the formal parts. She paused before asking her opening question. Toby's attention was fixed on her, as if he was waiting for his turn to speak. In previous interviews Maddie could recall him being sat right back in his chair with his legs straight out in front of him, his arms crossed over his chest and his face looking up to the ceiling. He had even pretended to be asleep at one point. He was wide awake today.

'You are aware that you are under arrest for burglary, following the recovery of stolen property taken from an address in Leonard Road, Langthorne. Did you commit that burglary?'

'Are you going to lock me up?' Toby pushed himself as far forward as he could. His eyes were fixed on Rhiannon, his stare intent.

'Can you answer my question, Toby?'

'If I admit to it . . . if I tell you I did it, will you lock me up?'

'I feel I should remind you, Toby . . .' the appropriate adult interjected, 'you can have legal advice, mate, if you feel you need to. It's not too late.' His voice matched his appearance: weak and wafty. Rhiannon didn't acknowledge him. She continued.

'Did you break into an address and steal these items?' Rhiannon reached into a bag she had put on the floor and pulled out the medals. They were sealed in a see-through evidence bag. The front was distorted by handwriting but you could still see them clearly.

'I want to be locked up!' Toby said.

'Because you nicked the medals Toby, or because you're scared of something?' Maddie cut in. The eyes that twitched at the sound of her voice were wider than ever.

'I nicked 'em, yeah. Okay. So now you got to lock me up. I hold my hands up: I broke into some old man's gaff.

I didn't know they were in there but I heard about some gold coins. I sold them. I gave them away cheap really. I didn't really know what they were. Some fella mugged me off for them.'

'What fella?' Rhiannon asked.

'I ain't telling you no more. Not until you tell me you're locking me up. I don't want to be going back out. Not now. There's nothing for me out there.'

'If you're scared, we can protect you,' Rhiannon said. 'But you need to tell me what you're scared of.'

'I ain't telling you nothing more. Not until you say you're sending me to jail. I've had enough of it out there, okay? I don't get to see my kid . . . I don't get to see my missus no more, 'cause her mum is in her ear saying that I ain't good enough. No one thinks I'm good enough. I just get used. People want something — they come to me. And I'm just the dumb fuck that goes through a window to get it. But look who's sat here! Look who's sat here now.' For a moment Maddie thought his anger was going to break with tears. He held it together.

'So someone put you up to it? You said you heard about the gold coins. Who told you about that?' Rhiannon didn't give him much time to relax, she could smell blood maybe. Maddie sensed it too.

'If someone made you do this Toby, you need to tell them,' the appropriate adult spoke again. Toby didn't even look at him.

'I ain't saying that. I shouldn't have said that part. I've said too much. This is about me. This in here is just about me, okay? I fucked up. I nicked the coins and I nicked them medals. I saw them and I took them. I wouldn't normally. I know they can be hard to get rid of. And people, they know them when they see them. They know they belong to someone. You can't argue with that. I got a few quid. So you have to lock me up, right? That's what you do, ain't it? So DO IT!'

Maddie sighed. 'This is a strange situation for me, Toby. I have to be honest. I mean, yeah, we're here to lock up bad people — burglars, definitely. But you're only seventeen. I can justify remanding you to the next court, but that might even be this afternoon and then the court will probably let you go anyway. You'll get bail to go back, but you'll be a free man for a while at least. Which is normally all you want. What's different this time? If you want us to keep you safe, then you need to speak to us. It doesn't have to be in here. I can talk to you after.'

'There are others. Jobs, I mean. I went out again. Later on. Word got round what I got, what I was good at. It was a different night. My mum . . . she has a garage. It's part of a block behind her house. It comes with the house. I keep stuff in there. From other jobs, not just this one. I did these other two. You need to lock me up — I can't help myself!'

'Where else have you committed thefts? Can you remember the addresses?'

'No. I don't know exactly.'

'What do you know?'

'Leonards Road, you said, yeah? That was the old man. But then I did some up in Hawkinge. Out of the town. That was on another night. I did two together up there.'

'How did you get to Hawkinge? That's a long walk, Toby, and you don't normally go too far.'

This was the first question Toby didn't have a snap answer to. He hesitated. He seemed to consider his options before he replied.

'What does that matter? I went there and I did the jobs. Campbell Road, near the speed camera. I did a couple places up there. One was about halfway along — white patio doors out the back. Are you writing this down? You need to be writing this down!'

'It's all on tape, Toby. You know how this works. Tell me about that job.'

'Like I said! Campbell Road. I went in through the back door. I went over the fences and through the gardens trying the doors. The first one weren't locked. Patio doors. Straight into the kitchen. They must have called you lot already? I got some phones from there and a key thing.'

'A key thing?' Maddie said. She was trying to keep up; this wasn't what she had been expecting at all. She hadn't even bothered opening her book to start with, but now she was taking notes.

'A thing for keys. And some phones. They looked old. I don't even reckon I could sell them on.'

'So why take them?'

'What does that matter? You ever done a job like that? You need to be in and out. You don't take your time price matching — you get me? I took what I could and I got out. I had a look when I could and it was shit. But it was me, okay? I can't be no more upfront.'

'Who lives there, Toby?'

'I don't know. I didn't see them. I was in and out. It was proper late. Everyone was asleep but me . . .'

'What about the other place? You said there were two jobs up there.'

'The other place . . . yeah, there was another place. You don't need to be asking me no more. Why you asking me about that? You need to get up there. These people will tell you what happened, I've given you enough. You need to charge me with breaking into their gaff and taking their stuff. You need to lock me up in jail. This is all you need to do. You don't need to be asking me no more questions.'

'What other addresses did you go to? What other numbers?'

'I don't know . . . another place along there. I don't remember numbers. I don't always see them. I went in the back door. I told you about the garage — you should be able to work it out.'

'Do you remember anything about inside? Anything distinctive?'

'Distinctive? What does that even mean? No. I went into two kitchens. I weren't looking for *distinctive*, yeah? I was looking for phones, laptops, jewellery, Xboxes — that sort of shit. Stuff I know I can move.'

'So how did you get up there, Toby?'

Toby threw his hands up in frustration. He looked like he stopped himself saying the first thing that came to his lips. His face twitched. He sucked in a breath. 'I got nothing more to say. You need to be locking me up. I told you enough. Send me to court like you said, yeah? I'll talk to them mugs. If you say they're just gonna let me go, I'll tell them what I done. There ain't no point going through it with you now. I told you enough. You should be doing your job. I ain't saying no more, in fact — this is over, yeah? I don't wanna talk no more.'

Maddie saw that the old Toby was back. He threw himself back into his chair, his eyes fixed on the ceiling. His bravado had returned, even if it was just temporary. Rhiannon tried a few more questions but she was wasting her time. He didn't utter another word and the interview ended a short time later.

Rhiannon showed the appropriate adult out, while Maddie walked Toby back to his cell. She pushed his cell door shut. She was back a minute later with a cup of tea. She pushed it through the solid hatch. He mumbled his thanks. She had to bend to see in, to make eye contact with him.

'You're a bit of a twat when you come in here normally, Toby. You always make it as difficult as you can. But I know why — we both do. This is all a game. You and me, we might have chosen different sides but we still play the same game. Am I right?'

Toby moved to sit on his bed. He perched on the edge and put his cup on the floor between his bare feet.

His right hand ran over his face and lips. 'Yeah, cops 'n' robbers, ain't it? Old as time.'

'I don't mind that, not now I understand that we have parts to play. I can even see that you're not such a twat after all. You're just playing your part, right? So I don't want to see anything bad happen to you. If you're in some trouble, some drug debt with nasty people or something you don't think you can handle, you can talk to me. Okay?'

'Okay, yeah.'

'I know you're scared of something. Once you're scared, it's not like playing a game anymore, is it? Then it's real life. This is real life, Toby. This is your life. Talk to me about what's going on. Off the record, on the record, I don't care. You might be surprised by what I can do.'

He didn't reply immediately. Maddie stayed silent. She wanted to force him to speak. She wasn't letting him off lightly.

'Lock me up. That's how you help me.'

Maddie stood back straight. She shut the hatch with a resounding clunk. She hesitated at the door, considering there might be something else she could say. There was nothing.

She huffed and walked away.

Chapter 7

The noise caught Grace out and she dropped her phone. She was on the toilet upstairs. The noise was the front door. The toilet door opened right onto the top of the stairs. It didn't lock. Craig had taken it off. He had to be back. He had started to turn up more and more. He liked to check she was home, and alone. He said it wasn't that he didn't trust her but that it was how he built trust in the first place.

'GRACE!' Craig's voice boomed up the stairs. Grace jumped and then she scooped up the phone in her hand. She stared down at it. She was going through the pictures of her injuries. She did it sometimes, to organise them and to keep her strong when things got tough. She wasn't allowed a phone. He had smashed up her last one. He had no idea about this one. The fact she had it was bad enough, but he would look through it, he would find the pictures, he would know what she was planning!

'Yes. I'm just finishing up on the toilet, Craig!' She tried to stay calm. 'Are you home for some lunch? I can make you some lunch!' She called back out. The toilet was sparse. There was nowhere to hide anything, let alone a large smartphone. She heard solid footfalls on the stairs; it sounded like he was taking them two at a time. Her eyes fell to a bin to her right. She stuffed her hand with the phone into it. It dropped inside, as the door was ripped open.

'Craig! I'm on the toilet!'

'You alone in here?' His eyes darted round the room. They had a corner shower unit. The curtain was pulled round to drip dry. He wrenched it back.

'Alone? Of course I'm alone! No one comes round here.'

'No one, eh? Not even those police officers from last night?'

'Police officers? Why would they come round here again? We told them it was none of their business.'

'I *saw*, Grace. Don't you think I didn't! I saw how you were looking at him. I know you fancied that big lad. You're with me, Grace. You need to remember that. It's a respect thing. I don't like how you looked at him.'

Grace's lips bumped together. She didn't know what to say. She wasn't expecting that and had no response. He stepped forward and loomed over her, bringing his head down so their foreheads were nearly touching. Grace felt so vulnerable. Her aching arm hung across her midriff, her knickers were pulled down and taut across the tops of her knees, her jeans were gathered around her ankles. 'And you don't even deny it!' He was spitting. He always spat when he was angry. She turned her head away.

'I'm s-s-sorry! I didn't realise I was even looking at him. I was trying not to—'

'You couldn't keep your fucking eyes off him, could you? And in MY HOME!' She felt a grab on her right shoulder. He stepped back and dragged her with him. Her skin squeaked and pinched against the toilet seat and she was thrown to the tiled floor. She could feel the coldness against her legs. She was on her side and looked up just as he threw his leg forward. She was hit with so much power that she skidded to the right and collided with the bin, which was sent sprawling towards the door, spilling its contents. The phone slid across the tiles and stopped behind the door. Craig had stepped back and was making snorting noises through his nose. He stared down at her, his eyes fixed wide and open.

She knew it wasn't over. She daren't look over at the phone. It was out in the open but it should be hidden from his view behind the door. One step in and he would see it. Then he would see what was on it. He would see what she was planning and then she didn't think he would stop, he would beat her to death right there. *He couldn't see the phone.*

She was still on her side. One of her legs was lifted in an instinctively defensive posture in case he kicked her again. He had caught her on the side. She couldn't feel it too much yet. Often she would feel it more later when the adrenaline wore off. He looked to be calming down and took another step back.

'You make me do it, Grace. You need to respect me. That's all I want, I just want you to respect me like I respect you. That means you don't go lusting after other men. You don't stare at them when they're in my FUCKING LIVING ROOM!' He had wound himself back up and stepped towards her. She had an instant to react, to stop him coming close enough to see behind the door. She lifted her leg towards him and kicked out. She pushed herself towards him with her right arm; her left still lay across her front, limp and useless. As she moved forward she was able to scoop up the phone with her right hand and bring it firmly into her stomach. She had never lashed out before. She didn't think he would take it well. He didn't.

She heard a roar. He was so angry he couldn't form words. She was lying in the door now; her knickers were tighter, now twisted higher up her thighs. She brought her legs up into a foetal position as she heard the door scrape. She felt a blow to her lower back that knocked the wind out of her. He was using the door, slamming it on her where she lay. The second blow followed quickly. The pain broke through the adrenaline as the door's sharp edges dug into her back. He slammed it again — and again, each blow harder than the last. He was working himself up into a frenzy. She didn't cry out, she didn't beg. She was getting good at being quiet.

The blows stopped. She stayed in her foetal position. She could feel her phone, still firm in her grasp and out of sight. She heard him step away then a noise that sounded like he slapped the wall. She chanced a look — he was facing away. She pushed the phone into the sleeve of her injured arm. She heard him step back over to her, felt his breath on her ear.

'You ever do that again and I won't stop. You understand me?'

Grace managed a jerked nod. 'S . . . sorry . . . I'm sorry . . .'

'You *make* me do this. I shouldn't have to. I don't want to.'

She nodded again then arched her head back away from him so that he wouldn't see an errant tear that she couldn't hold on to. She could see the toilet. The seat was hanging off at an angle. It must have come loose when she was dragged off. She heard the top step creak. He was moving away — down the stairs. The front door opened then slammed shut hard, enough to rattle the internal doors.

She tried to move to a sitting position but failed. Her side and her back were immediately shot with pain, enough to make her gasp. Her left arm was useless. She was still on her side. She reached down with her right. She wanted to pull her knickers up at least. They were tangled and it was difficult with one hand. She bit down on her bottom lip and grimaced as she fought the pain. They came up. They were still twisted but it was enough to cover her up a little. She put her head back down on the floor. She could feel the coldness of the tiles on her face. It was almost nice. She would rest here for a few minutes. She would have to try and get up again soon.

She needed to be making a start on dinner. It couldn't be late.

* * *

Maddie was aware of someone hanging beside her desk and half turned away from her. She needed to finish her phone call; it was important. Toby Routledge was still causing her work. She had sent a search team out with a hurriedly obtained warrant to search the garage he had mentioned in interview. They had found property. If it matched with what their victims had said was missing, it would make their case stronger, strong enough to charge him and put him in court for his case to be heard that afternoon. She was on the phone to a uniform patrol that could give him a lift. She turned to the figure to her left to make them aware she would only be another minute. Suddenly her call wasn't so important.

'H-Harry B-Blaker!' she stuttered. The officer on the other end of the phone expressed her confusion and Maddie had to explain hurriedly. 'Sorry, that wasn't meant for you. Are we sorted then? Can you just head back in? Go to custody — I'll make sure he's ready.' She spoke into the phone but she was still fixed on Harry. She missed with her first attempt to put the receiver back in its cradle. She had to break her gaze away to try again.

'Harry Blaker!'

'So you said.' Her beaming smile dropped away quickly. She suddenly remembered she was upset with him. Harry's face didn't seem to carry much of an expression at all. Just like she remembered. She stood up and felt immediately awkward; she didn't know what to do next. With anyone else she might have stepped in for a hug. Instead she stepped clumsily back. She didn't know what to say or do.

'If you're gonna hug me, you need to get it over with,' he said. That growling, stoic, emotionless tone. How she'd missed it! She stepped into him and gripped him tightly. She felt his hands press lightly on her lower back. He smelt of aftershave close up. His beard tickled her neck. She let him go but still held onto his arms.

'I like the beard,' she managed.

'I figured it might stop people staring.' He shrugged.

Maddie did stare. She felt like now she had permission. The raised, white smudge of scar tissue was still prominent under the beard. It looked like someone had rolled a patch of dough as thin as it would go, then stuck it onto his right cheek. It had a light pink outline and his facial hair was patchy over the scar tissue.

Detective Inspector Harry Blaker had taken the fragment of a bullet to the face. He'd been shot at from the side with a stolen police-issue, high-velocity rifle. The bullet had smashed into a car door frame and fragmented. A piece had ripped through the fleshy mound of his bottom lip and come out through his cheek. It had caused some damage to his jaw and knocked a few teeth out. His bottom lip was thinner on one side too, making his mouth in general a little lopsided. But he had been lucky. Very lucky. Maddie had, too: she had been hiding in the footwell when he had taken the hit, the sounds of bullets all around her and his terrified eyes and bloody face as he had slumped over was still something that regularly invaded her sleep. That had been nine months before. There were rumours that Harry was never coming back, that he might take the option of early retirement that was on offer, but Maddie had never believed it for a second. But she'd had no idea what he was thinking, given that he had virtually gone into hiding since the incident.

'What are you doing here?'

'I work here, if I remember right.'

'You're back then? To work, I mean?'

'Yeah. I'm only allowed a few hours a day apparently. Occupational Health are still treating me like a child, but at least they've let me in the building.'

'A few hours a day. Still in Major Crime?'

'Yeah. But I don't know what that looks like yet. I've been here twenty minutes and I'm bored already, despite there being a lot going on. This bomb incident is being led by CT and they don't seem to be in the mood for sharing.'

'You got that right. Two dead and scores injured I heard, but that's from Sky News — we've had nothing official. Suits me. I've got enough of my own stuff to be getting on with.'

'That's the problem for me right now, I don't have a workload yet.'

'It's got to be better than being bored at home, though?'

'I suppose.'

'You should be used to being bored by now. We could have helped with that too, but I got your message.'

'Message?'

'You weren't up for guests. That was what we were told. It made sense for the first month or so. I understood that you might need some time. But nine months later and still nothing? What's the matter with you?'

'Are you angry at me?' Harry seemed genuinely shocked. Maddie took a moment. She was angrier than she realised, she had felt her voice quiver with emotion when she spoke.

'Yes, I'm angry with you. I was worried at first. Then I was angry. After what we went through, what sort of bloke just locks himself up and doesn't talk about it?'

'I guess I didn't need it. I appreciated it, when I saw you at the hospital.'

'It's not just about you, Harry. I can't talk to people about that day, not like I can talk to you. That's what we do here, right? When you go through something, when you see someone you care about hurt in front of you, you spend time with them while they recover. You see them heal and you heal with them. That makes sense to you, doesn't it?'

'I guess I didn't think—'

'You didn't. Not about me. Not once.' Maddie felt her chest flush. She took a moment. Harry didn't reply. 'I'm glad you're back. You look well, too, I'm glad about that.'

'I'm better, Maddie.'

'Well, good for you. So what are you doing here, down with the peasants in CID?'

'I'm a spare part. Major Crime seems to have it all covered. No one knew I was coming back and now they're too busy to care. I figured you might know a thing or two about wiling away your days here. Seems like I might be doing that for a little while at least.'

'I see. Well, there's no wiling these days. CID is a busy place. I even managed to get a few of them smiling down here.' Maddie herself was back to smiling. Her overriding emotion now was happiness. Harry did look well. She had promised herself she would tear a strip off him when she did see him again, but she couldn't manage any more. Her anger was gone. Harry looked around. The office was buzzing with busy detectives and the desks were mainly occupied.

'You told me this was the last place you wanted to work.'

'It was. I didn't exactly get a list of options after . . . after what happened. Same old story . . . they still didn't know what to do with me. I'm enjoying it here, actually. It's been fun.'

'Fun?' Harry was still looking around.

'Well, yeah. Why not. More fun and games today actually. I'm against the clock . . . I need to get a kid to court in time for his case to be heard. He's down in custody. I think that's sorted though. Then I'm out to one of our DV victims. Not that she will admit it. Grace Hughes . . . I'm worried about her.'

'Not someone I know.'

'Let's hope that doesn't change.'

Harry looked confused.

Maddie clarified. 'I figure she has a good chance of becoming part of the murder statistics. Then you'll know all about her.'

'I see. CID pop in on victims they're *worried about* these days? I assume she's not supporting as part of an active investigation then?'

'She's not. It's something I've ended up championing somehow. We see these women who are clearly having a bad time at home but they're too terrified to tell us what's going on. I started actively visiting them. It's all off the books. Mainly I give advice on how to stay safe. If nothing else, these women need reminding that their lives aren't normal, that they don't have to put up with it.'

'It's not off the books, though. If they disclose an assault, you would be duty bound to act on that, surely?'

'Technically you're right. I've told the bosses that we talk theoretically and I get the women to talk about experiences a *friend* might be having. There's a little bit of discomfort around the whole thing, but it's the same as what victim charities do. The only difference is that I can be a bit more proactive and go and knock on their door. These women wouldn't talk to anyone if they could help it. But they need to understand that their partner might be escalating, that they might be in more danger than they could possibly realise. They can't just bury their heads and hope it will go away.'

'I see. You want company?'

'When?'

'On your visit? Maybe I should make the effort to get to know her while she's still alive.'

'I tend to go alone. It's part of making them feel at ease.'

Harry shrugged, but he didn't move away and he lingered on her.

Maddie cocked her head. 'You *are* at a loose end, Detective Inspector Blaker!'

'Maybe.'

'And asking to tag along with me? Only I'm . . . how did you put it back when I first came to you . . . ? Busy!'

'I guess I asked for that.'

'You did.'

'So, you can take me out. Show me just how much fun CID is. I promise I won't get in the way.'

'Are you even allowed out? Are Occupational Health cool with you leaving the nick?'

'No. It's been made very clear that I am grounded.'

'Well, okay then. You can tag along. But you'll need a nickname . . . Just so you understand your place in this arrangement, I think I'll call you *Kid*!'

Harry flickered a smile of his own. 'Don't push it.'

* * *

The knocking on the door made Grace jump and she felt the pain through her side and lower back. She was in the kitchen peeling potatoes. It was still morning but she was already pushed for time. Doing even the simplest of tasks was taking longer and longer as her arm got worse. Today she was struggling to stand straight. Her side was sore from the blows earlier, her ribs and back, too. She hoped that was all it was — a bit of soreness and some tender bones, something that would heal in a day or two.

The door thumped again. She was ready for it this time. She turned her head to the kitchen doorway but she was quickly back to peeling her potatoes. She wasn't expecting anyone; she never did anymore. At first, her dad used to visit her most days, but even he had given up. It got to the point where every time he came round they would argue. They couldn't just have a conversation. He would try at first, then he would start asking about Craig. He would ask if they were still fighting, despite Grace telling him a million times that they didn't fight. He would tell her that she needed to stand up to him, that he shouldn't treat her like that. He made her feel worthless. Like she was stupid, like she didn't know that already and she wasn't capable of looking after herself. He didn't understand. He couldn't.

The door thumped harder still and she huffed. She considered walking to the window to try and see who was being so insistent. She couldn't think who it might be. She shook her head. She looked back down at her potatoes. It went quiet. Movement through her kitchen window dragged her eye. She peered out to see a strange man stood in the rear garden. She felt her heart flutter in panic. She snatched up the knife from the sideboard and moved towards the door. She tried to control her breathing, tried to look like she was in control despite the shake in her hand. The man saw her. He held his hands out as if he was surrendering, as if telling her that he meant her no harm. He kept his right arm out as he leant with his left to pull the gate open. His movement was deliberate and slow. A woman she recognised as Maddie Ives stepped through the gate. She smiled warmly. Grace exhaled her relief but her body quickly tensed back up as she considered her situation: *She could barely walk!* They would ask her about it! Maddie would. Nothing seemed to get past her. She would know.

Grace threw the knife in the sink and made it to the patio doors. She unfurled the blinds on one side. They fell the full length, covering the left door panel. She stepped in behind it. She could see someone was stood against the glass.

'What do you want?' she called out. She hoped it was loud enough for them to hear. She heard Maddie reply.

'I just wanted to make sure you're okay.' Her voice was muffled through the glass. 'He's not here, is he?'

'No. But he might come back!' Grace called out, hoping they would take the hint.

'I've got people sat up the road. They'll call me if he does and we'll be long gone. I'm not here to make anything worse, Grace. I just want to talk to you. I would rather not do it through a patio door!'

Grace stood back. Her anxiety was getting worse. What if the neighbours heard? Maddie was having to raise her voice. They might be picking up the whole conversation. They might tell Craig everything that was said! She pushed her left hand into the pocket of her tracksuit bottoms, trying to ignore the pain and make it hang as naturally as it could. She spun the key in the handle and pushed it open. She backed away. There was a high stool under the breakfast bar. She perched on the edge, trying to ignore the searing pain in her lower back. It had subsided by the time Maddie's face poked through.

'Is it okay to come in?' she said.

'A few minutes. In case he comes back.'

'I understand. This is DI Harry Blaker, by the way. He's out keeping me company.'

'Why have you brought someone else? We spoke alone last time.'

'We did. Harry here is very experienced. He might be able to help.'

'I don't need any help.'

Maddie was still smiling. It looked warm and genuine but it dropped away a little. She started to look around the kitchen. 'You've started dinner a little early. Is Craig still working full time?'

'Yes. I like to get the chores done.'

'I get that. Is he still delivering?'

'Yes.'

'And you're okay?'

She had to shuffle her position. She could feel a pain in her side now. It was getting worse. 'I'm fine.' She timed shifting her position for when she spoke. She hoped it would mask her twitch at the pain. She reckoned she had got away with it.

'My colleagues came here. They said there was a disturbance at this address.'

'And I said there wasn't. We both said there wasn't.'

'I know that. They told me that too. Sometimes people aren't always honest about what has happened. They might want to protect people, maybe they want to play it down and just get on with their lives. Sometimes police involvement can make that difficult.'

Grace waited for a question or a point. It didn't come. 'Why are you telling me that?'

'I think that's what was happening here. You didn't want to tell us about what was going on, like last time. You said something similar to the police then but, when we spoke, you suggested that Craig had been violent to you in the past.'

'I shouldn't have said anything. He cares about me. He gets frustrated is all — it's only because he cares.'

'He still does, then?'

'No, that's not what I meant. After that time he was so sorry. He didn't recognise himself. He's been totally different since.'

Maddie wasn't looking at her anymore. She appeared to be looking around her kitchen. The man stood next to her was staring right at her. She felt uncomfortable. He looked older, fifty maybe. His head was shaved close and he had a beard that started at the ears. His mouth looked a little odd and she tried not to stare at the obvious scarring on one side of his face. He was frowning. His whole demeanour seemed stern. He spoke next.

'You're lying,' he said. 'About Craig. He still beats on you, doesn't he?' The man's voice was a low growl. Instantly it unsettled her. She met his eyes. His face seemed to soften a little. 'You don't have to put up with that, Grace. You don't deserve it either, no matter what he says.'

'He's fine. We're fine. I don't know what this is all about.'

'Sure you don't. You know why we're here. Sometimes we can't prove things and it feels like we're not doing enough. It's one of the worst parts of the job, a big reason why I stopped working the domestic violence side of the business. You should talk to Maddie. And I mean talk to her properly, with honesty. I put my life in her hands once and it ended up just fine. I'd do it again. Think about it.'

He fell silent. Maddie didn't speak either. She was looking out into the garden. Grace thought about earlier, about how angry Craig had been, how he had built himself up into a frenzy. What if he didn't stop next time? What if he went too far? She couldn't let that happen. Not before she had done what she needed to do.

'So what are the options?' she spluttered. She almost hadn't meant to. She regretted it the second it came out of her mouth. Maddie's eyes shot back to her and she looked energised. 'And I'm not saying anything to get him arrested.'

'Okay . . . I can give you an alarm. It's a button really. It looks like . . . hang on . . .' Maddie scrabbled around in the small bag slung over her shoulder. She pulled out what looked like a make-up mirror, folded shut and with a curved back. Maddie flipped it open. 'This links to the control centre. If you push it in, it will send help. It's totally silent. No one will know you pressed it and it just looks like a pocket mirror. It even has a little GPS thing in there. You get a few hours where we can track it, in case you're not at home.'

Maddie held it out. Grace took it. She ran it over in her hands. She felt the button and caught her reflection in the mirrored side.

'Craig doesn't like me wearing make-up. I don't really have much anymore. I don't think he would like me having this. He might even know that it's new.'

'Keep it in the bottom of a bag. He won't look twice. It just needs to be somewhere accessible. Our control room will send a response on blues and two's if you push it and I'll make sure they let me know too. Craig won't know it was you that called. It's just in case things get out of hand. And I think you know that could happen.'

'I don't know what you mean.' But Grace was considering it. If it got to the point where he wasn't stopping, where she thought' he might not stop at all, at least she could call for help. 'I'll hold onto it.'

'Great! That's all I ask.'

'Now, you two have to go. I can't have him coming back. I don't like that you've got people out looking for him. What if he sees them?'

'Don't worry. They know what they're doing. We'll go.' But she didn't leave immediately. She lingered on her still.

'Grace, did you get burgled recently?'

'What?'

'Burgled. Did someone break in here?'

'No! Why?' Grace felt a panic rising in her. She sucked in a breath to quell it.

'It doesn't matter. It was just a thought. We had a burglar up here do a few places. We only know about one of them.'

'We've never had any trouble up here.'

Maddie half turned towards the back door but she still didn't leave. She looked her up and down.

'You still have my number from before?'

'Yes.' Grace nodded.

'I assume you still don't have a phone. We talked about the phone box during the day or a neighbour. You can get hold of me.'

'Okay.'

'But if it's an emergency, if you think it's all getting out of hand, you press that button, okay? And someone will be straight out. He won't even know how — we'll tell him a neighbour must have called it in.'

'Okay.' Grace nodded. She managed a weak smile. 'Thanks,' she said.

* * *

Maddie spoke first but waited until they were some way down the drive.

'So there you are . . . the classic victim. I just hope she sees sense before he seriously hurts her. Did you see her face when she shifted on that chair?' Maddie stopped at the pavement.

'I did. She looked like she was in pain.'

'Her arm, too. The patrol sergeant said he thought she had hurt her arm.'

'She kept it in her pocket. It didn't look right. I was waiting for you to ask her about it direct.'

'She's not great at direct questions. I tried pushing it with her before. She backed right off and stopped speaking to me. That was the first time I've seen her since. I need to be careful around her. She was even more guarded today. I assume it was because you were with me.'

'None taken. The alarm is a good thing at least.'

'Massive. A real positive. I didn't expect to get that past her. She told me last time that she didn't have a phone anymore. He must have taken it off her. That started real alarm bells.'

'I bet. She said he doesn't like her wearing make-up either, that's another sure sign.'

'It is.'

'What do we know about this Craig?'

'We know he used to beat on his previous partner. He was charged with GBH with intent but CPS knocked it down to try and get the job home. It still went nowhere. She wouldn't support, but we did get her relocated out of the area. He doesn't know where she is. It was the only way to keep her safe.'

'Are you still in contact?'

'Not me, it wasn't my job. That was before my time. I was referring to the all-encompassing *we*. The police. I read through the notes before I met with Grace. His ex-partner was lucky, she got safe.'

'As long as *she* doesn't make contact with *him*. How many times have we seen that?'

'The report's very clear . . . the ex, she's terrified. I saw the CSI photos. I've never seen anything like it. The injuries on her body . . . she had broken ribs and a femur that was so badly bruised the doctors were amazed it didn't break. Do you know the force you need to worry a femur?'

'A hell of a lot.'

'They reckon he worked on it over a period of time. Probably beat her thighs with his fists. She said he did it to stop her walking far, to stop her going out basically. All her injuries were on the upper body or the thighs. Stuff that is easier to hide.'

'A real piece of work. I'm surprised the CPS didn't run it still, even without her support?'

'She didn't just withdraw support — she said explicitly it wasn't him. Then she got angry with the police when he didn't go down. The detectives that dealt with her said she turned real nasty towards the end. I think she was just scared.'

'Leaving him to move on to his next victim,' Harry said.

'I suppose she got herself safe. She wasn't thinking about what happens next or who else it could happen to. He's been with Grace for a couple of years and she's never reported a thing. Someone like that, they don't just stop. The only way he stops beating his partners is if we lock him up or he drops down dead.'

'I don't suppose we could be lucky enough for the second?'

'We certainly can't rely on it.' Maddie started walking up the road.

Harry slowed as she continued beyond their parked car. 'Are we not leaving?'

'Oh! Did I not mention the other job?'

'Other job?'

'Our burglar in interview. He said he did a couple of breaks in this area. We've only had one report along here — number 21. No one's been there yet to talk to them.'

'Can you not just send a DC up here? That sounds like a basic enquiry?'

'Welcome to CID Harry! You can't just be pointing at DCs and clicking your fingers. Most of the time there's no one in the office to point at. I just need to get an account. I'll get someone up here for a statement later.'

Maddie continued walking, trying to pick out the door numbers. She stopped at the end of a drive just a few doors up. A blue Ford hatchback was parked too far over and she had to walk on the grass to get to the door. She paused, waiting for Harry who was dawdling behind her, seemingly peering into the car. A teenage lad jerked the door open an instant after it was knocked. His face dropped immediately.

'Oh!' He grunted. He stepped away from the door, leaving it swinging open and called out, 'Ma! It's the Jehovahs!'

A woman appeared at the door, a minute or so later. She looked harassed. Her cheeks were flushed and she was holding laundry under her arm.

'I'm really sorry, I haven't got the time to be—'

Maddie held up her warrant card. 'Maybe your son should take a moment to ask a question,' Maddie said.

'Oh! Yes, he should. Sorry about him.' She rolled her eyes. 'Teenagers! Are you here about the break-in?'

'Yes. Do you mind if we step in?'

The woman stepped back. The layout looked the same as Grace's. The woman led the way down a corridor and into the kitchen. She appeared to hunt for a clear surface to put the washing down.

'Sorry about the mess. We're going on holiday tomorrow. You know what it's like the day before. Sometimes I wonder if it's worth all the hassle!'

'I know what you mean. Anywhere nice?'

'Yes actually. Lake Garda. At least I've heard it's nice — we've never been. It's a friend's wedding.'

'Ah, very nice, indeed. It's a stunning setting.'

'It will just be nice to have a few days away from here. It's worked out to be quite well timed really, what with the break-in.'

Maddie took out her notebook. 'I bet. I'll try not to hold you up for long. I'm DS Maddie Ives . . . this is DI Blaker. We do actually have someone in custody for the burglary here. I read the report and I know there is an appointment for one of my colleagues to come up and see you for a full statement. Do you mind just giving a quick list of what was taken? We're going to be searching this lad's place and it would really help if we knew what we were looking for.'

The woman huffed a little. Maddie was aware that her eyes lifted to the clock. 'Yeah, of course. I'm up against it a bit, but if you don't mind me stuffing the washing machine while I talk?'

'You go right ahead.'

The woman picked back up her pile of clothes and pulled open the washing machine. She stood back straight. 'Actually . . . JOSH!' she bellowed.

'*WHAT?*'

'Can you come down here please and talk to the police?'

'WHAT FOR?' The reply back down the stairs was instant.

'Don't be rude! They're here to talk about what was stolen. Some of it was yours. Can you come and tell them what it was?'

Maddie heard the huff, even from where she was stood. The same lad who had answered the door appeared in the kitchen. He hung in the door.

'Josh, is it?' Maddie said.

'Yeah.'

'Sorry you're a victim in all this. It's Haines, right? Your surname, I mean. I left the paperwork back at the police station.'

'Yeah.'

'Great. And what was taken that you can remember?'

'I had my Xbox down here with loads of games. It was ready to take to my dad's.'

His mother cut in. 'Josh is going to stay with his dad for a few days. He isn't too keen on weddings.' Her tone seemed a little frosty, like this had been the cause of upset in the house. Josh didn't return her stare.

'I was going to a gig. I had tickets. I didn't want to miss it.'

'You're not going now, then?' Maddie said.

'No. My mum says I'm not allowed'

'That's right. Josh here, at fifteen years old, thought the best way to ensure a bright future was to get caught smoking cannabis at school. He's currently suspended in his GCSE year. Something that might become permanent if I can't make his case at a meeting with the school next week. He seems to think it's funny of course. Maybe I should get the police here to take you down the cells — lock you up for a while. We'll see how funny it is then, won't we?'

'Whatever, Mum. Everyone does it. I just got caught.'

'Well, more fool you then. And now you want me to buy you a new Xbox and let you go to a concert in London. You live in a dream world.'

'Of course I do. And you're perfect. What is it? Two bottles of wine a night?' Josh turned away. Maddie heard the stairs thump as he made his way back up them.

The woman shook her head. 'Sorry about him. He has a very active imagination. It's been hard since . . . well, since his dad and I split up. This will be the first time he's stayed there, actually. It might be good for his dad to see what I'm up against at the moment.'

'Kids are never easy. It must be ten times worse when it's just you.'

'And the rest. So the Xbox you know about. There were some headphones too that belonged to Josh — *Beats* they're called. We got them for him last Christmas. There was a stack of games. I don't know what they're called but I can ask him again if you like?'

'Don't worry. Xbox and games is fine for now. If we find some games I'll ask him to confirm. The headphones I have. Anything else?'

'My iPad. It's white, but it was in a gold case. I had a smaller tablet too. A Samsung thing. It's old, I'm not even sure it even switches on. I lost some jewellery. Costume stuff, luckily none of the good bits. And we had a stack of letters. They were messed up but I think maybe one or two are missing. It was a stack of bills. Something I was going to worry about later. I have no idea why anyone would take them. And that's it, I think.'

Maddie closed her book. 'Thanks for that. Like I said, someone will still come out and take a more detailed report. It looks like we might get a charge on this one. I'll keep you informed. I didn't take your name?'

'Nicola. Well, Nikki, actually. Nikki Haines.'

'Thanks, Nikki. Can I take a number? Just in case no one has?'

'Oh. Yeah, I called in on this phone but you can take it.' She picked up her phone and spun it over to reveal a sticker with a phone number on the back. 'It's new,' she said in explanation.

Maddie jotted it down. Harry already had the front door open.

'You can get back to your packing now!' Maddie said, as they spilled out.

'I need to. We have a taxi picking us up at four a.m. tomorrow. It's all rush, rush!'

'Sounds like it. Have a wonderful time.'

They made it back to the car and Maddie checked her phone. She had left it under the armrest. It showed a missed call and voicemail from Rhiannon. It connected to the car and played through the speakers as they pulled away.

'Hey, Maddie. The hearing went ahead for Routledge this afternoon. He was first on. He went guilty, as we expected. The court has bailed him. He's on a tagged curfew and has signing-on conditions. He'll be back for sentencing in three weeks. I was thinking I would go round and see him later. Maybe he'll talk a bit more freely outside of custody. I'll speak soon.'

The call ended.

'Good timing,' Harry said.

Maddie was staring forward, her mind racing with options. 'It is.'

'And a good result? Unless I'm missing something?' Harry must have picked up on her sounding pensive.

'It is a good result. Especially with him. He's a slippery one. He never speaks to us in interview, but this time he did. I think I know why, too . . . he's terrified of something. He wouldn't tell us what. He was desperate to get locked up.'

'Sounds like a good idea to go and see him then.'

'It does. She's sharp — Rhiannon, I mean. She has a big future.'

'Someone you've taken under your wing?'

'I'm not sure she needs that to be honest. I like working with her. She's the perfect mix . . . the enthusiasm of someone brand new in, but the ability of someone with far more experience. I think she had a bit of a tough upbringing. She talks about it occasionally — but just bits, you know. What she did say sounded a lot like mine.'

'Like yours? How so?'

Maddie flicked a glance left. 'You interested in my upbringing, Harry?'

'Not really. I'm just trying to work out if I should get in a car with you again.'

Maddie chuckled. 'That's hardly something you can talk about. I remember the last time I got in a car with *you*!'

Harry turned away. His attention seemed to move outside of the window. He took a few seconds to reply — long enough for Maddie to worry that she might have upset him.

'You've got me there,' he said, eventually.

* * *

Grace stood over her chair. The vice was still covered. She always covered it over during the day. She didn't even like to catch a glimpse of it. She still couldn't even write its description in her diary; she could only refer to it as *the chair*. That didn't sound so scary. She dropped to her knees and leaned forward. She had her phone gripped tightly in her left hand. She pushed it under the seat cushion, far enough until she felt a solid strip of wood that formed a ledge. She had worked the stitching apart enough to fit a phone in it. She was confident it would stand up to the chair being frisked. Her diary, however . . . that was different. It was jammed down the side with a stubby pen tucked into its spine. It was out of sight and as far down as she could get it but it would be found easily enough if someone was looking. There was nothing she could do about that except not to give Craig a reason to search it in the first place. She needed to be able to reach it when she was sitting in the chair, when her left arm was clamped so tightly that she could barely move. That was when she usually wrote in it. It helped her cope with the pain, helped make the words flow. She could talk about how it felt. The phone was in its place. She pushed her fingers down to feel for her diary. She just brushed the top of it. She did

that maybe ten times a day. She liked to know it was there.
She liked to touch it. It was going to set her free.

Chapter 8

Frank Dolton swept through his front door into a grand entrance hall, his footfalls echoing around the open space. In front was his bespoke oak staircase that matched the material underfoot. He could still feel a breeze and hear the sound of raindrops bouncing off the carpet of fallen leaves outside. His front door was still open. He turned to it. His driver was standing on the threshold and he suddenly looked awkward. The floodlight covering the front door clicked off behind him.

'Sorry, sir, will I be needed any further?' he said.

'Oh. You have the thing, yes? With your kid. I think I'm in for the night, thank you, Peter. Just have your phone on you.'

'Very good, sir. I shall park the car in the garage.'

Frank spun on his heels and made towards the kitchen. 'Make sure you give it a wipe to dry if off!' he called out. There was a reply. He didn't stick around to hear it and it didn't matter anyway. He heard the front door pull shut.

The kitchen was immaculate. All the surfaces were wiped down and the fruit basket was freshly stocked. He never ate the damned stuff but it gave off the right impression. It was a large room with a vaulted ceiling that had panes of glass on both sides of the pitch. The rain ran down them in squirming rivulets. Three hanging lights dripped down from the centre to illuminate the island that contained the only item that was out of place in the whole room: a handwritten note.

Your evening meal is in the main oven. The accompanying vegetables are in the sides. Have a lovely evening. Sasha.

Sasha was a fine cook. He much preferred to be home in time before she left. Then she would serve the dinner immediately and clear away the dishes after. On days like today when he was late, he would have to serve up his own meal and stack his own dishwasher. He could always leave it on the side for the housemaid in the morning.

He took the plate out of the main part of the range cooker, careful to use the oven gloves, but it was warm rather than hot. He pulled back the wrapped foil to reveal a pork chop and a clump of buttery potatoes. He took an assortment of vegetables out of a smaller part of the same oven and slid them onto the plate. He hunted the fridge for the prepared pudding — Sasha's forte — then he remembered that he had asked her not to prepare puddings for a couple of weeks. The scales were tipping over twenty stone now. He was six foot four, but that was still some way over his ideal weight.

He devoured the meal quickly with a large glass of red wine. Then he hunted again for something that might constitute a pudding. He settled for another glass of red and carried it through to his study. His computer monitor came to life with a nudge of the mouse. Already he had new emails. He scanned through the list. One was from his accountant and there were two invitations to business seminars and a regular contact from a local estate agent who was constantly trying to prompt him into expanding his property portfolio. He would deal with them all later. A notification swept in from the bottom right corner: *Alexa would like to be friends with you on Facebook.*

He barely used Facebook — a waste of everyone's time. Occasionally he would post a picture of himself in his latest acquisition or when he was on holiday. His last two uploads were of a new sports car and from behind the wheel of his yacht. From time to time, he liked to remind people how well he was doing. But *Alexa's* profile picture popped up too. It was thumbnail sized, still large enough for him to make out an incredible female figure wrapped in black lingerie. His interest was piqued. He clicked on it. Facebook opened up on the woman's profile page. The privacy settings were tight, so he couldn't see if he had any mutual acquaintances. There were a few more pictures that were similar in tone to her profile picture. They looked like professional modelling shots. That was the problem with Facebook — you never knew what was true. Those pictures almost certainly weren't.

He clicked to close it. He should reply to his accountants, really. They needed some information before they could complete his tax return. He had been putting it off. He brought his email back up and opened the message. They wanted clarification on some of his expenses. There was a list of them. It meant going back through his diary and receipts. It was just about the only job he did himself. It could wait until tomorrow. His cursor chased across the screen to shut the computer down. Another notification snagged his eye: the same profile picture, the same woman. But this time Alexa had sent a direct message:

You don't want to be my friend? :(

He scowled. He didn't know how Facebook worked or how she might have known he had ignored her request. He clicked on the message. It took him to a different screen, still within Facebook. It was a messenger screen, like a larger version of text message conversations he had on his phone. Her message was at the top. A cursor blinked in the *reply* box. Idly, he typed: *I don't really do Facebook.*

The reply back was instant: *Shame. It has some nice features.*

He rubbed at his face. He took a swig of his wine. His second glass, and nearly empty already. He walked back through to the kitchen for a refill. He considered continuing through to the lounge and turning on the television or going upstairs for a shower and a change. It had been a long day and he felt like it was still clinging to him in a layer of grime. He was intrigued, though. He walked back through to his study. The screen had fallen dark but it was only asleep. Another nudge of the mouse and it was instantly bright. There was a new message: *I like your yacht.*

Made sense. She must have seen his profile picture and decided to make contact. In his experience money was a powerful motivator. This would be someone trying their luck, but he was no one's fool. He took a deep swig of his fine red wine while considering his reply.

How do you know that's my yacht? Just like I don't know that's your body.

Again the reply was instant: *You like the body?*

He smiled as he typed. *Of course.*

The screen changed. There was a beeping sound — a deep tone. The screen announced *Video Call from Alexa* and there was a trailing line after it. Below this the screen was split in half. The left side was filled with his own face and the right was a dark box. He hesitated. He'd held meetings before on Skype and similar services, but never on something like Facebook. His curiosity was getting the better of him, though. He clicked a button marked *Accept* but moved the cursor to hover over *End.* It couldn't hurt to see where this was going. The tone stopped. The screen to the right suddenly flashed with colour and then movement. Someone stepped back. The focus became clearer. Someone had moved away from the camera. It was a woman and she was standing in the same black underwear he had seen in her profile picture. It was the same body too.

'You picked up!' The lips that had spoken the words were half a second behind the sound on the screen. There was an immediate accent. Frank couldn't pin it down in those few words.

'I . . . er . . . I was curious.'

'And now? Are you still curious?'

He gathered himself together. 'Now I'm more curious.'

'I don't like it when people doubt me. This is my body. You can see this, no?' Eastern European he thought. He still wasn't sure.

'I can. I mean as well as you ever can over these things.'

'You want to see better? Maybe we can arrange this?'

Frank laughed. 'I don't meet with strangers. If you think that's a—'

'We do not need to meet. I find you attractive man. You find me attractive woman. We are in comfortable homes. Maybe we should enjoy this?'

Frank looked around even though he knew he was home alone. He could feel his heart beating a little faster. The woman moved further back. Now he could see almost all of her. She was in knickers and a bra; she had matching stockings and suspenders. He was a sucker for a full set — always had been. Her hands moved behind her back. She peeled off her bra to reveal her breasts.

'You see better now?'

Frank didn't have an immediate response. He took a moment. His mouth opened and closed a couple of times. 'I can see more, yes. Better, far better.'

She smiled and looked down her own body.

'You want to see better?'

'I always like to see better,' he said.

'You next then, Mr Frank.'

His eyes flicked to his side of the screen and he realised that he was leaning right forward, that his side of the screen was a cheek and one eye. He sat back. He broke away to look down at his shirt. A tie hung from it; he had undone his top button the second he had got into the back of his car to be driven home. He was in suit trousers and a pair of slippers. He was pretty sure he knew what she meant but he wasn't the sort to play those games. He took another swig of the wine. The glass was empty. He was starting to feel a bit muzzy. He would have one more. He got up for the kitchen. He needed to steady himself a little. He was drinking too fast. The next one he would take his time over. The bottle was still open on the counter.

When he got back to his screen the woman was stood with her hands on her hips. 'I thought you were running away! To mummy perhaps?' She pouted her lips.

He flashed angry. 'My mummy, yeah, something like that. Thanks for the show, okay, but I think I'm just about done.'

'A man like you? Done? I joke okay. You do not need permission. You take what you want. No man has yacht, has Ferrari, has big house and smokes big cigars without taking it. That is big turn on. It makes me want to touch myself. I like men who take what they want. Give me something to see and maybe I will.'

Her face was filling the camera now. She pushed a finger into her mouth, her cheeks dimpled around it. The finger slid back out and dropped out of camera shot. She bit down on her bottom lip and her eyes fell closed. He could guess where her hand had gone. He was meant to.

'Show me your chest,' she said. 'This is all I ask.'

Frank felt silly at the suggestion, but a little less silly than it might have seemed a few swigs of wine ago. Now he found himself beyond the point of curious, closer to the point of lust and tinged with a desire to show her that he did indeed get what he wanted. And he wanted to see more of her. He wanted to see what she would do, how turned on she was by him. Yes, it might stem from his money, but he could forget that. She wanted to see his chest. That wasn't about money.

Now he had made a decision, his fingers stumbled in his haste. He pulled his tie away. He unbuttoned his shirt quickly and pulled it open. His sleeves caught on his watch so he pulled it off and threw it on the desk. The woman's face had an encouraging grin. She stood back from the camera and turned away, bending to remove her underwear. She took her time. Frank found himself leaning in. The computer monitor held every ounce of his attention. She turned to face the camera. Just the stockings remained. She paced back towards it and leant forward until her face filled her camera.

'Show me what I make you do. This turns me on. When I am turned on I show you too.' She dropped into a seat. Her bottom half was now concealed by a table. She moved back smoothly; the chair was obviously on wheels. The underside of black shoes appeared at the bottom of the screen, one after the other, the heels pointed towards him. They were some distance apart. Her hands dropped. She edged further backwards, showing more and more of her legs. She was still biting down on her lip.

Frank was lost in the moment. He stood up and pulled at his belt. His trousers and underwear came down together. He was excited. There would be no hiding it.

'Grab your cock! Take it firmly and show me!' she goaded. He did what he was told. He leaned forward to support his weight with his left hand, his wine glass tipped, there was half left and it ran onto the desk. He didn't care. He leaned forward.

'That's it! Let me see!'

He was frenetic. A blur. He had to slow to hear her speak.

'Now, my turn!' She stood up — he could see her bare midriff. Her hand covered her up. Then the screen went dark.

He stopped what he was doing. He let go of himself and slid the mouse to wake it back up. Nothing happened. He banged the keyboard — the screen stayed black. He suddenly realised where he was, what he was doing. He reached down for his underwear and his trousers then pulled on his shirt. He could feel his cheeks flushing red — some exertion but mostly embarrassment. He sat back in the seat that he had pushed away behind him. The wine dripping on his deep pile carpet was the only sound.

He exhaled. 'What the hell am I doing?' He chuckled nervously and shook his head. He needed a shower. A cold one might be best; it might sober him up a bit. He stood up and felt a little unsteady. His computer made a 'ping' sound — an email notification. He scowled — the system had obviously crashed. He shook the mouse again and the screen lit up. It was back on his home screen. He checked along the bottom: Facebook wasn't open and Alexa would be long gone. It was for the best. Things had gone too far already.

He clicked the email notification. It was from an email address he had never seen before: "Alexa@friendofthedevil.net".

'Christ! She's keen!' Frank said out loud. But his mind was clearing a little now. He hadn't given out his email address and it wasn't visible on his Facebook profile. He still burnt with shame too. He had been lost in the moment, but the moment was well and truly gone. He opened the mail. It had *No Subject* at the top. The body of the email had no message either, just a file attachment with a downward arrow. He clicked it. His screen fell black again, just for a second, then it flickered white. A video played.

Frank slunk back into his chair. His screen filled with a high-definition video of a minute earlier — of him stood up and masturbating in his study. The video was two minutes long in total. His form filled half the screen. The other half was the woman who had called herself Alexa.

The transcript of the conversation between them played along the bottom of the screen at the same time. When the video ended, it closed and his screen showed his email. Another one had appeared. It was from the same address. He clicked on it.

Ten thousand pounds to destroy the video or the next email address I send it to is Mallory.shaw2@thunderstorm.com. And then every national newspaper and social media outlet I can find. I will send payment instructions. You have until 10 p.m.

Frank scanned the message. He lingered on his wife's email address and cursed. This was just what she needed — hell, he wouldn't put it past her to be the one behind it all. They were heading towards divorce. His solicitor had surprised him with hope of a far leaner settlement than he had dared consider. It hadn't been presented to her yet. She wasn't getting much, certainly nothing like she had boasted to their mutual friends. He was going to argue that she had walked out on him, that she had made the decision to end the relationship. He had a trump card, too: infidelity — an affair with some piss-poor builder at her gym. She was also claiming infidelity, but over a long period of time. He knew she had nothing to back that up. Not like he did. This would cause him problems but that wasn't why he suddenly burned with anger. He could cope with paying more money to his bitch of an ex-wife. He would earn it all back in a year. It was the social media and news outlet reference that he found himself reading a couple of times over and cursing himself again for being so damned stupid. He was close to being elected — so close. This would ruin everything. And that election opportunity was something he might never have again, no matter how much money he threw at it.

His email pinged again. He opened it up. It was the payment instructions. He would need to download something called *TOR*. There was a link that would take him to it. Then he could transfer the money via the dark web. He had heard of it. He had never contemplated having to use it.

He picked up the wine glass and walked it back through to the kitchen. It was all starting to sink in — how stupid he'd been! It wasn't like him. He was normally so closed. He got to the sink. It was deep and made of solid porcelain. He brought the glass down into the sink and it smashed into a thousand pieces. He turned to lean on the island, his breathing heavier. He needed that shower more than ever. He had never felt so dirty. He would use it as time to think. Then he would come back and deal with this.

* * *

Grace's Diary

Tuesday 5 February

Craig hasn't come home this evening and I don't know what to do.

He came home at lunchtime. He was so angry. I think it has been building up since last night. I was on the toilet when he came home. He said I was flirting with the police officers when they came here yesterday. I know I wasn't. I tried to not even look at them. I just wanted them to leave. I tried to tell him that I didn't do anything wrong but he wasn't listening. He had already decided that he wanted to hurt me.

He pulled me off the toilet and he beat me badly. He kicked me then he dragged me into the doorway and slammed the door into my back. I don't know how many times. It took me a long time to get up.

My back hurts now. It aches and earlier today I saw blood in the toilet bowl after I had been to the toilet. It was quite a lot.

It made me remember, it made me think . . . I still can't even say it.

When he was slamming that door I could see the look on his face. I didn't think he would stop. He was lost. His eyes glaze over and he just keeps hitting.

I have taken pictures on my phone. I will take some more when the bruising comes out. I hope this back pain goes away.

Today was the day you came to see me. I lied to you. I couldn't move very well. You came an hour after Craig hit me with the door. I was so scared you would know and you would make me talk. It wasn't the right time. And I know you will say that I should have told you, I know you will be angry with me. You said before that there's never a right time.

But there will be. And it is soon.

I'm going to go to bed. I found myself sitting in the chair, waiting for him to come home and tighten it, but it just feels crazy. He used to stay out a lot. I don't think he's coming home tonight.

I'm so glad I can write this in here. It still feels like I'm telling you. I know you will wish I had told you earlier, but I know you will understand.

And I know you will help me.

Chapter 9

Wednesday

Maddie Ives still had her moments where she missed her previous life in Manchester, but her early morning run was rarely such an occasion. This morning was among the more spectacular. A sunrise over the English Channel in a sky that was still in flux from a cold, clear night into a crisp winter's morning. The sea was to her left and Sandgate, the next town from Langthorne, was on her right. It was a thirty-minute drive from her CID office in Canterbury. She could have rented closer, but she liked the drive. It gave her time to organise her thoughts on the way in or clear them on the way home. She was almost used to the routine that the commute to work gave her. Rhiannon had introduced her to the area. She lived there, too, but her flat had a sea view. Maddie couldn't quite justify the price hike. Rhiannon had hinted that a relative was taking the edge off the sky-high prices by the sea, otherwise Maddie couldn't see how she would be able to afford it either.

She got back home just before 7 a.m. Her flat was at the end of an alleyway leading from the seafront and between a row of shops. It came out next to a deli and she had to sidestep the man who was opening its doors to set up. Delicious smells followed him out and she made a mental note to grab one of their breakfast bagels on her way back out. Having dragged herself out of bed for a 10k run, she felt she had earned it.

Thirty seconds later and she was changing her plans. She bustled back into her flat and breakfast was already waiting. It wasn't quite a bagel: it was a round of thick-cut toast with steaming coffee. That would do — particularly as it was served by Adam Yarwood, who smiled in greeting. He was already dressed in a crisp, white shirt, tucked into grey jeans.

'What's this? What are you doing out of bed this early?'

'I don't like what you are implying, Maddie.'

'What am I implying?'

'That I am lazy. That I waste my days rather than embracing them.'

'Well, you saw right through that. And why aren't you wasting your day?'

'I got some work. London. I got a message on my phone.'

'You plasterers are getting smarter.' She bit into her toast and eyed him closely.

Adam glanced down his designer shirt. 'I'm not working on the tools today. It's more of an assessment; quote stage. First impressions an' all that.' He turned away. His phone was on the kitchen bench. He scooped it up to check it. He had a suit jacket over the back of a stool. He put it on and pushed the phone into the inside pocket.

Maddie just assumed he was lying now — whenever he talked about work, at least. And he knew she wasn't fooled. It was like an arrangement they had. He was a self-employed plasterer by trade, his business was registered and he took on jobs when he could. But that wasn't very often anymore and his patch was four hundred miles away in Manchester. But Adam was getting work elsewhere with his brother, Leon Yarwood. Leon headed up one of the biggest organised crime groups in the north of England and, in a previous life, Maddie had been tasked with getting close to the gang and their inner workings.

She had been an undercover asset for Greater Manchester Police for ten years before she had messed it all up by saving a man's life. It had seemed like the right thing to do at the time. But she blew her own cover doing it, and the very next day she was moved to the other side of the country to start a new life and what felt like a whole new career as a customer-facing detective.

That was just over nine months ago. It already felt like a lifetime. It seemed that everything about her life had moved on — the only element that had followed her down was Adam Yarwood. She knew that one day she would have to face up to it — to them. Her employers couldn't know about her relationship, if that's what it was, and nor could his — one would see her dragged through a disciplinary process and the other might just get her killed. Maybe even him too. That was why she didn't challenge when he lied to her anymore, because that would be the point when they would both have to face up to it: the unavoidable elephant in the room. There was only one solution she could see, and she desperately didn't want that.

Adam faced her. He tapped his pockets and seemed satisfied he had what he needed. His visits were often fleeting. He would come down for a couple of days at a time. He sometimes talked about moving closer, but never seriously. He didn't stay at her place often; the risk was too great. But, just recently, she'd become a little more rash — a little less careful. She was making a mental note to rectify that when he kissed her hard on the lips. For a second she forgot every mental note she had ever made. He had that ability. He stepped back and his eyes twinkled their mischief. He pushed a strand of her hair out of her face with his knuckles, his hand resting to cradle her cheekbone.

'I'm taking you for dinner,' he said. 'In London. This little place I found. Sunday — you're off right?'

'Well yeah, but—'

'Sunday then!' he cut in. He had moved to the door. He pulled it open and stepped through it. There was no discussion, no set plan and certainly no details. Just like always.

The door pulled shut behind him. She lifted her own hand to her cheek as if he might have left something of himself she could gather up. She shook her head. She was being silly. She hated that he had that effect. She brought the hot coffee to her lips for a swig. Her eyes drifted to the clock.

'Shit!' She was running out of time. She slopped her coffee back down on the bench and made for the shower. She doubled back quickly when her phone emitted a whistle: her text message tone. She made it back before the screen dimmed. It was from Adam: *You look beautiful this morning.*

Her stomach fluttered a little and she felt her lips form a hapless smile. This whole thing was hopeless. As much as she floated to the shower, she couldn't ignore the feeling that always nagged at her whenever she dared feel happy about Adam: that this couldn't end well. And it *did* have to end.

For now, she needed to get to work.

<h1 style="text-align:center">Chapter 10</h1>

Major Crime was buzzing. Harry Blaker was aware that they had now been drafted in officially to assist with the aftermath of the explosions in the Roundhill Tunnels. It was the sort of incident that could jam up a whole police force, let alone a department and seemingly Counter Terrorism had run out of manpower too. Harry had seen the news, the incident was rolling twenty-four hours a day and talking heads were starting to demand answers. Harry knew the sort of pressure that could exert.

DCI Julian Lowe's office was mainly glass fronted and along with the man himself Harry could see a DC and Acting Inspector Carl Maddocks deep in conversation. Maddocks had been stepped up as cover for Harry while he was off. He was a nice enough fella, but he struck Harry as being a little out of his depth — too nice, perhaps, too busy trying to please the officers now under him, when his main focus should be on getting the job done.

Harry perched on the edge of a table and crossed his arms. He stayed out in the main office to let the meeting come to its end. Detectives were sweeping past him constantly in both directions, carrying blue files and loose paperwork, some chatting into phones, some calling out to colleagues. No one seemed to notice him. He would wait his turn.

Lowe's office emptied, leaving just the chief inspector. Carl Maddocks looked panicked when on his way out he saw Harry.

'Harry! I didn't know you were back! I'll clear out your desk just as soon as I can.'

Harry waved him away. 'You can keep it for now. You need it more.'

Carl nodded. He was still moving away. Detectives were making for him from across the floor and two questions came at him at once. Harry smirked to himself. He moved into the office and closed the door to the bustle. Julian Lowe was stood up but bent into his computer monitor. He looked up.

'Ah, Harry.'

'You wanted to see me, sir.'

'Of course I did. Sorry about the delay. Talk about timing, eh! Your first day back and it's as chaotic as I've known it.'

'My second, actually. I moved some stuff in yesterday. This is good timing, then. I can be a help.'

'You can. It was always going to be a positive to have you back, Harry. I did plan on taking you out for a coffee first thing — having a chat, you know, about how you are.'

'No need. I'm fine.'

Lowe stood up straight, his attention dragged away from his computer, his head rocked ever so slightly to one side. 'You're sure?'

'Yes.'

'You've been through a lot is all. I'm speaking with Occie Health later today, I want to understand—'

'I'm fine. Like you said, I've *been* through it. I just want to get back to work. It's already been far too long.'

Lowe smiled. It was patronising. 'Yes, Occie Health said you've been banging on the door for quite some time now to come back. I'm sure you understand that we couldn't have you back until we were sure you were okay. It wouldn't have been fair on you.'

'I understand,' Harry shrugged. He didn't. He had told Occupational Health it was a load of nonsense months ago. It was a tick-box exercise, his employer's way of being able to say they did what they could if he subsequently went off the rails. He told them that too. It wasn't about him; it was about protecting themselves. It wouldn't have helped his case any but he felt better for saying it.

'Okay, good. Well, something came in yesterday that I was going to task you with. I think it makes sense to stick with that plan, actually. You're better off out of all this.' He gestured at the window of his office and Harry looked out to the activity outside. He could see at least three people hovering close enough to the door to jump in the second he left.

'Maybe I can take some of the pressure off you, if you let me help?'

'It's beyond that, Harry. You'll just get sucked in and lost to this tunnel job like everyone else. It's a good thing no one really knows you're back. You can deal with something for me. Something that I would appreciate being nipped in the bud.'

'Go on.'

'Have a seat. It's a quick thing.'

Harry did as he was told. There was a knock at the door behind him. Someone had obviously been brave enough to do more than just hover. Lowe waved it away with a finger gesture that made it clear that he was asking for two minutes' peace. Harry considered he didn't have much chance of that.

'Frank Dolton,' Lowe said.

Harry recognised the name immediately. 'Frankie Fingers?'

'Well, yes . . . quite. I think he is soon to become Mr Dolton to you and I, Harry.'

'You think he's going to get the nod?'

'So it would appear. He's invested a lot of money in his campaign, although he is being pushed hard by some MP's other half, I hear. It's going to be a lot closer than we thought, but he's still the favourite with the bookies.'

'The favourite! Does anyone actually go out and vote in these things?' Frank Dolton was a local businessman who was in the running to become the county's independent police commissioner. These were relatively new roles and no one was really sure what they entailed. The senior ranks seem to recognise them as links between the police and the politicians that they answered to. Certainly, IPCs across the country had used it as a first step on the ladder to becoming a national politician. Harry was in no doubt that this election was nothing more than such a stepping-stone for Frankie Fingers and he would only be seeking political influence for his own gain. Independent police commissioner was an elected position, with the candidates funding their own campaign. In the past, the victor had generally been the one who had put in the most funding. And funding was not something of which Frank Dolton was short. His personal fortune was believed to be well north of a hundred million. Known as a local entrepreneur, he would be quick to tell you he came from nothing, but his nickname gave an idea as to how he had accrued such wealth. He was a man with fingers in many pies.

'It doesn't matter how many vote, just that more vote for Frank than the rest.'

'So what do you need from me?'

'Frank called me this morning. He was unhappy to say the least. It was 6:30 in the morning so I wasn't best pleased either. It seems he was the victim of a fraud last night.'

'A personal line to the chief inspector already!' Harry quipped. He knew Lowe and Frank Dolton were old friends. He also knew that Lowe didn't like people to know, or to show that they knew. He squirmed a little in his chair.

'Quite. I told him that he would need to go through the normal police channels, that there could be no special attention.'

'Okay. Is this the normal channel? You personally briefing a Major Crime guv'nor?'

'Well, no. Perhaps not. But your return has given me a bit of an opportunity. This is a sensitive matter. It needs to be handled as such.'

'Sensitive? Caught with his pants down, was he?'

'Strange you should say that, Harry. Mr Dolton got . . . chatting, to some young lady via social media. He was approached on a messenger system hosted via Facebook. I believe that somehow turned into a video call — I'm not really up on how it all works. Anyway, it appears that one thing may have led to another and both parties had indeed gone on to reveal their intimate parts to each other. It continued to escalate and there may have been an element of masturbation on the part of our soon-to-be-elected IPC—'

'And they sent him a video straight after and demanded money?'

Lowe's mouth flapped open for a second. 'They did. You've seen this before then?'

'I'm very aware it goes on. It's become common. What isn't common is finding the offenders. They can be anywhere in the world.'

'I know. I said as much from what little I know about this type of crime.'

'How much have they asked for?'

'Ten grand.'

'That's considerably higher than your average.'

'Well, our Mr Dolton does have a Ferrari as a profile picture.'

'So he's asking for it. What does he want done?'

'I'm not actually sure. He's made it quite clear that he has no intention of paying them for starters. He said that wasn't his style. He is of the opinion that this is a bluff and it will go away on its own.'

'Then why call the police at all?'

'Well, quite. He clearly isn't as convinced as he would have us believe. I think it's a bad time for him. People will be going to the polls very soon and this is the last thing he needs. I think he was running it past me to see if I'd heard of this sort of thing before as a way of deciding whether he has taken the right course of action.'

'He's probably right. That would be my opinion at least. You call these people's bluff and they slither away to pick on someone else. Chancers.'

'I agree.'

'But I wouldn't promise him that. They might release it just for the hell of it.'

'I agree with that, too. I said the same. He wants to know if there is anything that can be done to at least limit the possibility of this little *faux pas* coming to light. This would need to be under the radar — I cannot tell you how important that element is, Harry. He's not exactly broadcasting this as you can imagine. I told him that I would talk to one of my more experienced detective inspectors. That also means that if this gets out he will know that it was either you or me who leaked it, and I can tell you now that I will not be breathing a word. He insisted I provide a name, just so you know.'

'Well, thank you very much — the name drop, I mean.'

'He insisted. I said I had someone I could trust and who has the time to have a look. I've already started managing his expectations, though. I just need you to go and speak with him, see if there's anything obvious we can use. I don't expect there will be, so it's a few words of advice around what he shows as his profile picture and his security settings. Job done. He will be happy that he's had a Major Crime inspector out to him personally and that we've done what we can.'

'What have you got? From our commissioner I mean?'

'Not much. I'll send over what I have. I'll put his PA's number on there. Mr Dolton will be expecting you to call, so you can arrange a time that suits face to face. And Harry . . . I'll say again, this requires a certain element of sensitivity, okay?'

Harry's flat tone might have conveyed his apathy. 'Isn't that the reason why you gave this to me?'

Chapter 11

Grace woke suddenly. She felt like she was moving. Something had hold of her ankle in a grip so tight it was painful. The duvet was also close around her as she attempted to move inside it and she got a mouthful of cotton as she tried to breathe. She was dragged until she fell. The back of her head caught something hard, as did her injured arm, and she yelped in pain and surprise.

'WHO SAID YOU COULD GET INTO MY BED?' she heard Craig roar.

She pushed out her arms to try and get out from under the cover, but immediately felt blows on her body. She couldn't see Craig — she couldn't see anything; she could just about work out that it was daytime. She caught a blow to her head that made her ears ring. For a moment or two she didn't know which way was up. There were more blows, from which the pain may have stopped her from slipping unconscious. There was still something firm behind her and she leant back into it to slide down into her defensive foetal position. She brought her legs up and tried to protect her left arm, on which even the slightest touch was agony. The blows continued. She shut her eyes and tried to wait them out.

The shouting had stopped and now the blows stopped, too. She heard footsteps moving away. She didn't know if it was over. It seemed to be for now at least. She didn't move, not wanting to antagonise him, and concentrated on listening. She heard the distinctive swish of the shower curtain followed by the spray of water. A short time later the shower stopped and the curtain seemed to be ripped back again by someone in a hurry. Then came more footfall around her.

She stayed still. Her eyes were open now and starting to function. She could see enough through the fabric to make out the bedroom window as a block of light with shadowy movement in front of it. She could hear Craig making noises: animalistic squeaks and grunts that she had heard only a couple of times before, when Craig was so furious that he struggled to even articulate himself. He must have built himself up to it. She stayed dead still and mouthed silent words of prayer that he would just leave. He must have been out all night and he would be going to work. He had very early starts and normally rose before the sun. He had to be running late.

The footsteps were close to her now. She held her breath again. The snorts and grunts were replaced by muttering.

'You make me do this. It's like you *want* me to be like this. I swear you wind me up on purpose, mugging me off so I *have* to do it. I SWEAR IT!'

She twitched involuntarily at the sudden lift in volume. Then there was absolute silence: no more footfall, no more grunting. She considered the possibility that he was gone, but still she dared not move. She prayed for the sound of the front door.

The blow to her midriff came from nowhere. It rushed through the duvet so hard it lifted her off the ground and bounced the back of her head off something hard. She didn't feel pain; she didn't feel anything. Her peripheral senses closed in, but she could still feel her ankle being grabbed again, her legs being pulled roughly apart. She felt blows to her thighs on both sides, then she was tugged again so that she was lying flat. The duvet was pulled tighter down round her face and she struggled to breathe as the cotton was pushed into her mouth. There was another blow to her head — maybe two — before she felt her underwear digging into her skin as it was grabbed. Her hips were lifted off the floor until the material gave and she bumped back down. A weight pushed on top of her and she heard a grunt from close to her ear before there was another blow to the side of her head. Her legs were pushed further apart and she could feel a firm grip on her thigh. And then the darkness closed in.

* * *

When Grace awoke she didn't know where she was. She tried to move but nothing seemed to work. Something suffocating lay over her face and she was baking hot. She felt claustrophobic and trapped, and her hands lashed out in a panic. The something over her face was her duvet. She fought her way out of it and then felt silly for doing so. She was still on the floor at the foot of her bed. She stayed still for a few moments as the pain from her left arm threatened to overcome her. She lay flat and stared up at a bulb hanging in a shade that was criss-crossed with dusty cobwebs. She must have missed them. She used it as something to focus on as she waited for the pain to abate.

It was at least ten minutes before she could sit up. Her head hurt, her side and her back did too. Her nose throbbed a little, and when she put her hand to it she could feel a clump of clotted blood. She sucked in air, her mind flashed with the fear that had been the last thing she could remember. He had been here! She stopped still to listen. She couldn't hear anything; he had to have gone.

Grace tried to get to her knees, but moaned out loud as pain shot through both her thighs and her abdomen. She took another moment. She recognised the pain. It was a 'dead leg': internal bruising to her thigh muscles. She had lost count of the amount of times she had suffered it — usually when she had talked to Craig about going out. She couldn't walk well on it, certainly not any distance, but it would only last a day or two, then heal as if nothing had happened. From experience, she knew that the sooner she got moving around the sooner it would ease up.

When she tried to move there was a different pain too. She looked down to where she was exposed. She had gone to bed in a nightie and a pair of knickers. Her torn underwear was wrapped round her left thigh. Craig had forced himself on her before. Only once. That time he hadn't hit her, though, just held her down.

Craig was getting worse. Maddie had told her he would.

There was a clock on a bedside table that read 08:30. She didn't know how long she had been lying there. She struggled to her feet. Her muscles flared with pain, but she could walk. The stairs were going to be difficult. She tried the first, and when she shifted her weight onto her leading leg she was close to collapse. She had to grab the handrail. She sat down. Edging down the stairs on her bum was surely safer. Once at the bottom she was able to stand. She waddled gingerly through to the kitchen and considered starting dinner. She could get the basics done at least. She always felt a little less anxious when she knew it was started, then, if he came home, he could see that she had been there all day and that she had been working. She was expecting a delivery of shopping today too.

She used to go out to do the shopping, it would be her only trip during the week, but he had insisted on coming with her and she would hardly be able to breathe. She particularly dreaded the time to pay. The last time she chose a specific queue on purpose, where there was an older lady serving who had a cheerful exterior. She remembered being stood waiting with her head bent when a new till had opened up right next to her and a good-looking young lad had called out for her to come across. She couldn't refuse. Her anxiety had been so immediate and so strong she was almost sick right there and then. Craig was pushed right up against her the whole time. The man had noticed and stopped any attempts at small talk almost instantly. Craig had still had a go at her as they had walked out and started to lose control of himself. It got out of hand; someone called the police and he had later blamed her for that. It made her so weary. It just wasn't worth it. Now she ordered the shopping in. Craig still insisted the delivery time was when he was around. It was due early evening. She wanted to be moving freely by then at least — just in case.

She bent forward to check the contents of the cupboards for today's dinner. Both her thighs shot with pain. She straightened back up. It was no good: she would have to do a few laps of the house to get her muscles warmed up first, otherwise nothing was going to get done.

Chapter 12

'So this is where a millionaire hangs out during the day, is it?' Maddie said.

'I guess so,' Harry growled.

They had pulled onto a wide gravelled area where the pebbles were a mix of bright white, slate grey and black. It led to a red-brick, barn-style building that mimicked the numerous farm buildings that had lined their approach. On closer inspection, however, this was a new build, with sleek aluminium windows and a tiled roof with solar panels covering one side. It stood in expansive grounds laid to lawn. In the distance Maddie could see a real barn, this one far more dilapidated and authentic looking. To the left, the lawn sloped until it met a line of trees, while beyond them was a distant canvas of green and brown where the other side of the valley rose up sharply in the distance.

The gravel crunched under Maddie's footsteps as they approached from the left side of the building, which looked to be made up mainly of glass. There was a patio area with grey-painted rattan furniture and fixed umbrellas. The entrance door was glass too. Harry pulled it open for Maddie to step in.

The reception area wasn't manned. It comprised of four chairs around a glass table on which magazines were carefully arranged to look untidy. The chairs were arranged red-grey-red-grey. The attention to detail was a little sickly — where clinical met modern. Both officers stood hovering around the table rather than opting to disturb a chair.

There was no reception desk, just a sign on an aluminium pole that requested persons wait to be greeted. It was by an internal oak door that was soon pushed open by a stern-looking young woman. She wore a tight-fitting blouse tucked into a skirt over black tights. She wore black-rimmed glasses and Maddie wondered whether they had a prescription or were simply part of her look. This whole place stank of creating an impression.

'Can I help you?' She gripped a hardback book in her hand. Maddie saw the year was printed on the front: a diary, and a decent prop if she was looking to fob them off.

'I'm here to speak with Frank Dolton,' Harry said.

The woman fixed on him. She delayed enough maybe to prompt him to provide a bit more detail. He just stared right back until she started up again. 'I'm afraid Mr Dolton isn't available right now.' She opened up her book and her manicured fingers flicked at the pages, 'I might be able to book you in for something next week, but it really depends—'

'He wants to see me today.'

'You've spoken to him?'

'No.'

The woman huffed. She wasn't getting the detail she needed. 'So what makes you think that he wishes to speak with you?'

'He spoke to my boss.'

'And who is your boss?'

'Chief Inspector Julian Lowe.'

'Chief Inspector? Like a police officer?'

'Just like one, actually,' Harry said. Maddie hid her giggle behind her hand. She needn't have bothered, the woman hadn't yet cast her so much as a glance.

'And you are?'

'Also the police,' Harry replied. 'Maybe you could tell him we're here?'

'He has made me quite aware that he is very busy today. He specifically requested that I was to defer all requests of him to a more suitable time and place. Now, if I could just take—'

'Can you tell him it's about the masturbation thing?'

Maddie wasn't expecting that. Nor was the woman, judging by her reaction, but she seemed to get herself together very quickly. She closed up her diary and tucked it under her arm.

'Could you give me a minute, please?' She was gone before anyone could answer.

'What the hell was that?' Maddie said.

'We weren't getting anywhere near him. We will now.'

'And in what sort of mood! I get the impression this is not the sort of bloke that wants that sort of information given out to his PA.'

'You don't know she's his PA.'

'You're right, actually. Good point — she could be his wife!'

'She could.' Harry shrugged.

The woman returned, holding out a pair of visitor badges. 'If you'll come this way.'

Through the oak door was a wide corridor. Individual offices were off to both sides as they walked through, most were easily large enough for five or six desks; some had more and looked a little cosy. It seemed to Maddie that the building was occupied by several companies. They passed signs for an accountants firm, a marketing firm and some sort of communications company. Frank Dolton was right down the end. His office looked to be the largest and yet there was just one desk at the far end of the room. The left side of the room was almost all glass, taking advantage of the view out over the valley. Maddie had seen worse places to work. Frank Dolton had his name written in frosted lettering on the glass door leading in and on an aluminium nameplate on his desk. Maddie reckoned they were largely decorative — no one was coming in here unaware of whom they were meeting.

Dolton stood up from behind the desk. He was overweight, despite his attempts to conceal it with a dark-coloured, three-piece suit. His podgy face was the obvious giveaway. His brown hair was combed back and styled by a product of some sort and his bunched-up neck flushed red. He didn't smile as he proffered his hand to each of them in turn. Maddie couldn't tell if he was either angry or embarrassed.

'Thank you, Claire. That will be all.' He looked beyond them to the stern woman still stood behind them.

'Yes, thank you, Claire,' Maddie said, seeing if she could force the woman to at least look at her. It was the quickest of glances and the lips formed a pout rather than a smile. The glass door closing silently was like a starting gun to Frank Dolton.

'What the fuck are you doing here? When I spoke to Julian, I told him I wanted someone to speak to me off the record — away from prying eyes. So you turn up to my office telling all and sundry that you are police officers!' His voice was low and delivered through gritted teeth.

'You don't need the foul language, Mr Dolton. It's a pet hate of mine.'

'In my office, I'll swear if I want to!'

But Maddie noticed he didn't.

'So that is why we are here,' Harry said. 'You wanted to speak to someone, isn't that right?' His deadpan tone and face did nothing to appease Dolton.

'No! I don't know why you're here! This is not something that I wanted to deal with at my place of business. I'll be calling your boss just as soon as you people get off my premises. You can leave your visitor passes and be careful the door doesn't hit you on the arse on the way out.'

'I think there's been a misunderstanding,' Harry said. He held his ground. He had a way of looking like he was sizing people up when just in a conversation. He was doing it now.

'You bet your f . . . *damned* life there has. I didn't think Julian would be working with such amateurs — I actually thought more of him! Leave it with me, he said!'

Harry took a moment. He lifted both eyebrows high to show surprise. 'Then you have my full apologies.' He took his card out of his pocket. He turned it over to the blank side and took out a pen. 'This is my card. My colleague's details I'll put on the back, but she just came out for the ride. If you're upset with anyone, that would be me.' He turned his card back over and tapped his name. 'Now if you do want police help, you be sure to give me a call.'

'Came out for the RIDE! What the . . . *hell* is this? I called you people . . . I tell you something . . . when I'm elected . . . this is exactly the sort of thing . . .' The shade of red covering his face was distinctly darker. As was his mood. Maddie needed her hand again to conceal her smirk.

'You don't need our help?' Harry said.

'Not here! Not like this! I asked for your boss to come to my place this evening to sort something out. He said he might get someone else involved — Blaker, right? That's who he said. He never mentioned anything about anyone bringing along someone *for the ride*! This is a joke!'

'Did you expect a different treatment because you know the boss or because you might become the commissioner one day?'

'I don't like your attitude, Blaker.'

'I came here to help you, sir. Surely that's an attitude to be applauded.'

'And you couldn't come out to my place this evening, like I asked? You people are meant to be a twenty-four-seven outfit, for Christ's sake!'

'I'm not.'

Dolton's cheek rippled like he was biting down firmly. It seemed like restraint.

'I understand you might be the victim of an extortion or a blackmail?' Harry tried again. 'Is that right?'

'Yes. Well, maybe. But I don't wish to discuss it. I'll call Julian and see if I can get some professionals to deal with it.'

'Professionals?'

'Yeah. Not a couple off the street, turning up at my place of work unannounced trying to force a situation where I am required to humiliate myself in front of a woman I don't know from Eve and who just *popped along for the ride!*'

Maddie felt like she had been silent long enough. 'Humiliating yourself in front of a strange woman is the reason we are here, is it not?' she said. 'We both know what happened. We've had the briefing. This isn't unusual — I've dealt with a number of very similar cases. You've nothing to feel humiliated about. You're a victim. I suggest we get the details we need and then we can make a start on finding out who's really caused you all this upset. Because it wasn't either of us. Sir.'

Dolton's mouth flapped a few more times. He shook his head. He seemed to make a decision. 'No, you know what? I don't need you. I dealt with it. I did it my way, so it's done. I think I'll just leave it at that.'

Harry shrugged, 'I'm disappointed, sir. We might be able to do something, maybe even—'

'I think we're done here.'

Maddie knew that Harry didn't take kindly to being talked over. He fell silent, as if to give Dolton an opportunity to back down and apologise. He didn't take it.

'You have my number if you change your mind,' Harry said, at last.

Dolton pressed something on his desk phone. The outline of blouse and skirt was quick to appear in the frosted glass — *too* quick. Maddie was sure Claire must have been waiting just around the corner.

'Sir?' Claire said curtly.

'Would you show these people out?' Frank said. He sat back in his seat and shifted his monitor, clicking his mouse firmly.

Maddie allowed herself to be led away. She waited until they had lost their escort and were clear of the building. 'Thanks for that!'

'For what?'

'He's probably already on the phone to Lowe. Me and the DCI are already a little up and down to say the least. I'd rather he wasn't contending with complaints from the next commissioner with my name attached.'

'I'll tell him what happened.'

'What did happen?'

'I'll tell him his mate wants special treatment because of who he is, what he is and how rich he is. Life doesn't work like that. The commissioner, of all people, needs to know that.'

'That's exactly how life works!' Maddie said.

Harry fixed her with a fiery look. 'Well, it shouldn't.'

'Is that what that was about?'

'It wasn't *about* anything. He gets the same service as anyone. Or none at all.'

Maddie held up her hands. 'For what it's worth, I agree with you. It's just the DCI who might not.'

Chapter 13

Ian Hughes hesitated at the end of his daughter's drive. He hadn't been there for a while, and the last time hadn't gone so well. From being so close, all they seemed to do now was argue. He knew why. Her boyfriend Craig was why. His daughter was nothing more than an extension of him now. He was controlling, arrogant and moody and Ian had never hated a man more. He was pretty sure Craig felt the same about him too. Certainly he'd made it clear that Ian wasn't welcome at the home and Grace had ratified it, although he knew she did so under duress.

Seeing his daughter as regularly as he had always done was now impossible. He kept trying at first, at least once a week, but they were always 'on their way out' or 'busy'. Ian had almost considered giving up, but then he heard that Craig had got a new job that would keep him out of the house all day and he began trying again. He thought that, if he could get Grace alone, she would be the same girl he had known and loved her whole life with every ounce of his being — the more so since they had lost her mother. But she wasn't: she was distant, guarded and insecure. They argued. He kept coming round and trying, but she soon stopped answering the door when she was there on her own. It had been six weeks since he had seen her last. She might have thought he had given up, but the pull to see his daughter, even if just for a few minutes, was only getting stronger.

The drive was empty as he approached. Craig drove a silver Volkswagen estate car that he used for his job delivering parcels. He worked only until the late afternoon most days. It wouldn't be long until he was home. Ian had timed it like that on purpose. He knew Grace would want him gone before Craig got home. That might prompt her to answer the door. Even being told to go was better than not seeing her at all. He just wanted five minutes, but just to see her and to be able to confirm her existence was a start.

'Be calm, Ian. Be clever,' he muttered to himself. His eyes never left the front door. He just needed to see how she was, just a bit of small talk. Maybe he could lay the building blocks for some sort of relationship again. He sucked in a breath, walked to the door and pressed the doorbell.

There was no answer. He left it half a minute or so before he pressed it again and then stepped back. The blinds at the living room window were turned enough to restrict the view, but he could still see in a little if he pushed himself up close to the glass. There was movement, and his eyes were drawn to it. He could make out a figure. It was Grace. She was in a long nightie and was stooped over the sofa. Her head was turned away. He watched her push herself off and take a few steps towards the kitchen. She moved awkwardly, like someone who was in a lot of pain. She reached the next sofa and used it for support. She looked like she was recovering her strength to move again.

He thumped hard on the window. Grace turned as if she had been stung. Her eyes were instantly wide; they looked to be filled with terror as they met with his own.

Then she grimaced; the pain was clear on her face. He thumped again.

'GRACE! YOU'RE HURT?' he bellowed.

She shook her head and gestured with her hand. Her message was clear: she wasn't replying to him, she was telling him not to be there, she was gesturing for him to go.

He was going nowhere. He could see she was in pain. He moved back to the door and thumped as hard as he could. He tested the handle; it wouldn't give — double-locked. He pushed the door. It didn't have much flex in it but the panel that made up the bottom half of the door looked to be a weakness. She had a minute to open up or he was kicking it through. He knocked again. He pressed the bell too. A shape appeared through a frosted panel in the top of the door, long and white.

She pulled the door just a couple of inches, just enough for him to see her face. It was still tinged with pain despite her best efforts to smile. She looked tired — exhausted. Her eyes were heavy; her face was pale and red with a rash of spots. She barely looked like the girl he remembered.

'I need to come in, Grace. I need to talk to you. I can see you're hurt, what happened to you?'

'I'm fine, Dad! You can't come in. It's late. Craig will be home soon, I know you don't like to be here with him. I know you don't get on. Why don't you come back tomorrow morning? I'll have some time to make you a tea then.' She smiled again. It was empty, serving only to tug at the bags under her eyes.

'I'm not going anywhere, Grace. The sooner you let me in the better, if you want me gone by the time he gets back. I just need to be sure you're okay.'

'I'm fine! I told you that.'

'I heard what you said.' Ian stood firm. He stared his daughter down. She didn't have a response. Finally, she stepped back and he pushed the door wide open. She'd moved back to lean against the wall in the hallway. He stepped in. The house smelt delicious, like something spicy was cooking.

'I'm fine,' she said again.

'Let's walk through to the kitchen then. Once you've done that, you can tell me why you're still in your nightie at four p.m. I'm not going until we've at least done that.'

She hesitated. She had her hands behind her back. She pushed off. Her face flinched immediately. She gestured for him to walk through first.

He stood his ground. 'After you.'

She hesitated. When she took a step, it looked stiff and difficult. She took a couple more and her walking seemed to get better as she went. She walked down the hall to the kitchen. There were high stools under a work surface and she sat on the edge of one with her body turned back towards him. He moved past her to fill the kettle. It was stone cold. On the bench next to him was a slow cooker that was plainly the source of the delicious scent.

'Don't worry about offering to make your old dad a cup of tea! I don't think I've ever known you to have a cold kettle,' he quipped. He ran his gaze over her body again then raised it to meet her in the eyes. She was flushed red and he reckoned she was embarrassed. He was trying his best to stay calm about her being injured in the first place, but the fact that she was too embarrassed to even show it to her dad was eating him alive. The kettle overflowed over his hands where he wasn't concentrating. He moved it back and swore. He put it back down on the bench and sighed.

'Please. Don't boil that!' she snapped, seeking a way to stop him turning it on. 'It's had descaler in it . . . I still need to give it a proper clean.' Her eyes were still wide and they flicked from him to the kettle and back again. It had to stay cold.

'Did he do this?' His voice was low. He couldn't bring himself to say the words louder.

'What?'

'You heard me, Gracie. You heard what I said. You know I'm not stupid so you can stop pretending. I don't want to argue, but please . . .' He still wasn't looking at her; he was trying to stay calm. The sink was under a window and he looked through the spotless glass to a cheerful windmill that picked up a breeze in the neat garden. Its tiny, yellow sails whirled around and he watched it until they ran out of steam. That was his cue to turn his attention back to his daughter. She still hadn't replied. She was hanging her head as if she had done something wrong. Her hand was resting on her thigh and she was still perched on the edge of the stool. It wasn't the stance of someone who looked comfortable. There was a clock somewhere that had a loud tick; he counted nine of them until he broke away to open a cupboard. He took out two cups and put them on the bench — anything to keep him occupied, to stop him talking. He didn't want to push her away, to make her clam up. He had seen it too many times. He was quite literally biting his tongue. He started to look for a pan to heat water for the tea. Finally his silence worked. She was the next one to speak.

'I'm getting out, Dad.' Her voice was soft, so soft he almost missed it.

'What?'

'I'm leaving him. I know I need to. It's getting worse. But I have to do this right and I need you to leave. If you're here when he gets home . . .'

'Craig? You're leaving Craig?' He tried to keep his voice low. He knew he couldn't show his emotion. He wasn't angry with her.

'Yes.'

'He did this to you? He hurt you?' He choked down a sob of both rage and sorrow.

'I'm scared, Dad! I'm so scared. But I know him. I know how to handle him — after all this time, I know. I have to get out. I've been planning it for a long time. I've spoken to the police and they know what I'm doing.' She lifted her eyes; the skin around them was puffed up and red, standing out against her pale cheeks.

He swallowed hard. He could feel his heart beating strong and quick. He wanted to erupt, he wanted to burst out of the door right now and go find him. He wanted to tear bits off him until there was nothing left. He swallowed again. 'Where are you hurt?'

'It doesn't matter.'

'Gracie!' He checked himself. He lowered his voice again. 'Please, Gracie, where does it hurt? Do you need to go to the hospital?'

'I can't go anywhere yet, Dad, okay? I told you . . . I know what I'm doing. Please don't get involved. I've got a plan — *we've* got a plan. Me and the police. I've been talking to a woman — DS Ives — she's helping me get out. But it needs to be done right. I need to be sure that he can't come back for me.'

'Prison? You're talking about prison! What has he been doing to you?'

'Please, Dad! You will know. Soon everyone will know. I've written it down. Every single thing he's done to me . . . how it felt . . . what he said . . . what he threatened me with . . . it's all in a diary. DS Ives told me how to do it. And there are pictures. I have pictures of every scrape and every bruise. It's all they'll need. Please, you have to trust me. I will be in touch real soon and it can be like it was. I know I've shut you out and I haven't been very nice. I've shut everyone out. But you don't understand. If I talk to people other than him, if I go out to see people, it's so much worse. I have to do this right.'

'How soon?'

There were noises from the front of the house. Grace's eyes snapped to the kitchen doorway where she could see all the way to the bottom of the drive. Her eyes bulged in terror and she pushed herself to stand.

'Dad! He's back! His car! You need to go — you have to go now!' She limped to the back door. She tried the handle one-handed and flinched as she did so. The door didn't budge. She spun the lock in a panic and pushed it open. Ian hadn't moved. She turned back to him, her eyes still wide with fear and desperation.

'When does this end, Gracie? When?' Ian said.

'Please, Dad! Please, just go! He made me promise I wouldn't let you in! That I wouldn't see you!' Her voice was hurried and whispered.

'When?' he said again, his voice a growl. He wasn't moving until he got an answer. He could hear movement at the front now. Some shoes being kicked off, keys thrown on a table. Then a bellowed voice.

'GRACE!'

'Tomorrow! I swear! It's all been building up to tomorrow. I've got enough now but it's all hidden away. The diary of everything, the photos; I go tomorrow — the morning. As soon as he goes to work, I'm getting it all together and I am going . . . Please! You have to go!' She still stood by the open door.

'Now. Do it now, while I'm here.'

Her head glanced away from him, then snapped back just as quickly. 'Tomorrow! I swear! There are plans — please don't mess them up or he'll walk free and then I don't know what happens! The diary, the camera, it's all hidden. I have to do it right. I can handle him — it's just one more night! Please, Dad, this time tomorrow it will all be over. You have to trust me! You have to go!'

He took a step towards the door.

'GRACE! WHERE ARE YOU, GRACE?' Heavy footsteps clumped up the stairs. Ian had a choice to make. Craig was a big man. He would take some stopping, but he fancied his chances on rage alone. Or he could sneak out the back door, walk away and trust that his daughter would be safe — *for one more night*. And what if he did front Craig up and he couldn't handle him, he might knock him down first but then he would surely take it out on Grace too. He might find what she had been hiding. Ian's eyes rose to where the ceiling squeaked. The footfalls moved back to the stairs and he could hear Craig starting back down.

'Please go! For me!' Grace whispered. Then she raised her voice to call out. 'I'm in here, just finishing the dinner is all!' her voice was nervous, laden with panic. The footsteps sped up. Craig was back on the ground floor. It was decision time.

* * *

Craig burst through the door. He was flushing red and slightly out of breath. His eyes quickly searched the room and Grace waited until they rested on her.

'You didn't answer me?' he said.

'I did. You didn't hear me is all! How was work?' She leant back on the work surface, doing her best to appear casual. She had moved into the kitchen. The patio door caught in the breeze and creaked as it opened to its full extension. Craig's head jerked to it.

'You been outside?' he said.

'In my nightie! No, it was a little warm in here.'

He turned back to her. He lingered on her. She felt instantly uncomfortable, as if he would know she was lying. The breeze rattling through was cold; she had goose pimples everywhere. His eyes searched all over her. Then they rested on the two cups on the surface.

'You have someone in?' He moved closer.

She stood straighter. 'No.'

'Why two cups out? Did you not have chance to put them away before I got back?' he said. His tone was still low but there was an edge to his words that she had come to recognise.

'I wanted a cup of tea. I thought you might too. I was just waiting for you to get home. I don't boil the kettle when you're not here — like you asked.' He stepped to the kettle. She had got it back on its base. It had dripped from the spout where it was so full. Her eyes rested on the droplets of water and she bit her bottom lip. Craig made a show of resting his palm on the kettle to check the temperature. Over the last few weeks he had been insisting she didn't have hot drinks during the day. She knew it was part of his control: he reasoned that anyone coming over would have a hot drink — standard etiquette. If she hadn't made tea he could be happier no one had been there and she had been abiding by his rules. He had taken to dropping in at different times to test its temperature. He seemed satisfied, but he still eyed her suspiciously.

He walked past her and out of the open door into the back garden. She lost sight of him when he turned right towards the gate. Her dad had gone that way. She took a breath and mouthed another silent prayer that he had left and was clear away. Enough time had passed for him to be fully gone, but he could be stubborn — he might even have changed his mind completely and be on his way back. Her pulse was quickening; she could feel it in her temple when she bent down to get the dinner plates. Her thighs jabbed with pain and her arm was a perpetually dull ache but she knocked it gently on the corner of the unit and this was enough to take her breath away until the worst of the pain passed.

Craig came back in as she straightened up.

'What are you doing out there?' she said. She was still trying to be casual. She pulled cutlery out of a drawer next. There were potatoes baking, ready to be covered in homemade chilli con carne, Craig's favourite. She pulled the oven door open to check on them. When she turned back Craig was right on her. She stopped still. Her eyes were looking down. She could still feel his gaze boring into her. He was so close she had to turn her face to one side.

'Was there someone here, Grace? You know what happens when you lie to me. You know how angry it makes me. I don't want to be angry.' She could feel his breath on her cheek.

'What? No, of course there was no one here. Who would come here?'

He didn't move. She was still looking out to the side.

'Look at me, Grace. Look at me and tell me there was no one here.'

She turned to him. She had to push her head back against the wood of the units behind. She could feel the warm air from the oven rising up through her hair. The top of the oven was neck height and directly behind. She had to arch her back to keep it away from the heat. He lifted his palm and pushed it quickly towards her. She flinched, her eye slammed shut as she readied herself for the blow. It never came. He had gripped onto the oven's handle behind her. She felt the oven mitt fall onto her shoulder and then heard it slap against the floor. He must have knocked it from where she hung it over the handle. She opened her eyes and met his gaze.

'This is silly, Crai—'

'TELL ME!' he snarled. He then seemed to check himself and his head shook slightly. 'I just want you to tell me,' he said.

'There was no one here. Okay? Of course there wasn't.' She stared into his eyes. He lifted his free hand. It rested on the front of her neck. She flinched to his touch.

'You're not lying to me are you, Grace?'

'I'm not lying to you.'

His grip on her neck tightened — enough to pin her against the unit. Her thighs burned with having to stand straighter. His fingers tightened more. With his other hand he wrenched the oven door open and it hit her in the back and stopped so it was resting against her shoulder blades. The warm breeze turned instantly into a scalding heat that saturated the back of her neck. She struggled instinctively against his grip but he was too strong. She felt him kick her lightly as he adjusted his feet to get a firmer base. He was breathing faster.

'Who was here?' he snarled. His face was closer still, his eyes bright and intense. The heat was unbearable.

'No one! You're hurting me, Craig, you're hurting me for no reason!' She uttered the phrase Maddie had told her. It was supposed to be able to break through a fog of violence. Maybe it worked; he seemed to loosen his grip slightly. The oven was still searing against her neck and lower back. He hesitated for a second, maybe two, and then she heard the oven slam shut. He pushed off her neck and stepped back. She moved forward, just enough to be away from the heat. She rubbed at the back of her neck with her right hand, her left still hung useless. Craig turned away, strode out of the kitchen and was gone.

Grace moved to the side. She leant forward with her right palm to take her weight. The only sound was the bubbling cooker. She concentrated on lining up the plates, trying to ignore the burning sensation on her neck. She pulled open the cutlery draw. Serving the dinner became her focus. She was well practiced at getting on with things to take her mind off her pain and discomfort.

'Let me do that.' Craig was back in the room. He was smiling. He had a small bunch of flowers in his hand. He held them out as he walked over to her.

'Are they for me?' she said. She took them in her right hand. She tried to disguise the shake. They were beautiful: an arrangement of pinks and whites — and from a proper florist. She fought off tears — the sight of beautiful flowers combined with the shock maybe? Surely she was losing her mind.

'I got them for you today,' Craig said. 'I'll serve the dinner. You have a seat.' He pulled out a stool from under the counter. She limped to it. The seat scuffed under her as he moved it in. He ran some water into a plain vase and put it gently on the table next to her. He laid a pair of scissors down for her to use, then turned to the oven. She stripped the string and wrapping away from the stems then dropped them into the vase. The flowers stood high — too high — to be on the table; they blocked her view. Craig moved them over to the other side of the kitchen. 'You can put them where you want to later,' he said.

'Thank you. They're beautiful. But what did I do to deserve this?' She was uncomfortable. She couldn't sit in these stools for long. She was trying not to show it.

Craig cut into the potatoes. They spewed steam so he had to turn away, and he met eyes with hers. He spoke softly: 'You're good to me. I know sometimes we can fight — we're as bad as each other for that. But I know how lucky I am. Sometimes I like to do things for you. I should do more.'

'You work all day. I know it's difficult to—'

'So do you! You work hard here. I know that.' He moved to the table and leant across, his hands reaching out towards her. He took her hand in his. It was her left. As he pulled it gently towards him, she couldn't help but gasp.

'Is that arm really so painful?' he said.

'It can be. If you catch it wrong.' She forced a chuckle.

He stood back up straighter. He pulled open the drawer. 'There's only one thing for it then . . . It's gonna have to come off!' He lifted out a meat cleaver. She could see his grip was strong as he raised it. She flinched, nearly toppled off her stool. Then she saw him laughing.

'A joke! Just a joke. As if I would hurt you!' He laughed harder. Then put the cleaver back in the drawer and walked out of the kitchen. Grace exhaled. She could feel her pulse racing; her breathing was quicker too. She heard the stairs creak, and moments later there was a whooshing noise from the boiler in the utility room. She heard Craig coming back down the stairs and then he reappeared.

'I'm running you a bath. We can have a proper look at that arm. Is that why you're still in the nightie?'

Grace nodded. 'Yes, I'm sorry. I can't get it over my head at the moment. I didn't think you would mind . . .'

Craig clapped his hands. 'Of course I don't mind!' He turned his attention back to the two plates and finished serving the meal. He cut Grace's potato into fork-sized chunks so that she was able to eat with her left arm resting in her lap. She considered asking for painkillers. She'd done so before, but he'd said that he didn't like her taking pills. She actually believed that he didn't like considering that she was hurt. She did her best not to show her discomfort; it seemed to make him angry. Maybe today was different. She might ask later.

Craig took her plate. She'd not eaten much. Her appetite hadn't been good for a while now. He scraped the leftovers into the bin and stacked the dishwasher. He started it on a cycle and walked back up the stairs. The boiler went silent. He must have stopped the water. When he came back down this time he made straight for the fridge and opened a bottle of wine. He poured two glasses and handed one to Grace.

'Oh . . . I thought maybe I would take a painkiller. I don't think it's good with wine . . .' She didn't make eye contact, but kept her gaze down at the table. He didn't reply immediately. There was a silence for a few seconds. She was just about to relent, to change her mind, to say she wasn't in any real pain anyway when he spoke.

'I'll see if we have any.' He fidgeted in a cupboard, took away her wine and replaced it with a glass of water. He popped two tablets straight onto the table. She scooped them up and threw them into her mouth. The water followed. She finally looked up at him.

'Better?' he said.

'I'm sure it will be,' she said. 'Thank you. For looking after me.' Another sentence she had been given by Maddie. She had said that the key was to give constant reminders of how people are supposed to treat each other. Craig reacted with a smile this time. He walked back out of the kitchen.

He called back as the stairs creaked again. 'Your bath is ready!'

Grace grimaced as she pushed off the stool. She moved gingerly through the hall. Craig was already up the stairs. The bathroom felt warm and steam hung against the ceiling. The bath was deep-filled with a plume of white bubbles that was taller at the tap end. Craig put the lid down on the toilet and used it as a seat. He looked over at her expectantly — then slapped his palm on his forehead.

'Oh! Sorry, you need me, don't you . . .' He stood up. She was careful to pull her left arm through the sleeve herself, then she lifted the other arm and her side reacted with a twinge. Craig lifted her nightie over her head, leaving her stood in just her knickers. He threw the nightie onto the floor and stepped back.

'Jesus, Grace! You do bruise easy!' He expelled air through his nose, like he was forcing a laugh.

There was a mirror above the sink, and Grace was close enough to be able to see most of the way down her body. Her lower back and side were consumed by a dark purple bruise, which changed to a lighter pink around her hips. There were flashes of white too, where she had taken the impact from the sharp edge of the door. Her upper back was a bright red. That was new. She guessed it was from the scalding oven. Her long-sleeved nightie had covered her arm but she took her time to look at it now. She tried not to normally; the only time it was exposed was when she was sitting in her chair and then she couldn't look at it. She sucked in air quickly to choke off a sob. Her forearm had a kink and its skin was pale, as if it was washed out of all colour. She guessed the blood wasn't moving through it the way it should. She was pale overall but her arm was worse. There was bruising in a straight line along the bottom of her arm, this was the darkest purple yet. Her thighs, too, were bruised, a dark red that she knew would soon change to purple.

Craig was back sitting on the toilet, side on to her. His eyes roved all over her body but kept returning to her damaged arm. There was no hiding it. He didn't seem to know what to say, how to look. His attention shifted from her arm to the bruising on her lower back. She had bruises elsewhere. Some were older and yellowing, but still tender to touch — on her shoulders and legs mainly, but she had one in the shape of teeth marks on her breast. That was from around a week before.

'The bath should be just right,' he said.

She was still trying not to cry. This was the first time she had seen her body for a long time. It was like if she didn't look at her injuries, she could forget they were there — they wouldn't hurt so much. It was ridiculous of course. She bit her bottom lip. Suddenly, sinking into warm water seemed to her like it might be painful. Craig must have sensed her hesitation and he stood up. She pulled her knickers down one-handed and stepped out of them. Craig was still watching her every movement as she turned to the bath. She heard him move behind her. He supported her right arm. He was gentle but she still flinched at his touch.

'You're cold!' she lied. She stepped in. The warm water was soothing on her legs and midriff. She slid in further. Her arm ached a little more as her pulse quickened in the heat, but even that still felt a little better. She flinched when her upper back met the water where her scalded skin reacted, but she forced it under, her neck too. The pain eased quickly and soon she lay right back so that her hair folded in. She couldn't remember the last time she had washed it. Her eyelids drooped closed. Just her face and her bent knees were out of the water now. When she opened her eyes again Craig loomed above her. He was staring down. She suddenly felt vulnerable, she had forgotten herself. But he was smiling. He didn't seem to be offering a threat.

'I'll leave you to it for a while. I'll come back in and wash what you can't, okay?'

'Okay. Thank you.' She pushed herself forward to a sitting position and watched him out until he pulled the door to.

It was a good half hour before he returned. In that time, she'd heard a knock at the front door — their grocery delivery. Craig dealt with it. Afterwards, he was as good as his word. He washed her gently and they assessed her arm. She felt able to speak about hospital — maybe going while he was at work the next morning. He didn't shut her down, he didn't say anything; he might even have been considering it. He carried her to bed after her bath. He had a fresh nightie and underwear ready for her, then he left her to rest with the television on. An hour later he came up to bed himself. He brought her a hot tea and some more painkillers. She felt sleepy. She would need to get a good sleep. Tomorrow was going to be a long day. Tomorrow she was leaving him. No matter what he had done tonight, she knew him too well: every now and then, when he thought he had gone too far, he could be like this. She had seen his eyes all over her body, lingering on her broken arm, seeing just how much damage he had done. She would milk it. She would take the opportunity to get a good night's sleep and then he would get up and go to work in the morning.

And then she was leaving. She had to. She had promised her dad and she had promised herself. And everything was set up for tomorrow.

Chapter 14

Frank Dolton pushed through his own front door. Once again he was home long after the sun had set. Today he had given his staff the day off. He had found himself wanting to be alone more and more just recently. His driver had danced the equivalent of a verbal jig when he had called him on the phone to let him know he would drive himself home. Sure he had tried to conceal it, but Frank Dolton was astute enough to know a man punching the air on the other end of a phone when he was talking to him. He couldn't blame him. Frank was not a man who worked regular hours, meaning his driver couldn't either. Maybe he deserved a day off.

As did his cook, who didn't approve when he said that he would just order in takeaway. She was mumsy enough to suggest that he 'should be eating properly', but she hadn't put up much of a fight either. He knew he wasn't easy to work for. He wasn't easy to live with either. Hence he was stood in the hallway of a six-bedroomed mansion with no one to talk to but his reflection in the hallway mirror.

He tugged at the skin under his eyes. It stretched until he let it go again and then it crumpled back into puffy bags. He was looking old and tired. And fat. Hell, he was *feeling* old, tired and fat. He was best left alone when he felt like that.

Once in the kitchen, he threw the keys to the Bentley onto the burnished granite worktop and opened a bottle of Sancerre red, his favourite wine. Before the money, he had been a lager drinker, but he had invested in a wine cellar once it became necessary to host dinner parties for the right people and had discovered a love for red wine quite by accident. Now he savoured the smell of a freshly opened bottle and craved for the warm, muzzy feeling that started towards the end of his first glass. He had never really been able to handle his drink, even now that he was drinking more and more of the stuff. He kept telling himself that he would have a few nights off it altogether, but he certainly wasn't going to start tonight.

He avoided turning on any of the main lights. They were too harsh and he didn't see the need. Those hanging from the middle of the vaulted ceiling were decorative at best, bare bulbs with oversized filaments that glowed a copper orange — pretty to look at, but hardly efficient as a light source. He carried his glass back out into the hall. He would watch some television and then get an early night. The hall was darker still, just a lamp on a low table near to where he had come through the front door. His study was to the right of that and emitted its own glow; he must have left a light on. He popped his head round. The glow was a bright white. His computer monitor was facing away from him but it looked like it was the source. He walked in. He dropped into the chair at his desk, put down his wine and scowled at the screen. His home screen was showing: a photo of him with his arm around one of the pit girls at the Monaco Grand Prix. Sebastian Vettel's Ferrari was in the background, still wearing the blistered tyres in which he had finished the race. In the middle of the screen, just underneath his smile, was something he had never seen before: a digital clock. And it was counting down.

'Seventeen hours, forty-three minutes?' Frank said out loud, his lips turning to deepen his scowl. He looked around the room as if it might hold some explanation as to what the hell was going on. He had never seen a counter on this screen; he didn't even know his computer had the function. He did some quick maths: 17 hours 43 minutes was 2 p.m. the next day. He considered that maybe it was linked up to the calendar on his email account and he had some important meeting, but he couldn't think of anything significant.

'What the hell happens at two p.m.?' He moved the mouse and the screen flickered. The clock in the bottom right suddenly jumped forward a few hours as if it was a copy of the one newly discovered on his home screen. A symbol appeared next to his email icon: it showed that he had seven new emails. He opened it up; it was where he would find his calendar, too. Most of the messages were expected; things that could be dealt with later. One stood out — from someone called 'Alexa'.

His blackmailer was back.

He clicked on it. The message was in the same font as the day before. The subject line was *One More Thing . . .* He read the rest.

Mr Dolton,

I did not receive the money. This will not be good enough. I know more about you than you understand. I know to you one million pounds is nothing. This is what I will need now. This can go away but you will pay one million pound UK sterling. This is what you must do. You already have instructions how.

Twenty-four hours is 2 p.m. tomorrow. This is your time. This countdown is yours. This is more than a video ruining your politics now. I know you. I know your family. Because you did not pay, they are not safe. Do not pay and tomorrow I will demonstrate.

I'm watching you. Speak to the police and I will know.

Alexa

Frank pushed away from the desk and stood up. He moved to the window and pushed aside a heavyweight curtain. He peered out at nothing but his drive and the flanking equidistant lamps that ran off into the distance. He looked back over at the phone on his desk. He considered using it, but who would he call? He didn't know who these people were or of what they might be capable. He needed time to think. His eyes flicked back to the timer: 17 hours 39 minutes. The seconds were still counting down. His initial panic subsided quickly. He snorted and moved back out into his hallway. He wasn't about to be taken for a fool by some chancer who reckoned he was a soft touch and was making an idle threat towards his family. He had an elderly mother in a home, a dad who was long dead and a brother he only spoke to if he really had to. There was no way this person knew him at all. If they did, they would have chosen to threaten something he cared about, something that was worth a million pounds to him.

He missed out the living room and went straight upstairs. He would finish his wine in the bath and get an early night. Tomorrow he had another busy day.

He left the computer on. He didn't know how they had managed to interfere with his screen saver but he didn't care either. Tomorrow he would dump the thing and start again with a new one. Maybe get some expert to set up his security this time. And he would close down his social media, too. But all that could wait.

The timer continued ticking down in the darkness.

Chapter 15

Thursday

Grace . . . Grace . . . Grace!

It was her name. It was whispered so gently, like her mother had done when she used to have to wake her for school. She turned towards it. She still felt like she was in a haze of warmth. She'd slept better than she had for a very long time. Deep sleep. She couldn't remember any dreams, or more importantly any nightmares. Even her arm didn't seem painful. It was as if she was in a little bubble that cold and pain couldn't puncture. She opened her eyes. Craig stared back. He was smiling.

She breathed in deeply. She tried to say good morning. Her voice fell out in a murmur.

'I have to go to work,' he said.

She was suddenly awake, her bubble burst. 'What time is it? I missed breakfast! There's no lunch done for you!'

Craig was still smiling. 'It's okay,' he soothed. 'Don't worry. You needed your rest.' All the panic left her just as fast as it had come on. She slipped back to sleepy and warm. His face was softer than that she had seen for quite some time. She stretched her right arm. Her left was across her belly. As she closed her eyes in the stretch, she felt a hand push under her buttocks and another under her shoulders. She was lifted straight up in a strong grip. The sheets fell off her.

'It's okay, I can walk,' she said.

'I know that. Doesn't mean I can't help you down the stairs does it?' She was moving across the bedroom. He slowed right down and turned to the side for the doorway. She pulled her left arm in and it twinged a little. She would ask for another painkiller before Craig left. They got to the top of the stairs.

'I need to use the toilet? Don't worry. You get to work. I can sort myself from here. Thank you for last night — for being so good to me.' She was still sleepy, her voice still a murmur.

'I have to go. I don't have the time for the toilet.' Craig's tone had hardened suddenly. It caught her out and snapped her towards wakefulness. He was sideways again, taking her down the stairs.

'Craig . . .' she said, 'where are we going?'

He didn't reply straight away. At the bottom of the stairs he turned back on himself. He turned again to get her through the door of the living room. He wasn't so careful this time, and she felt her ankle bang off the wooden surround. As they moved into the room, her eyes fell on the chair. The blanket had been swept off. The vice was on show. She started to wriggle, but felt his grip tighten; it got so tight that it felt like he had a hold of every part of her.

'Craig, please! I can't—'

'You have to. I need you to stay here today.' He was out of breath, struggling to keep hold of her. She was still wriggling but could only kick out with her legs; everywhere else hurt too much. 'Grace! Stop it or this will hurt!'

He threw her into the seat. Her injured arm bounced off something. She cried out and he pushed his hand firmly over her mouth. His smile was gone, the softness gone with it. He pushed his face right up close to hers, his lips almost touching the back of his own hand. 'You sit the fuck down and you stop moving,' he bawled in her face 'or I swear you will sit in absolute agony for the rest of your *life*, DO YOU UNDERSTAND ME?' She'd felt some phlegm on her forehead and had slammed her eyes shut. She jerked a nod and he took hold of her left arm. She whimpered. His hand was still pushed tightly over her mouth and it made her breathing louder. Her arm was pulled away from her body. She felt the firmness of the steel underneath. He tugged up the sleeve of her nightie and it caught under her injured bone. She thought she might vomit with the pain, but did her best to breathe in deeply. She felt the first turn of the buttress thread and the rough edges of the plates slid smoothly towards each other, their touch was light and cold with the first turn. She knew the second turn was always the worst: once it was tighter, once the blood was restricted and the nerve endings trapped, it became a little more bearable, but that second turn was the one where she would feel every millimetre of movement.

The second turn came. She screamed into the palm of his hand.

Chapter 16

Grace finally had control of her breathing. Craig had been gone almost an hour. She had spent the time trying to calm herself down. Her panic came in waves. She was calm enough now to start looking around, to start thinking through her options. She couldn't get her mind clear; she just kept thinking over and over that this was her own fault.

He hadn't stayed long after he had trapped her in the chair. He never did. He always looked at her with the same expression: it was horror, she was sure of it. He didn't like seeing her in it. She had once considered that he didn't know how else to control her and that's what this was; she was convinced of it now. Before he left, he had said that he couldn't risk her going to the hospital, like she had said she would the previous night. He needed to be sure she wouldn't go. Talking about it had been a big mistake.

She had tried reasoning with him but he wouldn't listen. She promised not to go anywhere but he reiterated what he'd said: they wouldn't understand; they would ask questions and they would call the police. And then he left. She had begged him not to. She knew it was risky, that it could make him angrier, but she was desperate. She couldn't stay in that chair. Not today of all days. Not today.

Now she could feel every movement through her forearm. It was agony. She knew it would eventually go numb if she could keep it still and bear it for long enough. She would be left with just an ache — she could cope with that.

An hour had passed. There was a clock on the mantelpiece that had a loud tick and chimed on the hour. She scrunched her eyes shut and concentrated on counting the ticking in the hope it might help. The plates gripping either side of her arm still felt cold. She thought about what she had to do. First she would retrieve her diary. She hadn't written anything for yesterday but that didn't matter. She would find the time later — that wasn't her focus. Today was always going to be about leaving. She had built up this day for so long that she couldn't contemplate anything else. The phone buried in the chair was her way out. She should be able to reach it; she'd managed before from this position when she wanted to get pictures of herself trapped in the chair. But that was earlier on — when her arm was less damaged, less tender and painful. Getting hold of it today would be agony. She knew that, but she had no choice. Today, she didn't need it for pictures; today, it would secure her freedom. At last, she could be safe.

Twenty more minutes passed. Her arm had numbed a little and her breathing was back under control. She sat with her back straight and her right hand laid out on the arm of the chair, mirroring her left. She had to sit as straight as she could to limit her movement. Sitting in the chair for any length of time was exhausting. She was getting more desperate to urinate, too. She tried to block that from her mind. She looked up at the clock. It was nearly 9:30 a.m. Time to make a start.

She moved her right hand into her lap, shifting her weight a little so she could plunge down the gap in the chair on her right side. She leant a little, half an inch to the left. The pain was immediate. She screwed her eyes tightly closed. Her fingers found the gap and she pushed them down between the cushion and the arm. She felt the top of her diary almost immediately. Her fingers hooked over the top. She tugged it out in a smooth movement and trapped it on the right arm of the chair. She was back in her starting position with both arms out, her back as straight as she could get it, her breathing long and deep. She could feel her pulse beating in her injured arm and the pain was dropping away. She needed to be still for just a little longer.

It subsided enough for her to consider her next movement. She realised she was gritting her teeth. Sweat ran off her forehead and gathered in her eyebrows. It was cold enough to make her shiver. She suddenly felt cold in general. Craig didn't like the heating on during the day and she was just in her nightie. It made her need for the toilet worse, too. She breathed in deeply. This was it. She needed that phone. It was everything now. It was towards the back and centre of the chair. She would need to bend forward to reach under. She would need to put pressure on her arm. This was going to hurt.

She pushed her right hand under the front of the cushion this time. Leaning forward was excruciating and she had to stop. She let out a little whimper.

Her eyes squeezed shut as she shifted again, her hand pushing further to the back. She was more aggressive. The pain was worse but she gritted her teeth and pushed on. There was no other option. Her hand curled underneath the cushion, she could feel it under her buttocks. She shifted her weight forwards as best she could. She managed to reach the back of the chair; she needed to push just another couple of inches. She whimpered again, her head developed an involuntary shake, side to side, as if her body was telling her to stop. She pushed on regardless. Her fingertips brushed the wood of the shelf at the back and she could feel where she had unpicked the seam. With her eyes still tightly shut she leant further and her shoulder nudged something. She opened her eyes to the sound of her diary clattering to the floor where it had been knocked from the arm. She gave one last push and her fingers bumped against something solid — the side of the phone! She held her breath; she was nearly there. She needed to be careful. Her left arm was under more pressure than ever, her whimper was now a full-throated cry of pain. She wrapped her fingers over the top of the phone. She felt it budge. It shifted just a few millimetres — but it was *pushing away*. She stopped instantly. She couldn't bear this position much longer but she couldn't rush it and risk knocking the phone off its shelf. If it fell down the back, all would be lost. She edged forward again.

Suddenly her left arm was shot through with agony and she flinched. She must have reached a critical point; the angle was too sharp. Her right hand fidgeted — only slightly, but it was enough. Her hand nudged the phone. She heard it fall. It clattered against the wood then scraped against coarse material as it settled in the bottom of the sofa.

Grace froze. She was still leaning forward with her left arm so firmly held; everything was twisted at an unnatural angle. She moved to sit back up but took it slowly. The pain made her want to cry out again. She didn't. She got back to sitting up straight with her right arm mirroring her left. The pain wasn't going away this time; there would be no waiting for it to numb down.

She was losing her internal battle and was starting to panic. She dared to peer over the right side of the chair. Her diary had slid to the floor and bounced — well out of her reach, just like the phone. Craig would come home in a few hours and he would see the diary laid out in front of him. He would read the pages. He would realise that she had documented everything he had done to her and he would know that she planned to hand the whole thing over to a police officer named Maddie Ives. And while he read those words, she would be held captive in front of him by an iron vice — utterly helpless.

She tried to stay calm. Her breathing was getting quicker. She sucked in air. She told herself everything was going to be okay, that she just needed some time to think. There was still time. She still had a good few hours until Craig was due home. Today was still going to be her day of freedom. But now, despite months of planning, she didn't know how.

Chapter 17

Maddie huffed for the umpteenth time. She was staring at a load of numbers — crime stats, she'd been told. She'd been asked to make sense of them in the form of a report. She couldn't make sense of them in any form at that point, and when she lifted her eyes to find something better to be doing with her time, she saw Rhiannon.

'Oh! I didn't see you there!'

'I've been lingering. You looked busy. I didn't want to interrupt.'

'I can't tell you how much I am desperate to be interrupted right now. What's the matter? You look confused!' Maddie's desk was cluttered. Her notes and workings littered the side where Rhiannon stood. Her young colleague took her question as an invitation to swoop the paperwork out of her way, bunching them up and losing Maddie's place in the process. 'That's only an hour or two you've put me back, there, Rhiannon — nothing to worry about.'

'Sorry. I need you to look at something.' Rhiannon opened a file, took out two A4 photographs and put them down in the space she had just cleared. They were in high resolution and labelled the way a CSI photographer would. Maddie could make out someone's personal belongings, but they were laid out in two distinct lines on the scarred concrete of what looked like the floor of a garage or lock-up.

'Okay, so what am I looking at?' Maddie said.

'This is from the warrant this morning. This is Toby Routledge's garage, the one he gave up in interview.'

'Ah, okay.' She remembered how Toby had told them that they would find stolen property in a garage linked to his mum's flat. She looked again at the items. The first row of property had the fewer items: a couple of old-looking mobile phones and a Volkswagen logo key fob with a yellow cardboard tag tied to it. The second was longer: an Xbox with a pile of matching games and a couple of computer tablets; some headphones; items of jewellery — at least four necklaces and some rings. In both were scruffy-looking envelopes.

Maddie was feeling a little jaded. She hadn't slept well and so had given up trying and gone out early for a run for the second day in a row. She assumed the layout was something thc CSIs were doing now. She couldn't see why. 'He wasn't lying then.'

'He wasn't. But what do you make of it?'

'I don't know what to make of it, really. It matches up with what we know was stolen from number 21.'

'It does — the Haines address. Toby would have needed a car too, I reckon, so he probably had help. But what about how it's displayed? It's like he laid it out. That's weird, right.'

'What, this was how it was found?' Maddie was suddenly confused. She reached out to pick up one of the photos so she could study it closer.

'Exactly like that. They did pictures *in situ* first off. All the stuff is laid in two rows. And can you see the envelopes at the bottom of each row?'

Maddie nodded.

'We think that's mail from the two different addresses he burgled. Certainly, that row has post for number 21. He must have scooped it up from wherever people stack their mail while he was in there. It was like he's making sure we know where it's all from.'

'It's an investigator's dream!' Maddie said, but she was still scowling.

'It is. The other address was number 17 — Grace Hughes's place. You asked her about the burglaries didn't you?'

'I did. She said they hadn't been burgled there. I'll need to ask her again but, looking at what he got, it might be stuff you wouldn't miss. He said the back door was unlocked. It's plausible they don't even know.'

'It is. The fact that he didn't get much, though . . . that's odd, too, isn't it?'

'It is. Maybe Toby got spooked — or there just wasn't anything easy. We know he's not one for taking too many risks once he's in.'

'True, but if he was spooked, then they probably knew he was there.' Rhiannon pointed at the photo Maddie was holding. 'This piece of card here has a registration number on it that matches the car registered to the address — some Volkswagen estate thing.'

'Has the key been accounted for?'

'Again, it hasn't been reported, and you would certainly miss your car key being stolen. This looks like the keying it came with and they've taken it off. No one keeps the original key fob attached do they?'

'So why would you steal just a key fob?' Maddie said.

'VW keys are just a block of plastic these days. They look similar to this. Maybe he thought it was the actual key. I doubt he was turning too many lights on in there.'

Maddie considered this for a second. 'So what are we saying? Our serial burglar, Toby Routledge, goes out on the rob and by the looks of it has a reasonable night at one of the places he visits. Then he takes it to a garage and lays it all out so we would know exactly what he had nicked and from where. *Then* he tells us exactly where his little display is — in interview no less? The whole thing just doesn't make any sense at all.'

'Not with what we know about Toby, no.'

'I don't get it. It's not right.'

'He's determined to go to prison, that's for sure,' Rhiannon said. 'I guess the only person who can explain why is Toby Routledge. I planned on going round to ask him about that again, maybe he'll talk a bit more freely outside of the custody block.'

'I'll come with you.' Maddie stood up; the figures could wait. 'I assume you mean now?'

'Wait! I'm not finished . . . I remembered that Toby had conditions to sign on. He was due here this morning at ten a.m. I called down to Front Counter and they told me he didn't make it. They've got my number in case he turns up late but they haven't called yet.'

'So he's wanted?'

'Signing on is a court condition. He's arrestable with a transfer straight to court. He might even get his wish and get sent straight to prison.'

'Excellent. That's one wish I'll be very happy to grant.'

* * *

'Déjà vu!' Maddie referred to the climb up the stairs towards Toby's flat for the second time in just a few days. Maddie was ahead, Rhiannon just a few steps behind. There wasn't the room to be side by side. There still wasn't the room when Maddie got to the tiny landing that met directly with Toby's front door. She took a few moments to take it in. She was slightly out of breath and her thighs burned. Even the twenty-year-old Rhiannon was puffing out her cheeks.

Maddie lifted her finger to her lips to request quiet. She could still hear music from the ground-floor flat they had passed on the way in. The music was a sort of sped-up reggae — not to her taste and, she imagined, so niche that the chances of the neighbours enjoying it were slim to none. Besides that she could hear nothing else. There was a dusty mat outside Toby's door that she reckoned had been there some time and had probably outlasted a number of tenants. Places like this tended to have a high turnover of occupants. The mat was skewed at an angle as if it was taken for granted. The door itself was a solid slab of dirty white wood with only a flaked and tarnished chrome letterbox to relieve its plain though scuff-marked surface. The worst of the marks grouped together at a height that suggesting the door had been repeatedly kicked. They didn't look fresh. The sort of lifestyle Toby lived she reckoned someone kicking at his door would be a fairly regular occurrence. There was a folded-up buggy over to the left side, leaning tentatively against the wall with its filthy wheels pointed towards them.

Maddie had waited long enough. She pounded on the door. The letterbox rattled with each hit. She left it just a few seconds for an answer and when there was none, she hit it again. She also pushed the door at the top, middle and bottom. From how it flexed she could tell it was only locked in the middle.

'It's cardable,' she said. Her voice was low.

'Can we do that?' Rhiannon said. Maddie turned back to the door. She couldn't really, not lawfully. Police could force entry to arrest people if the circumstances were right, but they had to believe their target to be in there in the first place. Right now all she had was a solid door with silence behind it. There was nothing for her to *believe* he was in there at all. But this whole thing just didn't seem right: Toby's demeanour in custody was so far removed from what she had come to know of him it had actually caught her out; the photographs of his stolen property with direct references to where it had come from wasn't right either. And now he had missed signing on for his bail conditions. If the running theory was that he was ignoring court-imposed conditions so he could get sent to prison then he should have answered on the first knock with a bag packed — or even be sat on the front step with a cigarette on the go. But no answer? That really didn't make sense. Maddie couldn't stop her mind from conjuring up the worst.

'I'm going in,' she said. Rhiannon didn't argue. Maddie reached to her back pocket. This was where she kept her 'cards', which were actually A5-sized sheets of plastic cut in two and with well-worn edges. The design of some door locks meant they were susceptible to something strong, thin and malleable being pushed between the lock and its housing. If you got the movement right, you could part the two enough to open the door. This wasn't possible on modern doors, but on old wooden ones like this, it often would be.

She slid the card down the crack in the door until she felt it bump against the lock. She wriggled the plastic. It took a little manipulation and some whispered cussing, but finally she felt the lock move and then the door pushed in. Its squeaking hinges seemed as loud as a roar. Rhiannon had moved so close to Maddie that they were almost touching.

'POLICE!' Maddie paused for a response. 'THE DOOR HAS BEEN OPENED AND I AM COMING IN. POLICE OFFICER!' She followed her words through the door. She remembered the layout from their last visit, turned left into the living room and stopped to take it in. There was no one there. A dirty curtain pulled across the window was the only difference she could see. The open pizza box was still on the low, cluttered table. Disturbed from its feast, a fly lifted off the crust. The clothes dryer was still propped against the wall, the same baby clothes lying underneath it.

'MADDIE!' Rhiannon's voice from the other end of the flat sounded urgent.

Maddie turned and made for it. The front door still hung open and she stepped around it. 'Where are you?'

'I'm in here. I found him!' Rhiannon's voice came from the bathroom.

Maddie swept in. It was compact. A small, frosted window was directly in front of her, a sink to her left, the bath tucked behind the door with a shower head hanging limply over it. The bath was full of water. Toby was laid out naked inside it, his head closest to the door. His wide eyes looked up from the bottom, his face entirely submerged. The water level was so high that the slightest movement would have spilt it over the side. There was no movement. Toby was as still as a stone.

'Shit,' Maddie exclaimed. 'Stand back!' She moved her arm across to stop Rhiannon getting closer. Maddie had seen an electrocution in a bath before and the water had been still very much charged when they had arrived. She cast her eyes round the room. There was no sign of any electrical source thrown in the water. No other obvious hazards either. She risked plunging her own hands in and water immediately cascaded over the sides. She felt her knees and feet soak through as she leaned over to try and get a grip. The water was freezing. Toby's skin was too — and slippery. She scrabbled to get her hands underneath him so she could try and lift him. He was a dead weight. His eyes were still open and they seemed morose as they looked up at her, like she had disturbed his peace. He slipped out of her hands and his head bobbed back to the bottom. She knew the air was out of his lungs and that he had been there a while. She knew it was hopeless.

'We need to call it in!' Maddie said. Rhiannon had taken a step away and was already barking into her radio. Maddie's mind was shutting out the din, she could only focus on those eyes staring out from the under the water. Just a few key words from Rhiannon's update registered: . . . *seventeen-year-old male . . . in the bath . . . not breathing . . . Toby Routledge . . .*

Maddie shook her head to clear it. She tried to take hold of him again. She positioned herself so she was stood behind his head. She took a better grip this time, hooking her hands under his shoulders and wrenched backwards. Now his slippery skin was assisting, as it met no resistance from the smooth edge of the plastic tub. Toby moved up and over the side, his weight shifted suddenly and his pale body banged into the door as she lost control and had to step out of the way. He fell to the floor and the bathroom door was pushed shut, his hip resting against it. Her eyes fell to the court-imposed tag displayed prominently around his ankle. She stepped back and gasped for breath. Toby had come to a rest on his shoulders with bent legs angled towards the ceiling. His upper body was straight, his posture unnatural — like a toppled mannequin. Rigor mortis. She had known from the first instant that Toby Routledge was dead; rigor mortis confirmed that he had been gone a while. Four hours was the rough figure they were taught for the muscles to start stiffening up. The water had slid off him in a crescendo at first but now it drummed on the floor in multiple drips. His expression looked sadder now and she could hardly tear her eyes from his.

She needed to get out.

Chapter 18

Ian Hughes's hands still gripped the steering wheel, despite the car having been stationary for almost an hour. It was 1.20 p.m. He knew Craig went back to his depot most days between one and two. He'd sat outside and watched him pick up his afternoon deliveries a few times now and each time he had planned on getting him alone. He wanted to speak to him, to tell him what he thought of him. But more than anything he wanted to teach him a lesson. But each time he had bottled it and ended up watching him leave while he thumped the steering wheel in frustration at his own weakness. Craig was a lot bigger than him and no stranger to violence — Ian was sure of that. But Ian had been building up to this. He had anger on his side — fury, in fact. And it had worsened after his last visit to his daughter. He couldn't even think about the man without his heart racing, his veins flooding with adrenaline, readying him for the fight. Previously he had let him go. The last time he had got as far as following him for the first few deliveries. But then he went home like every other time, promising himself that there would be another chance.

But this was his last chance. Grace was leaving him today. She had told him that. She might already be with the police now and soon they would arrest him. He should go away for a long time. He hoped they would throw the book at him. British justice seemed to come down hard on men who beat up their women. But whatever they did, it wouldn't be enough and it wouldn't be *him*. He wanted to dish out some punishment of his own first and he wanted to look into the bastard's eyes while he did it.

Ian wore a hooded top with a large pocket running across its front. The pocket was stretched; the brass knuckleduster made a real dent in the material. He'd had it for ages, since he was a kid. Then it was just a prop, something he would show off to his mates. It soon got thrown into a drawer but he never dreamed he would ever use it for its actual purpose. He was not a violent man. His wife had been the fiery one; she'd always said that he was too easy going, that people could walk all over him. But everyone has a breaking point.

A silver VW estate car rolled past. The parcel depot was on the outskirts of Ashford, a large, bleak-looking warehouse with constant comings and goings. He knew the car. He knew it was Craig. It rolled across the front and then turned to go round the back where it would stock up with parcels for the afternoon. He had seen Craig come out with his car so full he would barely be able see out. Today he was only gone ten minutes, and when he reappeared the windows were clear — a quiet day.

Ian had parked his car in a row of others against a chain-link fence that marked the perimeter of the depot. He slunk in his seat a little as the VW moved back across his path, albeit on the other side of the fence. He could see Craig's face side on: he was looking straight ahead and didn't seem to be paying attention to what was around him. Ian couldn't see anyone else in the car. It turned left and came right past him. Ian had borrowed his mate's car, a dark blue Vauxhall. He didn't think Craig knew his own car but he wanted to be sure. He couldn't risk relinquishing the element of surprise.

He pulled out from his parking spot. Numerous car dealership forecourts lined both sides of the road. Craig continued over the roundabout ahead that took him past a McDonald's and then took a right towards the town centre. Ian was able to hang a few cars back. The traffic was steady. He took one hand off the steering wheel to feel for the brass lump in his hoody. It was still there. Even through the soft material it felt solid and unforgiving. Today, he would need to be the same.

They continued along a two-lane A road past a shopping outlet and left the mainly industrial area to move into a housing estate. The area looked bleak and tired in general, with grey-fronted council houses on both sides. There was just one car for cover in front of him now. He saw Craig's brake lights through its windows. He backed right off. Craig passed a house with a three-seater sofa rotting in the front garden. This was the last house in the row before a gap where a square of concrete wrapped round a dismal-looking pub. Craig pulled onto the hard standing and parked his car in a bay near to the entrance. A man in a thick jacket and a woollen beanie hat looked up from rolling a cigarette at a wooden table with a shredded umbrella leaning through its middle. He seemed to acknowledge Craig's car. Ian pulled in, too, but he continued to the furthest end of the car park. There were two cars up on ramps among a few more that looked like someone was storing them for later. Much later. The two cars either side of his had grass and nettles pushing up under their grills. He checked his mirror. Craig was already out of his car and striding into the pub. He looked like he was in a rush.

Ian walked across the car park and the man with the beanie hat looked up. The cigarette was between his lips now and his cheeks sucked in as he lit it.

'Alright,' Ian said. He was aware his voice sounded tense. He held his right hand firmly into his front pocket where he had already pushed his fingers through the thick brass. The man offered a nod.

The entrance was via two slim wooden doors that fell back together with a clatter. It was a big place. The bar was directly in front. A woman sat behind it on a stool with a newspaper laid out in front of her. A freshly poured pint was still settling on the bar. The stool beneath it was pulled out, whereas all the others had their feet hooked over an iron rail that ran along the bottom of the bar. Bunched up untidily on top of the bar was the jumper Craig had been wearing moments earlier. The barmaid looked up. There was no other movement, save for the energetic lighting of a fruit machine pushed against the wall on the right. A brown, battered-looking door was just beyond it. It had a sign that read *Toilets*.

'What can I get you?' the woman said. She folded her paper up and pushed it away.

'I, er . . . I was meeting my mate. I think he just came in here?' Ian pointed at the newly poured pint.

'In the loo. Can I get you anything?' She looked him up and down. He didn't belong in here and they both knew it.

'Oh . . . Yeah, I'll have the same.' Ian stepped to the bar. His wallet was in his back pocket and he had to take his fingers out of the knuckleduster to get to it. His fingers were so tense it took a few goes. She was busy pouring his drink when he dropped a five-pound note on the bar. He looked over to the toilets and sucked in a breath. He could feel his heart pounding. The rage was still there, but now there was an undercurrent of nervous tension. This was it: what he had been waiting for. He had thought this through enough times: he always planned to go in hard and fast, to get some shots in. He needed to get him down on the floor and then he wouldn't stop. He pushed his right hand back into his hoody pocket. His fingers found their place in the solid brass. He stepped towards the toilets.

* * *

Grace had been sucking in her breath. She let it out suddenly in a rushed sob. The pain had caused a feeling of nausea so strong that she had leaned over, her mouth trailing over the side of the chair, waiting for the inevitable. It didn't come. She recovered a little. She had two problems. The pain in her arm was unbearable; it came in waves and each was worse than the last. She couldn't do much about that. The other issue was her bladder, which felt like it was fit to burst. She was fighting it now and in extreme discomfort. She'd had pain for a couple of months when she went to the toilet. It stemmed from when she had been pregnant. She had confirmed it by a home test and told Craig straight away, hoping it might act as a wakeup call, that it might change the way he treated her. He had been happy at first. It lasted a day. After that, Craig was worse than ever. He beat her — and she was sure he targeted her lower body. Her miscarriage was inevitable, as was his refusal to let her see a doctor. She had somehow made it to the toilet and then she'd sat with her back against the door, sobbing all night. Craig had stayed downstairs. Every now and then she would hear him get up for something, he would pause the television. But he didn't speak to her. He didn't say a word all night, even when he had gone to bed, leaving her to spend an uncomfortable night on the toilet floor, too scared to move.

The next day he'd acted like nothing had happened. He was as nice as she had ever known him to be. He'd taken the day off work and they'd gone for a walk; it was a sunny day. She had struggled a bit at first but it got better. They still hadn't talked about what happened — certainly not about why. Now, urinating could still be painful, but holding it in was agony. She knew she was going to have to let it go.

She took one last look around the room, desperate for an alternative. There was none. She pushed her right arm into the seat cushion to assist with lifting her hips. It was an immediate sense of relief. Then she balked at the feeling of a soaking warmth and the smell of urine. She had to lower herself back down. She sobbed openly.

She focused on her breathing, concentrating on getting it deep and rhythmic. But though she'd found this to help in the past, it didn't seem to make a difference today. She had been trying to free her arm for a few hours now. She needed to rest, but she was going to have to try again. She looked down at her arm. It had swollen, noticeably so since she had started. She was getting rougher as she got more desperate. Nothing she tried seemed to work. She couldn't pull it back, her elbow was against a metal plate and pushing it forward just pinched her skin and worsened the pain. The only way it might move was by wrenching it straight up. She had to be quick and powerful and hope that somehow it came free. There was no point waiting for the pain to die down. It wasn't going to.

She would do it on the count of three.

Her right hand had developed a shake. She noticed it when she moved it across and pushed it under her left arm. She would lift her left arm and try and push it up with her right at the same time.

'One . . . two . . .' She abandoned the attempt with a sob and her body slumped forward: she wasn't ready; the pain was so bad — she couldn't imagine how much worse it would get. She looked up at the clock — it was just gone 1 p.m. She still had the luxury of time. She didn't have to panic just yet. But the sooner she did this the sooner she got free — the sooner she could get something for the pain.

She focused back on her breathing.

'One . . . two . . . THREE!' Her last word was screamed, she wrenched upwards with all her strength. Her left arm flexed from the middle of her forearm with a sickening crunch where something gave. It wasn't the vice, she was still held tight. The pain seemed to consume her whole body and the nausea was back in an instant. She barely had time to turn her head to the right before she was violently ill. Another wave of nausea quickly followed, she couldn't catch her breath, she wretched again, a little more fluid came out but it was mainly coughing and spitting foul-tasting mucus. Saliva hung from her lips. Finally she could get a breath. She lifted her nightie to wipe her mouth. She dared look at her left arm. Her forearm was now misshapen enough for her to see a raised lump. The pallor of her arm was a shocking white with the exception of the angry red where the dimpled jaws held tight.

She looked away. The sight of her injury and the pain made her feel sick again. She leaned back over the right arm of the chair. Her eyes fell to where her diary was still lying open on the carpet. She gave another whimper. She wanted to give up, to just sit still and try and cope with the pain. But Craig would be finishing at around 4 p.m. He would be home soon after. She couldn't imagine what he would do. She didn't want to.

The pain didn't matter. Somehow she had to make sure she was not sat there when he got home. She summoned as much energy as she could to yell for help. She knew it wouldn't do any good. Her neighbours worked during the day — most of the road did — but she was desperate, she had to do something.

* * *

Ian pushed open the first door to be presented with a short corridor and two more doors. There was also the distinct smell of public toilets. Both doors were off to the left. The one labelled *GENTS* was the furthest away. The carpet thinned out the closer he got to the door. He rested his left hand on the handle while his right made a tight fist around the thick brass of his weapon. He pulled open the door.

Craig leant over the sink, fiddling with his face in the mirror. Ian saw Craig's eyes shift to see who was coming and they made eye contact for a brief second. Craig started to turn. No words were exchanged but he must have read the intent in Ian's face.

Ian moved forward and swung his right hand with all he had. He was aiming for Craig's face. Craig was already moving the top half of his body away and Ian wasn't quite quick enough. The metal grazed something soft then made contact with something firmer. Craig shouted out in pain and surprise. Ian was close enough to see Craig's head jerk back and blood slither from his nose. *He'd hit him!* But there wasn't time to assess his handiwork. Craig recovered quickly, hunkering down and throwing himself forward. His right shoulder caught Ian under the chin, closing his mouth so firmly that he heard as well as felt his own jaws clatter together. Craig's full weight followed right behind the blow. Ian was lifted off his feet and felt himself falling backwards. His back and head bounced off something hard that then gave behind him. He heard the door smack off the plastered wall and he forced his eyes open to see the corridor he had just walked through — but as a blur. He was sent sprawling onto his back, the wind knocked out of him. Craig landed on top of him and quickly shifted his weight to sit up. Ian felt a strike to his thigh, then another quickly. He was trying to get his breath but no air was coming in. He felt himself grabbed by his hoody, a big bunch of material in a bigger fist. He was dragged to his feet and bundled back through the toilet door. There were more blows to his upper body and to his face. He was starting to feel them through the adrenaline and still he couldn't breathe. He flailed out with his right hand but his eyes were blurred, he could only make out the white of Craig's T-shirt. He missed hopelessly.

He was grabbed again. He felt himself shoved through another door and pushed backwards until his legs met something solid and he folded to a sit on a toilet. It was a slim cubicle. There was no real room to swing his arms but it would have been useless anyway: he was still struggling even to breathe. Suddenly he was hit hard in the face, the hardest blow yet. It was with the underside of Craig's shoe. Ian looked up groggily. Craig had his arms out, anchoring himself against the cubicle walls and he kicked out again. Ian took the blow to his chest this time and was propelled into the solid porcelain of the cistern behind him, which stabbed brutally into his kidney, before taking another hard strike to the face — then another. His blurred vision was now starting to fade altogether.

The blows stopped. He managed to rush a breath in but his stomach felt nauseous.

'WELL?' Craig's face loomed over him. He realised that Craig had been yelling at him for some time. He hadn't made out any of the words. He felt his head loll as if his neck muscles would only work on one side at a time and he still hadn't quite got his breath back. He had lost the knuckleduster somewhere. He lifted his right hand to his face. It came away bloody. He had no idea where the blood was from.

'WHAT THE FUCK?' Craig shouted.

Ian smiled. He took his time. His whole body was suddenly racked with pain. He knew he was beaten, but it didn't matter. Not now. He lifted his head. Craig's face was still blurred round the edges and a blackness seemed to be coming in from all sides as he loomed over him.

Ian's hands relaxed and fell into his lap; he was resigned to his defeat. He spat to the side, his saliva tinged red as it bubbled on the cubicle wall.

'You're a piece of shit, Craig. A bully. Nothing else. Someone had to teach you a lesson . . .' He sucked in another breath. He could only speak softly and even that took effort.

'And this is my lesson is it?' Craig sounded a loud, mocking laugh. Ian reacted to the sound with a flash of anger but he couldn't even lift his arms, let alone act on it. 'You're a sad, pathetic old man and you know what? Your Grace knows it, too. She doesn't want anything to do with you any more!'

'You don't know Grace . . . *She's* the one teaching you a lesson,' Ian growled. 'She's played you for a fool, Craig!'

'You think? She does what she's told when she's told. It's taken a while and she's had to learn the hard way, but now she won't have a bad word said about me. You reckon you can say the same, old man?'

'She was right! You really don't have a clue do you?' Ian managed to rock forward so that they were closer still. 'Where do you think she went today — right after you left for work?' He inhaled through his nose. It made a snorting noise. His mouth had a metallic taste, but he still managed to twist it into a grin.

'What are you talking about?' Craig was close enough now for Ian to make out something different in those eyes: a flash of doubt maybe?

'She's had enough. She's been building up to it for a long time. I came here today because it was my last chance before *they* take you away. You're right. I am a sad, pathetic old man. But you will be too by the time you come out of prison!' He managed a chuckle.

'Prison? What are you talking about — prison?'

Ian's head still lolled a little. He managed to lean back and get some stability from the wall behind. 'She's been keeping a diary. My Gracie. She's written down everything you've ever done to her, every finger you laid on her. And if that isn't enough, she has pictures too! You didn't know that, did you? She's got pictures of every cut, every bruise, every little blemish you ever inflicted on my daughter. They'll be enough to send you down, Craig, I'm right about that, aren't I? She's been hiding a diary and a camera right under your nose this whole time, you *stupid* fuck! Your best bet is to go straight from here to hand yourself in. The police will be looking for you by now, Craig.'

Craig stepped back. His face was red with exertion but it looked to have changed shade. When he leaned back in to speak he spat a little globule of white phlegm.

'You're right. I didn't know about her little diary or her bit of photography. I didn't know that at all, the cheeky little *bitch!* But I do now. You remember that. You remember it was you who told me!' Craig stepped back. His arms pushed out for the sides of the cubicle again. Ian saw Craig lift his foot. He saw the foot lash towards him sole first. Then the blackness closed in.

* * *

The barmaid was replenishing bottles when she heard the first bang, followed by an angry shout, then another bang. She made her way to the end of the bar nearer to the toilets. She knew better than to get involved but she held her phone in her hand in case she needed to make a call. Those sorts of sounds weren't exactly out of the ordinary in this place, but generally that was on a Saturday night, when she had other people around her to make sure she didn't get caught up in it. She was on her own today. She had learned to handle herself since taking this job but right now she still felt vulnerable.

Suddenly the door from the toilets was flung open and it bounced off the wall. She saw Craig appear. He popped in a couple of times a week at least, always at lunchtime. She only knew his first name. She turned away, hiding the phone behind her back, trying her best to act disinterested. She could see from his expression that he didn't want to be questioned. It wasn't just his expression either, the bloody stain that started at his nose told her the same. He strode the length of the bar. When she dared look over, he was staring forward, his hands were bunched into fists and his arms swung as if his chest was tensed. He was veering left, towards the door and away from the bar.

'You not stopping for that pint, love?' she chanced.

His eyes flicked over to her. They were unblinking, they seemed opaque and fixed, as if he was looking through her rather than at her.

'I have to get home.' His voice was a low growl. He barely slowed his pace. His head snapped back to the main door and then he opened it roughly. It was raining now, mixed with sleet and hard enough for her to hear it as well as see it. He didn't close the door behind him. She watched him step into the freezing wetness, unflinching in his T-shirt and jeans as he strode out of sight.

'That is one angry man!' She gave a nervous chuckle and walked around to close the door and stop the draught. She should go and check on the older man, but first she stopped at the window. Craig's car was moving off quickly — a silver estate. She clocked the number plate as best she could. She would check the old fella first. She knew better than to call the police before she was asked to.

Chapter 19

'How you doing, kid?'

Maddie was sitting on the top of the stairs, her bum on the small parcel of carpet that served as Toby Routledge's landing with her legs on the next step, hugging her knees. She let them go immediately in response to Harry's voice. He came out of Toby's flat, which she and Rhiannon had entered a couple of hours earlier. There was no reason for her to still be there, not after she had called in the reinforcements, but she hadn't left yet. It didn't feel right — leaving before he did. Toby Routledge was a piece of shit, a thief who had often targeted the elderly, robbing them of their possessions so he could get his next bag of cannabis. But Toby was essentially lazy. He saw breaking into houses as quick and easy; it got him what he wanted — it wasn't personal. He didn't dislike the occupants and Maddie reckoned that if he could have seen an old man's pain when he awoke to find his military service medals missing, he would be uncomfortable — sorry, in fact. And he was just seventeen years old. Good person, bad person . . . he hadn't had the chance to make his final choice.

Harry had sat himself down next to her. She saw his legs appear as he trailed down the steep staircase. His shoes were doing their best to burst out of the blue forensic overshoes that only came in one-size-fits-nobody. She had hesitated long enough.

'Alright. You?'

'Tough find that. Just a boy really.'

'Yeah.' She gritted her teeth. 'Just a boy.'

'You know him well?'

'I wouldn't say that. It was just cops and robbers stuff. He was a regular. We had a few games with him.'

Harry sniffed. 'You'll hear cops saying things about Toby, like he got what he deserved and good riddance. They don't mean it. We all know it's a waste of a life in there. No kid deserves that.'

'I know. I know it's part of coping.'

'It is. So, how do you cope?'

'Find who was responsible, I suppose.' She turned to Harry; he was looking at her intently. His face creased a little.

'Foul play for you, then? No hesitation.'

'Yes.'

'There's no clear evidence of that. The devil, if he had an advocate, would say Toby fell asleep in the bath. He was a known drug user . . . maybe he took a downer — something he hadn't had before. I've seen it happen.'

'He was terrified when I last saw him. He was worried about something — about *someone*. I think this was it. This was what he was worried about.'

'That won't be enough,' Harry said.

'It won't. When I got in that room, the water was brimming — I mean to the very top. But the tap was off and he was laid down. No way he could have shut that tap off without disturbing the water. The floor wasn't wet when I went in, either — not noticeably. And there was nothing around the edge . . . no soap, nothing to wash with and certainly no drug paraphernalia. And where are the clothes he was wearing? I know his place is a mess, but there would be a pile of clothes, the one's he took off, his boxer shorts in the bathroom or thrown on the floor somewhere. I had a quick look, there was nothing like that.'

Harry turned away. He smirked a little.

'What?'

'I agree,' he said.

'Harry Blaker . . . agrees! Well, that was worth the nine-month wait on its own!'

'I worked with some good detectives when I was first in and I was taught a valuable lesson about deaths. You always have to ask yourself a question at a scene . . . what *isn't* here?'

'Well, that is helpful.' Maddie rolled her eyes. She wasn't in the mood for riddles.

'It will be when you take the time to think about it. You're right about his clothes. No evidence of drug use and where's his phone? Do you know a teenager these days that doesn't have a smartphone with them twenty-four/seven?'

'We took a phone off him the day before, but I get your point. He would have replaced it in an instant. Is that why you're here, then? To pass on your wisdom?'

Harry groaned as he got to his feet and turned towards the flat. 'Nope. I'm here to open a murder investigation. Why else would I be here?'

Maddie managed a grin. 'Because you've got nothing better to do!'

'Well, now I have. This is my case, apparently.'

Maddie suddenly turned serious. 'I want to be involved, Harry. I don't want to be shut out of this one. I understand that I can't be in there now, I get the forensics bit, but I want to—'

Harry held up his hands. 'I've already cleared it with the boss. Go back and type up your statement with all that happened here. Be detailed. I'll come and find you when I'm back. We'll talk about what we do next.'

Maddie's couldn't help but smile. 'You've missed me, haven't you.'

'Nope. You know this kid and his background. And I'm still not allowed out on my own.'

'So it's a marriage of convenience? That's still a marriage, Harry, you know that, right?'

'It's beginning to feel like one. Take that as you will.' His growl was back. He stepped back into the flat.

Maddie stood up and leaned to the door. 'Happiest day of my life, Harry!' She started down the stairs. She felt like she could leave now, knowing that Toby was in good hands.

Chapter 20

Grace sobbed so hard it came out as a snort. Her body slumped and then straightened immediately as the pain tore through her arm. It wasn't coming free. She was no closer than she'd been five hours before when she had first started. Her throat was sore now, her voice all but shouted out. Her eyes moved around the room, desperate for something she could use. There was nothing in reach.

Her eyes fell to her nightie. It had ridden up her thigh. Her skin was pimpled as if it was cold. She wasn't feeling the cold or the damp cushion anymore. Maybe she was beyond that. She forced herself to look back at her arm and at the iron vice that held it. She had to run over every detail. That was how you found weaknesses, by studying every element. That seemed to make sense. She had never really looked at it. She had never really wanted to get out of it before; she knew the repercussions would have been so much worse. Taking the time to study it might help keep her calm. She focused on the device, talking out loud and describing what she was seeing.

'It's cast iron. Matt grey, painted . . .' she managed, her voice croaking and breathy. 'The metal plates of the vice

169

are long . . . shiny and black on the outside. Dimpled on the inside where they touch my skin . . . raised teeth on the edges — I can feel their grip . . .' She shut her eyes for a second. The pain came in waves, and every now and then she had to suck in a breath and hold it until it passed. It was just a few seconds. She carried on.

'The plates are screwed to tighten them.' She leaned to the left. It increased her discomfort but she needed to see it all. She could see the mechanism that was locking her in. Her voice was still strained.

'There's a handle . . . matte grey. There are . . . one, two, three, four, *five* spindles to the handle. They twist to tighten it. They will twist to undo it. I cannot reach them with my free hand . . .' She stopped abruptly. Her whole body was screaming at her to move back to sitting straight, to take the pressure off her left side. She held her position for just a couple more seconds, still looking down at the five spindles on the handle. She had an idea — it came to her all at once. Maybe it could work? It had to work! She suddenly felt a little rejuvenated. It was something at least. But it was going to take some time. She checked the clock. She needed to rest — just for a little while.

'I have time. He doesn't even finish work for a good few hours.' She spoke out to the empty room. It made her feel better. It made her a little calmer. 'You still have plenty of time,' she said again.

* * *

Sergeant Tim Betts was staring out of his driver's window when the radio sounded. An emergency call had come in — a fight at a pub. The offender had left the scene and they were still broadcasting details of the car, a silver VW Passat. They gave the last-known location and a general direction of travel. The pub was in the next town over. Tim had sat up straighter, but now he relaxed back into his seat. Someone would be closer. Their car was ticking over where they had stopped for a takeaway coffee.

It had been a busy shift. He went back to staring out of his window, hoping they would be left alone for the half hour it would take to finish another day. The broadcast was still going on.

'The informant only got a part reg and said a name for one of the offenders was "Craig", we have a possible match on PNC for a VW Passat, colour silver, with the RO from 17 Campbell Road, Hawkinge . . .' The chatter was just washing over Tim now; he was only half listening — until Vince Arnold snapped to attention beside him.

'Tim! 17 Campbell Road! That's our wife beater from the other night! He might be heading home. That's not far from here.' Vince didn't need much of an excuse to get excited.

Tim picked his coffee back up. He took a larger gulp than originally intended, then pushed the lid back on. So much for being left alone.

'And you want to head up there?'

'Well, yeah. I was desperate for an excuse to nick that fella the other night. This is fate!'

'It's a part reg and a *possible* match. I don't think it's a nicking yet.'

'Don't mug off fate, Tim! Bad things happen when you do that! It's gotta be him! The fella's a thug and the witness got what? Five out of seven digits right *and* a first name!'

Tim shrugged. He couldn't argue. He put his cup in the holder. Hawkinge was just a couple of minutes up the motorway from here — the next junction. They might as well make progress. He put the blue lights and siren on — maybe a little early. Tim looked up to see the milkshake of a young lad, who had been walking across the front of their parking bay in McDonald's, spreading out over the damp concrete. Tim put his hand up. The lad waved back — still with a shocked expression and a grimace at the sound. He stepped out of the way.

'Zulu One, show us attending the area of the h/a for that last broadcast. We know the male. He might be heading home.'

'*Zulu One . . . thank you for that. All received.*' Tim heard other patrols over the revving of the engine, they were calling up to go to the pub where the informant was. His eye flicked to the clock.

'Part of me hopes it isn't him. I've got plans with the missus tonight.'

'Ah yes, the new flame! And you're at the time when it burns the brightest of course. Does it make you feel better if I promise you I won't make you late off?'

Tim smiled. He felt the front wheels scrabble for grip as he came off a roundabout. 'It never has in the past.'

Vince laughed heartily. 'Don't you worry. Today will be different.'

* * *

Grace dared not breathe as she leaned to her left. The pressure on her arm was as bad as it had been at any time, but she was coping. Having something to focus on was helping. Even the simplest task was taking time. She had removed her underwear one-handed. Shifting her weight to slide it under her buttocks had nearly made her vomit again but she had managed. Now they trailed from her right hand, the waistband swinging against the spindle on the left side of the handle. If she could hook it over, if she could pull it up, then surely it would loosen the clamp on her arm? It had to. It was her only chance.

She moved back to sitting straight. She couldn't breathe when she was leaning over; the pain was too much. She sucked in a deep breath. She needed to start again. She leaned left, her eyes shut as the wave of pain came again. She opened them to see the spindle. She lowered her underwear, still holding her breath. The waistband fell over the spindle on the first attempt. She pulled it taut. She leaned back to sit straight, still holding the material firmly in her right hand. She pulled — gently at first. She thought that increasing the pressure slowly might stop them from tearing. The spindle didn't move. It couldn't be that tight. It didn't need to be. It was the thread that held it shut. But it wasn't budging and the material was stretched as far as it would go. She would need something stronger. Her nightie might do it. If she could twist it up to increase its strength it might be enough. It had to be. She sat back straight. She needed another rest. She needed to think. She looked at the clock. She still had plenty of time. She just needed to stay calm.

* * *

Vince saw the silver Volkswagen first. Tim was drawn to his excited pointing. They were parked on some rough standing at the bottom of Spitfire Way — a steep hill that led up to the village of Hawkinge. Two roads led into the village from this end, but both came off the same roundabout. Tim had known that if their target was heading home, he would have to come this way. When he did arrive he certainly wasn't hanging around. It was lucky Vince was switched on or they might have missed him completely. The Volkswagen was already over the roundabout and picking up speed on the hill when Tim joined the traffic. He had no choice but to put the lights and sirens back on. They were only a few minutes from the VW driver's home address and Tim would much rather stop him before he had the chance to get behind a locked door.

Traffic was steady on the hill, where two lanes merged into one near the top before another roundabout. There was also a set of traffic lights for pedestrians to cross to a supermarket. The lights were on red.

'Subject is held at the traffic lights, top of Spitfire Way,' Vince announced into the car's radio set. 'We are attempting a stop.' Tim had turned up the radio and the acknowledgement was loud — as was the next contact.

'Go ahead, Control!' Tim could tell Vince was tense. He was leaning forward, fixed on their target vehicle ahead. They were edging closer, just two cars behind now and both of those were trying to push over to the left to get out of their way. The Passat was the first car held at the lights. When they turned to green he would have a clear run. Tim was ready if he did. A mother pushing a pram with one hand and holding a squirming toddler with the other walked across in front of them all. She would have no idea that she was the starting gun for a police pursuit. Tim had long since killed the siren, leaving just the lights sending his message. She got to the other side. The traffic lights blinked orange. The Volkswagen moved off, but it stuttered and shifted clumsily to the left. He was getting out of the way. He was letting them past. He couldn't know they were there for him.

'Get in front of him! Block him in!' Vince was more excited. He talked over radio operator and Tim missed what she said. He pulled the car up roughly across the front of the Volkswagen. It wouldn't stop him making off if he really wanted to, but he would be in no doubt they were there to speak with him. Vince's window slid down and both officers stared across. Tim could feel his heart in his chest.

The driver was staring forward. He took his time to turn and acknowledge their presence. He looked furious. His window eventually rolled down and Tim saw that he gripped the steering wheel tightly with both hands. When he turned to look over at them, his chin was lifted in a show of aggression, the corners of his mouth curled in a sneer. There were remnants of dried blood around his lips and on the lower half of his face. There was no doubting that he'd been in a fight. It looked like Vince was going to get his way: the chance to nick him for something at least.

'You need to pull over — for a chat,' Vince said. Tim could hear the glee in his voice. 'Over there.' Vince lifted a thick finger and pointed to a lay-by that was the first exit off the roundabout. The driver's window slid back up. Tim edged the patrol car right, allowing the Passat to move off. He made sure he was right behind him. The pace was just above walking for now.

'Not the talkative type, is he?' Tim said.

'Suits me. I'll do all the talking.'

'Zulu One, confirm you received my last?' The radio operator was back. Tim pressed the button on the dash to reply.

'No, sorry, Control, we were just talking to our subject. He's pulling over. We should be with him very shortly. Can you still keep the other patrols rolling this way until we have a confirmed stop-stop and he is out of the vehicle?'

'Received that. My update was in relation to this incident. The other patrols are with the informant. The other involved person has already left. The witness cannot confirm a fight has taken place, just that two males were both seen with injuries and she had heard some shouting from the male toilets. We have no details for the other party. At this point we do not have any offences unless you get something from your male.'

'Oh, fuck off!' Vince exclaimed. 'He needs to be arrested, surely!'

Tim huffed. 'For what, though? We don't have the other party, there's no allegations.'

'Affray! We don't need a victim for that.'

'No, but you need evidence of a fight.'

'He's got a bloody nose!'

'I saw that. We'll ask him what happened. If he says he got a punch on the nose in a pub fight then we'll get him in and I'll call the other patrol to put a bit more effort into finding this other fella. It probably won't go anywhere, but at least we get to upset him.'

Vince was the one who looked upset. 'What do you think the chances are of him talking to me about how he got his nose bust?' Vince said.

'Slim.' Tim had been watching the movement of the silver Volkswagen the whole time. It had come to a stop in the lay-by he had indicated. There were no signs of the driver's door pushing open. He could see the front wheels too, they were angled outwards, how you might sit if you were still considering making off. 'We might get a proper offence anyway,' Tim said. 'I'm not sure he's planning on hanging around.'

Vince looked at the back of the Volkswagen as they pulled up behind it. The brake lights were still showing too.

'Let's hope you're right. Don't you drive off without me!'

'What, and leave the brains behind? No chance.' Tim rested his hand on the handbrake, he kept the car in gear but he was hanging back. He wanted enough room to be able to swing out or to react if the subject decided to ram them in reverse. Tim could hear that the Volkswagen's engine was still running when Vince opened his door. He had a strong feeling that their subject wasn't about to play nice. He watched his colleague walk the long way, around the back of the patrol car, to come up the driver's side — wary of him suddenly reversing and trapping him between the two vehicles. Vince got to the driver's window and bent in to speak. The brake lights went off. Tim had his own window down and he heard the Volkswagen's engine cut out. He relaxed a little and put his car into neutral. He might be getting off on time after all. This could be a very short conversation. Part of Tim was disappointed, of course he was, but at the same time he reckoned the subject would come to their attention again. Tim was a strong believer in karma. One day their wife beater was going to get what he deserved.

* * *

For the first time, Grace allowed herself a little bit of hope. She had managed to strip off her nightie and fashioned a twist of material that might just be strong enough. She lowered it towards the spindle, leaning a little further still, putting more pressure on her left arm, but it worked. She snagged the handle and tugged it cautiously. Even with some strength in reserve she was damned sure she felt movement.

Her left arm didn't feel any looser, but she accepted it might not instantly. It was in a constant state of pain; it was swollen in some parts and numb in others. She leaned to the left, far enough to see down the left side of the chair. The spindle on the right was slightly higher than it had been. *It's working!*

She dared to expel a breath of air but bit quickly down on her bottom lip. She couldn't celebrate yet. The jaws were still too tight to lift her arm up and out. But she was closer. She got a firm hold of the material again. She wrapped it once round her right fist for better grip. She closed her eyes and braced herself. She pulled the makeshift lever straight up. A shot of added discomfort broke through her left arm. She considered it was probably blood rushing into where it had been forced out, as the plates of the vice loosened. She used the pain to pull harder. She felt a definite give through the material. Her left arm wasn't working, she tried to lift it but it wouldn't respond. She could see the plates had parted a little. Enough maybe. She used her right arm to scoot underneath her left, then yanked at it roughly — no point being careful now. Her arm lifted. It bumped and scraped against the unforgiving iron — *but it came free!*

She was out.

Grace snapped hastily to her feet, still holding her left arm limp in her right. She was too quick: the blood rushed from her head and she felt dizzy, her vision suddenly tainted with darkness and her ears buzzing. She took a moment until she felt steady, until her head cleared and she felt like she could move. She assessed her arm. It was disfigured, worse than it had been, with a pronounced lump halfway along her forearm. There was no time to ponder it now.

Her eyes flicked to the clock: 1.53 p.m.

She scooped up her diary then headed up the stairs. She needed to wash; just her lower body would do. She snatched the shower head from the wall and shivered as the water arched out of the spout. She was back out before it had chance to get warm. Getting dressed was difficult with just one arm and sore legs, but she was in a hurry and she didn't care so much anymore. She put on some jeans, a loose T-shirt and a jumper. She had lost so much weight that none of her clothes fitted her properly anyway. She swept back out of her bedroom without looking back. There was no emotion attached to this house, nothing positive at least. She had never really moved in, not in her heart. There was not a picture on the wall or ornament on the mantelpiece that made it hers. It was nothing more than a carpeted prison to her, and right now she was fleeing it.

She plunged her hand into a small bag on the way out of the bedroom, filling the pockets of her favourite coat with a few bits of make-up, bits she hadn't been allowed to use for months. There was no time to apply them now. She walked carefully back down the stairs and into the kitchen where she grabbed the boxes of painkillers that were stacked up at the back. Craig counted them at night — part of his control over her. Next she tugged open the kitchen drawer with the knives in it. She selected the sharpest and paced back through to the living room. She dropped to her knees. She struggled to lift the sofa from the front. She needed the phone that had fallen into the bottom of the sofa. Among other things she needed the pictures saved to its memory. They documented her torment and catalogued her injuries. The next person to see them would be DS Maddie Ives. And then she would know.

Grace pushed the sofa backwards using one arm and her shoulder. It proved heavier than she expected, and the cast-iron vice on the side added to the weight significantly. She slashed the full length of the underside with the knife. A heavy object fell out — *the phone*. She scooped it up and let the sofa fall back, leaving the knife handle poking out from underneath.

She stared down at the phone in her hands, watched the screen light up when she turned it on. This was it. This was when she set herself free. She brought up the panel of numbers on her screen. Her fingers were shaking, but she was careful and the digits built up on her screen until she hovered over a symbol of a green telephone. She hesitated, lifted her eyes away from the phone and to where she had parted the blinds so that she could at least see the outside world. She heard a car. She could see it now, too. *It was silver!* It slowed, then the engine revved a little and it carried on. It wasn't him, but it was a reminder that he could come back at anytime. She stayed at the window, attracted by the movement of a woman pushing a buggy with her head bent. Grace had seen her a few times. She didn't look over at her house; she never did. No one did. No one cared if she lived or died here. And she would die here if she stayed. She knew that. If things carried on as they were, Craig Dolton was going to kill her. Maddie Ives had told her that straight the first time they had met. She had to do something, something that would last. The clock chimed behind her: 2 p.m.

It had to be now.

Her attention moved back to her phone. The number she had typed was still on the screen. She pressed the green button to make the call. It came through the speaker. It played the note of each digit in quick succession. The phone rang. Just once, then it cut off. She sucked in a rushed breath. *That was it?* All that planning? All that build-up and that was it? One ring and then silence? She didn't know what else she had expected.

The enormity of it hit her all at once. She dropped the phone and suddenly she couldn't breathe. The phone clattered and bounced, the screen stayed lit. She brought her hands to her mouth.

There was no going back now.

* * *

Tim saw Vince push away from where he had been leaning on the subject's car door. Even in that movement he could tell that the outcome of the conversation was not what Vince had been hoping for. It had been short, just as Tim had anticipated. Neither of the men were talkers. The rear brake lights of the Volkswagen flickered as the engine started. The subject could carry on to his home address, a minute's drive from here, and Tim would make his date after all. Vince was stomping back to the police car. He walked along the front this time. Tim looked away to find the talk-button on the dash to update Control of the outcome. His head jerked up at a bright white flash that split his windscreen into a million squiggly lines, followed by a sudden noise.

The noise was all consuming. A deep *woomf* that seemed to come from everywhere, like the loudest thunder he had ever heard. Tim's eyes slammed shut and instinctively he turned away as the Volkswagen was consumed by the brightest orange. He tried to look back; his windscreen was nearly opaque, but his window was still open and through it he could see a large cloud of smoke and ash that rose to the sky in a rolling, squirming ball of white, black and grey. Objects thumped, clanged and pinged off Tim's car as he felt the whole thing lift and shake on its suspension.

Instinctively he pushed his door open and rolled out. In his haste he got caught up in his seat belt and the palms of his hands were first to strike the tarmac. The next thing to hit him was the heat. The Volkswagen was still engulfed in a wall of fire that roared, whooshed and whistled and forced him to look away. He lifted his hands to shield his face and scanned for his colleague, his shocked and confused mind trying to recall where he had seen him last. He took a step towards the front of his car but he had to turn back, the heat was too intense. He stumbled around the back. He could see Vince now, not far from his passenger door. He was on his back, his eyes scrunched tightly shut, his face a fixed mask of shock, his legs and arms wriggling like an upended insect. Tim ran to him, instinctively grabbing him under the arms and wrenching him backwards away from the searing heat. Something popped loudly, sparks shot from what had once been the front of a Volkswagen Passat. Vince's feet scrabbled to propel them both backwards. Tim kept going until he reckoned they were far enough away to be safe. He looked around to take in his surroundings. They were now on the side of the road and cars had stopped beside them. The startled occupants had stayed in their seats. Bits of fiery debris were littered across the road and out into the field on the other side, where they still burned.

Tim shook his head to try and clear it. Flames still roared from the Volkswagen's blown windows. The blast had come seemingly from out of nowhere. He pressed his emergency assistance button.

* * *

Grace stared at the phone where it lay for a second; she didn't want to pick it up. She was going to have to. It felt heavy in her hands. The keypad was still showing the last number dialled, the eight digits that would change her life. She still had one more number to call. One more number that she had committed to memory, rigorously testing herself so she would know it when she needed it, just like the one she had dialled before. She typed it in.

'Hello?' A bored voice answered this time. It didn't even make one ring.

'Hello.' Grace had meant to say more but her throat was so dry it cut out completely.

'Can I help?'

She swallowed a couple of times. 'Yes. I . . . er, I need a taxi please. From number seventeen Campbell Road. The name's Hughes.'

'Sure. Where can we take you today?'

'The . . . away from here . . . please.'

She could hear tapping on the other end of the phone that stopped abruptly.

'Sorry?' was the nasal reply.

'The train station!' Grace snapped.

'Okay. Can I take a number?'

'No. I won't have a phone. This is a . . . a friend's.'

'Okay . . . well, the driver will normally send you a message when he is outside is all? Can he send it to your friend's phone?'

'No. No, I will be waiting.'

The woman hesitated. 'Well, okay then. It'll be ten minutes.'

Grace hung up. She moved back over to the chair. Her lips formed a snarl as she looked down at it. She bent down and picked up the duvet that Craig had thrown off that morning. She bundled it back over the arm, covering the vice. She still couldn't stand the sight of it. She would never have to see it again. Not that chair, not this house and not that man. She walked to the front door and pulled it open. The sudden burst of light hurt her eyes and a chill nipped instantly at her face. She slipped on the coat she had been carrying under her arm and lifted the fur-lined hood. She left her injured arm hanging limp under her top two layers. She stepped out, leaving the front door swinging open. It was snowing now, the flakes were small but still delicate and they fell with that delightful *hushing* noise she had always loved. She lifted her face, closed her eyes and felt the flakes bump off her cheek like an icy embrace. She felt herself smile. She had loved the snow when she was a little girl, and for just a second she was one again. She hoped it would fall harder, with bigger flakes, the sort that could cover everything in a layer of thick white so that, for just a short time, it would look like a blank canvas, like the world was starting again — a sign from Mother Nature herself that maybe she could start again, too.

She got to the end of the drive and carried on walking. The virgin snow swirled around her feet now, like white dust. She would wait for the taxi down the road.

Away from this place.

Chapter 21

Ian Hughes parked the car hurriedly. He was two hundred metres from his daughter's address but he had passed it already. He knew Craig's car wasn't there.

He pushed open the driver's door. His shoulder complained as he did. He didn't know if it was stiff from him throwing his useless punches or if it had taken a hit — probably a bit of both. He hadn't had time to assess his injuries, save for a quick look over his face in the rear-view mirror, prodding bits that were tender and trying to direct his anger away, rather than towards himself. There would be time for that later. Right now he needed to know Grace was safe.

He jogged along the pavement. There had been some snow but not enough to settle. It was a quiet street and nothing was moving. He could hear a police siren in the distance and slowed to see if it was coming closer. If anything it sounded like it was going further away. He paced up the drive of 17 Campbell Road. The jog and the tension increased his heart rate; he could feel it pulsing through the swelling on his face, his lips and cheek particularly. He had to stop and lean on the porch for a second. He had been feeling dizzy off and on since his return to consciousness on the floor of the toilet cubicle. He couldn't afford to pass out again. His head cleared and he looked up. The door was open.

He stumbled forward, his mind immediately conjuring scenarios of Craig returning home, of Grace still being here and him dragging her out, bundling her in the car and taking her somewhere where they could be alone and he could vent his anger.

The front door banged off the wall. He hadn't realised he had pushed so hard and the noise made him jump.

'GRACE!' he bellowed, the panic rising in his stomach. He moved through the ground floor to the kitchen. A cupboard was open, some cough medicine hung out of it, threatening to fall. He took in the rest of the room; nothing else looked out of place. He moved into the living room. There was an instant and distinct smell of vomit. He moved close to the small sofa in the corner, opposite the window. A thin duvet was thrown untidily on one of the arms. Under the other arm was a stain that looked to him like the source of that smell. The seat cushion was disturbed. A white nightie made a bundle on the floor, the ends bunched like they had been twisted together.

'GRACE!' he shouted again as he sprang from the living room and onto the stairs, taking two of them at a time. The bathroom door was open; he shot a glance inside then kept on moving. At the end of the landing, he burst through the door into the master bedroom — there was no one there. He could see a few items of clothing discarded on the floor: some balled up socks and a couple of tops. A make-up bag spilled its contents over the dresser, as if someone had plunged in a hand to grab what they could. The house in general had that look: like someone had left in a hurry. He started to feel calmer. The scenarios in his mind were no longer quite so bleak or horrific. He even allowed himself a little smile. Grace had done what she said she would: *She's left him!*

He moved to the bed. A piece of neatly folded paper lay dead centre on the crisp white duvet. It was good quality writing paper, the sort you might save for special occasions. He unfolded it and recognised Grace's handwriting, even if it was messy — rushed maybe?

Craig,

I have left you. You hurt me every day and you know that you do, deep down, no matter what you tell yourself.

And we lost our baby because of you. And you know that too. No amount of taking it out on me will change that. You killed your unborn child. OUR unborn child and I think you meant to.

I'm not sorry. This is not my fault and I won't be back.

You need to know that.

Grace.

Ian sucked in air. She had done it. He folded the paper and put it back carefully. His hands balled into fists but he resisted punching the air. He'd done enough of that for one day. His mind suddenly made sense of the note. Her unborn child? She had been pregnant. His hand rose to his mouth and he suppressed a sob. She'd lost it. He took a moment to peer around the room. All the beatings, all the stress, all that his daughter had been through in this house. He'd barely had a clue.

He moved back down the stairs and slipped out the front door that he'd left open. He felt sure Craig hadn't been home yet. Maybe he had done the decent thing and gone to the police station? Ian snorted in contempt. He shook his head. That man had never done a decent thing in his entire life.

He got back to his car and caught his reflection in the window. His left eye was all but swollen closed, his cheeks were puffy and his nose looked out of shape. He would go home and clean himself up. Grace might even be waiting for him. She would be furious with him at first, not just that he put himself in danger and got himself hurt, but for his intentions too. She didn't believe in violence as a way to solve problems. He had always been so proud of her principles.

He could still hear sirens. It sounded like they had multiplied. There had to have been an accident up on the main road. He'd take the back way home. Despite his aching shoulder and his throbbing face, he drove away with a smile and a lighter heart. Finally, his daughter was safe. She was safe and she was free.

Chapter 22

Maddie read her statement back over. A police officer's statement is always so dry, so devoid of any emotion. This one detailed the discovery of a teenage boy, his life snuffed out in his own bath having expressed his fear and foreboding when he was in police custody just twenty-four hours earlier. But it read as a list of cold facts and observations in strict chronological order. Nothing more. All the feeling, the human emotions — they were all stripped out, as things police officers weren't allowed to take into account or even have.

At least it was finished.

It hadn't been easy. Maddie felt like she needed to put in every detail of her interaction with Toby when he was in custody. She knew it would count as a 'death in police contact', a label that was automatically assigned to any death in which the deceased had been in contact with police in any manner in the twenty-four hours that preceded their death. It meant referral to an independent investigative body and a whole lot of questions. There would be a poring over the details — every one — to establish if she could have done anything more to prevent his death. She wasn't worried. She would be prepared at least — she intended on poring over the exact same things just as soon as she could. She would be doing it to console herself that she wasn't in some way responsible for Toby Routledge's death, doing it so she could live with herself. The independent investigation would have a different motivation: they would be looking to ascribe blame, even if there were none to find. Maybe this was why police officer's statements were so devoid of any human emotion — they were too busy covering their arse.

As part of her preparation, Maddie wanted to go down to custody. She knew that all areas of the custody suites were picked up on CCTV — sound and vision. She wanted to be sure that her conversation with Toby through his cell hatch had been captured. She knew she had tried to get him to talk, for his sake, but she wanted to see it again herself. She wanted to be sure.

Custody was eerily quiet. This was rare: even if it was 3 a.m. it would often be a hive of activity; at least *something* would be going on. There was no one in the back office, so she walked through to the desk where prisoners were booked in, usually the busiest part. There was no one there either. She could see down one of the long corridors lined with cell doors. She was looking for the standard officer pacing the corridor, doing checks and answering buzzers, moving prisoners to see their solicitor or to be brought to the desk to be charged. There was nothing. Everything seemed to have stopped. Then Maddie heard movement to her left and walked towards it. A floor-to-ceiling cupboard door was open and the posterior of a well-built woman stuck out from where she was bent over. Beyond her was a stack of blankets.

'Hey!' Maddie said.

The woman straightened and turned. Her outfit was all in one and navy blue. An upside-down watch hung from her top pocket and she had a pen tucked behind her ear. Maddie recognised her as the custody nurse.

'Hey!' she said back.

'Where is everyone?' Maddie asked.

'The skipper's here somewhere. All the officers got called out. There's been another explosion — like in the tunnel, I think. Didn't you hear?' The woman eyed her as if she should know already.

'No. I was . . . I had to finish something so I locked myself away. Only for an hour, though . . .' She felt like she needed to explain. The nurse still looked at her expectantly. 'Don't worry. I'll come back down. It was nothing urgent. I should go and see if I'm needed for anything.'

'I guess you should.' The woman gave a curt smile and turned back to her cupboard.

Maddie's next stop was Major Crime. Harry's desk was empty, but he bustled in as she was on her way back out. The rest of the Major Crime detectives were elsewhere.

'How's it going?' Maddie said.

'It never rains . . .' he mumbled back. He approached his desk but didn't sit. He pulled a ringing phone from his pocket, pressed a button that silenced it and put it back in the same pocket. He looked up and beyond Maddie and she turned to see Chief Inspector Julian Lowe walking towards them both. He swept past her and greeted Harry.

'Sir,' Harry snapped back.

'Well, this is a shit storm, Harry. Are you up to speed?'

'Not really, sir. They've only just carried my murder victim out in a body bag. I know there's been another car gone up, that's about it.'

'There has. I'm going to need your help. A *just* job, really, that's come out of all this.'

'I've been making calls all day to get resources for the Routledge murder. I'd scraped the bare minimum an hour ago. Now I'm getting nothing but calls back telling me they've been taken off my investigation to work your new explosion. If you take me away, sir, there's not going to be anyone left.'

'I know all that, Harry. No one is making decisions lightly, least of all me. This is a pretty unique set of circumstances.'

'It is. But I know how this works. I break off for a *just* job and then suddenly I'm up to my hilt in the bombing investigation, I'll never get back to Toby Routledge.'

'You have my word, Harry, I just need you to deliver a message and then I'll get you back to young Toby. I'll try and get you help where I can but these bombs are taking over, as you can imagine.'

'DS Ives is here right now, sir. She found Toby so she's involved already. I need to keep her on-board.'

'Fine. Assuming you have capacity, Maddie?'

Maddie nodded. She had been doing her best to stay in the background.

'Okay then. You and DS Ives work the Toby Routledge job. You said the "m" word — we're not considering suicide at all, then?'

'No.'

'I couldn't be so lucky. Murder investigation it is, then — and I will get you back to it. I just need you for the next hour is all.'

'What can I do in an hour that's so important?'

'I need you to deliver a message. To Frank Dolton.'

'Frank Dolton? I thought this was related to the explosion?'

'It is. The victim . . . It was his brother.'

* * *

Maddie got another sense of déjà vu as the white and grey stones crunched under the wheels of their car on the approach to Frank Dolton's place of work. They didn't know for sure that he would be there. They had talked about calling ahead to confirm, but agreed that it was best just to turn up. Men like Frank Dolton could wrap themselves in so many layers you might never get near them. They might need his staff to see their faces when they said it *was* urgent.

At DCI Lowe's direction, Maddie had made a call to the Gold Command, who were running the tunnel bomb incident and who would inevitably be leading the response to this second incident. He had said she should get an understanding of the victim and of how the incident had played out before they delivered the news of his death. The person manning the phone at Gold Command must have been quite shocked when, after they'd confirmed the identity of the victim to her, she'd muttered, 'Oh, that's fantastic!' It had needed a hurried explanation and a little bit of convincing that she was still the right person to deliver the message. She had given her assurances that she would let Harry do the talking.

When they arrived, Harry led the way in. The entrance foyer was exactly as it had been: the same faux-untidy display of magazines, the same pattern of chairs, the same feeling of clinical discomfort. Claire took a little longer to arrive this time but her expression was the same: stern and disapproving. Maddie noted that she wasn't holding her diary — this time she wasn't even prepared to book them an appointment.

'Can I help you?' she said.

'I need to speak to Mr Dolton as a matter of urgency,' Harry said.

'I'm afraid that won't be possible. Can I take a message or a number?'

'No,' Harry growled.

'Then I'm afraid I can't help you.'

'I'm not here for your help.' He stepped past her and pulled the door.

'Hey! You can't go in there!' Her voice took on a squeal. She stepped back out of his way, though, and glanced at Maddie. Maddie shrugged and followed. Harry was already striding up the corridor that ran through the middle. Claire ran after them, telling them she was going to call security. Maddie didn't recall seeing any. All the eyes in the glass offices turned towards them as they swept through. Mr Dolton's door was shut but she could see him sat behind his desk. He stood up as they approached. He looked furious.

'What the hell? Did you just push through here? I don't know who you people think you are! I told you, I did not wish—'

'WE'RE NOT HERE ABOUT THAT!' Harry's voice was powerful when it was raised. He came back a little quieter but with no less authority. 'We need to talk to you about a different matter. It is very serious and it will not be easy.'

Frank Dolton was still puffed up with red cheeks and still standing. He leaned forward on the desk, taking his weight through his knuckles.

'Claire, would you give us a moment please. And this had better be good. I am a very busy man.'

'Maybe you would like to have a seat, Mr Dolton,' Harry said, his tone instantly softer.

Frank hesitated. His eyes never left Harry. Maddie heard Claire huff as she made her way out. Frank straightened his back and then his suit. He sat down. 'What is this about?'

'Your brother . . . Craig Dolton.'

'Craig, yes.' Frank shrugged.

'He was killed in a vehicle explosion earlier today.'

Frank took a moment. His expression took a second or two to register surprise then he moved back in his chair as if he'd just taken a blow. His lips parted, then clamped shut again. Then he seemed to force a cough and his eyes flickered to his wristwatch. His shocked expression seemed fixed.

'I know this is very sudden and very difficult news,' Harry said. 'This is always a difficult part of the job for me. Maybe we can get you a drink of water or something?'

Frank shook his head. Finally he spoke. 'What happened?' The arrogance and agitation were all but gone.

'We don't know for sure. The vehicle he was travelling in exploded. There was a police witness to the incident. Right now we are considering that it was a device of some sort that has caused the explosion, but we cannot be certain. I'm sure you can imagine that this will all take time.'

'Device? You mean a bomb?'

'Yes,' Harry said.

Frank leant back into his chair. 'Jesus! A bomb! Like the other day?'

'You mean in the tunnel? We have no idea if the incidents are linked, but I would expect that to be a line of investigation.'

'Craig . . . When did this happen?'

'Around two this afternoon, sir,' Maddie spoke up.

Frank turned to her. His eyes looked heavy but they suddenly widened a little. 'Two p.m.?'

'Yes. As the DI said, there was a police witness, so it was called up pretty much as it happened.'

'Police? They were there?'

'He had just been stopped. He was assisting us with our enquiries.'

'Assisting . . . Was it about Grace again?'

'You know Grace?' Maddie couldn't resist.

'I've met her. Only a couple of times. The police were involved with them before. They argued a bit, I think.'

'How do you think she'll take the news?' Maddie pressed.

'I don't know, really. They had their problems — what relationship doesn't? I don't think it was the most harmonious relationship. I think she used to wind him up — she knew how to press his buttons maybe.'

'She pressed his buttons?' Maddie said. She could feel her heckles rising a little. As if the tiny form of Grace would ever look to press the buttons of an eighteen stone lump.

'Yeah. At first. But the last time I saw her he seemed to have got her in line — you know what I mean? That was a couple of months ago. He only brought her out with him when he wanted something. I guess he thought I wouldn't want to say no to him in front of her.'

'In line?' Maddie said. Her anger came on stronger. Her tone must have carried something that Harry picked up on. He stepped in closer to her as Frank continued.

'Yeah, she wouldn't say boo to a goose, really. She barely looked at me . . . she would just lurk in the background, her tail between her legs, like a dog that's been beaten too much — know what I mean?'

Maddie felt Harry's arm across her midriff now. She pushed against it as she took one step forward. 'I don't think I do.' Maddie's voice shook a little with rage. Frank Dolton seemed totally oblivious. Harry interjected quickly.

'He was with police for another matter. Nothing to do with Grace — it was all bottomed out. We will need to take some details . . . a statement covering the last time you spoke with your brother . . . anything you might know about him that could be relevant — that sort of thing. I'll get a detective to come and see you for that. Now probably isn't the right time.'

'No. I'm not sure I can think straight right now.'

'Is there anything important that you think we might need to know now?'

'Important?' Frank said. He lifted his hands to his head. He eyes had a glazed look as he flicked them between both detectives.

'Anything you think might be relevant. Has Craig upset anyone recently? Does he owe any large debts that you know of or is he mixed up in anything that might explain if and why someone would choose to target him?'

Frank was shaking his head. He still held it with both hands. 'You have to understand . . . me and my brother . . .

we've never really been close. I don't know much about him anymore. The only person I know he owes a lot of money to is me. The only time I heard from him was when he needed more. The last time we spoke was when he moved into one of my houses. He's never paid a penny in rent. He seems to think that's what brothers do. I guess I never really chased him for it.'

'That's your house they live in?'

'Yeah. He thinks it's his, though, I'm sure of it. He came to me for the deposit for the place. He said he was looking to buy it but was never going to get a mortgage. He knows I'm always looking for more properties, so he asked me to buy it so he could rent it off me. He said he would struggle to pay the deposit back so that would make better sense. He didn't even have a job then. I told him if he went out and got a job I would help him. He got something doing deliveries. I think he still works there . . . *worked* there, I guess. So I bought the house and he moved in. I even leant him some money for furniture. I asked for the rent and sent him an agreement to sign and return. I've not had replies to either.'

'How long has he been there?'

'Two years? I'm not sure. Probably longer.'

'So he owes you two years rent. That is a lot of money,' Harry said.

Frank lifted his head and sat back straighter. 'Not to me it isn't, Inspector, and it certainly isn't something I'm upset about, if you're looking for motives here, I mean?'

Harry lifted his palms as if he was backing down. 'I'm always looking for a reason someone might harm another. I'm a murder detective. When I find out who did this, you'll be glad I work like that.'

'Well, I didn't have anything to do with it.'

'I'm sure you didn't. And I'm sure you'll comply fully with any further questions we might have.'

'Of course.'

Harry pushed off the back of the chair. He hadn't attempted to sit and now looked ready to leave. 'Is there anyone you would like me to call for you? Anything we can do?'

'No. Thank you.'

'Do you still have my card?'

'Yes.' Frank opened his drawer. He pulled out the card Harry had left the previous day and dropped it on the table. He seemed to fix on it.

'Okay then. If there's anything you need from me or anything you think might be important, you can call me on that number. It doesn't matter about the time of day and it doesn't matter if it isn't relevant in the end. Sometimes the smallest thing can become very significant.'

Maddie thought Frank looked hesitant, like he was going to say something more. Harry may have sensed it too; his gaze lingered on the seated man.

Finally, Frank lifted his eyes from the card. 'I know where you are,' he said with a nod.

* * *

The door to the building had barely shut, Maddie's feet had not yet left the rubber mat to find the fashionable gravel, but she couldn't hold it any more. '*Like a dog that's been beaten too much!* That's what he said.' She let the phrase hang in the air the way it had been hanging in her mind.

'I heard it too. The man's a pig, but this wasn't the time to tell him.'

'When is the time?' Maddie said.

Harry stopped walking. 'You would have told him then? In there? As part of that message?'

'I was going to challenge him on it, yeah. No harm in that.'

'That wasn't what we were there for. It wasn't the time to give the man a lesson in respect.'

'Respect? It's beyond that Harry. He knew what was going on. If you stand by and watch someone suffer at the hands of another, you're no better than the offender.'

'I agree, Maddie. But he wasn't getting that message today, no matter how you said it.'

'Because his brother just died?'

'Yes, because his brother just died.'

'Bullshit. And I've seen people affected worse. I don't think that man gives a shit about anyone but himself.'

Harry fixed her in a stare, using one of his silences.

Maddie wasn't backing down. 'And I don't care that you don't like the bad language. Some of the people we come across . . . some of the people we work with . . . there's no other way to describe them.'

'Then don't.' Harry continued walking towards the car and Maddie followed. They didn't exchange another word until they were back onto the main road. Maddie spoke first. She was looking out the window as she did, thinking out loud rather than looking for a conversation.

'He knows more about his brother than he admitted. There's more to it all.'

'I'm sure there is. This Craig sounds like he upsets people.'

'You mean like me?' Maddie turned to flicker a smile. She was trying to lighten the mood.

'No. I mean like someone capable of extreme violence.'

'Like strapping a bomb under his car? You don't think it was random then?'

Harry shrugged, 'I don't know enough about that investigation. That won't be for me to worry about anyway, I've done my part. I'll update the boss and check in with the team doing house-to-house round Toby Routledge's block of flats. I need to see how much they did before they got pulled away.'

'What then?'

'We need to go and see his mother, but we'll do that after.'

'After?'

'I want to swing by the hospital. There were two officers caught up in the explosion. Superficial injuries, I think. But we should show our faces.'

'Hospital? I read there were police witnesses but I didn't know there were injuries?'

'Minor injuries. But it can't hurt to stick our heads in.'

Maddie stared at him until he returned to her gaze.

'What?'

'I just didn't know you cared!' She chuckled.

'It wasn't so long ago that I was hurt doing this job. I remember how it feels when your mates turn up. It was everything.'

Maddie turned away. She felt her cheeks flush. They hadn't talked about it, really; it was as if neither of them knew how. She recognised that this was probably as close as Harry Blaker would ever get to showing his appreciation.

'You're welcome, Harry,' she said.

<h1 style="text-align:center">Chapter 23</h1>

Frank Dolton bundled through his own front door less than twenty minutes after the two detectives left. He had given them a few minutes to get clear, hanging around his own reception area, watching them stop in the middle of his car park for a chat about who knows what. They had left eventually and he had been only two minutes behind them.

He swung his front door open and turned off the hallway into his study. His computer screen was dark. He had to stop and calm himself before reaching for the mouse to awaken it. He realised he was breathing heavily and sweating profusely.

The screen blinked on. It was his home screen again, and the same picture of him and the glamour model. He was really beginning to despise his own smug grin in that picture. The timer was the same, too: the same font, the same design and it was still ticking down.

'Nineteen hours forty minutes,' he said out loud. The door to his study swung open and made him jump. A plump, middle-aged woman filled it. She stopped and crossed her arms. It was Sasha, his personal chef.

'Well, I hope you're not expecting dinner just yet, Mr Dolton. You need to call ahead if you're going to be early. I told you that.'

'You did. No need to worry.' His attention moved back to the screen. There was a notification telling him he had new mail. Sasha hadn't moved away. 'Can I help you with anything else?'

'No.' Her arms fell apart and she tutted — but she did move away. Frank clicked to bring up his email screen. Nine new messages. He skimmed the senders. His eyes rested on the one from 'Alexa'. The subject read: *Now you listen* . . . He clicked the message open.

Frank Dolton,

So now you know what I can do.

Three days ago in the tunnel was a demonstration. I did not need to hurt people that day. Today I needed to hurt your family, but they are not important to you, I see that now. Tomorrow all your people will hurt.

There is another device. It is on a vehicle. It is already in place. This person is not lucky. It is set for 12 noon, tomorrow. If you do not pay, I will make sure it is known that you did nothing to save your people. Not good for commissioner!

But I think maybe this is not enough. Maybe you do not care for people. So you will see there are attachments to this message. I found them on your computer. Some you have tried to delete but they are still there. You will know what I can do with them.

You did not care about brother, but I know you care about your fortune. I know you will pay for this.

£10 million. This is the money to destroy this information. This is the money to save your citizens, to be next commissioner. To be hero man, but man who gets richer in secret.

I release this information to press, to police, to the world. Tomorrow. 12 noon. Unless you pay.

Alexa

There were lots of attachments. He clicked through the first few and they opened at different places on his screen. Documents, photos, signed contracts, he recognised them all. Some were recent, some much older. He slunk back into his chair. His breathing was still fast and heavy, sweat still clung to his forehead. He wiped it with the arm of his jacket. He didn't need to open the rest. He didn't need to look at any of them in detail either. He knew what they were and he knew what they meant.

'You're working too hard, sir.' Sasha swept into view. 'You're looking old before your time.' She held a cup in one hand and a plate in the other. 'I made scones. I've been harsh on you recently. I'm only thinking of you — we need you to be healthy. But this is a treat.' She put the tea and scones down on his desk. Frank couldn't speak. He nodded. She took it as enough and left.

His right hand fell to his pocket and he took out his wallet. He fished out the card he had been given by Detective Inspector Harry Blaker. He took it out and ran his finger along the name. He stopped on the phone number. He knew he should call. This was serious. There was another device out there. But once he did, once he picked up that phone and said those words, there would be no taking it back. And then everyone would know.

He stood up, strode back through to the hall and turned to the door. He would go for a drive, clear his head a bit maybe. He couldn't think straight. Not with that damned timer ticking down in front of him.

Nineteen hours, thirty-six minutes.

* * *

In the hospital, Maddie embraced Sergeant Tim Betts. Harry Blaker stepped forward and reached out for a handshake, but Tim declined politely. 'Sorry, sir, sprained wrist.'

'Nothing too bad, then?' Harry said.

'Nah. I sent the junior out first, of course.'

'Less of the *junior*!' A voice boomed out from behind a white curtain just beyond Tim. They were in the area of beds that was part of the accident and emergency department, where they put the minor injuries that they couldn't deal with immediately. The curtain *whooshed* back and a harassed-looking nurse swept out and moved quickly away. Maddie was left staring at Vince Arnold. He wore a big grin but it dropped away pretty quickly; he must have picked up on her shocked expression.

'Now this *is* a sight for sore eyes!' he bellowed. 'Couldn't keep away could you, sarge?'

'I had no idea it was you!' Maddie spluttered.

'Of course you didn't! It's okay, you know. You can tell me. What . . . did you get blue-lighted over here when you heard?'

Harry stepped through the curtain and Vince took up his handshake. Maddie had seen them interact before: it was clear that there was a lot of mutual respect between them.

'How you doin', boss? Nice to have you back. You know, after all that happened.' Vince still talked too loud.

'Couldn't keep me away. All the good ones get hurt at some point,' Harry said. He stepped back as if he was taking in Vince's form. He was sitting up in a black uniform top with a zip at the top that hung open. His eyes were red and streaming. His face had been wiped clean, but there was still blackening around his ears, both of which had a yellow-tipped plug just visible that might have accounted for his increased volume. Maddie cursed herself for not making herself aware of the details. She had no idea the officers had been so close to the car when it went up. It must have been terrifying.

'I've always thought that, boss. I got frazzled eyebrows and a ringing in me ears. That's about it. Not enough to keep a good soldier down. Not like my skipper out there, the man who got caught up in an explosion and managed to sprain his wrist taking his seat belt off!'

Tim stepped in behind them. 'You need to change the record, mate,' he said, jovially. 'And the doctor's just dropped back the results from your brain scan. Turns out you still ain't got one.'

'Very good! You been out there for ages thinking that one up?'

Maddie stepped closer to Vince. He must have seen the intensity in her and his smile dropped away.

'You okay, Mads?'

'You were close enough to see him?'

'See him?'

'Craig Dolton, you saw him?'

'I saw him. I was talking to him. We were done and I was walking back to the car. Next thing I know all hell broke loose.'

'He was in there? He was definitely in there?'

'Mads, the man went up. No doubt he was in that car, in the driver's seat. I walked away and I heard the engine fire. It pulled away — then it went. He was in there. He's long gone.'

Maddie reached for his hand. He squeezed it gently. 'I'm glad you're okay, Vince.'

'And I'm glad you're the one on the case, Mads. They damned near ruined these good looks. That should be a crime on its own!'

Maddie grinned — the way she always grinned when Vince spoke. She couldn't help it. 'I'd best get back to it then.' She paced back through the busy ward with Harry at her side.

'You didn't have the heart to tell him the explosions are someone else's problem?'

Maddie was still good-humoured. 'It doesn't matter anyway. That man hears whatever version he wants to hear.'

* * *

Toby Routledge's family home was not somewhere Maddie had been before and neither had she met his mother, despite the numerous interactions with her son. Sharon Lyons had always refused to come out in support of Toby when he was in custody. Maddie hadn't been sure of the reason, but just moments after knocking she could hazard a guess. The first of her reasons answered the door. The other one was scurrying around in a baby walker.

'MA!' The first girl looked around twelve years old and hadn't developed her late brother's response to police officers yet. She stepped back immediately, allowing the door to swing open so she could shout up the stairs. It was a couple of minutes before Sharon Lyons appeared. Her bare feet slapped against the exposed wood of the stairs on the way down. She was careful to avoid the spiky carpet grips that were still in place. She looked red in the face. Her hair was pulled back and tied roughly. She wore leggings and what looked like a man's fleece top with the sleeves pulled over her hands. She stopped two steps from the bottom. Her whole demeanour was of someone who was agitated and on edge. And she hadn't said a word yet.

'Miss Lyons?' Harry said.

'Yeah. You coppers?'

'I'm Detective Inspector Harry Blaker and this is Sergeant Ives.'

'So? What do you want with me? You lot don't think you've done enough?'

'What do you mean?' Harry said. Maddie thought it was a brave sentence the instant it fell from his lips — the verbal equivalent to lighting blue touchpaper.

'What do I *mean*? He came to you, didn't he? He told me he came to you. When he got out of your place he said he had asked for help but he got nothing! Just like he always got from you. I know he was trouble, that kid, trust me on that. I know better than anyone. But when he asked you for help — you did nothing!'

'That isn't quite true . . .' Maddie stepped in a little.

'You calling my boy a liar? 'Cause he ain't here to talk about it now, is he? He can't be giving his side of the story — you lot made sure of that!'

'I saw Toby. I was the last police officer to speak with him and I asked him over and over what he was scared of. He *was* scared too. I'd never seen him like that and I met him a fair few times.'

Toby's mother fixed Maddie in a stare. Maddie gave her a moment to think, to be the next to speak.

'So you knew he was scared and you still did nothing about it?'

'He wouldn't talk to me about it. I just about stopped short of begging him, Miss Ly—'

'Well, you *should* have begged him!' Toby's mother's voice was raised enough to silence both officers. She walked the two remaining steps and turned into a room off to their left. Maddie exchanged glances with Harry. She shrugged and stepped in to follow her through. The youngest child was a little baby girl. She was dressed in a nappy and a pink T-shirt and thumped her baby-walker enthusiastically into the sofa. She giggled as the sensation rippled through the plastic surround and made her chubby cheeks wobble. She lifted her giggle up to Maddie, then her little legs propelled her backwards so she could do it all over again.

Sharon Lyons was at the other end of the room, where bright daylight leaked through a large window and framed her in silhouette. She was facing away, her right hand splayed and resting against her right cheek. A neat spiral of cigarette smoke now rose from between her fingers, only dissipating when it hit the yellowed ceiling.

'How old?' Maddie asked.

Sharon didn't turn round. She didn't move. 'Eleven months.'

'She looks like she's enjoying that walker!' Maddie chanced, still trying to lighten the mood. There was a pause. Maddie knew this was where she either softened and talked to them or they were ordered out. Sharon Lyons decided to soften. She turned to face back into the room.

'She's never happier than when she's bumping off something. Shoulda been a boy, that one. I guess I've run out of boys now.' She looked empty of emotion rather than sad. Her face was ashen, her body straight and stiff rather than sagging under the strain of the last few days. She was coping at least. Maddie guessed she was used to having to.

'Can we have a seat?' she said. 'All of us, I mean. You might have some questions for us?'

Sharon gestured at the sofa. The movement made a kink in the line of smoke. Maddie sat down and Harry next to her. Sharon was still by the window. She pushed it open a little and winter reached through the gap in the form of an icy breeze.

'Sorry. I shoulda opened that earlier.' Sharon wafted the smoke like it might make a difference. The air was already beginning to thicken with a white haze.

'It's your home, Sharon,' Maddie said.

'I don't have questions. Nothing you can answer. A couple of your lot were round here earlier. They said he had been found. They told me how. They said it was being treated as suspicious because of his age, but there weren't nothing there to suggest any foul play or nothing. Like he might have just slipped under and drowned. I asked them how that was possible, how a healthy, strong boy like that just . . . slips away. He don't. Not my Tobes. Since he left here, I don't reckon he's used that bath the whole time. I'd never get him to sit in a bath. He was in and out of a shower if you were lucky, like most boys. He shouldn't even have been in there. I told them something ain't right and they wrote it all down in their little books and they told me they would get answers. I don't reckon you got any of them answers yet, have you?'

'No.' Harry's standard abruptness was cutting.

'So what you doing here?' Her anger was coming back.

'Probably asking some of the same questions, Miss Lyons. I'm what's called the SIO — Senior Investigating Officer. Basically, that means it's my job to find out what happened. I take that very seriously. I'll have a look at what they wrote down but I like to speak to the people that matter myself.'

'I don't get why I matter.'

'When did you see Toby last?'

She took a deep suck on her cigarette. Her hand had a shake to it. She coughed when she breathed out. It was rasping, like the early sign of something serious. She had to take a moment to get her breath.

'Two days ago. He had some washing. I only ever saw him when he needed me. But I never minded that. Rather that than never at all.'

'Were you close?'

Sharon's lips creased into a smile. 'I don't reckon you get too many mums who got a good relationship with their seventeen-year-old boy — not day to day, you know what I mean? Day to day we bickered — we got on each other's nerves. That boy put me through a lot when he lived here. Constantly getting nicked, and at all times of the day and night. You lot round here searching the place, asking to come in to check he weren't here, no matter what I said. And me pregnant or with a newborn or just trying to get on with my life. It never mattered. You lot were going to do what you were going to do. I blamed the police at first . . . you wouldn't have got me sat talking to you a year ago. But then I worked it out. It was Toby bringing this to my doorstep. So I got him out. I warned him. I said one more night like it and he was gone. You lot turned up less than a week later and that was it. It weren't fair on me and it weren't fair on his sisters.'

'We are intrusive,' Harry said. 'We don't turn up when it's convenient and we see it all the time — the family getting the brunt, I mean. It's tough.'

'It had to stop. But it ain't easy kicking your son out. He didn't talk to me for a while, but I thought maybe it would do him a favour. He would have to run his own house, see what that was about. The council got him a little place. Someone pulled some strings at the Social. They did it to help me out. He never saw what people were doing for him. He only ever saw people as having it in for him. We were just starting to get better. He would turn up with his washing but he would stop for a bit, have a cup of tea. Play with his sister. I could see he was missing us. Then he got different. It was sudden.'

'Different?'

'Yeah. Like moody. More moody than before. He was talking about how he weren't a bad person and he was trying to be good. I thought it was just part of growing up. But it seemed to change. He seemed to get scared — more and more.'

'When was this?'

'Last couple of weeks. He didn't want to go home and at first we argued, but then I said to him he could camp out if he needed. He crashed on the sofa. He probably stayed here more than at his place in the last week or so. But then you lot sent him to court and he got that tag thing to monitor a curfew — he had to be in his own place before six. He told me he wanted to stay over here. I could see he was scared, but if he stayed here I knew what would happen . . . I knew you lot would come for him late at night again. I didn't want him getting nicked no more. I told him that. I said he had to do what the court said and he had to sort out whatever shit he was in. We argued.' Sharon turned back to the window. Maddie heard a sniff like she was upset. She considered standing, going over to her and comforting her. She stayed seated for now. She would give her some space.

'The last time I saw my boy, we argued. That's the hardest thing . . .'

'He knew you loved him. He still knew that, of course he did.' Maddie tried to be soothing.

'I know that. I do know that. I told him I loved him. I said that was why I was doing it. But if I hadn't, if I had let him stay here on that couch . . . the worst thing that woulda happened would be your lot sticking him in the back of your car. Maybe the court woulda sent him for a stretch in the young offenders. Nothing major. Safe, at least.'

'What was he scared of, Miss Lyons?' Harry said.

'I don't know. I been wracking my brain. I know a lot of people. I put the word out, trying to find out who he's upset, what he owes and who to. I got nothing back. A few weeks ago I heard he was working with some older fella, but no one seems to know who that was. I thought I knew all his mates. This fella was driving him about so he could screw some new places. I didn't ask him about it. If I had, he woulda shouted the house down, I know that. And I know he was using the lock-up. One of the neighbours saw him coming away.'

'Lock-up?'

'Yeah. It's a garage really. It comes with this place. It's in a separate block. Your lot searched it, day before yesterday. I can't remember the last time I stepped foot in there. He's had the keys for years. He always made me promise I wouldn't talk to the police about it when they came here. I never did. I was surprised when they turned up and said that he had told you to look there. They already had the keys. They said Toby had given them over. They found stuff too. I had some paperwork to sign and it listed a load of stuff. All nicked, they reckoned. I know he weren't perfect. I knew he was out screwing places but I reckoned it was scrap metal — shops maybe. Not people's houses. I guess I just hoped. He weren't a bad kid. Seems a strange thing to say. Easily led.'

'I think you're right. I don't think he really considered what he was doing. But he was always good at covering his tracks. He gave us the right run around. Not this time, though, he just gave it all up. He told us what he was up to and where to find it.' Maddie paused, she watched for any reaction. 'Why would he do that?'

Sharon perched on the arm of the sofa closest to the window. There was a glass ashtray on the other arm. She squashed her cigarette into it. She kept hold of the ashtray. It was nearly full.

'We didn't always get on. The older he got the further apart we got, but he was starting to come back. He was starting to grow up a bit. No matter how much we argued, how much we upset each other, I always understood him. If he turned up angry or got angry I always knew why. He had a lot of front too, but I seen him scared a few times before and I always knew why. This time though . . . I had no idea. He wouldn't talk to me either. We had a conversation a couple of nights back. Must have been Sunday night 'cause I'd watched a *Poldark*. He was on the sofa there and I was going to bed and he said, "Mum," he said, "remember that I'm a good lad really, no matter what people say. And a good son. Don't ever forget that."

'It sent shivers down my spine it did. I made him promise he weren't depressed or nothing, or sick or dying or nothing like that. He promised me. He just said that he wanted to say that. He said he loved me. I ain't heard that since the first day he got nerves at the gates of his primary school.' Sharon bowed her head. She sniffed again. She put the ashtray back down and reached into her pocket. She lit another cigarette in a smooth movement and raised her head to blow the smoke upwards.

'I don't care what you say about him falling asleep or taking drugs, or fitting and slipping under in that bath, or about how there's no foul play. My boy, he knew something was coming — and then it came. He needed help and I just don't think he knew how to ask for it. He ain't never asked for no one's help before. Toby weren't like that. Too proud. Even at seventeen. And look where it got him . . .' She faded out again. She stood up. She picked the ashtray back up and walked through to the kitchen. She sidestepped her tiny daughter in the walker who was now transfixed by *Peppa Pig* playing softly on the television. Maddie felt a nudge as Harry got up and followed her. They walked into a messy kitchen. The floor was sticky where the flooring had been pulled up and not yet replaced. It had left black rubber stains on bare screed. There were remnants of cat biscuits and a dog bowl with floating hairs. Sharon was bent over the bin, tipping ash. Harry spoke.

'Miss Lyons, I don't know what impression you have from my colleagues, but personally, I'm not happy with the circumstances of your son's death. Right now I am treating this as murder and I'm in charge, which means we're all treating this as murder. I don't know who or why, but this is Day One of our investigation.'

Sharon lifted eyes that were swelling with tears. She ran the back of her hand across them. 'Okay then,' she said.

'I'll keep you informed. We have an autopsy that may give us some answers. That will be in the next day or so. But there are other lines of enquiry too. We will find out what happened.'

Sharon forced a laugh through her tears. Maddie was a little taken aback. 'Sorry, I don't mean to laugh. It's just Toby, he always said you lot always find out. He said you have a knack. I guess he'll be looking down on us all now, hoping he was right.'

Maddie smiled. 'I reckon he will.'

Sharon managed a weak smile back. 'Well, you will let me know when you find your knack, won't you?'

'No problem.'

* * *

When they stepped back out, the snow clouds had cleared and the sun was low enough to force Maddie to shield her eyes as she walked back to the car.

'She's had a tough few years or ten.'

'Seems like it.'

'What more is there to do today?'

'Not much. You're due off shift. The way I see it, if we head back in we've got more chance of getting caught up in the tunnel job. There's not much more we can do today. I tasked Rhiannon with having a quick look through what came from the door-to-door stuff. Maybe we got lucky and there was some disturbance at Toby's place. I also tasked a team to go out and find his associates, we need to find out what trouble he was in and who with. I think most of the team I tasked I lost to this other job, so it's possible none of that got done. Go home, Maddie. Tomorrow I should know what still needs doing and who I've got left to do it with. It might just be me and you.'

'You could do a lot worse. You tasked Rhiannon?'

'Yeah. I know she's one of yours but she comes highly recommended.'

Maddie chuckled. 'I didn't think you'd listen to my recommendations.'

'And she was the only spare detective I could find.'

'You just couldn't let me have that, could you?'

'If they're not done, tomorrow is CCTV reviews, knocking doors, media appeals — the standard stuff. Someone needs to do it and I would prefer it wasn't a senior detective. We're better used elsewhere.'

'There's a compliment in there somewhere.'

'Then it was accidental. I'll drop you back. Go home. We'll start again at seven in the morning.'

'What happened to you doing four hours a day and staying in the nick, anyway?'

'Two explosions and a murdered boy, Maddie. I won't tell if you don't.'

Maddie shrugged. 'My lips are sealed.'

Chapter 24

Friday

The 7 a.m. meeting was a short one for two reasons and both stemmed from the same issue: first, there was very little to update; second, Harry Blaker was in a foul mood. Harry led the meeting. Maddie was present, along with Rhiannon and two other detectives from Major Crime.

Toby Routledge was on the autopsy table later that day. That was an important step. The initial CSI report gave a confident summary of drowning as the cause of death. They had also found some evidence of bruising on his shins and significantly they were at places that could be attributed to thrashing against the solid side of a bath, but it wouldn't be enough to prove foul play beyond any reasonable doubt. They would need more defensive wounds. Injuries sustained at the time of death didn't always show externally, but they would show on the inside. When Toby's skin was sliced down the middle and peeled back, they could only hope that it had some secrets to reveal. The flat also had numerous sources of DNA and fingerprints, but it was noticeable that there was nothing in the bathroom. Another case of what was *not* at a scene. Someone had cleaned up.

The verbal summary of the door-to-door enquiries in Toby's block and neighbouring blocks reported that there was nothing of significance. Maddie was disappointed. She knew the area and the people that occupied it and she didn't think for a moment that they could be relied upon to talk to the police without a little encouragement. Maybe there was something there to revisit. The same pair who had knocked the doors had also identified a parade of shops nearby where there might be CCTV covering anyone on foot walking towards his flat, but it was a long shot and there were no resources to follow it up. Inevitably, the two Major Crime detectives had quickly been tasked by Julian Lowe to do a couple of 'just' jobs in relation to the latest vehicle explosion. Maddie knew they would not be coming back and Harry's mood had blackened even further.

When the meeting ended, Maddie offered to pick up a takeaway coffee and stepped out for a walk while he calmed down a little. She was frustrated too, but she could appreciate how their investigation was further down the priority sheet than a car bomber who might not be finished.

She went back to her own desk with her coffee. Harry had refused one with a wave of his hand. She saw an opportunity to spend half an hour doing some work on the reports she was being pushed for.

It was still early and the office was quiet. The opening of a door down the far end of the office was enough to stoke her interest. Even from this distance, she recognised Jim Sutton; he was unmistakeable. He handled the post for the station and Maddie was pretty certain he did it on his own, having never seen anyone else doing it. All the officers had pigeonholes in a rack halfway up the office. He had a cart with a squeaky wheel that he pulled behind him. As he stopped at the trays, Maddie was amused that he hadn't noticed her.

'Don't you ever take a holiday, Jim?' Her amusement increased as he jumped at the sound of her voice.

'Sergeant Ives! I didn't see you there. I do apologise.' He pushed his glasses up his nose. He always referred to everyone by their formal rank. Maddie had given up correcting him. And he always apologised. She had given up correcting that too.

'Don't you worry. I'm an early bird this morning, Jim. Shame, I've just been out for coffee, I could have grabbed you one.'

'Very kind, Sergeant, but I don't really drink it, see. It's not good for my sleep.'

'Very wise. Anything for me this morning?'

Jim put his finger in the air like he needed a minute. He dipped his whole torso into a large, white sack and presently emerged with a brown paper parcel and two letters. He walked them over. 'Just these two bits, Sergeant. At least you can be sure they're not bills here, eh!' He put his hands on his hips. Always the same phrase, whenever he brought her post.

'No, it will be far worse, it will be more work!' She gave her standard reply and he seemed delighted as usual. He whistled as he walked back to his trolley and was gone a short time later.

Maddie handled the parcel. It was from an external source and it felt heavy. The postage mark was local and the address handwritten. The sender had used her full title. She pulled it open at one end and a small plastic memory card fell onto her desk, the sort that could be pushed into a mobile phone as extra storage. She had no idea who might send her a memory card. Certainly she wasn't expecting one. A second item was bigger. It wouldn't slide out at all. She ripped more of the envelope. It revealed an A5-sized hardback book with a plain cover. She opened the front page to see a handwritten message.

Maddie inhaled sharply. She realised immediately what it was. Grace had taken her advice! She flipped on another page. It was dated. The first page was late November. Grace had called it *Day One* in brackets. That day was a short entry.

Craig got back from work. He was angry. I don't know why. I did ask but he told me to mind my own business. He talked down to me. He said it was adult stuff that I shouldn't worry about. He was really nasty. I didn't push it. Craig got undressed. We were in the kitchen and he just took his trousers off. He demanded oral sex, right there and then. He said that was what women did for their men when they had been at work all day. He told me to get on my knees and do it. I was too scared to say no. He kept slapping me on the back of the head. He called me 'Good Grace', and he kept saying that I knew what I was good for.

When he finished he went for a shower. He got changed and went out. He didn't speak to me again.

I wasn't going to do this. I wasn't going to write it down, I didn't think it was a good idea, but I do have to tell you, I know that. He's getting worse. Tonight was the worst he's been. I cried in the toilet after so he wouldn't know.

Maddie sat back and ran her hand through her hair.

'Jesus, Grace,' she uttered. She flicked ahead. Trying to see if there were any contact details — a telephone number. There wasn't. She remembered the update from yesterday. The patrols had gone round there to speak with her, to break the news. They had found a note that was meant for Craig and evidence that she had left in a hurry. She was being treated as a missing person. Maddie was sure that Grace would know that he was dead. The news was full of the bomb incidents and they were giving the description of the car, the location and the fact that members of the public had seen a thirty-five-year-old, white male in the car just before it had gone up. It was rolling news; you couldn't miss it.

Maddie didn't think that changed much. She still expected Grace to get in touch with her specifically and she doubted she would have to wait long. It had to be a strange time for Grace. Maddie had experience with victims who had suffered years of abuse at the hands of a partner and finally reached a point where they had asked for help. Suddenly the police would swoop in and remove the aggressor and the victim would feel totally lost — beside themselves, almost. Years of being controlled, of being told what they could and couldn't do — and then absolute freedom, just like that. It was often baffling, overpowering almost. Some started wanting their partner back. Mistaking their confusion and dependence for love. For Maddie it was hard to believe that the two lines could blur but she had long since given up trying to understand the workings of the human mind. Abusive partners don't just bruise the skin of their partners, they get right under it.

She picked up the memory card. It was a standard size and she had a device that transferred the images straight from the card onto her computer. The instant she slotted it in, her screen came up with a prompt asking if she wanted to view the files or print them. She selected the *print* option. The printer at the end of the row of desks clunked to life.

Maddie wanted to see Grace soon. She would tell her that she was there to help and that she was still going to need it. She should read the diary first. She owed Grace that, to be able to understand fully what she had been through.

She turned the page. The pain and horror dripped from even the first words.

* * *

Grace cussed under her breath. She had flinched at a sudden sound, glass bottles being tipped from a bin into a lorry. She knew that was what it was; she had passed the lorry on the way in. Flinching meant tensing her sore muscles and this caused her pain. But she couldn't help it. She hadn't been able to relax since she had left the house yesterday. She had gone to a hotel. It was cosy enough: the double bed and the bath were nice; she was alone and she felt safe; she thought that was all that would matter. But she was wrong. She still had the constant feeling of anxiety and it seemed to be worsening as she had come to realise the enormity of what she had done. She tried to ignore it. The first night was always going to be tough, but she was through that now. Things should start getting easier.

She was stood at the communal entrance to a solid, flat-fronted block of flats. The entrance was a brown, wooden door with glass slats. This close she could see the wire running through the glass to toughen it and the metal lip round the outside that beefed up the door's strength overall. Even the buzzer system was just a row of numbered buttons with no hint at the identity of the occupants behind them. Grace knew the measures were necessary. The building was assigned as a women's refuge. From the outside it was nondescript, no one outside would know its function — at least no one *should* know. That was its most effective security measure. Finally the speaker crackled.

'Hello?' The voice sounded unsure. Grace stepped a little to the left and ducked her head so she was looking straight into the camera.

'Sally! It's Grace!' There was a pause. For a second Grace held her breath. Months of planning had brought them to this point, but maybe the ramifications had set in. Once she moved through that door and stepped over the threshold, Sally was part of it. She had been from the start in truth, but unlocking that door was acceptance of it. Grace stared at the camera, silently whispering for the door to be opened.

The door made a clacking sound followed by a buzzing. Again Grace flinched, as if the noise was something of which to be fearful. She tugged hurriedly at the door and moved inside from out of the cold. She continued up two flights of stairs until she got to another door — brown wood with glass inserts — and another buzzer system to get past. She could see a small landing beyond it. A woman walked across it, she pushed the door open. Grace stood still. Whenever she had considered this moment she could never be sure quite how it would play out.

'Sally?' Grace asked, tentatively.

The woman's face broke into a beaming smile. She stepped forward and wrapped Grace in a tight hug. Despite her relief it was agony and Grace couldn't help but wince.

'Oh, shit! Did I hurt you?'

'No, it's okay. It's just my arm.'

'Of course. Sorry, I forgot. Let me see . . .' Sally's eyes searched for the damaged limb. It was hidden away under a jumper and a coat. 'Oh, don't worry about it — here, come in!' She stepped back and pointed towards a front door that was hanging open. It had the number 6 on the outside, matching Sally's instructions. Grace stepped in. It was a small flat but neat and tidy. The kitchen was to the left. She could see a living room to the right side with a long window. They were both in the hallway. Sally seemed to be unsure of what to say, Grace could guess what it might be. She was right.

'Have you done what we discussed?'

'Yes. Everything.'

'The diary and the memory card?'

'It's gone. I sent it yesterday. I put in one last entry, something she needed to know and then I sent it. The memory card, too, with all the pictures on it. They were in date order. Maddie Ives is the detective I've been speaking to. She's a sergeant. She might even have it all by now.'

'Well done, Grace! You did good, girl!'

'The next bit will be hard. When I go and see Maddie. When I have to sit in front of her and tell her I don't know anything about Craig . . . You were right, I need some time to get my head straight before I talk to anyone. I think about what I did . . .' Grace started to break down and sucked in a rushed breath. Sally grabbed her by the shoulders and stared intently into her eyes.

'You did what you had to do to get safe. There was no other way. Trust me! Look at me, here! You don't want to be living this life — in someone else's flat, never feeling truly safe, and only here until someone else needs it more. I don't go out, Grace. I can't work or have something simple like a Facebook account in my own name, with my own friends! I'm tired of being in fear. We shouldn't have to fear anything anymore.'

Grace felt tears on her cheeks. She couldn't remember the last time she had cried openly. It felt good to let go. She felt Sally hug her tight, while mindful of her damaged arm.

Grace got herself together — enough for her vision to clear. Sally was chewing on her lip; she looked concerned but her face broke into a reassuring smile. 'Was the hotel okay?'

'Yes. Thank you for sorting that. It was so nice, I had a bath and a big bed!' Grace started to remove her jacket and gasped as she did so.

'You need a hospital with an A&E. There's one ten minutes from here by cab. You need to get that arm sorted. You'll feel better — stronger even, if you're not in constant pain. And that works too. You left him. You ran away to a hotel, you didn't know what to do with yourself. Then you went to the hospital and got sorted in a town as far away from him as you could get. That explains the delay in going to the police—'

'I can't!' Grace surprised herself with the ferocity in her voice. 'Not just yet. The doctors and nurses at those places . . . they're like the police. It's an interrogation. I need to be sharper.'

Sally took hold of her again. She was gentle. Grace's head was turned slightly to one side. This was the first time they had met in person. They had talked via a messaging app on Grace's hidden phone, and that was it. Sally had tracked her down on social media — early on, when she was still allowed to access it. Sally was the only person who really understood what it was like to live with somebody like Craig Dolton, who knew the constant fear. Grace didn't know if she had ever felt closer to someone than in that moment. She was struggling to speak. Sally spoke instead.

'Don't worry. We have plenty of time, okay? Viktor will be here with the money later. By this time tomorrow you will have enough to start all over again. Your new life has already started, even if it doesn't feel like it yet. For both of us, too.'

'I'm sorry. I just need to get him out of my head. When I called that number — the number you gave me — the phone just died. I didn't know what to expect, but not that. I saw the news, Sally. I know he was in that car. They as good as said it, but I already knew. I can't explain it. You told me the call might just arm it, that it would only go off when the car was moving but I knew it happened straight away, I just knew. When that phone cut off it was like he was so much a part of me that I felt him go. I just felt free. And now . . . now I don't. I can't explain it. I don't know why.'

'I know, Grace, I know exactly what you mean. You've lost everything over time . . . your life, your identity, your ability to make a simple choice. He took that all away. But he's gone now. Maybe that feeling you have, maybe it *is* freedom — you just forgot what that feels like.' Grace felt the grip tighten on her shoulders. She felt reassured. A little stronger, perhaps. But she did need to go to a hospital. There were parts of her that were not going to be fixed by time and kindness. Sally was right: she needed to start looking after herself.

Chapter 25

When Maddie stood up she was in a daze. She hadn't finished reading yet but she needed to break away. She had never read anything like it. Her head was shaking. The diary was still clasped in her hands. She dropped it on the table, as though the horror of it might have the ability to take on a physical form that could soak from the pages and be absorbed through her skin.

'You okay, kid?' Harry's standard growl. He was stood, a dark figure in her peripheral vision. She didn't acknowledge him at first. 'Sorry,' Harry said, 'the kid thing . . . force of habit.'

She took a moment. When she did raise her eyes to him he suddenly looked worried. He reached out with both his arms as if he was trying to steady her. 'Jesus, Harry!' Her voice was a coarse whisper. 'I had no idea how bad . . .'

'Are you okay? You look washed out.'

'We need to go out.'

'Okay. You want to sit and have a sip of water first, maybe? Some sweet tea?'

'No.' Maddie did feel a little light-headed. It lasted just a few steps then her walk became more determined. She felt her body flush with anger. She had scooped the diary up on her way — the pictures too, which had gathered in a stack in the printer tray. She heard Harry behind her on the stairs. He didn't say anything more. Maddie got into the driver's seat. She opened the diary and passed it over to Harry and started the engine. Harry took the hint and started reading. She pulled away.

It was a twenty-minute drive to 17 Campbell Road, Hawkinge. Maddie didn't speak. Suddenly it was as if she didn't know how, as if there was nothing she could say. Harry made a few noises between turning the pages: a few sighs, a couple of tuts and some muttering under his breath. She pulled straight onto the drive. The door was still ajar. She knew a search team was due to go in there. Craig Dolton's murder was being treated as a terrorist incident until they knew better. Counter Terrorism searches could take days and they hadn't even started this one yet. It was a specialist job for a specialist team, of which there was only one available to the county and they were still in the Roundhill Tunnels, bagging up debris and photographing scorch patterns on the walls. Craig was deemed to be a random target of the same offender. His home was a belt-and-braces measure and not considered a priority. She walked straight up to the cold-looking, uniform officer sat on the doorstep who greeted her with a look of surprise. He stood up stiffly. He had to pull the snood down that was covering his mouth to speak.

'Good morning,' he said.

'DS Ives and DI Blaker. We need two minutes in there is all.'

He looked unsure. 'Okay. I'll need to put you down on the scene log, can I just take—'

'Two minutes. We won't touch anything, you have my word.'

The officer hesitated but seemed to take the hint. 'Well, okay then. I'll start my watch!' He chuckled nervously. Maddie was already stepping past him. She walked straight into the living room and made for the sofa at the end, opposite the window. She saw the duvet bunched up on the arm just as Grace had described she had concealed it when the police came round. Maddie stopped. She noted the stain on the floor under the other arm. The seat cushion had a darker stain, too, as if a puddle had been left unattended. She pulled the duvet off. The vice was revealed.

'Oh, fuck!' She took a step back, her hand rose to her mouth. 'It's real!' Her voice was close to a squeal. 'That piece of shit!' She felt her veins flood with rage. Suddenly she wished more than anything that Craig Dolton was still alive, so she could find him and kill him all over again.

Harry moved closer to the chair and leaned in to inspect it. Maddie turned away. Her eyes stopped on the window. She looked at the squared view of the world. In her diary, Grace had talked about watching car lights flickering past at night, about dreaming of being free, of being outside the house. Of *this* house.

'I need to find her,' Maddie said.

'Okay.'

'All this . . . it was going on when I saw her.'

'It was.'

'I could have stopped it.'

'You can only stop what you know to be happening. She chose not to tell you about it.'

'I knew there was more. I told her I knew. I could have pushed her harder. I could have done more to let her know that I could make her safe, to make her trust me.'

'She made her choices. And you're the one she sent this to.'

'I should have done more.'

'Beat yourself up for mistakes you make, not the ones you don't. We'll have a look at where they are with finding her. See if there's anything we can do.'

'Fine then.' Maddie turned away. 'I'll get the search team to make sure we get our own photos of that chair.'

'They will anyway, Maddie,' Harry called after her. 'You know this changes the emphasis on her, right?'

'What do you mean?' Maddie stopped her march back towards the front door.

'From what I've read, no one could have hated that man more.'

'You think she killed him! You think she's capable of strapping a . . .' Maddie ran out of steam. Her head dropped. Her mind was suddenly clouded with confusion. She couldn't think straight; she couldn't think of Grace as anything other than a terrified victim strapped into that . . . thing.

'No. I don't think she's capable, but she disappeared on the day he went up. You know it's a relevant line of enquiry.'

Maddie didn't say anything. It was best she didn't react. She knew she was still full of anger; this wasn't the time to talk about it. When she was calmer she might even agree. Grace would have to be spoken to, that would happen whether people knew how Craig had treated her or not.

'So we head back. We find out where they are with finding her and see what's left to do. I would rather be the next copper she sees. It's going to be difficult enough without someone immediately demanding where she was at the time of his death. She needs to be handled right.'

'She does. But we still need to ask those questions.'

'I get that, Harry!' Maddie snapped.

'Of course you do. You've become quite the expert in nine months of investigations,' he snapped back. Maddie watched Harry walk past her to the front door. She choked down her response and sucked in a breath. She took a moment to look around the room until she was back under control. She reminded herself she wasn't angry with Harry and that he was probably right. And that pissed her off, too.

Chapter 26

The bus route dropped Grace around one hundred metres from the entrance to the hospital marked *Accident and Emergency*. The Queen Elizabeth, Queen Mother Hospital, or QEQM as it was known, was Margate's largest medical facility and was not somewhere she had been before. It was still instantly recognisable as an NHS building. It had the standard red brick with a solid, square design and a jumble of signs and directions in every colour. Foot traffic was heavy. Everyone seemed to be moving with their heads bent, their attention on whatever was playing through their headphones or smartphone screen held out in front of them.

She walked past a group of smokers clumped around a low wall just off from the main door. Some hung off the railings of a sloped path that looked to be newly installed. Still no one looked up. She was thankful. She just wanted to blend in. She needed to get fixed, to get something for this pain, and then she needed to get back out of there. Sally had soothed her anxiety a little but it was steadily increasing since she had left the flat. She could barely remember the last time she had been out on her own.

Craig never let her. She made it through the wide entrance doors into the open-plan foyer. The reception was directly in front, with the seated staff separated from the public by smeared glass. A man was leaning forward; he made eye contact with her and looked expectant.

'Can I help?' His voice was filtered through a speaker system that made it sound almost robotic. He was older, and much of his greying hair looked to be bursting from his nose. He pushed his glasses back with one finger. 'Can I help?' he said, again, his impatience clear.

'Yes. I need to see a doctor. I think I've broken my arm.' Grace wiped her forehead where a layer of sweat had formed and turned quickly cold.

'Okay.' His eyes fell to her arm. It was by her side and under a layer of clothing. 'I need to take some details.'

'I wrote it down,' Grace cut in, thinking straight away that she needed to calm down. 'I mean I wrote it all down to make it easier.' She spoke slower and more deliberately. 'I'm in a lot of pain.' She slid a piece of paper towards him and flickered a reassuring smile. There was a thin gap under the glass. The receptionist snatched it up and eyed her again. She watched him work on his computer. It took a few minutes. She had written it down on the way over to limit the need for conversation. She was glad she had.

'If you'd like to take a seat.'

She thanked him. She wiped at her forehead again and ambled over to the row of plastic seats while looking around her. Nobody was paying her any attention. The seating area was large and the people were spread out. She dared to hope that she wouldn't be there long.

* * *

Maddie made it back to her desk. She bent over her computer and fired it up. She couldn't sit, even though she might be there a little while. There were a number of computer systems that might have information on the search for Grace and she would need to check them all.

Harry had taken a message to go and see the chief inspector. He said he would come over when he was done. Maddie's phone was ringing. It had been ringing the whole time she had been back at her desk. She clicked to load up the first system. It was taking its time. She looked away from her monitor to her phone's screen. The ringing stopped. It was Front Counter. The phone displayed four missed calls from their number. She picked up her phone and returned the call. She intended to tell them that whatever it was could wait. It was picked up on the first ring.

'Maddie!' She recognised the voice instantly as one of the regular counter staff: Lisa Harriett. She sounded urgent.

'Hey, Lisa. I'm sorry but I'm really busy up here. Is it something that I can help with later?'

'I don't think so.' Lisa lowered her voice. 'We have a gentleman down here who has your name from somewhere and he won't leave until he speaks to you. He looks all beat up and he won't tell me what it's about.'

'Beat up?'

'Yeah. His face, he looks like he's been fighting. He doesn't look like the type though, know what I mean?'

Maddie didn't have the foggiest, if she was honest. 'Okay, can you tell him that I'm a little busy at the moment. See if you can take a number and I'll give him a call just as soon as I can.'

'I did try that. I called up an hour ago and someone from your team answered and said you were out. I told him and he just said he would stay. He said he's already been sent over here from Langthorne — he went there first. He's been sat there ever since. I don't think he's going to go anywhere.'

Maddie huffed. 'Did he give you his name?'

'Yeah, it's Ian . . . Ian Hughes. He said he was here about his daughter, Grace?'

Maddie had been getting frustrated with her computer. Nothing seemed to be loading and now she wondered whether she might be trying to open too much at once. Suddenly it didn't matter.

'Grace?'

'That's what he said.'

'Tell him I'll be right down.'

Less than a minute later, Maddie pushed through the door into the public area at the front of the police station. She was a little out of breath having almost broken into a jog.

'Ian Hughes?' she asked of the only seated person in the public area.

He stood up immediately, looking nervous and awkward. 'DS Ives?'

'Yes.'

'Is she here?'

Maddie's face must have shown her confusion. 'Is who here, sir?'

'My daughter, Grace? You know Grace, right? She said she was coming to see you?' He was looking at her intently now, as if he thought she might be hiding something. Maddie suddenly felt a little uncomfortable. He looked like he was holding his breath, waiting for good news.

'I'm really sorry, I haven't heard from her. Did she say she was coming down here?'

'I saw her two days ago. She said she was. She was keeping a diary. She said you told her to?'

Maddie held up her hands. 'Okay, okay, Mr Hughes, I know your daughter. I told her to keep a diary and it arrived today by post. I've been out to the house. I need to speak to her, but right now I can't find her.'

'He's dead, isn't he?' He seemed to study her closely now for her reaction.

'Who?' She knew very well who.

'Craig. He's dead.'

'I am aware that's a possibility. I know the local media have suggested a name but the official identification—'

'He's dead, and it was merciful,' Ian cut over her. 'He went up in a car explosion, right? He wouldn't have even seen it coming. He's not answered for what he did.'

'And what was that?' Maddie said.

'I'm certain now that I don't know the half of it. I saw how she was. She could hide the bruises and tell me lies but I saw the limps and the grimaces and the way she couldn't even look at me. They lost a baby, too, because of that monster. Did you know that? She was hurting every day. I couldn't get her away from him.'

Maddie had her hands back in the air, surrendering to his onslaught again. 'Mr Hughes, please! I couldn't get her away from him either and I can tell you it was eating me up inside, too.'

He came back slower and softer. 'It hurts that she didn't talk to me about it. I know she would have told her mother. We lost her. A few years back. Grace didn't take it well. Neither of us did. But there was a positive to come out of that — it made us even closer. Right up until that piece of . . . But now I don't know where she is. In her head I mean. She finally plucks up the courage to leave him, she sends you everything and then he's gone. Just like that. I need to speak to her. I need to know she's alright.'

'I do, too. We're doing what we can to find her. She's a priority right now, I can assure you of that.'

'I know my Grace. At least I used to. I reckon she'll be taking a bit of time. She'll come and see you when she's ready, but it will be you she comes to. She seemed to be clear about that.'

'And when she does I'll make sure she lets you know she's okay.'

Ian paused. It was clear he had something more to say. His eyes roved around the room before they rested back on Maddie. He leaned in a little closer.

'Was it bad?' he said.

'Was what bad, Mr Hughes?' Maddie was stalling.

'The stuff she wrote . . . the stuff in that diary . . . Was it bad? I know it was worse than I thought.'

'It came this morning. I've not had a chance to read it properly, but I will. I owe her that.'

'You must have at least flicked through it. You must have an idea.'

Maddie sighed. She wasn't going to be able to fob him off. Images of horror, pain and a cast-iron vice all flashed to the front of her mind. It wasn't for her to tell Grace's father. She didn't know if Grace would either. He chewed nervously on his bottom lip. He needed some sort of answer.

'I flicked through. Your daughter has unbelievable strength, Mr Hughes, and ultimately she won. She made it through. Now we have to all be there for her and we have to make sure he doesn't have a legacy. For us he may be gone, for Grace it will take a lot longer.'

Ian's face shuddered like he might break. 'Thank you. I'll leave my number. Please, the second you hear from her, you will let me know?'

'I will. And, Mr Hughes . . .' He was scribbling his details on a scrap piece of paper, using the counter to rest on as he turned to her. 'You need to call us in the future — if you have concerns, I mean. Not try and sort it out in the toilets. You're not that sort of man.'

He flushed red. 'Turns out you're right. I got one in, though. I might even have broken his nose. With all that's happened, I'm glad I took that chance.'

* * *

'Grace Hughes?'

Grace jerked at the sound of her own name. She was still sitting in the firm plastic seat. Her head had been down and she'd been focusing on her breathing as a way of coping with her aching arm, while watching the constant passing of shoes along the section of floor in

234

front of her. She'd been there an hour and the movement had been constant in both directions. She lifted her eyes to a thirty-something woman in a light blue nurse's uniform. She was ten metres away and surveying the waiting room, waiting for someone to react. People still bustled past her, stepping around the obstruction.

'Grace Hughes?' she called out again, a little louder this time. She had a friendly face and her tone was patient and warm, even in just a couple of words. Grace suddenly felt a little sick. She didn't want to be speaking to anyone. She knew there would be questions about how it had happened. She couldn't talk about it. Not yet. Maybe this was all a bad idea. She could get some painkillers from the chemist, enough to get her through the next couple of days and then she would come back. She bent her head. Her attention was back to the floor. Then a pair of plain, black shoes stopped in front of her. Tights rose up out of them. She could just see the bottom of a light-blue dress.

'Grace Hughes?' It was the same voice but quieter, more reassuring. 'The fella behind the window there remembers you. I'm Becky Davies. I'm a nurse here. He said you might have a broken arm. Want me to take a look?'

Grace lifted her eyes. Becky Davies's smile was even warmer close up. She had short hair dyed a dark shade of purple and pushed over to one side. 'I don't know if it's broken,' Grace said.

'Well, you haven't had the training I've had! It must hurt pretty bad for you to think it might be. Come through and we can have a look.' The nurse took a few steps, giving Grace some space to stand up and get herself together. They moved away from the waiting room and down a short corridor that was wide enough for workstations either side. Some had staff stood at them, clicking through computer screens and writing notes. Becky stopped at a bed with a wraparound curtain. A high-backed chair was next to it. Grace took up the offer to sit and the chair had an immediate chill that seeped through her coat. The nurse pulled the curtain around. Grace could hear voices from the other side, it sounded like the beginning of an argument.

'Can we get to your arm? How many layers are you wearing?' The nurse was a few paces away, still giving her space. Grace appreciated it. She took off her jacket. That was easy. Her jumper was more difficult. The nurse stayed where she was and she didn't offer to help. She lifted it enough so her arm was exposed.

'That top's going to have to come right off, I'm afraid. I can help if you need it.'

Grace hesitated. She only had a bra on underneath; once she took her jumper off, all of her injuries would be on show.

'It's a little chilly in here,' Grace said. Her attention was half on the curtain too. The voices outside were seemingly louder, more aggressive — male and female. The female was starting to shout. The nurse must have seen her looking beyond her, towards the noise. She rolled her eyes. 'It's just a few minutes. I can't check you over properly with your top on.'

Grace considered her options: she could be insistent or she could leave. She didn't feel strong enough to do either. It was tough lifting her jumper over her head one-handed but she managed it. The nurse pulled the sleeve from her good arm and then it was off. Grace looked straight ahead. She knew the bruising to her side was looking worse; it had come out in a deep blue that was quickly turning purple. Her lower back was bruised, too, and the skin on her upper back and neck was still an angry red. Her arm throbbed.

She saw the nurse's expression change, it was subtle at first, but less so as her eyes flicked over her body. She only spoke to ask Grace to sit back down. She was asked to rest her arm on a flat, black surface, like a miniature dinner tray. It was cold and painful but she did as she was told.

The nurse ran her finger gently along it then brought Grace's other arm over for a comparison. Grace stifled her reaction the best she could.

'Okay. Well, you were right. We have a broken arm for sure.' Nurse Davies lifted her eyes to meet with Grace. 'Is he here? In the waiting room or outside?' Her smile had faded.

'What do you mean? Who?'

'You're covered in bruises. They vary in age and they're mostly in places that you can cover up. This injury to your arm, you haven't just done this either, have you?'

Grace didn't answer. She had expected questions and she was ready for those, but these weren't questions.

'You get to know what signs of domestic abuse look like,' the nurse said, 'and you've ticked just about every one of them. The only thing that's missing is the abusive partner sitting next to you, making sure you tell me that you fell down some stairs, or that you're clumsy around doors.' She stopped talking. There still wasn't a question but it was clear that Grace was supposed to talk next.

'I left him.' Grace's voice was almost a whisper. The raised voices from outside the curtain were starting to move away. A different male voice seemed to be pleading with them to leave.

'Well then, you made a good decision. Why didn't you speak to the police?'

'Who said I didn't?'

'Because they're not here. And they would be. They would want a copy of your medical records. They would be taking pictures and statements. They like to do it at the hospital so they can get it all done together. Trust me, I've seen it enough times.'

Grace had nothing to say. She didn't want to talk about it. She hadn't come here to talk about it. But Nurse Davies wasn't finished yet.

'If you have the strength to leave him, maybe you should go the whole hog? Speak to the police. No way he should be getting away with this. His next girlfriend won't thank you.'

Grace's gaze slipped back to the floor. 'It's complicated.'

'It isn't, Grace. Life never is — not really. The person that did this to you should answer for it. See, simple!'

'It always is when it's someone else. You and my dad would get on well!' Grace suddenly flashed angry. This wasn't her fault — none of it. What he had done, why he had done it, that he chose to do it to her — it wasn't her fault. Her dad used to make her feel like it was. Like she was letting him do what he wanted. She hadn't been letting him do anything; she just couldn't stop him.

She pulled her jumper roughly back over her head and pushed her right arm through one of the sleeves. Nurse Davies was talking again, she was soothing, the warmth was back in her voice. But Grace was done talking about it. She didn't know what treatment meant for her but she was certain it would mean spending a lot more time in the hospital and right now she was starting to feel very trapped. The aggressive voices on the other side of the curtain were back. They were louder still and now included shouted threats and insults. There was a scuffle of feet and something metallic knocked onto the floor. Nurse Davies was still talking but suddenly Grace couldn't separate the sounds, they were just a swirl in her mind. Grace was shutting down, the mental equivalent of going into the foetal position. She needed to be somewhere else, anywhere else and she needed to be alone. The sense of panic was rising.

She moved forward as quickly as she could. She felt her left shoulder collide with something — it could have been the nurse. The pain was excruciating and it served to power her legs. Her right hand swung at the curtain. She moved out and turned right, back the way they had come in. She kept her eyes down, focusing on shoes again. She was pretty sure she walked right through the middle of the man and woman who were still arguing. She ducked low, desperate to disappear.

She kept her head down until she made it to the entrance. There was a steady stream of people moving both in and out. She was held up. She could see the sunlight and feel the cold breeze. As soon as she made it out she turned left, away from the hospital buildings and towards the road that had brought her here. She took a path that cut through the lawns. The breeze still concealed the smallest of snowflakes but now they felt sharp on her face as she strode into them. She pulled her coat tight. She hadn't done it up; there hadn't been time.

The hospital grounds ended at a steel fence. There was a bench next to it that she fell onto. She needed to stop. She needed to think about what she could do next. Her arm hurt. She did nothing to hide the pain in her expression. She leaned forward, fastened her coat up and hugged herself as tight as she could with one arm. She was only sat there for a few minutes when her vision picked up the familiar black shoes and tights: Nurse Davies. She was still smiling and it still had its warmth. In contrast she looked freezing cold, a thin, navy cardigan the only addition to her uniform and she gripped it tightly around her.

'Hey, Grace. I figured we got off on the wrong foot and that was my fault entirely.' She moved to sit next to her. Grace didn't complain. She didn't say anything.

'I remember when I started in all this. Nursing, I mean. Back then it was all about healing the sick and injured — what you would expect, really. That's enough to worry about. Now though, now we need to be picking a whole list of things. Domestic violence included. I can spot it, too. It's obvious once you know. But I'm not so good at talking to people about it. I guess I just say it like I see it. I see someone in harm's way and expect a conversation on how we get it sorted. You probably think it's none of my business . . . that I should just make you better. But it is my business, and I am trying to make you better. I can treat a broken arm. I can fix it and you might say that's my job done. But if you come back in here tomorrow, or next week, or next month with something I can't fix, with something none of us can fix, then I'll have failed you. Am I making sense?'

'I think so,' Grace said. Nurse Davies was close enough to her for Grace to feel her shiver. 'You're freezing cold. You should go back inside.'

'Will you come with me?'

'I can't right now. I don't seem to be able to do busy places. I need time and space.'

'I guessed you might say that.' She lifted something from the bench beside her. Grace hadn't seen her carrying it. It was a navy blue tube with a white strap. Grace recognised it as a sling. 'This will give you a little more protection. It will also compress it a little, which is what you need. It's going to hurt going on but trust me, it will be better in the long run. We need to straighten that arm and that can only be done in surgery. This is the next best thing.'

'Thanks.'

Nurse Davies started pulling her arm around. She closed her eyes and gritted her teeth. She felt the sling slide up her arm. It was pulled tight by Velcro straps that doubled back through a plastic loop. Her hand gripped round the curved bit at the end. The nurse did her coat up too.

'And these.' She reached into her pocket and pulled out a rattling pillbox. 'These are painkillers. The best I can get you if you're intent on leaving. There are better ones but I can't justify letting you leave with them. These are pretty strong. No more than four a day. Read the box for times, okay?'

'Thanks.' She took the box.

'You're sure you won't come back in with me to get that fixed properly?'

'I will, just not right now.'

'That's a real shame. I figured you might have had enough of living in pain. You don't have to, you know. I can try and make it quieter — try and get you a room for a bit. No promises.'

'Thanks. I really appreciate what you've done. And I'm sorry, I know it looks like I'm not helping myself sometimes.'

'Well, nothing is ever as simple as it seems from the outside. Twenty years working for the NHS should have taught me that.'

'I was hoping simple lives do exist — for other people, I mean. It gives me hope.'

'You can certainly make your life simpler. Fixing your arm is just the start for you, Grace. But it must hurt like hell. You can't think straight when you're in pain.'

Grace stood up. She pushed the pills into her pocket.

'You do have to start sometime, though. Promise me you'll be back soon.'

'I just can't face it right now. I thought I was ready.'

Nurse Davies got to her feet. She still held her arms tightly across her front, her cheeks flushed with the cold. 'I guess that will have to do,' she said.

'Thanks.'

The nurse shrugged and started to walk away. She called out as she did so, 'That's what I'm here for!'

Grace lifted the bottle of pills. She struggled a little with the lid. She had already had some of the tablets she had taken from the house today. These would surely be stronger. She tipped two out and swallowed them dry. By the time she pushed the pillbox back into her coat pocket and looked up, the nurse was out of sight.

Chapter 27

Grace mumbled her thanks to the taxi driver and walked back towards the communal entrance to Sally's flat. The snow was now more like sleet and it was getting dark quickly. She fiddled in her pocket for the key. It had a black, plastic fob on it that would get her through the communal door. It got caught up on her pocket and, in her haste to pull it out, fell to the floor with a clang. She cursed and bent to pick it up. The action made her arm throb.

She continued to the door but stopped suddenly. She didn't need the fob: the door was loose, creaking in the breeze. She peered through to the corridor beyond. There was moisture on the floor where the sleet was blowing into the communal area. It looked like it had been blowing in for some time. This was supposed to be a secure building, which was the whole point of it. The door had been locked when she had left.

She pushed the door open wider and stopped still to listen. She couldn't hear anything out of the ordinary — the only noises were the clicks of the lights coming on above the stairs, bathing the hall in a dirty-yellow sheen.

She took the steps in front of her until she got to Sally's landing. This had been locked earlier, too. Now it was wedged with some folded-up paper that had been forced under the door holding it all the way open. She stopped again to listen. Still nothing. She stepped closer to Sally's door. There was no noise at all. Grace readied her key, but tried the handle first. It opened with one twist. The hinges groaned a little as she stepped in.

'Sally?' Grace called out. The movement of the door obstructed her view, but she could make out a light source in the living room. She stayed behind the door for now, anticipating a cheery greeting from Sally, and an enquiry about how her hospital visit had gone. It didn't happen. The silence remained.

She looked left into the kitchen. The fading light through the window was enough for her to see that it was neat and tidy. She had only cast a glance in there earlier but nothing had looked out of place. Straight ahead of her was a large cupboard with shoes arranged neatly along the bottom. Again nothing looked disturbed. She stepped further in and peered around the door — slowly, deliberately. The door to the living room was open and she could see the end of the long sofa. The main light was on and it made the early evening look darker through the window behind. Still nothing was out of place, but still no Sally. Maybe she had popped next door or taken some rubbish out and they had just missed each other? That might explain the wedged doors. She looked down at the keys in her hand; maybe the fob was the only one Sally was issued with? She felt a little better, told herself that she was just being silly. There was nothing to be worried about. No one knew she was here and, even if they did, no one remained to do her any harm. She wouldn't have to be here long. Soon she could leave. She could start a new life somewhere quiet, where no one knew her. Sally had arranged it all. She had been so precise. Grace had known all along exactly what she had to do. She liked that, she always had — clear instructions.

She undid her jacket and let it fall open. The sling was effective: her arm was pulled tightly against her midriff and it made it a lot more bearable. She walked around the door and into the living room. It was spacious and it opened up in front of her. On the right side was a display cabinet with some trinkets and old ornaments in it. To the left, beyond where the television sat on a low table, was a door, the top half of which was glass. She assumed it led to the bedrooms. As she moved into the room, she saw a smaller sofa against the wall, near the door. A magazine was on the floor that looked like it had fallen off the arm. She got closer. On the other side of the chair, a mug lay on its side, a brown stain spread from its rim and it still looked damp.

Why would Sally not clean up a spilled cup?

She felt her heart beat a little faster. She had been suppressing her fear, dismissing the feeling in that flat as ridiculous — her own anxiety making something out of nothing. She couldn't suppress it any longer, the atmosphere in there was thick with panic — and not just hers.

She crossed the floor swiftly and made it back to the front door. Her hand reached out for the handle. She paused with her fingers gripped round the cold metal. She couldn't just leave. Not without knowing that Sally was okay — or at least without being certain that she wasn't there. And where would she go? She turned her head back towards the lounge. She heard a thud. It sounded like it had come from below her — the flat downstairs. There was another one straight after. She was more certain, now: the sound was not coming from inside the flat. She breathed out and took her hand off the handle. She *was* being silly, and all because of some spilt tea or coffee. She knew she was more on edge than normal. She needed to check the flat. She needed to be sure.

Back in the lounge she stopped again at the upturned cup. It looked like it had been almost full. She bent down next to it. The carpet was thin, but still deep enough for the wheels on the sofa to make small, distinctive dents. The wheels now rested an inch or so outside of these impressions. There were scrapes on the wall too, black marks that stood out against the white plaster. They looked fresh. They were level with the top of the sofa and she felt sure they had been made by it being pushed against the wall with some force. She moved to the internal door. There were glass panels running down as part of the wall either side. They were slightly smoked; it was a dated design. Through the glass she could make out a corridor with the same cheap-looking carpet and illuminated by the same, yellowed bulbs. The internal doors were off-white and flimsy looking. The two she could see were both closed.

She pulled the door open and crept across the hallway to stand against the furthest door. She would work her way back. She held her breath and listened . . . nothing. She considered calling out again. Maybe Sally was having a lie down. Maybe she would hear her now. She would wake up and ask her why she looked so damned frightened. Then she would tell her to stop being so damned silly! She shook her head. She couldn't call out. She didn't know what the answer might be. She wasn't sure she was able to call out anyway. She pushed the handle down and the door pushed in — this one groaned, too, and the sound seemed like the loudest thing she had ever heard. She didn't push it hard; the door only edged open, enough to light a sliver of the darkened room beyond.

A woman's bare foot hung over the end of the bed. She could see a flash of red nail polish. There was no movement.

'Sally?' Her voice was strained, broken for the first part of the word. She cleared her throat and swallowed. There was no answer, no movement. She pushed the door harder. More was revealed. She recognised the clothes Sally had been wearing: dark-coloured leggings and a fleece top that had felt warm and soft when they had embraced. She was lying on her front. Grace couldn't see her head — not quite. She would need one more step. She pushed herself forward. Her hand fumbled for the light switch and then every inch was revealed.

Sally's head was turned towards her, her eyes wide open and unfocused; they made no effort to see who was entering. Her mouth was open — as wide as it could be — her tongue lolled out from the side and her neck had a dimpled red line round it. Everything else was white — as pale as death. Grace felt the scream build; it rushed through her and she sucked in air to fuel it, but before she found her voice, something slapped across her mouth. It stayed firm and she was dragged backwards so hard that she was taken off her feet. She hit the floor with her upper back, not as hard as a freefall but hard all the same — enough to knock the wind out of her. Her mouth was still covered.

'You don't say a word! Make noise and you lie next to her, understand?' It was a man's voice, thick with an accent, the words hissed directly into her ear. She could feel the breath, warm and moist. She felt herself pulled, half dragged, back through the door and into the living room. She was thrown into the same chair she had just inspected. She felt it move back on its wheels and it bumped off the wall beside her. Her mind flashed with a realisation that incorporated the dent in the carpet, the spilt cup and the scrape on the wall.

This was where Sally had started.

Chapter 28

Maddie was glad to push the door shut to her apartment. She kicked her shoes off into an untidy heap by the door and the wooden flooring felt instantly cool under the feet. The thermostat for the heating was on the far wall, where the kitchen merged with the living room. She switched the main light on and made for it. She turned the kettle on next and was back out of her bedroom in a snug pair of pyjamas before it turned itself off. She dropped a teabag in a mug and poured water over it. The shrill ring of her mobile phone was enough to make her slop the water over the sides.

'Dammit!' She lifted the phone. The screen showed the number and she recognised the code as being from the Maidstone area. 'Hello?'

'DS Ives?' It sounded like a young woman and there was a low din in the background as if she was in a call centre of some sort.

'Yes.'

The woman must have picked up on the uncertainty in her voice. 'Sorry to bother you. I'm Helen from the FCR. Is this a good time?'

The FCR was the Force Control Room, where Lennockshire Police fielded all their emergency calls.

'Oh, yes of course. Sorry, you just caught me out a little bit. I was expecting you to start selling me PPI refunds. How can I help?'

'I'm not sure, really, Sarge. We've had a call in from a nurse. She was talking about a woman who came into hospital with an injury and discharged herself. The nurse is worried that she didn't get the treatment she needs and our record has a note for you to be informed. Grace Hughes — does that mean something to you?'

Maddie had moved to the window where she had a view of snowflakes falling past the street lights of Sandgate's High Street. She now spun to face back into the room.

'Grace Hughes! She means something, yes. What do you know?' Maddie had marked up her record when she had given her the GPS alarm, so she would be informed of any contact with the police.

'Well, that's about it, really. She went into the hospital in Margate this afternoon with an arm injury. The nurse thinks it was broken. She also noticed other bruising — all over her body, she said. She suspects she is the victim of domestic abuse, so she called it in.'

'She did the right thing. Is she still at the hospital?'

'Grace? No, she—'

'The nurse, no sorry, the nurse.' Maddie pulled open a drawer and rummaged for a pen and a notepad.

'Oh, I don't know.'

'Did she call in on a mobile number?'

'She did, yes.'

'Can I take the number? I'll give her a call.' Maddie scratched down the number and gave a hurried thanks.

She had taken her name too — Becky Davies. She underlined it while she listened to the ringing tone. Something for her hands to do — a nervous tick. The phone was answered. Again a female voice, this one sounded a little more harassed.

'Hello — is that Becky Davies?'

'Yeah, who is this?'

'Becky, I am Detective Sergeant Maddie Ives. Thanks for answering my call and thanks so much for calling in today — about Grace Hughes?' Maddie gave her a second to remember the name.

'Grace, yes. I saw her today.'

'I've just been called about it from our control centre. Grace is someone I have been working with for a little while. She is someone we have assessed here as being at high risk of coming to some serious harm. Her boyfriend . . . well, he's a piece of shit, Becky.'

'I guessed that. She's in a right state.'

'The call taker got some information, but I just wanted to run over it again with you, if I can. We don't know where she is right now and I just want to be sure she is safe. There's some noise in the background, can you hear me okay?'

'Yeah. I'm on the bus. Just on my way home. There's not really much more I can say though.'

'I appreciate that. Tell me where you work and how you got to see Grace today.'

'Where I work? I'm an A&E triage nurse at QEQM in Margate. I do the initial assessments and referrals. Grace presented with a pain in her left arm. She was really struggling with it. She was sweating. Her whole movement looked awkward, to be honest. When she showed me her arm I was quite shocked. There is a break in the middle of her forearm, probably the radius. The colour presentation around it suggested that she's suffering blood-flow issues — and has been for some time.'

'Some time?'

'Yeah. We get training on how to spot people in abusive relationships. One of the big signs is an old injury. The abuser stops them going to hospital until it gets so bad they have no real choice. It was what made me call. That and the other bruises . . .'

'Other bruises?' Maddie said. She heard a sigh down the phone.

'Yeah, she was covered, the poor cow. Her back and side was the worst. Some new, some looked older. I don't reckon she could move any which way without it hurting.'

'Was she alone?'

'I'm pretty sure she was. She said she was and I spoke to Neil out on reception. He said he didn't see her with anyone while she was waiting. I saw her after she left, too. I caught up with her outside and she was alone then. I tried to get her to come back and get the treatment she needed. I managed to give her some stronger painkillers at least. I probably shouldn't have done that.'

'Your secret's safe with me, Becky. Did she say she was coming back?'

'I asked her to. She didn't commit to when, but she will need to get that arm sorted before it becomes very complicated. She'll be in constant pain.'

Maddie moved the phone from her ear for a brief second. There was a beep telling her she had another call. It was Harry. He would have to wait; this was important.

'I don't suppose she gave you any clue where she might be staying?'

'No, none at all. She walked away from the car park though so I guessed she was local, if that helps?'

'Did she give any contact details? A phone number?'

'No. I didn't see her with a phone either. Usually you call out to the waiting room and nine times out of ten people look up from a phone. I didn't see her with one.'

'Okay, it was a long shot. Thanks for your help. You did the right thing calling it in. I've had people tagged before on the hospital system. If I remember right you can put a note against her name asking for the police to be informed when she turns up. Can you put that on Grace?'

'I can, yeah. People don't always see it or do what it asks, but I will make sure it's on there. I'm back on at seven tomorrow morning — I'll do it first thing.'

Maddie took a second to think. 'Don't worry. I'll get our control centre to make contact with the NHS tonight. I'd rather get that on there now. She might even have gone to another hospital.'

'She might. She left when I asked her about her partner. She just clammed up. I can be a bit of a bull in a china shop. I don't get why you'd stay with someone who does that to you, but people don't want to hear it, do they?'

'They don't, no.'

'You're really worried about her, aren't you?'

'Yes. She needs help. Thanks for trying.'

They said their goodbyes. Maddie made the call to her control centre straight after to get her record flagged. Then she had the call log from Becky Davies's initial report sent to her email so she could check that nothing had been missed. Her phone beeped with a message from Harry:

Meeting 7 a.m. tomorrow. No need to call back.

She smiled to herself. As much detail as she had come to expect. She moved back to her window where she had left her mug. It was still warm. Her thoughts moved back to Grace and what this information meant. It meant nothing on its own, but she would run Grace back through the police systems — see if she had any links to Margate. She couldn't remember seeing any. She would call her father, too — maybe Ian Hughes knew of a friend or a relative over there, or maybe she had even got in touch with him. It meant going into a police station. The closest was only fifteen minutes away but she could see the snow was starting to thicken. It would be much longer if she had to walk. She would drink her tea first at least. Then she would need to get changed again.

Her door thumped. It sounded more like someone had fallen into it, rather than knocked. She put her mug down and pulled it open roughly, ready to berate the person responsible.

Adam Yarwood had a wide grin. He also had a white carrier bag in one hand and a satchel hanging from the other. His door key was in his mouth.

'I ran out of hands!'

'Did you kick my door?' Maddie tried to be stern but couldn't hold back a chuckle.

'Sorry. Nice pyjamas. I know I didn't make an appointment but I figured you might be pleased to see me?'

Maddie flushed a little. They weren't at the point where she would wear these in front of him. Not yet. Something smelled delicious. It was coming from the white carrier bag. She suddenly realised how hungry she was.

'You can leave the food,' she said.

'Fair enough. Would you like me to carry it in for you too?'

'Yes. That would be acceptable.' Maddie stepped out of the door and Adam strode in. He dumped the bags on the table, then his keys. He sat down to remove his shoes.

'Oh, you're staying then, are you?' Maddie did her best to look serious.

'Like you had better plans than a takeaway with the likes of me.'

'I was just going back to work, actually.'

'Dressed like that?'

'Well, no. I was going to get changed.'

'Come on, Maddie! I've never seen anyone more *in for the night*!' Adam stood back up. He opened cupboards and readied plates and cutlery. The delicious smells got stronger as he emptied the carrier bag and pulled off lids. She didn't think she could achieve much tonight anyway.

She would look at Grace and any Margate links first thing in the morning.

'Fine,' she said. 'I'm still getting changed, though.'

Chapter 29

Grace took a deep breath. She had felt the impact of falling into the chair through her arm. She needed a moment for the wave of pain to pass but the man had no intention of providing it.

'Make noise and I will hurt you. Understand?' The man was close; once more she felt his breath on her face. She turned sideways to be away from it and opened her eyes. He stepped back and his eyes moved over her whole body. 'You are Grace?'

She nodded.

'Then I know you are one who does what she is told. You are here for Sally?'

She nodded again.

'Who else knows you are here?'

She shook her head. A tear fell onto her cheek and she gently rubbed it away.

'Do you have phone?'

'Are you going to hurt me? Like you hurt Sally?'

'Do as you are told. Maybe she did not.'

'Are you Viktor?' Grace said. She chastised herself inside for her voice sounding weak.

'I am Viktor. Sure.'

'What do you want from me?'

'Where is your phone?'

Grace was trying to think fast, trying to be one step ahead but she couldn't think straight. This wasn't how it was supposed to play out. 'In my pocket,' she said. Lying already seemed pointless.

'Hand it to me.'

She took it out. He snatched it from her and checked the screen. 'It is switched off?' he said.

'Yes. I switched if off before I left the house, just like Sally told me.'

'You did not switch back on?'

'No.'

'At no time did you switch back on?'

'No! I didn't need to and she told me not to.'

'Give me jacket.' Viktor said.

'Why?'

'GIVE JACKET!' The sudden volume caught her out. She shuffled to pull the jacket off one-handed. She lifted it up. He snatched it off her. He searched the pockets, pulling out the make-up items she had grabbed from her house. His eyes ran over each one. He twisted out some lipstick, then twisted it back in again, he opened a tub of powder and a small mirror. He put them back into the pocket. He did the same with her purse. He threw the jacket to the far end of the longer sofa, out of her reach.

'The phone's off. I didn't bring anything else. A few bits of make-up. I did what Sally told me to.'

Viktor pushed the phone into his pocket. His face was a sneer. He leaned in closer again. Grace braced herself against the back of the chair.

'Of course you did. Like a good little girl! You really do not know, do you? You do not know what Sally was doing with you?'

'She was getting me free.'

'And now — you are free, are you?'

'Are you going to let me go? I just want to go. Sally said to come here and to meet you. She said I would get some money, enough for me to set up a new life. But I don't want anything. You can keep it.'

'Oh! I can keep it! I know this! Ten million pounds is good money for me. But Sally, she thought I was worth less than half of this. She needed me. For explosives. For access to the cars — I sent boy burglar in for the keys and then set explosions. He got your keys too so I could put explosive under husband's car. But Sally, she convinced you to be the one who set it off. She said it was easy. You hate him.'

'He's not my husband.'

'Now he is nothing.'

'I just wanted to be free. Sally said I could have some of the money to help me set up. To start over. She said she was getting it from Craig's brother. I didn't know how much. I don't care, either.'

'Give you money to start over? She did not need you. Why give you money? She was not your friend.'

'She understood. She found me when I was with Craig. She was kind to me. She went through the same things I did. She knew what it was like. I was going to leave him, just like she did. But Sally made me see that there would be someone else — someone next. I couldn't live with myself. But she made me see there was another way. She was kind. She booked me a hotel and made me go to the hospital . . . And you . . . you killed her!'

Viktor sneered. 'She talked with me. She uses you. Your phone. Contract has your name. She used your details. You make call to bomb from this phone. You have reason to want him dead. She make sure the police will know it was you.'

Grace shook her head. 'That's not right. The diary — she knew all about it. She told me to send it to the police with pictures — to write a note saying that I was leaving him and to go to the hospital. She told me to speak to the police, to tell them everything that had been going on so they would understand. It would just look like I was leaving him. She was making sure I wasn't involved.'

'On the same day he go boom! Ha! You dumb bitch! Sally was using you, yes? She needed you to access brother's computer. She got you to provide police with motive. You send book of bad things he does, photos too — she tells me this. He clamps you to some chair, hurts your arm. You want him dead. This is not difficult to believe. She made sure you bring your phone today, yes? She insist. And it turned off so no trace your journey here? She book hotel in your name. Uses your account you gave for money to be sent. You blow up boyfriend then spend nice night in hotel! Why not go to police. Sally tell you not to, right? This was never for you. Not for your freedom. This for her!'

Grace was still shaking her head but she was less sure. His words were swimming around in her mind. Sally had been very adamant that she brought the phone, that she switch it off. She was clear on her instructions with the photos: she had told her how to save them straight to the memory card so she could just take that out and send it off. Most phones didn't have memory cards; Sally had chosen it specially. It had come with a messaging application on it and Sally's details already in it. They had talked. Her instructions were simple: she needed to make the call to detonate at 2 p.m. The time seemed really important to her. Grace hadn't liked to ask why. She just thought it was symbolic, maybe.

'She told me to keep the phone on me so we could destroy it. She wanted to know herself that it was destroyed. And for safety.'

'Safety?' Viktor laughed loud.

'Your safety is not for her. She was not going to give you money. She was getting you here and I was supposed to remove you. Just like I removed boy who got car keys.'

'Remove?'

'Dead. All of them. This is what Sally said. She did not want witness to plan. We have agreement for half of money left. She told me it would be easy. She knew rich man would not pay to stop his wank video on webcam, but it was good test, to be sure we had his computer and his attention. She knew he wouldn't pay for brother either, so you would get your chance to make him go boom. But she said he would pay for his freedom and for his money. She was right!' Viktor's eyes lit up over a wide smile. 'Ten million! She used you to get rich. And to kill man she hates. Then you are no use to her.'

'Sally . . . she said that Frank knew what Craig did to his women. He turned a blind eye. He bought him that house. She told me he even gave him the money to buy that . . . that chair — to have it adapted into what it was. She said we would make him pay for what he did, too. She didn't tell me how much. She said I would get enough to go somewhere else. That's all I wanted . . .' Grace couldn't stop the tears. She didn't wipe them away either.

'She had you, did she not? She had you believing. This was her plan. Now she is dead. She told me about you. She told me how you would just do what you were told, how you were good at that. She would have you dead already, but me? I have different idea.'

Grace suddenly lifted her eyes. They met with Viktor. He had been pacing. He was stopped in front of her now. He was running something through his hands. For the first time she noticed he was wearing skin-coloured gloves. What he was holding looked like strips of plastic — cable ties.

'You don't need me either, do you?' Grace's voice was a whisper. Resigned. The boy who had helped him set the bombs, the woman who came up with the idea in the first place . . . If he was to be believed, they were both dead and by his hands. She was the only one left.

'You are wrong. I have job for you.'

'What job?'

'Sally, she make plan for you to be blamed — for the police to come for you. This was a good plan.'

'You want me to take the blame? For everything? They'll know. They'll ask questions I can't answer! I can't take the blame for you!'

He held his hands up for her to stop. He was smiling and shaking his head as if telling her not to worry, that everything would be okay.

'I help you disappear if you do what you are told. If you do not — if you are bad — then I will not help and I will get angry. You do not want me to get angry. Sally, she make me angry. I choked her until she was dead. I used cable tie. I used *this* cable tie. I tie this around your hands — your DNA yes? Yours and Sally's. You came here and you killed her. You killed husband with your phone. You got access to computer at brother's place and you set bombs. Everything pointing at you. You understand?'

'I . . .' Grace couldn't find any words. She was trying to make sense of it all, trying to work out how she had got into this situation.

Suddenly he took hold of her good arm. He was rough and she cried out in surprise. He slammed his hand over her face again, silencing her instantly.

'We stay here until early morning. The building is busy now — people come and they go. We leave first light. I cannot be seen here. We take Sally. You will be silent. Unless you would rather I tie down the other hand?'

Grace shook her head into his hand. She could taste the rubber from his gloves. He pushed off her, turning her face as he did so. She closed her eyes as he grabbed her arm again. She felt the cool plastic wrap round her right wrist then it was yanked across to the radiator. The plastic was pulled tight and he stepped away. She was now pulled tightly against the radiator; it was solid. She looked away from him, down at her left arm. It was still tight against her chest in the sling she had been given by the kindly nurse. She couldn't get it out, not with one hand. And even if she could it was totally useless. She hung her head. She was back in a modified sofa, back under the control of another. And back in a situation that she was convinced would end with her coming to harm.

Chapter 30

Saturday

Grace took a few moments to realise who and where the voice was coming from. As her eyes fluttered open and she made eye contact with a stranger, her panic was instant. Her right hand twitched against something, it was restrained, tied tightly. Her left hand flashed with pain as she tried to lift it in her panic.

It came back to her at once: this was no stranger; it was Viktor. He had secured her to the radiator. She must have finally fallen asleep. The room was still dark and Viktor was an outline. He had said he wanted to leave at first light. It clearly hadn't quite arrived yet. He clicked on a lamp up on a shelf that she hadn't noticed before.

'Leave time. We must be silent. I warn you not to cause me problem. You know what I can do.'

He pulled a knife from his pocket. The blade folded out of the handle in a slick movement. He cut the cable tie. She was trying to think. She couldn't just accept that this was it, that she had come so far and been through so much for it all to end with him. Her eyes moved to her jacket, lying in a heap on the floor on the other side of the room.

'I need to freshen up. I can't go out like this!' she blurted.

'We do not have time. This is the time to go, before people wake.'

'You want me to blend in. Look at me! I should at least stick a bit of make-up on or people will stare — and not just at me. I know I look pale and rough. People have called the police before when I was out with Craig and I looked like this. He never let me wear make-up. Let me have a shower and put some make-up on. A few minutes!'

Viktor's eyes ran her up and down. 'A few minutes.'

'My coat — the make-up things from the pocket. Can I have my coat?' She pointed to where it lay. He walked over to it and scooped it up but he seemed to change his mind. He threw it back down immediately.

'She will have. You can use what you find.'

'Come on, Viktor. It will be quicker. Girls have their own — you know how it is. There are different skin tones and—'

'Okay!' He snatched the jacket back up from the floor and threw it onto the sofa next to her. 'Skin tones! Like I care about this. Be quick. I check bathroom already. The window is very small. You might make it out . . . then you have three-storey fall. Keep window closed. I will be listening. If I hear window open I come in and maybe I will help you get through!' He laughed heartily. Grace struggled to her feet. 'And leave your make-up things in bin in there. This will be good. Police will find them. They will know you were here even more. You take nothing with you.'

Grace nodded and turned towards the corridor. The bathroom was the furthest door from the living room. She shut the door and exhaled loudly. She could feel her heart racing. She didn't have long. She turned the shower on as hot as it went. It came through quicker than she expected. By the time she had struggled to get herself undressed, the room already contained a heavy mist.

* * *

Harry moved to the back of the briefing room. That suited Maddie; she followed him, keeping her head down until she found a seat. She had been in since just after 6 a.m. The intelligence system had shown nothing to link Grace with Margate. She hadn't called Ian Hughes yet; she would give it an hour or so. Harry himself had suggested she wait until after the meeting, saying that it would be worth waiting until she had all the information. Other than that, he had told her nothing about what might be contained in the early morning briefing. She had heard rumours the previous day, that the CT team were taking a step back, having found nothing to link the bombings with any known terrorist organisations. It was suggested that Gold Command would soon be handing the lead back to Major Crime and, from a conversation she had overheard at the coffee machine just a few moments earlier, this meeting was expected to be part of that.

Looking around the room that could make sense. She recognised a couple of officers who had shown up in the last couple of days and had made it clear they worked as part of Counter Terrorism — as if that made them special. Their body language this morning was relaxed. The man in the row in front of her sat with his arms stretched out along the back of the chairs on either side, his legs were crossed towards the man with whom he was laughing. The only coppers looking tense or even interested were detectives she recognised from Major Crime. Some worked in Canterbury Police Station where the briefing was taking place, others were from further away. They all had their books open, ready to take notes, and they all sat up straighter as someone walked to the front of the room and asked for attention. The man in front of Maddie was still laughing; the only change in him was that his laughter was a little quieter.

'Good morning. Thank you all for coming.' The man now stood at the front was tall, in his late fifties, and wore a sharp-looking suit. He embraced the group, looking relaxed and authoritative at the same time. Maddie didn't think this was his first attempt at addressing a room full of police officers. 'Some of you will know me and may know the content of this briefing. I make no apologies for that; you are here to receive an update on Operation Minotaur and for those who have already been involved, to make sure that nothing is missed.

'I'm DCI Ian Clark. I work in Counter Terrorism and I have been the SIO to this point. Operation Minotaur is the ongoing investigation into the detonation of three explosive devices in the Roundhill Tunnels, just outside of Langthorne. It has been a massive operation from a resource and investigative point of view and at this point we are able to state that there are no links from this incident to any known terrorist organisation or activity. We have had the usual crackpots calling in and claiming responsibility on behalf of numerous terror groups, but nothing has been confirmed. We did have someone claim the attack on behalf of the independent nation of Glaucoma, but we're not looking into that one too seriously.'

He paused for a smattering of nervous laughter.

'So, with terrorism no longer suspected to be the main motivation, this operation will be led by Lennockshire Police from this point and specifically Detective Chief Inspector Julian Lowe.' DCI Lowe stepped in from the wings. Maddie hadn't noticed him to that point. He nodded. He had his hands thrust firmly in his pockets and wore the expression of a man suddenly under pressure. Ian Clark still had the floor and he continued.

'DCI Lowe is fully up to speed — he has been involved throughout — but we deemed it right that we provide you all with an update as part of any handover. It is important to understand that the resources of my team remain available. We still have search teams carrying out their work and they will continue to do so until finished.

We also have our expert in all things explosive here and he will remain available too. He is perhaps the best man to provide the update at this point. Mark, if you would.'

The man who had seemed so relaxed with his arms along the tops of the chairs snapped to his feet. He moved to the front and nodded at DCI Clark before turning to address the room. He was shorter than Maddie had reckoned when he was sitting down. His eyes were bright with excitement; his hair was shorn close to his scalp and had a hint of red to it. He stood with his feet slightly apart and his arms fell behind his back like he was 'at ease'. Maddie could tell a soldier when she saw one.

'Good morning. I am Mark Buchanan and some of you I know. A little bit about me . . . I am a civilian officer now but I was a cop for twenty years and I retired around five years ago — so thank you all for continuing to pay into my pension pot!' There was a ripple of laughter. Buchanan's eyes were still bright with mischief. He pulled his arms apart and round the front to wring them together over the beginnings of a pot belly as he now paced. 'Before I was a copper I was in the military and I did tours all over the world. I spent a lot of time in Ireland, both as a solider and a copper and, sort of by accident, become a bit of an expert in all things explodey. I'm almost freelance now; I go where the explosions are or where they might be and I was asked by your CT unit to come down here when the first devices were activated in the Roundhill Tunnels in Langthorne.' He spent a few silent moments looking up and out. He had a captivated audience, Maddie was sure of that. It seemed that he liked to be sure, too.

'The Roundhill Tunnels then . . . I'll talk about that incident first. We've spent a lot of time in there over the last few days, although it is still early in the investigation and we're certainly nowhere near an evidential package. Today, then, is merely conversational — merely my current thoughts and opinions, given to assist you and maybe direct you in your investigation. With that in mind, this is perhaps a good time to remind you that this briefing is marked confidential. And I do ask that nothing is written down — or, if it is, not removed from this room. You will be searched on the way out!'

Another ripple of laughter. This time, however, it was accompanied by the sound of dropping pens and closing notebooks. The officers Maddie recognised from Major Crime seemed to lean in, their expressions suddenly much more interested. The word *confidential* invariably had that effect. Buchanan moved off to one side as a projector screen behind him lit up white momentarily and then was filled with a high-definition image. It looked to Maddie like a clump of dark metal lying in the road. She could see the tunnels in the background, unmistakeable despite being out of focus.

'This is the site for the first explosion. My early conclusion is that this is a VBIED — a Vehicle Borne Improvised Explosive Device. We've been able to find debris from the device, enough to identify some components, and I can tell you that it was an adapted phosphorus grenade. A phosphorus grenade is standard issue in the British Army and also readily available on the black market — if you know which stall to go to. I've used these myself and I can tell you that you don't want to be anywhere near one when it's angry. It burns quick and it burns hot and it's the perfect choice for lighting up a secondary power source — in this case, the vehicle's fuel tank. Petrol . . . diesel . . . it doesn't matter a jot. It'll go up big style and it'll make a lot of noise and a lot of smoke. And that brings me onto the methodology . . .' Buchanan took time to do another sweep of the room. He needn't have bothered; his audience was hanging on his every word.

'The vehicle you see on the screen was empty when the device was activated. We believe the occupant of this vehicle pulled the car across both lanes, halting the traffic behind. According to witnesses, he then stepped out of his vehicle and walked back through the middle of the queuing cars. He was seen placing two packages as he went. One under a vehicle that we know to be a red Ford Focus and which we also suspect had contained an accomplice. Certainly the occupant of that vehicle was seen leaving the car and walking out of the tunnels prior to any of the explosions. She is described as a white female and I will come back to her a little later. So the initial device was activated and, around thirty seconds later, so was the second device, under the red car. We believe this was a frag grenade — that's your standard anti-personnel weapon. It will take out a vehicle quite happily but is a little more centred — something I'll cover in a second. And then comes the nasty part . . . A third device is placed under a civilian vehicle. We believe this to have been a random placement. A thirty-two-year-old female and her baby son were the occupants of this vehicle. Fortunately the young woman was switched on. She has described how she saw a man bend down by the red Ford and then at the rear of her own car. She heard the first explosion, then saw the Ford go up and figured she could be next. Turns out she was right. The woman was able to get herself and her baby out in time but she sustained considerable injuries and as I speak she should be under the knife having shrapnel removed from her spine. Something that she agreed to delay so she could give us her account. She is a hero and you will remember that every time you deal with her.'

Again he paused. He had been excited to this point. Now he was more circumspect. It seemed to Maddie that this pause was mainly for him, as if he was gathering himself together for the next bit. He visibly puffed himself back up.

'Our running theory, then . . . We have found debris consistent with mobile phone activation for all devices. We may have enough by the end of the search to be able to identify one or some of the phones. This was an attack designed to terrify first, to injure second and to kill as a last priority. That would make sense with using the fozzy grenade on the first car. It went up big and loud. There would have been lots of bright, white smoke — you wouldn't have missed it. It was designed to send a message to the people in the tunnel behind it. That they needed to get the hell out of there. The second device reinforced that message and then the third device . . . maybe that was their way of saying that they weren't too concerned about targeting members of the public, even if they did give them a fighting chance first. You will have seen from the news no doubt, that we have two fatalities, one from a blast wound and one unfortunate soul from wounds caused by shrapnel. And we have scores injured. Despite that, we were incredibly lucky. Any questions at this stage?'

The room was in stunned silence. The tension was tangible, frustration hung heavy in the air. Mark turned towards the screen. He clicked the pointer to scroll through some more scene photos. The next was a shot of the inside of the tunnel, looking right down the middle. The area was lit brightly by floodlights, which had been placed wherever there was a gap. The cars were in a mostly neat line, but for their doors hanging open and the debris littering their windscreens and road. The screen clicked onto what was left of the second vehicle. Then there was a shot of a male, slumped forwards as if he was hugging his steering wheel; the picture was from behind. His head was an odd shape, with a lump on the left side. Maddie strained to make it out; it could even be that his hair was just ruffled up.

'Our only victim still in his car . . . Andreas Mitz, a German national. That has caused us some issues as you can imagine. We have been in regular contact with the German embassy and their Foreign Minister, who is concerned that one of their citizens might have been killed in a terrorist incident in a foreign country — which brings me to the motivation. Following the tunnel bombing, we were waiting for someone to claim responsibility. No convincing claim came forward from the usual suspects. All our sources were silent — here and abroad. Then we had the second incident . . .'

Buchanan clicked his pointer again and the image on the screen changed.

'This is the fourth car bomb, which yesterday claimed the life of a local man, Craig Dolton. Mr Dolton was a two-minute drive from his home address and was being stopped by the police at the material time. We know then that no one dropped a package under the vehicle on this occasion. Sorry — I should say that all of the three vehicles in the tunnel had the explosive device underneath them — external. Mr Dolton was killed when a bomb exploded from *inside* his vehicle. The blast patterns are quite different as you can imagine. Of note, from this location you can almost see the Roundhill Tunnels, albeit this is a different road that leads over them.' Buchanan paused. Maddie tried to make out details in the photograph. Again it was a dark husk of scorched metal, but the contortion in the roof and panels overall where the explosion had pushed outwards was clear. She found herself shaking her head. *The killer must have had access to that car.* She turned to Harry, who met eyes with her briefly. He had been quick to point out that Grace would be a suspect. This new information could only add to his theory. Buchanan continued.

'Again, we know this was a grenade device, but the bomber has made some amendments to all of the devices. The standard grenade activation you will all be familiar with, up to a point at least . . . A pin, pulled from the body, primes the weapon. But not like the movies. No soldier will pull a grenade pin out with his teeth, not twice at least.'

More laughter round the room.

'It's awkward. It's designed to be.'

Buchanan mimed the pulling of a grenade pin. He bent forward, the backs of his hands coming together, his elbows pointing out. He then pulled them apart. He lifted his right hand in a tight fist. His eye fixed on it, as did every other set of eyes in that room. He licked his lips before he started up again.

'The body of a grenade is about a pound in weight. It feels lovely, sits nicely in the palm of your hand. All the while you hold onto that clasp, nothing's gonna happen. Let go of it and you've got about four seconds before all hell breaks loose. In this case, our man decided he didn't want to be holding his weapon. He didn't even want to be near it. So he took out the pins, the clasp too, and replaced it all with a mobile phone primer. It's actually easily done. I mean, it takes a steady hand — you wouldn't get me showing you, put it that way!'

There was too much tension in the room now for laughter.

'For him though, activation was simple. A simple phone call . . . *boom!* From what we can tell so far, all four devices are identical in their operation. The phosphorus grenade used for the first detonation is the only one of that type. Craig Dolton is interesting, as the device that took his life was already inside his car. For how long? Why it was there? What's the story? That's your job to understand. The one thing I can be certain of is that the two incidents are linked. You're looking for the same person. All my years of experience tells me that bombers create bombs in a way that is as individual as they are. And for that reason, you need to understand that anyone who sets a bomb wants only one thing . . . No matter what they say, no matter what they demand in exchange for *not* detonating — they *want* that device to go off. It is the only way to cover their tracks. We're getting pretty good at piecing them back together, but we're not quite there yet. Bombs are hard to make — even simple adaptations like these. It takes time touching, breathing over and sweating on the device. You will leave forensic evidence. A bomber will know this, but they will also know that forensic evidence is lost the moment it detonates. So I will say it again . . . the one thing every bomber wants when they create a device is for that device to reach its potential — to explode.' Buchanan held up his right fist as if he was inspecting it. When he released his fist and spread his fingers it was like breaking a spell. Maddie saw heads move, some turning to the person next to them, some shaking, there was a murmur of low voices too.

'Right, I will pass you back to the boss, who can talk to you about where the investigation is right now. Unless there are any questions?'

There was another stunned silence. Buchanan brought his hands together in a sort of bow. Ian Clark was already moving in behind him when Maddie called out.

'Sorry! Can I just ask . . .'

Buchanan had made it to his seat but turned to face her. He looked a little surprised. 'Sure.'

'Why would he use a phone? For the first three, I mean? If he was there?'

'What do you mean?'

'The first three in the tunnel. The phone makes sense to me for Dolton. You could be anywhere. But in the tunnel, could you not just set the grenades on timers?'

Buchanan nodded. 'You could.'

'And evidentially, that would be better wouldn't it? That way you would have no worries about your phone being traced.'

'You wouldn't. We've had the same conversation and it's something that we won't get a definitive answer to until we speak to the bomber. But I would say it depends on what they were trying to achieve. A timer is not a very precise method and it doesn't allow for a Plan B. Maybe they needed that.'

Ian Clark was stood beyond Mark. He looked impatient.

'Okay?' he said.

'Yes, thank you,' Maddie said.

Ian took up the talking. The twisted husk of charred metal, all that was left of Dolton's car, remained on the screen behind him.

'There's been a lot of work going on as you can imagine. Too much to list up here. You will be given your own individual briefings, depending on what part you are to play. A key focus has been phone work. We've been able to get a data dump from the mast that covers that area. We requested all of the cellular activity going through that mast at the material time. It was a lot as you can imagine, that mast is the main source for the town. From triangulation we were able to largely drill down so we were left just with the phones that had been moving — that is the phones that were in the vehicles on that road. From that point we were able to identify three phones that were switched on just prior to the explosions and then disconnected from the network within a very short space of time. Any savvy bomber will know that if we can identify the phone that detonated the device then we will look to track it backwards to get a picture of where it's been. You can get round this by only turning the phone on when you need it. We can be sure that was what happened in the Roundhill Tunnels. We are still working on finding out where the phones were purchased and by whom, but they are burner phones, as you would expect — no contract. My guess is we won't be able to link them to anyone quickly. The phone that armed the device that killed Craig Dolton, however, that had to be turned on earlier. The CT analysts are still working on that. They'll provide a very detailed product, but the early indication is that the device connected to the network while at Craig Dolton's home address the previous night. He lived there with his partner . . .' Ian now turned towards the screen. It changed. A picture of Grace appeared. She was smiling. She looked fuller in the face, her skin tone was healthy, her hair longer and straightened. She was smiling and her eyes had a sparkle. She looked happy. So different to how Maddie had seen her last.

'This is Grace Hughes. She is Craig Dolton's partner. This picture was provided by her father and is a couple of years old. She doesn't have any social media that we could find. It's quite likely that she wasn't allowed it. We have been provided a document by Inspector Blaker that was received into this police station having been sent by Grace on the day of her boyfriend's death. It is a diary. It gives a detailed account of her treatment over several months at the hands of Craig Dolton. It is not comfortable reading. The very last entry is only two days old and details Craig knocking Grace Hughes unconscious and raping her. As I have already discussed with Harry and DCI Lowe, this document elevates Grace Hughes to where we must suspect her involvement in the bombings and the murder of three persons. We believe a male walked away from the first vehicle and subsequently laid another device. We now have reasonable grounds to believe that Grace Hughes was the female seen walking from the second vehicle in the Roundhill Tunnel. She also has a strong motive regarding Craig Dolton's death and, of course, easy access to his vehicle. DCI Lowe will provide you all with a document with some key details about Grace. Our main task now is to find this woman. Harry and I have also discussed the action plan for if she should be located and I urge you all to read that part carefully. In summary, she is to be treated as extremely dangerous, and her arrest will be carried out by armed officers only. Firearms are having a separate meeting this morning where officers will be made aware that they are authorised to take the necessary actions if she is seen in possession of a mobile phone and does not obey commands.'

Maddie spun to Harry as if she had been stung. He was still peering forward. He would be aware of her stare. She held it. Her mouth fell open. She burned hot; she could feel it in her neck and cheeks. There was more to the briefing, an update on Grace's associates and movements among other things, but Maddie wasn't listening anymore, she didn't take any of it in. She couldn't wait for it to finish, and when it did she was the first one out of the double doors. She almost fell through them and heard them clatter off the wall behind her. She heard Harry's voice, too.

'Maddie!' he called out. She kept walking. She could see daylight through a glass panel in a fire exit at the end of the corridor. She made for it. She pushed this one just as hard. It was early morning and the temperature was still below freezing — it took her breath away. The black path had a thin layer of glittery frost that crunched under her feet as she walked towards the car park. She was making for a coffee shop she had used before as a bolthole. She hadn't needed one for a while. Not since her first weeks after transferring down to the area. She'd felt lost then, out of her depth and lonely. Harry had been a big part of getting her past that. Now he was the reason she needed it again.

* * *

The coffee shop was already busy. The cold weather and the early morning combined to cajole people through the door for a hot drink to start the day. Maddie had to join the back of a queue. She kept her head down. She was trying to calm her thoughts, trying to work out how they had got to this point: where Grace Hughes was wanted for murder, with firearms teams specifically assigned for her arrest. Ian Clark's words repeated over in her mind — *she should be treated as extremely dangerous and firearms are authorised to take necessary action if she is seen in possession of a mobile phone and does not obey commands.* Maddie knew what that meant. It meant Grace was in a lot of danger. It meant she would need to find her first.

'Black, no sugar.' Harry Blaker's voice filled her ear. She jerked her head towards it, her lips parted to snarl a reply but he was already moving away. She stared at his back, her teeth gritted. He had the collar on his wax jacket pulled up, his hands pushed firmly into deep pockets. He took a seat at an empty table at the far end and pulled a discarded newspaper idly towards him. He didn't look over. She had to break from staring at him. Someone was talking to her from behind the counter; they were asking her what she wanted.

Maddie put both drinks down on the table. She didn't sit. Harry sat back from his paper and looked up.

'Are you going to sit down so we can talk about this?' Harry said. Maddie didn't want to. She wanted more time; she knew she was still furious.

'I'm so angry.'

'I know that. It wasn't quite like the boss made it sound.'

'Oh, really? Because it sounded like you went running to him with Grace's diary, with her heart and soul poured out on that paper, and you used it to bolster your theory about how Grace sought some diabolical revenge for which she should be shot. Is that *not* what happened?'

Harry's head moved right and left like he was checking around him.

'This might not be the best place.'

'What if they do shoot her on sight? What if they kill her? And for what? What do we actually have? Circumstantial evidence at best. There's no way she was responsible for what we just saw.'

Harry was still fixed on her. 'At least sit down, Maddie.'

She sniffed, pulled the chair out and perched on the edge.

'I'm worried about her too,' Harry said. 'You're not the only one. You don't get the monopoly on that—'

'You met her once! Five minutes in her kitchen! I've been working with her, building her trust. I told her I would keep her safe. I gave her my word. I'm not saying I'm the only one who can care about the girl, just that other people don't know the half of it — they can't! I've seen what he's done to her and I've read those words. What she went through . . .' Maddie was starting to run out of steam. She was aware that she had cut him off, that she wasn't letting him talk. 'I did warn you. I'm angry.'

'I read it, too. I met her, too. Yes, it was only five minutes, but don't think I don't care. I know that you think a lot of her. I know you want to help her. But we have to look at it as police officers, not—'

'Don't start patronising me! Don't start telling me what I'm thinking and why. I'm not some rookie that just walked in off the street.'

Harry sat back and he put up his hands as if he was surrendering. The anger that had rushed back left just as quickly. An apology shot to her lips. She held it back.

'When we look at this as police officers we see a woman who has been through hell at the hands of Craig Dolton. *Raped* the night before. Beaten until she lost her baby. Then we see him murdered the same day that she finally leaves him.'

'Surely you can see that could well be circumstantial, that the bomb incidents are linked but the victims are random — part of something much bigger. Besides, where is she supposed to have found a grenade when she wasn't even allowed out of the house? When she wasn't allowed to talk to even her neighbours? She wasn't physically capable of making a bomb anyway, let alone putting it in his car. And she's a victim, Harry. I've never seen more of a victim than her. She's terrified, just the thought of doing something to harm her abuser would be enough to send her over the edge.'

'I hear what you're saying, but we just don't know. We have a lot more questions than answers. Grace gives us some of those answers, Maddie, and that brings us to the obvious question . . . where is she? If she was leaving her abusive partner to get herself safe surely she would come to the police — she would have come to you.'

Maddie rubbed at her face. Her climbdown was complete. She had asked herself the same question — of course she had. 'I don't know. I do know that she's scared and confused — she has to be. She must know he's dead, the whole world does by now. I don't know why she hasn't made contact. I think maybe she's taking some time out from it all. She's got herself somewhere safe and she's just getting her head straight before she makes contact. Who knows *what* she's thinking! Maybe she's put two and two together and is scared she's in the frame. I don't know.'

'We need to find her. We knew that earlier, so nothing's changed since before that briefing this morning.'

'The tactics have! Clark and Lowe in there want to send twitchy firearms officers to front her up and shout in her face. I think she's had just about enough of that, don't you?'

'I know, Maddie. It's not ideal. I said that I didn't think it would be necessary, but he's twitchy himself. Can you imagine the fallout? If she detonated another device because we took a softly, softly approach?'

'Why would she detonate another device? Jesus, Har—'

'I know! The commanders need to be doing everything they can to stop her if that is her intention. It's how you survive in that role.'

Maddie finally relaxed enough to take a swig of her coffee. Now she was calmer, she knew Harry was right — not that she would admit that, not here. She needed to get back to work. She needed to be the one who found Grace. At least then she could be sure how it would end. She pushed down on the plastic lid to secure it on her drink.

'I need to get back to work . . . Dammit!' Maddie's phone was vibrating in her pocket. She lifted it out. The display showed the same prefix for when she had received a call from the force control room.

'Hello.'

'DS Ives?' The low din in the background, the clattering of keys — the voice was different but she recognised this as the FCR calling her again. She stiffened a little.

'Yes.'

'Sorry to bother you, Sergeant. I'm calling from the FCR. We've had an alarm activation. One of your DV alarms. It's assigned to Grace Hughes and the notes say to let you know.'

'Grace Hughes! Yes. Where is it showing?' Maddie made eye contact with Harry. He stood up immediately. She started walking to the door.

'A block of flats in Margate, according to GPS. It's called Rolla House — opposite a bowling alley on our mapping system. This Grace Hughes is marked up as a firearms response only. We do have a firearms patrol on their way on immediate status but they're coming from Maidstone. Did you want me to ask them to make contact with you when they know a bit more?'

'Yes. Can you also show me en route, too, please? And send through the log with the address on it.'

'Of course. I will mark you up as attending.'

'When was the activation?'

'Forty minutes ago. We were sending a local patrol but the inspector up here stood them down. There's a very clear response plan for this woman, firearms only, and they were on changeover so not close.'

'Okay, let's hope they're closer now.'

She pushed her phone into her pocket. They were already out and walking the pavement. 'Grace must have pushed the button I gave her. She's still in Margate. Which suddenly makes sense.'

'How does that make sense? We couldn't find any links over there.'

'They just gave a building name. Rolla House. It's a women's refuge. That's where they moved Craig's ex. I remember it from her notes.'

'Craig's ex? You think they've been in contact?'

'I do now.'

'I'm parked in the front yard.'

Maddie had her phone to her ear. It was ringing. She spoke hurriedly to Harry before it was picked up. 'No need. I saw Vince this morning. He came in for his early turn and they've grounded him. He doesn't know why. They've seized his clothing too. He's moping about somewhere in a spare uniform. If he has a marked car he can drive us. We'll get there a lot quicker.'

'That is certainly true. But you said he was grounded? So not allowed out?'

'Unofficially, and he's not sure why. His ears have a bit of a ring, that's all. I just don't think they know what to do with him. He'll jump at the chance, I know he will.'

'I get that. But he's grounded, Maddie.'

Maddie tutted. The phone had rung out. She pressed to call Vince's number again.

'He is. But then, technically, so are you, Harry.'

Chapter 31

Maddie grabbed the phone vibrating in her pocket. The interruption was almost welcome: she had been staring out the car window, and an assortment of worst-case scenarios regarding Grace had been flashing through her mind.

She assumed the ringing phone was someone calling her back with an update. She had called in her theory about the women's refuge and Craig Dolton's ex. She thought better than putting it out over the radio. She had stayed on the phone while they had run checks and confirmed that Craig's ex-partner was shown as living in the Rolla House building, flat number 6. They had reminded her of her name: Sally Tomms. They would pass the message onto the firearms team so they could check that flat first. That was around twenty minutes ago and the only response since then was a message passed on from the armed patrol telling them to remain by their vehicles when they arrived. No chance of that. She almost dropped the phone in her haste to answer it now. The number was concealed.

'Yes!'

'Maddie, bad time?' Maddie took a moment to put a name to the voice. It was only a moment. Superintendent Alan Jackson's voice had a distinctive rasp at the end, as if conversation was being squeezed from him. He had been her boss up until a year before in Greater Manchester. His call now was totally unexpected.

'Boss, a little out of the blue is all!'

'Can you speak?'

'We're on our way somewhere. I could call you back when I can talk better?' He wasn't a man who called for no good reason but Maddie could do with keeping this line free. She hoped he would get the hint. He didn't seem to.

'This should just take a minute of your time Maddie. I've just come out of a meeting, I wanted to call you straight away.'

'A meeting?' Her interest was piqued.

'Yes. There's some movement up here. We've had a bit of a restructure of our covert teams and the long and the short of it is there's a vacancy for an inspector. I've been talking to your bosses down there, Maddie. It seems you've made a real impact. Julian Lowe was singing your praises for a piece of work you've pioneered with victims of domestic violence. He has no hesitation in endorsing you. Seems you'll be returning with a very impressive portfolio.'

Maddie took a moment. 'That's good to hear. It's not a portfolio piece — hardly pioneering either — it's just being able to take off our policing hats for a meeting or two.'

'I wasn't suggesting it was only something you were doing for promotion! No need to be defensive. We'd like you back. I can't guarantee you'd be out on the ground like you used to be, but you would be leading those who are. We're in a state of flux up here. It's an interesting time.'

'A state of flux? What does that mean?'

'The picture up here is changing. The OCG's that were prominent when you were operating up here are starting to fall apart. There's always a cycle. The Yarwoods, for one, seem to be imploding. One of the brothers seems to be on his way out and the other's been hospitalised in London. And that's just one of the gangs! We've put some other big players away too. It seems to be quite unsettled up here right now, all the gangs seem intent on filling the vacuum.'

'Hospitalised?' Maddie said. She tried to keep her voice level. She'd barely heard a word since that one. It didn't have to mean much of course; these days, *hospitalised* could be a sprained wrist or a funny turn. But she knew the Yarwoods; she certainly thought she knew Adam well enough. He would have to be dragged to one of those places — or taken there without his knowledge. She bowed her head, waiting for the superintendent to expand.

'Hospitalised, yeah. He's in a bad way apparently. Beaten half to death over a plastering contract if you believe the stories around it!'

'Plastering?' Maddie's head snapped up. Suddenly she felt her breath leave her body, her heartbeat quicken.

'Plastering. The brother, unfortunately, but it'll have to do. He turned up in King's Hospital with his skull caved in. They've got a group in for it. Seems he muscled in on some contract for a new office block. A lucrative contract for a *real* plasterer — no idea what a drug dealer, using plastering as a front, wanted with it! Seems he bit off more than he could chew anyway. This other crew beat him round the head with baseball bats. Who knew plastering was so competitive! I've called a surveillance team in. Leon Yarwood is due to head down with his mum on Monday, and I think they said his sister. Is there a sister you know of?'

'Sister . . . Yeah, there is,' Maddie murmured. She had been in the same room as her on a couple of occasions. Hateful woman. All designer labels in pastel pink and sunglasses indoors. Never worked a day in her life and leeched off her drug-pushing brother.

'Sister it is then. Leon's out of the country at the moment. We have him in Spain but making his way back. One source says he fled there after some threats were made. I spoke to the medical staff at Kings . . . his brother's in an induced coma. They can't assess him properly until the swelling's down or something. I say switch him off now — save the electricity bill!' The superintendent chuckled.

'Adam . . .' Maddie's voice was still a shocked whisper.

'*Adam* Yarwood, that's it! Couldn't remember it for the life of me! He'd dropped right off our radar. We had no idea he was even out of the county. The running theory is he has some bit of stuff on the go down south. He was found with an engagement ring in his pocket. A receipt, too. From the same day. Whoever she is, she certainly dodged a bullet! I've got a meeting up here later today to see how we manage the fallout. We'll need to get behind Leon and his family in case of repercussions. We plan to pick him up from the airport. The offenders have no confirmed links to the drug world, but it's a line of enquiry the Met have taken on. Of all the dangerous people his brother could upset, he ends up with his skull smashed in by a group of labourers with baseball bats! Karma can be a bitch I suppose.'

Maddie could feel the emotion welling up through her. She wanted to scream out, to stop the car. She wanted to run. She couldn't be here — she needed to be anywhere else.

'Maddie, you okay?' The voice this time was the bassy tone of Harry Blaker. He was leaning round from his position in the front. She managed a jerked nod, she pointed at the phone. Harry lingered for a moment, but he did turn away.

'Sorry, boss, we're just about there. I'll get back to you.' She had to squeeze the words out from a throat that felt like it was tightening with every passing moment. She ended the call before he could make any response. Harry's head appeared again.

'Anything we need to know about?'

Maddie cleared her throat. It didn't feel any looser. 'No. Manchester. They've got a job for me if I want it. That's all.'

'And that's terrible news, is it?' Harry said.

'No, no!' Maddie somehow managed to sound brighter. 'I just don't need anything else to think about right now.'

'You're right. We're here and we need to be focused.'

Maddie stuffed the phone back in her pocket. Then sucked in a lungful of air. She was here for Grace. She would deal with one person at a time. They pulled into a car park with numbered bays and she saw that two firearms cars were already parked up. Both cars were silent and empty; their occupants would already be sweeping the building.

Maddie stepped out and took time to run her eyes over the building. It was bland and flat-fronted with windows of different shapes and sizes in what seemed to be a repeat pattern. It was of brick, mainly, but the windows and doors were framed in dark brown wood — typical of a nineties build. Looking around she assessed they were in a rundown part of Margate, close to a road that was steady with cars. On the other side of this road was an empty car park that led up to a warehouse-style building labelled as a bowling alley, which fitted with what she had been told from mapping. The frontage looked tired: the 'H', in *Hollywood Bowl* had slipped to rest at an angle; the car park was punctured with weeds; the lines marking the bays were mostly rubbed out. She would have assumed it had shut down were it not for the catering vehicle with its door open to a side entrance.

Their chaperone wasn't long in coming: a tall woman, her sidearm hung on her hip and with her primary weapon, a rifle, across her front at an angle.

'Hey!' she called out, cheerily.

'Hey,' Maddie said. Her eyes had glazed, her attention drifting elsewhere for a few seconds. She scolded herself mentally; she needed to focus.

'The building is clear. We've knocked everyone up and we got to speak to someone in all but two flats. One of them we've been able to ascertain isn't occupied. The other one was the address we were given . . .' The woman reached for her notebook.

'Number 6?' Maddie said.

The woman nodded. 'Yeah. In the circumstances we have forced entry. There's no one there.'

Maddie let out a breath. She tried to consider what that information meant. Grace wasn't there. But she must have been there and she had been concerned enough to press her panic alarm.

'We spoke to FCR,' the firearms officer continued. 'They're still showing a GPS signal pinging at this address. We haven't done a good search but if I'm honest I don't know what we're looking for. They said you would?'

'Yeah. I gave it to her. Can we come up and take a look?'

The woman led the way. She still held her rifle like she was covering the trigger. There was probably no other way to hold it comfortably but it made Maddie nervous. She hung back a little. Harry was with her. Vince had stayed reluctantly with the car.

'You okay?' Harry whispered into Maddie's ear.

'Yeah, of course. Just worried about Grace.'

The flat was two flights up. The landing had another door with a buzzer system. It was wedged open now.

'Was this door secure?' Maddie asked.

'No, it was like that when we got here. We haven't touched much to be honest.'

Maddie stepped onto the landing. One thing they had definitely touched was the front door to flat number 6. It had been forced inwards. The sides were splintered and the letterbox had come loose with the force. The steel enforcer that had been used for the job was still out on the landing. The officer gestured for them to go in first. Maddie took the lead. In the living room, she was met by another officer holding his rifle with the same intent. He nodded at her and must have recognised Harry, greeting him with a nod and a polite 'Boss'.

Maddie peered around. The flat seemed small overall, but tidy. Everything seemed to be in its place. The living room was the largest space and at its far end was a door leading into a hallway. It had glass panels on the left side so she could see most of the hall and at least two doors that came off it. She moved towards it.

'Are these the bedrooms?' she called out.

'One bedroom and a bathroom,' came the reply. 'It's all been checked.'

Maddie didn't doubt it. The first door was almost directly opposite where she entered. She pushed it open to reveal the bathroom. Again, it was all in order as far as she could see. There was a bath on the right with a shower hung over it. The bottom of the bath looked damp and the shower still dripped. On the opposite wall was a sink with a small cabinet above it and a window over the toilet to the left of that. It was cold. The window was pushed wide open and the blinds shuffled in a freezing breeze. Her eyes dropped to a small bin where a lipstick stood at the bottom, held up by a white plastic bin liner puffed with air either side of it. She stepped back out.

The next door was the bedroom. It was big enough for a double bed and a small, fitted wardrobe with doors that slid into each other to reveal a neat rack of clothes behind. There was an empty cup on a bedside shelf. It had a tea stain in the bottom. So far it was the only thing that looked out of place. There was a crease running up the middle of the bed, too, as if it had been made and then had something laid on top of it. Someone this tidy would have just needed to run a hand over the crease to remove it.

Maddie couldn't quantify it, but something didn't feel right.

'Not much here,' Harry growled.

Maddie had to agree on the surface. 'Except a panic alarm — somewhere. She wouldn't have pressed that lightly, Harry. There's something wrong.'

'Maybe it was an accident?'

'The button's on the inside. It's possible, just not likely. And why leave it here? And where is Grace? Or Sally for that matter — the woman who actually lives here.'

'All we are getting from Grace are more questions,' Harry said, his frustration clear.

Maddie walked back out into the hall and cast her eyes left again, running them over the bathroom as she continued through the flat. She got back to the front door. There was a neat row of shoes running under a cupboard that was fitted into a gap opposite the front door. Inside were coats, a handbag and a hoover. A quick search of the bags and coat pockets revealed nothing. She went into the kitchen: again, nothing out of place, not even a dirty cup or spoon in the sink. A bottle of spray bleach was out on the bench. It bubbled from the nozzle and there was a patch where it had dripped — as if it had been used recently. Harry was back in the living room. He shrugged.

'I guess we get a search team in, just to be sure the alarm is here and to see if there's anything else we can use to find her.'

Maddie was trying to think. 'It's a make-up mirror. There was nothing in the bedroom . . .' She walked back through the door. She heard Harry call out to her but she ignored it; she wanted to bottom something out. She walked back into the bathroom, trying out scenarios in her head: if you were scared, if you wanted to press an alarm and you didn't want someone to know and it was disguised as an item of make-up, you would need to be somewhere where it wouldn't look out of place. She thrust her hand into the bin. There were other items of make-up in there, but no alarm. She straightened up and fixed on her reflection in the mirror over the sink. The unit was deep and doubled as a cupboard. She pulled it open to find it busy with items: toothbrushes, make-up wipes, bottles of shower gel and soap bars. She moved them around and pushed them aside. Her hand fell on something smooth in the corner, pushed behind a plastic beaker. She pulled it out.

It was the alarm.

Maddie stepped back and held it up. Her eyes flickered back around the room. Her mind rushed with scenarios, none of which seemed plausible. It had been hidden, but why hide it? Sally might have known what it was, perhaps? Maddie didn't know if she had ever been issued with one. So did this mean Sally was a threat to Grace? Why would that be?

'She was leaving me a message. She must have been. Why else?' Maddie spoke out loud despite being alone. Harry hadn't followed her; she could hear his voice as a low vibration from the other room. It sounded like he might be on the phone.

She pulled out the rest of the contents of the cupboard and started to rest the items in the sink. She changed her mind when she noticed the hot tap dripping, flattening the cotton wool.

The hot tap!

Maddie emptied the sink hurriedly and pushed everything back into the cupboard. She had to hold the cabinet shut so the stuff wouldn't spill back out. Now she was in a rush. She turned the hot tap on fully. She looked up at the window. It was square and the top third was wide open. She pulled it shut and did the same with the bathroom door. She stepped back. The steam started to build and the mirror started to mist. She bit down on her lip as something appeared at the bottom right of the mirror. The mist built from the bottom and the something became a line that moved diagonally across the mirror. The line ended in an arrowhead, pointing towards the window. If this was Grace, if this was her message, she had needed a bigger canvas.

Maddie snatched at the curtain that was draped inside the bath. She spun the hot tap to turn the shower on full. It came through loud and hot. She heard a thump on the door just a few seconds later. Harry's voice on the other side was agitated.

She pulled the door open. 'Come in and shut the door!'

'What the . . .'

Maddie pointed at the mirror. Letters and words were starting to form on the window. Harry fumbled with the door. It bounced off his heel the first time but then he got it shut. They both moved closer to the window. The words weren't clear. Maddie quickly tugged her long, black jacket off. She reached up, pushed the window open, bunched her jacket up and held it out of the window so that it spread out against the glass on the other side. The window now had a darker backdrop. It still wasn't easy. Harry pulled the light switch. It was enough for them to make it out.

ANOTHER CAR BOMB
BOY BURGLAR PLANTED
BLACKMAIL FRANK D
VICTOR KILLED SALLY
HE WILL KILL ME. PLS HELP.

Harry still had his phone in his hand. Maddie hadn't noticed it before. He lifted it back to his ear.

'Sorry, sir. I'm going to have to call you back.'

* * *

Vince stood out of the car as they approached. Maddie was just below breaking into a jog to keep up with

Harry. They were both using their phones. Maddie's call was over with quickly. Harry's update was still underway. He sounded breathless as he barked orders down the phone. He wanted a full forensic search of the flat; it was to be treated as a murder scene until they worked out what had gone on there. The firearms teams were holding the cordon. Maddie had to smirk as he explained how to take the pictures in the bathroom.

'You need to run the taps — the hot taps,' he was saying. 'Yes, that's exactly what I said . . . the hot *taps* . . . Yes! I've got a picture . . . It will make sense . . . I'll send it through, but we will need the CSI to get something evidential.'

He put the phone down as they got into the car. Vince looked expectant. Maddie got in the back seat. Harry finished on his phone and turned to speak with her. 'So what are we saying? Just so I know we're thinking the same?'

'Grace is in danger. Sally is already dead. Viktor was responsible. We should assume he was here and that he took Grace when he left. And Toby Routledge was used to plant the devices.'

Harry ran his hand over his shaved head. 'Well, okay then.'

'But the tunnel devices . . . I thought they were placed at the time?'

'In the tunnel, yes. The one under Craig Dolton's car was *planted*. We knew Toby did two break-ins on Campbell Road. We had the addresses, Grace denied it, but one was Craig Dolton's . . .'

'What?' Harry prompted

'Grace . . . she denied it . . .'

'She did. We need to find her, Maddie.'

Maddie's head continued to spin. 'And the key fob . . . the stolen property from Dolton's address . . . It looked like nothing. Worthless. A few old phones and a key ring.

A Volkswagen keying. Toby was trying to tell us. He was trying to tell me.'

'He could have just told you.'

'He was terrified. I guess he thought that if we worked it out, maybe he would be off the hook. He was in it too deep and he had no idea how to get out.'

'I guess he didn't want to be blowing people up.'

'That wasn't him at all. He laid out the stolen property. He took mail with the addresses on them. The burglary was a front, Harry. He was there to get access to their cars.'

'For *Viktor*.'

'Yes, for Viktor.'

'So we have another device and we know where that is, don't we?'

'The car at number 21. I called it in already — to the control room. They're deploying the right people, but we might just have had a stroke of luck there. She was going away, remember?'

'Yes! She was! Lake Garda for a wedding.' Harry was suddenly animated.

'I tried calling her direct, too. Her phone's switched off — but that's hardly a surprise. The house should still be empty. She said she had an early morning taxi coming. That car should still be sat there. We'll have confirmation soon. I told them to get hold of one of us as soon as they get eyes on.'

'I remember it. It was parked badly. What are they doing with it?'

'I was put through direct to Gold Command. When they confirm it's there they'll put in a two-hundred-metre cordon and evacuate the houses around it. They were going to call MOD as soon as they got off from talking to me.'

Harry was rubbing his head again. 'And who's this Viktor?'

Maddie was shaking her head. 'I bet I know. When Toby was nicked a few nights ago some fella got himself involved. Vince, here, nicked him. We got him in for drunk-and-disorderly. His name was Viktor. It's too much of a coincidence. It has to be him.'

Vince had been sat in the driver's seat, taking it all in. He chipped in now. 'I meant to tell you about him. His prints came back from the European databases. He's wanted abroad — some blackmail and kidnap thing. Heavy stuff. Me and Tim were gonna go out looking for him when we had some downtime. He gave an address a few doors up from your boy. The *Viktor* part was right, but he gave us a duff surname.'

'It didn't come back at the time? He would have had prints taken in custody.' Harry's tone was thick with frustration.

'We took his prints, but searches on foreign databases still ain't automatic. You have to fill out a form and justify it. It costs money, apparently, every time you submit one. I always do it — you never know. But it takes a little while. Normally they're still in by the time we get the details back, but he was out first thing with a ticket — we don't interview for D-and-D. We made a few enquiries about him with our Hungarian colleagues. This fella ain't nice.' Vince flicked through the pages of his pocket book. 'Viktor Lizawski,' he read.

'We had him in custody,' Maddie mused. She shook her head. 'Thinking back . . . Toby's body language . . . the fear I saw in him . . . it came on after we had the run in with Viktor. His whole demeanour changed.'

'You think this Viktor did it on purpose?' Harry said.

'It would make sense. If he was living nearby he could have seen us there and hatched some sort of plan to get himself nicked for something minor. That way he gets his opportunity to remind Toby not to say anything to the police. Jesus, Harry, when I think back, this Viktor said exactly that! Right in front of me! I didn't think anything of it . . .'

'Why would you? We couldn't know he had an agenda. We know him now though, don't we? This time he won't be leaving quite so quickly.'

'Finding him won't be easy now. Even assuming he doesn't know we're onto him, he still has Grace. He'll be trying to stay low.

'He will. We still have one good line of enquiry from in there: *Frank D*. Seems Mr D knows more than he was telling us after all. Maybe he can fill in the blanks.'

'Where's he?' Vince said.

'Work or home. Both are Canterbury area. We go on blues.'

Vince gunned the engine. 'No other way to travel.'

Chapter 32

From the impression Maddie had gained of Frank Dolton, his house seemed to suit him perfectly. Stout gates barred access and there was a polished metal panel off to the right demanding that you press and ask for permission to enter. The gate was held up by brick posts at either end. On top of each were matching stone boxer dogs. The gates themselves were made up of black metal railings with faux-gold tips. They yawned inwards before Vince even had the chance to drop his window. Dolton must have had a phone call; he was expecting them.

Maddie had called the number she had for Frank as they left Margate, expecting it to be his direct number. Instead she recognised the voice of Claire, his stern PA. It seemed that Claire was still very much the point of contact for her boss, even on a Saturday. She had been quick to explain that Frank was away on business until Monday at least. Her response sounded well rehearsed, the first part of her response uttered far too quickly: *Well, you won't find him at home, I'm afraid.* Maddie had told her not to worry, that it could wait. But it couldn't wait and she was now pretty sure where they would find him.

The front door opened. Frank's figure all but filled it. It was noticeable that he stepped out quickly and closed the door behind him. The handshake was firm but his palms felt a little clammy.

Harry spoke first. 'Mr Dolton . . . Maddie you already know, of course. This is PC Arnold.'

Frank looked past them to the marked car that Vince had pulled at an angle across his gravel drive.

'Do you have to leave that there?'

Harry shrugged. 'Yes.'

'I assume you are here with an update about my brother's death?'

'Well, not really, Mr Dolton. If I'm honest, I was rather hoping you would be providing us with an update about that subject.'

Frank's eyes darted over all three of them. They lingered on Vince before switching back to Harry. 'Are you here to arrest me?'

'Why would I be here to arrest you, Mr Dolton?' Harry said.

Frank seemed to hesitate with his reply. 'That's what the police do, isn't it?'

'There's a lot more to it than that,' Harry said.

'Well, I don't know what you're talking about. I am waiting for you to offer some clue as to who killed my brother. This is a difficult time for me. If you don't have anything of use then I must ask you to leave. I am a very busy man.' Dolton was fidgeting the whole time, the stones crunching under his feet. Maddie reckoned they were the same three-colour stones that furnished the approach to his office building. It was clear that he had no intention of inviting them back into the house.

'I can assure you we are very busy, too,' Harry replied. 'It seems there is a little more going on here than you told us previously. Maybe you know a bit more about how your brother died? You need to tell us what you know.' Harry used silence for the point to hit home. Maddie watched

Dolton closely. It looked to her like his face was losing colour. He took in a couple of rushed breaths and his lips bumped together like he was struggling to find a reply.

'I don't know what you mean? Explain yourself!' The second part of the sentence was delivered with much more force than the first. Harry gave him another few seconds of silence. 'Well, come on! You can't just come round here, with your accusatory tone, and not back it up!'

'Maybe not. I want to help, Mr Dolton.'

Dolton's lips pulled back over his teeth. Maddie couldn't tell if it was anger or fear. 'I'm sure you do,' he said.

'But I can wait here until the search team arrive in their large, highly visible van, to carry out a full search of your home. Maybe someone sees it and tips off the press? I appreciate that could be damaging for someone in your situation. Or we can have a chat inside and work out how we can help each other out.'

Dolton came back angrier still. 'You think you can search here? I've never heard anything so absurd in all my life! You don't appear to have a warrant!'

'I don't need a warrant to search your home, sir. Not once you're under arrest for conspiracy to murder. Then I can search it under section 32 of PACE. As a future IPC I'm sure you're aware of the basics of law?'

'Arrest?' Dolton was floundering again. 'I'll call Lowe, I'll call him direct and have you removed!'

Harry lifted his phone. He pressed a couple of buttons. 'That's his number. You can call him now. Do you think I would come here without his knowledge? This is very serious, sir. But then you know that already. So why don't you drop this ridiculous act and tell me what you know. I know this has been a tough week for you. We might even be able to help each other.'

Frank stared at the phone, but his hands stayed by his side. He sighed.

'Look . . . Look, I've dealt with it, okay? I'm not making any complaints. I'm the victim here, there's no need for any of this.'

'Dealt with what?'

'I assume you know *what?*'

'Humour me.'

'We already spoke about this. There were some chancers trying to extort some money out of me. I've dealt with it.'

'There's more to it, Mr Dolton. You don't think I'm on the verge of arresting you for dropping your trousers on a webcam do you?' Harry used another pause.

Dolton seemed to think about this for a second. He huffed a couple of times before he spun on his heels, pulled his keys from his pocket and strode into his house. He left the door open. Harry walked in after him. Maddie and Vince did the same.

Dolton continued through to the kitchen at the far side of the property. Maddie's eyes wandered around the interior as they followed. It was impressive. The whole place screamed money and its layout was clearly designed around showing it off, creating a powerful impression of the man of the house.

Now though, the man of the house was stood in the kitchen, slumped forward onto an oval island that seemed to be holding him up. He pushed a half-empty glass of red wine to the middle. The open bottle was near to it. His movements looked slower, more laboured; it was as if he had run out of steam all of a sudden.

'Bit early to be having a drink?' Harry said.

'It's been that sort of week.'

'A problem shared, so they say. I think you could do with telling someone else what is going on.'

Dolton suddenly looked tired, like a man who might have gone a couple of days without sleep. His heavy eyes hunted the kitchen surfaces.

'Can I offer you anything to drink?'

'No. I have a feeling we might be up against it a little bit, Mr Dolton. I have information that suggests the residents of this area are facing a bomb threat and that you know something about it. Now, you may be a victim or you may be in collusion. Either way, you need to start talking to me or you will be leaving here in cuffs. And very soon.'

'I like a man who talks straight,' Dolton said. He chuckled a little. It was empty and Maddie recognised someone who was stalling for time. 'Well, where do I start?'

'From the place that allows us to save lives, Mr Dolton. And quickly.'

'Yes. I suppose that would make sense. But you should know that I've dealt with the matter. This is all over — you have my word.'

'All over?'

'I was the victim of a crime. You know this — we talked about it. There was some escalation after we spoke. These people wanted more and more money. In the end we came to some arrangement, I paid some money and they have gone away.'

'Gone away?'

'They took over my computer. Had you come here first rather than my place of work I might have been able to show you. As it stands my computer has now crashed and appears to be beyond repair. I guess they thought they would have the last laugh, maybe it was punishment for taking my time.'

'Show me.'

'Show you what?'

'The computer . . . where is it?' Harry turned back towards the hall. He started across the kitchen.

'Looking at my computer . . . that would constitute a search, would it not?' Dolton called out.

'Yes.'

'Then you'll be needing a warrant.' Dolton reached in his pocket and pulled out a mobile phone. 'I think I should take some advice from my solicitor. I'm pretty sure you can't—'

Harry stepped back to Dolton and his hand shot out and grabbed Dolton's wrist, tight enough to make him shout out. Harry twisted it and Dolton arched his side, it looked as if he might drop to his knees. His phone clattered onto the slate floor. Harry stepped in closer. He dragged Dolton's arm behind his back and bent it upwards. Dolton rolled forward. He cried out again, this time more in pain than surprise.

'Vince . . .' Harry said. Vince took cuffs from his vest and snapped them on. 'Frank Dolton, you are under arrest for conspiracy to murder. You do not have to say anything, but it may harm your defence if you do not mention, when questioned, something you later rely on in court. Anything you do say may be used in evidence. Do you understand?'

'What! This isn't my fault! I'm the victim here!'

Vince kept a firm hold of his cuffs. Dolton was still leant forward. Harry walked round so he was in front of him. He stooped to look him in the eyes. 'Right now, I don't care what you are, just that you're in my way. Arrest for conspiracy to murder means I can tear this place apart. And I will. Unless you wanna suggest where I should be looking. A man like you has secrets, Frank, am I right? We will find them — all of them. Tell me what you know about this bomb. Right now, that's all I care about.'

'And you'll let me go?'

'No,' Harry growled. 'But I might not look for anything else.'

Vince lifted the cuffs higher, adding to Dolton's discomfort. The strain showed on his face.

'Look, okay! But I don't think I can help. My computer. Nudge the mouse to wake it up. It's useless, you'll see. In the study.'

Harry stomped through to the hall and Maddie followed. Vince kept hold of Dolton, who was forced to walk still stooped forwards. Harry stopped in the middle of the hall, his head flicking from room to room. He made for one to the right of the front door. Maddie saw that it was laid out like a study.

Harry gestured at the wide-screen monitor on the desk. 'You're better with these things, Maddie.' She took the hint, moved in front of it and pressed the keyboard. The screen stayed mostly black but there was a grey box in the middle. It simply said: *12 noon.*

'Twelve noon, Frank, what does that mean?'

'It was my deadline.'

'Was?'

'Was. Twelve noon today. I had to pay by then.'

'Or what?'

'I don't know. I don't know what they were going to do, but I had a deadline yesterday too — that was two p.m.'

'When your brother was killed,' Maddie muttered.

'Yes. I didn't take them seriously. I thought it was chancers, so I just let it run down. Then they killed my brother. They told me they had set the bombs in the tunnel too, a few days earlier. It was all over the news. I could see what they were capable of. So I paid them.'

'How much?' Harry said.

'Ten million.'

'For what?'

'For what? What do you mean for what?'

'Your brother was already gone. Why would you pay them now? I don't have time for half-truths, Frank.'

'They said there was another bomb. That's all I know.'

'Where?'

'Random. They said it was under some car, somewhere.'

'How? How did they talk to you?'

'Email. Alexa or something, that's what she called herself.'

'What do you care?'

'What do you mean?'

'About some random bomb?'

'I'm not a monster!'

'You didn't save your own brother. You don't care about anyone else. Ten million is a lot of money — even for you. But it wouldn't be about the amount, would it, not for you. Someone is getting one over on you. You would need something much more important than the death of a stranger to allow that to happen.'

'That's it. That's all I know, okay? I paid them. You remember that. I stopped them.'

'You think you stopped them? How come your computer still has a deadline?'

'It crashed. It was counting down before. It crashed, then that time came up, but it's over! I did what they asked. I transferred the money and then it started deleting stuff. Some programme was running, I watched it all happen. I couldn't do anything. It took seconds. But they have what they want.'

'You're wasting my time.' Harry strode out of the room. He was back in seconds with Dolton's phone. 'Vince, you got an evidence bag?'

Vince nodded. He took a bag out from one of his vest pockets. It was crumpled and he shook it open. Harry dropped the phone in it.

'You can't just take that!'

'I'm taking everything. My next call is digital forensics. They will send a full team and we will get everything. We'll go to your banks and your accountants for all your personal dealings and your company's accounts — every single asset you have and where it's come from. I won't rest until we have it all. Here, your work, everything.'

Dolton's cheeks dimpled where he was biting down. He had been standing a little straighter, but he slumped forward again, his head shaking. Vince still held his cuffs. Harry continued.

'Your wealth is all you care about,' Harry said. 'That and the status that comes with it. If *I* know that, I reckon these people knew that, too. They know something about you, don't they? Something that threatened your way of life. Some dodgy dealings from your past maybe?' Frank's head was still shaking from side to side.

'I need to speak to my solicitor. I have that right.'

'You do. It will delay everything, but you do. You make that decision and you can call for legal advice from the police station. The forensic teams, the financial teams, they won't get anything before twelve today, before this deadline. If people die because you were trying to protect yourself, I will make sure the judge, the jury, the whole world knows what you did. That you had the chance to help and you didn't. We will find whatever you think you're hiding. Telling us now gives us a chance to do something about it.'

Dolton's head stopped rocking. He stared at the floor. 'Okay . . .' he said. His voice was quiet, almost too quiet to hear him. No one replied. He took another few seconds. 'I told you about the Facebook thing. The woman who got me at a weak moment. I'd had a glass or two of wine.'

'Okay.'

'The countdown started from then. I got an email saying I had to pay the ten grand or they would release the video to humiliate me. They seemed to know I was in the running for a public office. I didn't pay. They upped the stakes almost immediately. The timer reset. I got twenty-four hours and a message telling me that my family were in danger too. They wanted a million this time. Quite a jump. It smacked of desperation on their part. The message itself wasn't very specific, there was no suggestion they even knew my family. It just confirmed to me that they were chancers and they'd seen from my pictures that I'd got money. I thought if they knew me, if they knew anything about my family they would know that there were other things far more valuable to me than that. I ignored it.'

'And you think they killed your brother?'

'I know they did. I got a message.'

'And a new deadline?'

'Yeah. And then they wanted ten million.'

'And what if you didn't pay? That's what's missing, Frank. That's what I will find out. Don't make me do it the long way. I promise I will make you suffer if you do.'

Dolton looked over at Harry, and Maddie could see that his eyes were full of fear. 'You have to understand, Inspector, I just paid ten million pounds for this information to remain secret. I'm more than a little reluctant to release it now — and to the police, especially.'

'You're out of options, Frank,' Harry said.

'You might think so. I have solicitors. They can make this all very difficult for you — maybe even impossible.'

Harry lurched forward again. He grabbed Frank by the scruff of his collar in his big fist. He spun him round and pushed him firmly into the office chair. The chair rolled back a little. Harry leant in, his big hands slapping on the arms of the chair, his face pushed up close to the seated man who was squirming in discomfort, his hands still clamped together behind his back.

'I was in a briefing just a few hours ago. We saw pictures. Pictures of the inside of that tunnel and of your brother's car. Dead people, Frank — what was left of them. A woman running with her baby with shrapnel sticking out of her spine. That was what I saw, but do you know what I heard?' Harry almost spat out his words as he pushed Dolton as far back in the chair as he could manage.

Dalton shook his head.

'The briefing. The man giving it, he knows his stuff. He said that the one thing *every* bomber wants to do is detonate his bomb. That's the evidence, Frank. A bomb is like a signature and it *will* go off. You haven't stopped a damned thing. All you've done is funded the next one.'

'I thought . . . I just thought, if I paid them—'

'You thought, if you paid them, you might get to save your own skin. You just paid ten million pounds to the people who killed your brother. I hope it was worth it.'

'Nothing will bring him back.'

'What do they know, Frank? Last time I ask you.'

Dolton hesitated.

Harry only waited a moment then snatched his phone to his ear. 'Take this piece of shit away!'

Vince loomed over the seated man

'I washed some money, okay?' Frank blurted. His face twitched immediately, almost like he hadn't meant to. Vince stepped slightly to the side. 'I washed some money for some people. It was a long time ago. It was a mistake, a big mistake. I didn't expect to be paying for it almost a decade later.'

'Money laundering?'

'Yeah.'

'How much?'

'I don't know, I really don't. Hundreds of thousands, okay? A couple of brothers — drug dealers. They had some cash to get rid of and I was in the property game. I had some land. They put up the money to have some places built on it. When I sold them I gave it back and it was clean.'

'And you made a nice profit I'm sure?'

'I'm a businessman. I saw an opportunity.'

'So the brothers, who are they?'

'Dead, I heard. Or at least one is. Overdose. The other is three years into a life sentence by now. I had nothing to do with them since that day.'

'So someone else knew?'

'My computer. These people got into it, to take control of my webcam and install their timer — or whatever they did. They must have had a bit of a look round. They got hold of some documents I thought I'd deleted. Some bank statements, too, and paperwork confirming the house construction and sales. It would have been enough to show what I did. They sent it all attached to an email, showing me what they had. They were going to go public with it.'

'So your brother wasn't worth a million pounds to keep him alive, but your freedom is worth ten million?'

'My freedom!' Dolton snorted. 'My freedom is just the start. The money laundering was just the start. I have a number of very powerful allies who are heavily invested in me holding a senior office as the independent police commissioner. They've been part of getting me this close, putting money up. The commissioner role . . . well, it's part of the job to spend the budgets, to decide who to spend it with.'

'So your mates were going to get the police contracts and you would be getting kickbacks for your trouble?'

'I'm a businessman, Inspector. I told you that already. If that information were to be released, then not being elected would be the least of my problems. The money laundering is something I could fight. Even though my business was built on that money they wouldn't be able to take it all away. I might even avoid jail. But these emails they have obtained . . . I've effectively promised favourable allocation of contracts worth a lot of money, but always in exchange for something. I've spoken direct to business leaders — important people, the sort who take their reputation very seriously. They would be exposed at the same time as me.'

'So it was worth ten million pounds of your money.'

'I would have made that back in twelve months of being commissioner. And that was before my own businesses saw any growth.'

'I need to see everything. If you paid these people then there will be a trail. We can follow the money.' Harry pulled away and turned to Maddie. 'Can you call this into Gold? We need a full team here now, digital forensics, the lot.' He moved back to Dolton. 'I need to know what the threat was specifically and what confirmation you received when you sent the funds.'

Dolton was shaking his head. 'The computer . . . it's totally dead. I was diverted to the dark web using something I had to download from the internet. It was all on an email. It will all have been deleted when the computer crashed. Your digital people will struggle. I spoke to my IT expert in the office, I told him a hypothetical story. These people directed me to a site on the dark web to transfer funds.'

'Go on.'

'I gave him the address. You can't search this dark web, but if you have the address you can go straight to a site. He had a look. He said it was a data scrambler. I don't really know what that means. He explained as best he could to a dinosaur like me. They gave me a list of digits to pay the money into, they looked like a standard sort code and account number, but when you type them in the coding on the site reads those numbers as different numbers altogether. Only the person who programmed it can tell what they are. I just followed instructions. I didn't know what I was doing. I did what I was asked. Afterwards I typed the site's address back in — it was gone.'

'Jesus . . .' Harry stepped away. Maddie had taken her phone out. She was waiting for Dolton to finish before she made her call. She knew a bit about currency exchanges on the dark web. Enough to know that it left no trace. If they could get into the computer and if the email trail hadn't deleted itself then there was an outside chance they could get information on where it was sent from to start tracking the source. There were things they could do, but it would all take time. Maddie moved so she could see the monitor. Time was not something they could rely on. Twelve noon was just over an hour away.

Harry fiddled with his own phone. It had been pinging and had rung at least once. She still had her phone in her hand from Harry's instruction but she was frozen to the spot, trying to work out where they went next. Harry looked up, the screen of his phone shone against his shirt. His face was suddenly ashen.

'Maddie . . . the car at 21 Campbell Road . . . it's not there.'

Chapter 33

Josh Haines rolled the window down a little further. Thick white smoke arched through it.

'Dan, you got your window down back there, mate? It's like an Amsterdam coffee shop in here!'

Josh heard laughter from his two mates in the back. He could feel the cannabis having an effect. He leaned back in his seat and let his head roll to the right so he was facing out. His eyes moved around the shuffling greenery. He smiled at the branches as they dipped and waved at the car with their leafy fingers. He grinned back.

'What time we heading back, Josh?'

The question drifted over him. He didn't look away from the scenery. He had always liked the woods. He found them calming; nature moving in unison with a gentle shushing noise. He could sleep here. Finally the question registered — what time were they leaving? He needed to get the car back to his house, then get back to his dad's before he got in from work. He looked at the clock on the dash: 11.35 a.m. They were around a half hour from his house. He would give it a few minutes for his head to clear.

'We do need to get back. Leave the windows open for a bit. I don't want the car smelling of weed.'

'Maybe we should get rid of this then!' The chuckling voice was of a girl this time. Alison Woolgar was in the front passenger seat next to Josh. He looked over at her. She was so pretty. His face slipped into a lopsided smile — he couldn't help it. He would never have dreamed of taking his mum's car out just a few months before; he could get into so much trouble. But it was all for Ali. As soon as he saw her look of amazement and the beaming smile when he turned up in it, he knew it was worth the risk. She had called him *badass*! He loved that. It had been easy too. He and his car had blended effortlessly into the choked roads and motorways that took them to their concert. Now he was just a short drive from home. He would drop the two mates in the back off first. Then park the car on his drive and head over to his dad's. Ali had said she would come with him, they could watch Netflix. She had suggested it! He had never been with her on his own before; she had never shown any interest.

Now she was holding a large, clear bag of cannabis. Her pretty eyes were rested on him. There was still a lot of stuff left. Enough for another couple of meets.

'Keep it sealed, Ali. It'll be cool. We can all meet up again to finish it off, yeah?'

He heard a cheer from the back.

'You got some place to stash it, Josh?'

Josh thought about it. He didn't really. The last thing he needed was his mum finding drugs in his room. But Ali was still looking over at him. She was biting down on her bottom lip and then she tucked an errant strand of auburn hair behind her ear. He didn't want to say no, not in front of her.

'Yeah, leave it with me. I'll drop you boys off and then stash it at my house.'

'You not dropping Ali back?'

'No, he's not. We're going to his dad's,' Ali said.

'Ah, I getcha!' There was laughter from the back and then a wolf whistle. 'You have fun, then, won't ya!'

Josh could feel his cheeks flushing a little.

Ali didn't look embarrassed at all. She was turned towards the back, unfazed. 'You're just jealous!' she said.

Josh could have punched the air. She was keen, very keen.

He started the ignition. It was time to go. The trees waved them all goodbye.

Chapter 34

The scenery was a blur outside Grace's window. Things seemed to be all in a rush now. It didn't make sense. They had left the flat as the first morning light was struggling to break through the layers of grey clouds. It was obvious why: Viktor needed to move Sally.

He had wrapped a winter coat around her and put the hood up. He'd also messed up her hair, so it fell over her face before he threw her over his shoulder like he was carrying out an old sack. Grace was forced to follow him down the steps. She had tried to hang back, but Viktor whispered for her to keep up — there was venom even in his whisper. She couldn't look away from Sally; the eyes that peeked out from behind her tousled hair seemed so sorrowful. Every step down shook her hair aside and loosened her hood until it was as if Sally was staring right at her.

The effort to conceal Sally was hardly necessary: Grace didn't see or hear another soul in the block or in the short dash across the frosty ground to where Viktor had parked a red saloon car with its boot up. He dropped her in the boot with a thud — like you might discard a heavy bag of rubbish at a refuse centre. She landed with her eyes up, her face now completely exposed. Still Grace couldn't look away. It had been snowing, steady flakes — bigger than the day before: a thick flake whirled past her eyes and it floated into the boot, falling end over end until it rested gently on Sally's nose. It didn't melt. Sally must have been just as icy cold. It was Grace's last image of her before the boot was slammed shut. She shivered now at the memory.

She had been ordered into the car and they had driven to a lay-by, where Viktor had parked fifty metres away from a catering truck that was handing out hot breakfast rolls and coffee. It had a steady stream of customers. Grace wasn't sure how long they sat there. Viktor let the windows steam up until she couldn't see out. She closed her eyes and tried to sleep while Viktor looked busy on his phone.

Now they were moving again and on the motorway. Viktor was leaning forward and Grace was sure they were travelling too fast for the conditions. He was hogging the outside lane and muttering at every car in front of them, pushing up so close behind them that they were almost touching. The cars soon moved out of his way, their drivers peering over at her when they passed. She considered mouthing something at them — a plea for their help — but she was sure she would be ignored and the risk was far too high. She still didn't know what Viktor had in mind for her. She still had no idea why he had brought her this far. She finally found the temerity to speak and hoped this wouldn't distract him too much on the perilous road.

'Where are we going?'

He was still leant forwards, eyes narrowed, with one hand gripping tightly around the steering wheel and the other just as tightly around the gearstick. The snow was now whipping straight at the windscreen, curving away at the last minute as if they were being propelled through little beams of light. The windscreen wipers were on constantly; dragging against bone-dry glass, they squeaked and juddered every time. Viktor didn't seem to notice.

'We need to leave.' His attention stayed straight ahead.

'Leave? Leave where?'

'Here. England. I take you to my country. I know people that can make sure we are not known people. Make us disappear.'

Grace didn't know quite how to respond. The panic, which had subsided a little since her experience in the flat, started to rise up again. 'But I don't want to leave! I can't leave here! What will I do?'

'Not go to prison. This is what you will do! This is favour. I help you.'

'Help me? Sally . . . she said they would have no idea, she said I would just be able—'

'Sally?' He laughed aggressively. 'Still you talk about Sally like she is friend of yours. You are silly girl. Sally and me had a plan, not Sally and you. Sally and me had a plan and Sally was making sure you were not going to be well after this plan.'

'I don't understand. I don't understand why she would want that. And I don't understand why you needed to set the bombs in the tunnel. You didn't need to do that. You killed innocent people!'

'We needed to make a noise, to make confusion. I wanted to be sure brother would pay money. The documents, the bad money was one part of it, but if he did not pay, one day maybe the bomb will be for him, this is who he is dealing with. He had to know I am bad man. And the explosions, the chaos! I like this! The police, they go look for terrorist people, not for simple man like me!'

He took his eyes away from the road for a second to glance over. He was beaming, his eyes wide with delight. There was no doubt that he was enjoying himself. It made her feel sick.

'People died!'

'People died. Your boyfriend died, too. You did this. I gave people chance at least. Empty car at front, then empty car in middle. Sally parked this car in tunnel. She enjoy it too — she tell me this! The people, they all had chance to leave but some were too slow. Natural selection maybe!'

'Jesus . . . Why am I still alive, Viktor? You don't need me.'

'You would not be. If Sally was here . . . if she was driving car. You should know that. She knew Frank Dolton would not pay for brother — for family. She knew she had you in her control. She could make you call to detonate. She knew you would come to her place after — you do as you are told. So she told me I get rid of you. She said it was to be suicide. You gave Sally bank account details. We transfer one million from untraceable source then string you up by the neck to be found. Police think you could not live with guilt maybe? No links with us. All on you. The nine million left never found. Half each she said. I did not like this. I have all the risk. Bribing on computer, sourcing grenades, pushing them under cars. It is big risk. She does nothing.'

'So you killed her?'

'I do not like to share. I get the feeling you will not be asking to share!' He grinned and Grace stayed silent. 'Do not worry. I will make sure you have money for new life — *good* money. But not here. The police, you are wanted. You cannot be free here. I know you are victim too. Not like Sally, she made plans for you, you not deserve.'

Grace was back to peering outside of the window on her side. A sign for Dover flashed past with a symbol for a ferry port next to it. It was three miles away.

'But I don't have my passport! They won't let me through without a passport!'

Viktor grinned again. He leaned over to push a button on the glovebox and it fell open with a clunk. A passport was lying on top. She opened it up on the first page. It was hers. 'Burglar boy. Sally . . . she tell you to leave back door unlocked so he could get car keys. But I also say to get passport for you. I always knew I would take you. Make you safe.'

'I can't . . . I can't go away. I don't know what I'll do.'

'You can.' There was menace back in his tone. 'And you will. I make sure of this, too. There is one more bomb. When we are clear of tickets, when we are through to board, you can make a call. The bomb, it arms at twelve o'clock. Twenty-five minutes from now. This is under a car. It arms, but will not detonate until car is moved. This car, this is Ian Hughes's car. This is who Sally told me. This is your father, no?'

Grace felt her breath leave her all at once. Her hand flashed to her mouth. He glanced at her, and in that brief instance she felt like he was looking deep into her soul.

'I can see this is right. You can stop him moving car, Grace. You can make call. I do not need to hurt him. But you need to do what I say. You understand? I only did this to make you see. You need to do what I say to be safe. You cannot be safe here. When we go through tickets, you can call your father. I give word, okay?'

Grace still held one hand tightly over her mouth. Her injured arm was still wrapped against her chest. She nodded her head in a jerk.

'Good girl.'

Rob Ford chewing gum was maddening. It was maddening to watch, it was maddening to listen to and it was maddening that, right now, it seemed to be the only thing he was doing. Rob was a forensic media technician, one of a team of four for the area, but, for Harry at least, he seemed to be the go-to guy. Maddie could only watch as he stared at the screen of his laptop, sighing at regular intervals, while it scrolled through lines of white letters and symbols. It was all gibberish to her.

They were in Frank Dolton's study. Dolton himself had been taken away, despite his protestations. The plan was to interview him as soon as possible, but they all knew it wasn't going to help. Their 12 noon deadline was only twenty-five minutes away.

The blue lighting of Rob Ford to the address was a desperate move, a faint hope that he might be able to get something they could use in time. But from his facial expressions and the severity of his chewing, Maddie's hope was getting even fainter with every passing second.

'What are we looking at?' Harry said. He had been pacing behind where Maddie was stood over the desk and this was the third time he had asked this same question. Rob looked up from his laptop and sighed. He played with the wire that trailed from the side of his laptop and chased round to the back of Dolton's computer.

'This isn't ideal, Harry. Remotely I mean. I can do a lot more back at the office.'

'None of this is ideal. This is where we are and this is what we have.'

'So you keep saying. Maybe we should do something about the tension in here. No one should work in this sort of atmosphere!' He grinned towards Maddie. She didn't return it.

'Can you tell me anything about that computer?' Harry asked.

Rob sighed again. 'I can tell you it's been attacked and I can tell you it's crude.'

'Crude? What does that mean?'

'Crude like amateurish. There's some pretty high-tech stuff out there right now but this sort of takeover could have been done ten years ago.'

'Takeover?'

'It's a keystroke device. Like I said . . . amateurish.'

'Keystroke device? Talk layman, Rob, you know this isn't exactly my area.'

Rob twisted the tower that was stood alongside the monitor and gestured at a row of plugs behind.

'What are we looking at?' Maddie said.

Rob had a pencil behind his ear. He pulled it out and used it to point at a black plug with a wire trailing away under the monitor.

'This is the connection to the keyboard. Only it isn't just a keyboard plug. The plug is longer than it should be. Someone has run the keyboard through a logger via the USB port. The untrained eye wouldn't look twice, but for me it stands out instantly.

'So what does it do exactly?' Harry said.

'It's as it sounds. It records the keystrokes and transmits them to another source. All you need to do is come in here, clear the cache, plug your keyboard in through this device and *boom*! Sorry . . . poor turn of phrase.'

'Clear the cache?'

'The history and all the saved . . .' Rob sighed again, then tutted. 'Say you need to go into your email account. You would type, say . . . *Hotmail* in the search bar. Then click about until you're logging in. You get asked for your login details which you type in, username and password. This device would record all of that activity and ping it out to an external source. The person receiving that then knows what email account you use and your security details. Effectively they have complete control. That's one example. Going onto your banking site, unlocking your computer in the first place, sending emails, searching for porn — it's all recorded on there. It transfers it out as a string of typed characters, but you don't even need to worry about deciphering that. You can run it through some software and it will give you a complete picture — everything you need to take over the user's life.'

'It's not remote though?'

'Well, not initially. You have to physically unplug the keyboard and push this little fella in the back of the computer, for the keyboard to be plugged back into it. But everything from that point is remote.'

'Any way you can tell me where that information is transmitting to?' Harry said.

'I will be able to find the device. I'll kill the main power in here and it will be one of the power sources left that is still giving off a signal. Your man will have to have hidden something in the room that picks up the signal and sends it back out — maybe even using the Wi-Fi in the house. I can interrogate the router too.'

Harry grunted. He was back to pacing. 'Interrogate the router and looking for signals. This isn't going to be quick, is it?'

Rob leaned back in his chair. 'Not twenty-five minutes quick, boss. And finding that device is not likely to get you any closer to who planted it — not if they've got any sense. The computer has been corrupted remotely. Judging by the simplicity of how it's been taken over, it may be that I can restore the contents, but there's no way of knowing at this point. It will take time. I would say days.'

'That's not something we have. Maddie?' Harry left her name hanging in the air. He stopped his pacing to look directly at her. He wanted ideas.

Maddie was struggling for them herself. 'He has staff. Someone had to have access into here to put that device down in the first place. I'll get a list.'

'I agree, but it's a slow time enquiry. Is there anything here that gets us closer to the person responsible for crashing this computer in the next twenty minutes?'

'Nothing I can think of.'

'Grace would make that list, of having access I mean. It's possible at least.'

'We will be sure to ask her,' Maddie stopped the words *if she isn't gunned down first* from completing her sentence. Harry moved on quickly.

'We can't stop it. There's no time. We need to be out looking for this car.'

'Okay. I know Vince would agree. He's chewing the steering wheel out there. He's called to check in three times in the last twenty minutes.'

Rob had insisted Maddie turn her radio off while he did his work — something about the signal interfering. Vince was outside, listening to the search for the car on his radio, keeping her informed. He was on the phone to her immediately after it was announced that the Haines car was now a vehicle of concern, and it was clear that he was desperate to be part of it. Officers had gone over to the house to sweep the car for explosives, but the car had vanished. A search revealed this same car had been captured by ANPR, the automated number plate recognition technology used by police, heading London-bound the previous day — towards the venue. It had also been captured coming away this morning, but ANPR coverage was patchy at best. That was at 0947 hours this morning, heading in the general direction of home. Since then . . . nothing. With Nikki Haines out of the country, officers had got in contact with her ex, and what he suspected had happened to it was not good. Joshua Haines had bought four concert tickets on a credit card registered to his dad. His dad knew he was planning on going and had given his blessing, but he was now convinced that Josh had taken his mother's car. Every available resource with a vehicle had been sent out across the southern part of the country, while efforts were ongoing to speak to the boy's mother; contact had been made with the Italian police at Lake Garda so they could find and inform Nikki Haines. The team's biggest concern right now was that if the car had been headed directly home it would have been there by now, which left them hundreds of square miles to search for a car that could be carrying explosives.

'Let's get on the road then. Any updates from Gold?'

Gold Command had also taken responsibility for leading the vehicle search. This included contacting every associate they could find for Joshua Haines via known friends and neighbours, social media and his school — any source that might know something about Josh, about where he was right now and, just as importantly, who he might be with. If they couldn't get hold of him, maybe they could reach someone else in that car — assuming they were still together. Maddie had heard nothing. She needed to get back to her radio.

'I've not been able to listen in. Vince should be able to give us an update.'

'I'll leave you to it here, Rob. If anyone turns up, the housekeeper or whatever, can you take their details and pass them on to me straight away. And don't let them in. You'll be on your own for a little while.'

'You do realise I'm not one of your detectives, Harry, right? I'm not even one of your coppers. I can't be telling people to do anything. More importantly, I just don't want to.'

'I get that. I know it's not ideal but we can't spare anyone up here right now. I'll try and get that rectified.'

'I'll do what I can.'

'I'm sure that will be enough.'

Harry swept out. Maddie cast one final look at Dolton's computer. The sullen grey box still consumed the middle of the screen and it still contained their deadline. She passed a grand-looking clock on her way out. They had twenty-two minutes.

Chapter 36

Josh Haines suddenly stiffened in his seat. They were on the M20 motorway and hadn't long joined it again after coming off to drop his two mates home. It was just him and Ali left and they were just twenty minutes from home, twenty minutes from returning his mother's blue Ford hatchback to where she had left it on the drive and walking away as if nothing had happened. He had even taken a picture on his phone so he could make sure it was in exactly the same place. He was doing 70 mph, bang on, careful not to speed, not to be erratic in his driving — nothing to stand out, nothing that might draw attention to him and the fact that he was some way short of being old enough to drive it legally. He was in the middle lane and in a stream of traffic. The inside lane had been concealing a marked police car, tucked in close to the front of a lorry. He was coming up to overtake it. He hadn't seen it until it was too late, he couldn't brake now, he couldn't move over either. His only option was to try and be inconspicuous, to continue smoothly past. There was no reason for them to even give him a second glance. He knew that he looked older than he was. He just needed to stay cool. He flicked his attention to the rear-view mirror. His eyes had been a little red and puffy but the effects of the cannabis had all but worn off. He took a deep breath.

'Josh! The police!' Ali had seen the car too. He looked over to her. She also moved to sit up straighter, her head fixed forward; she looked unnatural. Josh held in his breath and his mind rushed with what was at stake. Right now the fact that he was driving at fifteen years old was only half of a story completed by the significant amount of cannabis stuffed in the glovebox.

His car slunk past. It seemed to take an age. He watched his speedo intently: it was stuck on 70 mph. He reckoned the police car must be doing sixty-eight. Finally he was clear. The stream of traffic he was in all moved over to the nearside, the same lane as the police car. Josh did the same. His eyes moved to his mirror. He was still pulling away, slowly but surely. He just needed to get out of sight and he would put his foot down a little more, get a little distance between them. There were two officers in the car. They didn't seem to react and he continued to edge away. He let out his breath.

The blue lights flicked on.

'Shit!' Josh said. 'The lights are on! They want me to stop!'

'Maybe it isn't for us?' Ali was hopeful, desperate more like. She spun in her seat to peer out the back. The police car had suddenly gained on them, the female cop in the passenger seat must have seen her movement and immediately pointed to the nearside. They flashed past a sign for an upcoming exit. Josh knew they wanted him to take it. The police car surged forward and pulled out. He snatched his head right as it pulled level. The cop was still gesturing for him to come off the motorway. Nervously, Josh gave a thumbs-up. The police car slunk back and took up a position close behind.

'What are we going to do?' Ali's voice broke with the tension. He met her panicked eyes for just a second.

'I'll get done! For the cannabis! I can't get done!'

Ali pulled open the glovebox. The clear plastic baggie of drugs was immediately on display. The police car moved back in behind them. 'You have to pull over Josh! Maybe they won't look in there.'

'Of course they will!'

'I'll chuck it out the window!'

'They'll see, Ali! They're right up my arse!'

'Well, fine, then! What else is there?'

Josh considered their options for a second. His panic-stricken mind settled on what seemed like the best one. He pushed the accelerator to the floor.

'Josh, don't!' Ali squealed. It was too late. The car was already picking up speed; the police car seemed to drop away. Josh had seen the news and heard stories, they don't pursue kids. He could lose them. This could still work out okay.

* * *

'Shit! I told you!' Thomas Inge was driving the marked police car, his colleague Amy Moses was in the passenger seat. 'I told you they would make off if we put the lights on!'

'We had no choice.' Amy had dropped the radio handset and raked around the floor to pick it back up. Thomas quickly checked the clock: 11.38.

'Are the other units in position in front?'

Thomas's question was ignored. Amy was updating their situation on the air. He cursed. The whole force was out looking for this car but it seemed like no one had considered what could be done with it once they found it. The decision had been made to pull it over immediately. Units had been sent behind them to close the road off, they were going to isolate the car and call out the Ministry of Defence to deal with the threat of the explosives. They needed the car stopped and the kids away from it as early as possible. Thomas had voiced his concerns about putting the pressure on them, about making them panic, but Gold Command were convinced that a fifteen-year-old lad with no previous police record would immediately pull over at a police officer's instruction. He could tell from the pause on the radio that they were back to not knowing what to do next. Amy spoke into the radio again to prompt a reply.

'Zulu Three to Control . . . confirm you received my last? The vehicle is now making off. Two occupants, a white male driver and a white female front passenger. Driver matches the description for Josh Haines. The female looks to be the same age. Our speed is now ninety, that is nine zero miles per hour. The traffic is medium, the conditions are below freezing and the snow is now heavier but does not appear to be settled on the surface. At this time the risk assessment is medium.'

Medium my arse, Thomas thought. He had never liked chasing cars, he thought he would, but he had seen some things: he had seen them end badly. He didn't think he could cope if two fifteen-year-old kids lost it in front of him.

'We need to back off. I don't want to be putting him under pressure. It's kids in there! We were supposed to have patrols in position already.'

'I agree.'

So did the radio operator. They would have taken advice from the inspector based at the FCR and the message transferred back was to ease off and to keep the car in sight. They were trying to get marked vehicles in front of it so they could box it in. They were promised an update on when the cars were in position. Thomas checked the clock again. They had twenty minutes. That was enough time to get a row of police cars in front and for the tactic to play out. *As long as nothing went wrong.*

Josh Haines, it seemed, had a different idea. The blue Ford suddenly jerked left. It ran over the thick white line and zigzag markings, kicking up a trail of dark spray as it went, careering up the slip lane. Thomas had to accelerate hard to be sure it stayed in sight.

'Zulu Three to Control . . . vehicle is left, left at the Ashford slip. That is left, left at the Ashford slip — standby for direction of travel.'

Thomas swore again. The slip led up to a busy roundabout. The blue Ford slowed enough for them to get closer, but it didn't stop, instead it squeezed between two rows of cars waiting at a red traffic light to join the roundabout. Thomas heard the sound of car horns as it spewed out onto the bustling roundabout, clipping something hard enough for debris to scatter over the road after it. Thomas watched in horror as it looked to be going too fast to make the left turn, it rocked up onto two wheels but somehow made the turn. All four wheels planted back down on the tarmac. And then it sped out of sight.

The police car was now at a standstill, loitering at the back of the two rows of cars, the blue lights reflected off every sign in the dark morning, the siren bounced off the stationary cars in front to whine back at them. When the Ford had pushed its way through, the two rows of cars had become untidy as each driver tried to get out of the way. It meant that there was no longer a way through. The noise and lights from the police car seemed to confuse the situation more: drivers were reacting by edging forward, closing the gaps even tighter.

'We're gonna lose them here!' Thomas shouted. He beat the steering wheel as he tried to see through the gaps but couldn't.

The blue Ford was gone.

Chapter 37

Maddie pushed open the front door and almost collided with Vince coming the other way.

'You okay, Vince?' Maddie said.

Vince glanced from her to where Harry was stood next to her. He looked to be struggling to get his words out.

'I was just coming to get you. Rhiannon couldn't get hold of you and called me. They've had a call in. Anonymous. They think it might be Grace.'

'Grace has called in?'

'No'. He shook his head, still struggling to get his words out. '*Someone* has called in. They think it might have been *about* Grace. It's not a confirmed sighting, but Gold are convinced enough to send firearms to intercept. There's no way they can be sure, not from what I heard—'

'Vince!' Maddie cut over him. 'From the start . . . what's happened?'

Vince tutted. 'The control room took a 999 call. It was from someone talking about a woman down at Dover Port. She's through the border controls and waiting to get out on a ferry. Apparently this woman is anxious and she's talking about setting off a bomb using her phone. She was overheard talking about how she's done it before. The port have shut the front end but they can't evacuate until we have control of her. They don't want her to know anyone's onto her — they're worried it might push her to do it.'

'They think the bomb is at the port?'

'That's their assumption. There's not been a mention of where it is.'

They got into the car, Maddie slipping into the rear seat. Vince started up and was already pulling away with Harry belting up in the passenger seat next to him.

'Do we have a description? Informant details? Anything else?' Maddie barked.

'I don't. I told Rhiannon I would get you to call her. She should know more.'

Maddie already had her phone to her ear. It rang once.

'Hey. You've had the update then?' Rhiannon sounded tense.

'An anonymous call about a woman at Dover Port threatening to set off a bomb on her mobile phone. Gold have put two and two together and come up with Grace. That's about all I know.'

'I can't tell you too much more. I can only see what's going on the log — it's being run from elsewhere. It could just be someone having a mental health crisis.'

'What makes you say that?'

'The reports are of a young woman acting odd, muttering to herself, that sort of thing. The informant dismissed her as crazy, but then she was challenged direct. She said she can detonate a bomb just by using her mobile phone. She's telling people she'll be making a call at noon. *Then everyone will see*. The log describes her as constantly checking the time and muttering to herself.'

'Okay, can you mark up the log that we're attending. I don't want to draw attention to us going by calling up on the radio.'

'You're heading to the port?'

'Yes. We can't do anything more at the house.'

'Do you think it's Grace?'

'It can't be,' Maddie said, but she knew her voice betrayed her.

'You don't sound so sure.'

'I don't know what's going on. It doesn't make sense for it to be Grace.'

'There's more going on the log — hang on.' Rhiannon started mumbling and Maddie could hear the sound of a clicking mouse. 'There's a description come up . . . *Dark hair, slim build, a loose hooded top and leggings, open jacket . . .* and *one arm in a sling.*'

'Okay . . . I guess that changes things. The certainly sounds like our Grace, doesn't it?'

'So what is going on?' Rhiannon said.

'I have no idea. We're heading there now on flash. Hopefully I'll get some answers soon.'

* * *

Grace tried to keep her head down. She increasingly found crowded places difficult to deal with and the coffee shop at one of the world's busiest shipping ports was a hub of noise and movement.

They had passed through the border controls easily enough. Viktor had held both their passports open and the bored operator had waved them through. Grace wasn't even sure he had looked in the car. After the controls, the Port of Dover opened up to a huge mass of flat, grey concrete with vehicle traffic and people in high visibility clothing moving in every direction. Viktor seemed to know his way around, his confidence plain as he navigated the maze of white and yellow lines until they emerged onto a flat expanse of concrete, surely the size of twenty football pitches and divided up into narrow straight lanes. Viktor had taken them down one with a few cars parked at the far end. They were all in a line; it was the queue for the ferry. He had parked behind a high-backed van and the lanes either side of the car were largely empty. Grace had seen fifty or more articulated lorries parked in silent formation on the far right of the expanse. Directly in front was the huge blue-and-white ferry, its steel ramp reaching out like a forked tongue to rest on the hard standing. Traffic was moving down it in a steady stream. Each one announced their arrival on UK shores with a thump of metal on stone as they moved off the end of the ramp then turned right to filter away. The two huge docks either side of it were empty but she could see another ferry skulking silently towards it in the distance. The docked boat would be replenished and readied for the return journey to Calais. Viktor had told her that once they were in France they wouldn't need to worry anymore. He had also told her that they had time for a coffee, that it would do her good. He had pointed to a building over to the right hand side of the loading lanes. She had declined initially, but it quickly became clear that he wasn't giving her a choice.

'I need to make call,' Viktor said. They had just walked into the building that was signed up as *Passenger Services Building West*, and now he was keen to walk back out again. 'You stand here. You do not move.'

Grace tried to remonstrate, but he was already moving towards the door. They were still near the entrance. He had pointed to a space right next to the floor-to-ceiling glass window at the front of the building. She took her place. She looked out where Viktor stood in snow that was falling thicker and faster. His breath was visible as he talked into his phone.

He came back in. His call had been less than a minute long. His face was flushed red with the cold. He blew into his hands.

'You sure you not want coffee?' he said.

Grace shook her head. 'The time, Viktor . . . I've done everything you said. Please, let me make that call. I'm coming with you, I swear. I won't make any trouble.'

'I get coffee first. Patience!'

'I've been patient!' Grace snapped, but she backed down immediately. She was getting desperate. 'Please, Viktor. Just let me call him now. What if I don't get him the first time? He can be a nightmare with his phone. He doesn't always take it out.'

'Ah!' Viktor clapped his hands together, suddenly beaming as if he was thoroughly enjoying himself. 'In England, you say *the fickle hand of fate*. I heard this. I asked for this to be explained so I know what it means. I love this! Here it is . . . the fickle hand of fate is here! Your boyfriend was bad man. He was chosen. People died in tunnel — they were chosen. Maybe your father is not. You will have time to call. But say a word to one person and your father will know nothing. You understand?'

Grace nodded. Viktor led her over to the counter. He ordered his coffee: black, as strong as they could make it. He then led her out of the front of the building, taking a dog-legged route, his attention lifted to the CCTV cameras that jutted out from the lip of the roof. Grace stuck close. Her desperation was starting to consume her; she had to fight to keep it down. There were a couple of huge digital signs towering over the lanes where they had parked. They were standing at each end with angry red displays that looked like they were branded with fire against a sky that was now a constant blur of white. They told her the ferry departure times; they told her it was -3°C. They told her it was 11.56.

'Please, Viktor! Let me make this call. You gave me your word.'

Viktor was looking away from the building now — back over towards the port controls they had passed through. He looked back to her. 'I keep my word. You can call.'

Grace couldn't keep her desperation at bay any more. 'My phone!' She thrust out her hand.

Viktor felt in his pocket and fished out the car keys. 'I put your phone in armrest. Your father is only number saved on there. Just press his name!' Viktor chuckled and threw the keys. Grace caught them and, for a second, was rooted to the spot, her eyes on Viktor.

He waved at her. 'Shoo!' he said.

Her eyes lifted to the clock. Three minutes now. She broke into a sprint.

* * *

Maddie snatched at her phone, Rhiannon's name was written across the screen.

'Rhiannon!' Maddie was fighting to hold on to the car's grab handle with her other hand. They were coming down Jubilee Way, the main route into Dover Port. It was a steep hill and fast as a result. They flashed past an escape lane on the nearside, the deep sand that filled it had a top layer of white snow. The road surface too was starting to whiten, despite the heavy traffic. It would be slippery, maybe even with patches of black ice. The road here continued out from the cliff face on stilts, Dover's busy shipping port was a long way below and the sea was now visible as a mass of tumultuous grey in front. The protection from the sharp drop towards it was a flimsy-looking Armco barrier and a low, mesh fence. Maddie could see Vince's strong arms tense to get them around the long, sweeping right curve. She had to push the phone to her ear to keep it in place as Rhiannon spoke.

'There's an update. The informant gave a part-reg for a vehicle this woman's in. I found a match on ANPR going into the port, Gold have done the same. It's a hire car — a red Audi. It's hired out in the name *Grace Hughes*.'

'Okay then . . . What is the reg?'

Rhiannon relayed it and Maddie wrote it on her palm.

'There's more. We've done eborder checks. Grace has a ferry ticket booked. She's leaving the country on the next ferry.'

'Okay . . .' Maddie didn't know what else to say or what to think. All the information was pointing to one thing: to Grace setting bombs, killing her ex-partner along the way and blackmailing his brother. Maddie had only met her a couple of times, she didn't really know her or of what she might be capable. Maybe this was all possible. Maybe she had been completely wrong about her. Still, it didn't sit right.

'Anything more you need?' Rhiannon said.

Maddie had been silent long enough. She peered into the front of the car where Harry was listening intently to the radio; there was no time to confer. She spoke back into her phone: 'I don't really know . . . So she kills Craig, blackmails his brother and flees the country. But before she's out, she sets another bomb and detonates it from her phone, and she's shouting about it at a busy port near to a car booked out in her name . . .' Maddie was thinking out loud, her words getting faster and louder; she was winding herself up. This wasn't right. 'Is she travelling alone?'

'It's a vehicle ticket. That allows her a car and up to four people. She's the only one named on the booking.'

Maddie licked her lips. 'Hang on.' She moved the phone away. They were approaching the entry to the port, Harry was talking into the handset. She called out, 'Vince! What did you say Viktor's name came back as? He used a different surname, didn't he?'

'He did. I can't remember right now, Maddie.'

'You have to. It's important.'

Vince fidgeted. The car slowed for a barrier where they were now entering the port. The approach on blues had got someone's attention and the barrier lifted before he needed to work his window. Maddie heard a zip and then a pocket book flew from the front. It dropped into her lap.

'It was two days ago! I always underline surnames!' Vince called after it.

Maddie snatched it open. She flicked through pages of barely legible scrawl. Two days past, a *Viktor* was written, the surname that followed was underlined: *Lizawski.*

'Rhiannon, take down this name: Lima, India, Zulu, Alpha, Whiskey, Sierra, Kilo, India: Lizawski. First name Viktor. Can you see if there's any travel booked in that name? His date of birth is the second, of the third, nineteen seventy-nine.'

'Hold on, I'll run the search again on eborders.'

Maddie waited. She knew it was a clunky system. It was a database that showed all booked travel out of the UK. It handled a lot of data and didn't do it quickly. 'He's booked in! The same ferry, but as a foot passenger. He's there somewhere!'

'I bet he is!' Maddie said.

'What does that mean, they're working together? Why would they be travelling separately? And why is he reverting to his real name?'

'When was his ticket booked?'

There was another pause. 'Just now — like in the last ten minutes or so. It's not even updated with the full details yet. It shows as an online booking.'

'He's a foot passenger, Rhiannon. We only run pre-booked vehicles and named passengers against police databases. By the time his name is washed through he'll be missing in Europe and we won't have a hope in hell of finding him.'

She peered forward. The port had opened up in front of them. Harry was still talking on the radio but he was bent forward and she couldn't make out the words. She called out for Vince to push forward towards where she could see a ferry unloading in the distance. It was the only one docked, and a small queue of cars was forming in front of it. She turned her hand over so she could see the registration number scrawled on her palm. Grace was last seen with a red car — it was their best chance of finding her. She still talked into her phone.

'They're not working together. She's here under duress — she has to be. Why write his name on the window for me to find?'

'Only she can answer that,' Rhiannon said.

Harry turned to face her. He looked serious. She moved the phone away from her ear.

'We need to hold here,' Harry said. 'It's a direct order from Gold. A Firearms patrol is here already. There's another just entering the port. They have a visual on Grace — she's been ID'd. She's just run the length of the parking area to a red vehicle. They've reported that she has something in her hand but a car's obstructing their view. They have to assume it's a phone. That's a turning point, they're waiting . . .' He tailed off and his eyes dropped. He plainly couldn't look at her. His jaw creased. 'The car with the kids up in Ashford . . . they've lost it. We're out of options. I'm sorry, Maddie . . .'

She felt her stomach twist tight. She knew exactly what that meant. The firearm patrol's *obstructed view* meant through a sight on a high-powered rifle. Maddie stared down at the radio in her lap. It was busy with voices, she could try and tell them what was going on, that Grace wasn't the threat, but there was so much to communicate; she wouldn't be able to do it in time and there was a lot of nervousness about — they wouldn't just take her word for it. Grace had told them about Viktor and Maddie was now sure that Grace hadn't booked that ticket or hired that car. And she wasn't about to willingly detonate a bomb either. But everything pointed to that. It was supposed to. Suddenly everything made sense. Grace wasn't here to travel, she was here to die, and at the hands of a police marksman. She was the end of the trail, so Viktor could slip out of the country while everyone's attention was elsewhere.

Maddie lifted the phone so she could see the screen. Her call was still connected. She could hear Rhiannon's tinny voice, small and distant, she was saying her name. At the top was the time: 11.57. It flicked over to 11.58. Two minutes. There was no time for orders over the phone or explanations over the radio. They were just waiting to get a clear shot and it was all over. Maddie hung up her phone.

* * *

Grace made it back to the car but slipped on the thin layer of snow that had now formed on the concrete, crashing to the ground. She felt the pain through her arm and it was enough to stop her for an instant — but only an instant. She scrambled back to her feet. The snow was falling thick and hard and the wind was brisker here, freezing cold and blowing straight off the sea with nothing to repel it. She had unlocked the car remotely some way back, now she tore open the passenger door and thrust her hand to the armrest. She raised it to access the storage area underneath. Her phone was there! She grabbed it, backed out of the car and bent over the phone. The wind direction was against her, blowing snow into her face. She squatted low, using the car to shield her from the weather. It made her thighs burn almost immediately and she let one knee drop to the floor. It was sodden and freezing cold but she barely noticed.

She steadied herself enough to unlock the phone. It took a couple of goes. She pressed for the phone directory — it was as Viktor had said: *DAD* was now the only one listed. He must have deleted everything else in case she got hold of it.

'GRACE! STAY DOWN!'

Her head snatched up. Sergeant Maddie Ives was a few feet away, she was beyond the rear of her car and she skidded to a stop. Her arms were out towards her, palms up as if she was already trying to reason with her. She was gasping heavily and she could hardly speak.

'What are you doing here?'

'Put the phone down, Grace!'

'I can't!'

Maddie turned to look across to where Grace knew the border control area was on the other side of the car.

She started to get up to see what she was looking at so intently.

'STAY DOWN!' Maddie screamed, and took a step closer.

Grace dropped back to her knee. 'What's going on, Maddie?'

'Listen to me! You have to stay kneeling. Then we can talk, okay?' There was genuine fear in her voice.

Grace checked her watch. She was just about out of time. 'I don't have time to talk!'

'There is a sniper! They're here to kill you, Grace — as soon as they can get a shot!'

'What? Who?'

Maddie lifted her hand. It had a police radio in it. Suddenly it was blaring.

'DS IVES! THIS IS A LAWFUL ORDER . . . GET THE FUCK OUT OF THERE! WHAT ARE YOU DOING? FOXTROT TEAMS . . . MOVE FORWARD AND ENGAGE THE TARGET!'

The Police. Armed police. They're coming for you, Grace. They don't care that I'm here. You need to throw the phone down or they will shoot you right here.'

'I can't! I have to call my dad. I *have* to! There's a bomb under his car. He's already killed people, Maddie!' Grace's panic and desperation flooded back. She didn't have time to explain. She didn't have time to make Maddie understand. She just needed to make the call, then she could tell her why.

'You have to trust me, Grace! There *is* a bomb but it's not your dad in danger. It's a bunch of kids in their mum's car. They don't have a clue . . . You dial that number and you'll kill them all.'

'DS IVES! THIS IS YOUR FINAL WARNING.' Maddie spun a dial on top of the radio. The sound of the voices diminished and then she threw the radio down. She lifted her arms out, high and wide. She still faced Grace and her stare had real intensity.

'MADDIE! WHAT THE HELL ARE YOU DOING!' A man's voice. It came from behind Maddie and a little further away. It was the man who came to her house with Maddie before — the surly-looking one. He sounded furious now.

Maddie raised her voice but didn't take her eyes off Grace.

'TELL THEM TO BACK OFF, HARRY! IT'S NOT HOW IT SEEMS!'

'I CAN'T CALL THEM OFF!' the man shouted back.

Maddie was still staring right at her. Grace's grip on her phone was tighter than ever. The time was now.

The air fizzed. There was a loud noise and a thudding sound like something had been thrown at the car. She saw Maddie squat instinctively.

'GRACE! DO NOT MOVE! THEY'RE TRYING TO FORCE YOU OUT! STAY THERE!'

'Why are they shooting at me? I haven't done anything!'

'If you call that number, you will kill a car full of teenagers, Grace. You have to trust me!'

'Trust!' Grace snorted, her eyes suddenly streamed tears. 'Trust! I've been trusting people my whole life. Look where it's got me!'

The air fizzed again. The thud was closer this time and it made a different sound, as if it had struck something firmer. Maddie still didn't look away from her.

'I know, Grace. But I told you I would keep you safe. I gave you my word. This is how I keep it. I'm the only one stood between you and a bad day. You have to believe me.'

'Viktor, he brought me a ticket . . . he was taking me somewhere safe. He killed Sally but he didn't kill me. He said he would take me somewhere safe . . .'

'Viktor needs you to die. He hired this car *in your name*, he booked the travel tickets *in your name* and I'm pretty certain he just made an anonymous call to the police telling us you're about to detonate another bomb. He's forcing the police to take you out. He needs the trail to end.'

Grace's lips quivered. She was so exhausted. Her head shook. She didn't know who to believe. 'I killed Craig. I had to make a call. I knew he would die. Sally told me about the bomb. I wanted him dead. But I didn't kill anyone else. I didn't do anything else! I just wanted to be free!' She raised her tired eyes to Maddie. 'Sally's in the boot . . . Viktor strangled her. I thought he was going to do the same thing to me.' Grace's head was shaking, the events of the last twenty-four hours whirled around in her mind. She needed time to think. She didn't have any. She looked up to see Maddie glancing at the rear of the car.

'Of course she is,' Maddie said. 'You're being stitched up for that, too. He needed you dead though. So you couldn't tell us what really happened. Throw the phone away, Grace, and I'll walk you away from here. No one gets hurt, I promise.' She stepped forward. She was almost touching the rear of the car now.

Grace was lost in her panic. 'I can't lose my dad. What if this is how I save him? He loves me so much. He calls me his princess!' She snorted a laugh. 'He's the only man who ever has! That's all any of us want, right? To be someone's princess . . .'

'It's the least you deserve. And you can have that. Please, Grace, you have to trust me.' Maddie stepped forward again.

Grace started to speak, to tell her not to come any closer.

'ARMED POLICE! ARMED POLICE, DO NOT MOVE!' Grace could hear boots pounding the ground towards her. She spun to the sound and a masked man appeared beside the van in front, his weapon fixed firmly against his shoulder — it was pointed directly at her. She tensed, still gripping the phone tightly in her hand.

'HANDS WHERE I CAN SEE THEM!'

Beyond him, etched high over his head with its blood red display, was the digital clock. The huge numbers ticked over to 12 noon. She had delayed too long. It had to be now.

Her eyes dropped to the phone. Her thumb twitched to make the call. She heard a man shout — and in the same instant she felt a blow to her right side that took her clean off her knee. Her head banged off the side of the car on the way to the ground and she heard her phone clatter along the ground.

'SHE'S DROPPED THE PHONE!' Maddie screamed. 'SHE HAS DROPPED THE PHONE!'

Grace felt herself grabbed roughly in what felt like a hug, with strong arms wrapped round her chest and back in a crushing grip, including her injured arm. She could barely feel any pain. She looked up, her vision was closing in, but she could see it was Maddie who was hugging her tightly. Her head lolled backwards. She could see the black boots of the armed officers on the ground — they were much closer. She squinted upwards to see weapons pointing at her, and the nearest man was still yelling. Maddie was screaming right back. The surly man was suddenly there too; he was shouting and pushing the masked man away.

She closed her eyes to it all. All she was aware of now was the freezing cold ground.

Chapter 38

After

Vince forced himself to slow down as he tugged open the door leading into the passenger terminal. This building was more central, was closer to the border controls and was where foot passengers were directed before they could make their way onto the ferry. He had been given hurried instructions by Maddie as she'd pushed open the car door, with Harry talking over her, warning her not to be stupid. His words had fallen on deaf ears: Maddie had sprinted away from their car and Harry had bundled after her, leaving Vince still sitting in the driver's seat. Though he could have done with the chance of asking for a bit more clarity, he'd got the basics: Viktor would be waiting to board the ferry as a foot passenger and he needed intercepting.

Vince knew he should have called up for other officers to accompany him — it had been part of Maddie's instructions — but that part he'd ignored: Gold Command were running the show and so, technically, every decision should be run through them. In his experience that meant everything slowed down, with the final decisions being taken by the most risk averse. He didn't have the time to bring them fully up to speed either: the ferry was about to start loading its foot passengers; he had to act now. And besides, if Gold Command were given the opportunity to be involved in the arrest there would be no way that Vince, as a response officer from the next town over, would get anywhere near the action — it would be a firearms team for sure. And Vince wanted this. He had walked Viktor into custody once already and he had been taken for a fool. This was personal.

The waiting area was busy. It was a wide, open area with two large, supporting beams in the middle with benches wrapped round their thick base. The benches were full of people and their baggage. There was another clump of people at a coffee pod over to the right. There were vending machines against the far wall and the toilets were off to the left.

Vince attracted attention: an out-of-breath police officer in full uniform having wrenched open the door and now scanning the room with fists clenched. Everyone suddenly looked guilty — a natural reaction. But only one man moved. From the far bench, he stood up and stepped away. He walked with his hood up, his head bent and with an obvious limp. He looked to be making for the far exit. He didn't look back. Vince set off after him immediately. His footfalls echoed through a room that had fallen as silent as it was still.

'VIKTOR!' Vince's voice now filled the space. 'ARMED POLICE! ONE MORE STEP AND I OPEN FIRE!'

The man in the hood stopped. He stayed facing away, his arms by his side.

'PUT YOUR HANDS IN THE AIR, PALMS OPEN!' Vince was striding forward.

The hooded man raised his hands slowly. Vince could see they were empty. He was still facing away.

'TURN ROUND SLOWLY! KEEP YOUR HANDS IN THE AIR! NO SUDDEN MOVEMENTS OR I WILL OPEN FIRE!' Vince was almost upon him. The man turned slowly. His face was a sneer, his jacket hung open, Vince recognised the man he had arrested just a few days before and scanned his waistband and pockets for weapons.

Viktor was appraising Vince, too, his eyes roving all over him. His hands dropped back to his sides. 'You do not have gun!'

Vince was now close enough. He threw his right fist with everything he had. It was as if he had thrown a breeze block, with all his weight and momentum behind it. He felt Viktor's nose crack and his head whipped backwards. His body followed quickly, his legs folding beneath him. Viktor was laid out on his back, his arms flailing slowly, his face streaming blood. Vince reached down to take a firm hold of both Viktor's hands. He dragged the cuffs from his vest and knelt over Viktor with one knee close to his hip. He paused long enough to tense his bicep in front of Vince's blinking eyes.

'Some coppers are armed. And some have guns,' he said. 'Oh, and you're under arrest.'

* * *

From Maddie's elevated view, the port seemed to be enjoying business as usual. The police had one of the original buildings on the site that served as their base and Maddie found herself in its loft space, which seemed to function as the break room. It had a small kitchen off to the side and the main area was hogged by a square table, where mismatched and untidy chairs had it surrounded like an unruly group of outlaws. There was a sorry-looking sofa, too, the sort that wouldn't look out of place discarded in a front garden or hanging out of a skip. It faced a small, flat-screen television that Maddie had clicked off straight away. She'd been here almost an hour and had spent the time pacing, punctured with short periods of staring out of the window.

The traffic was incessant. The double-glazed windows and the vastness of it all gave a sense of detachment, as if she was looking in from the outside. Some of the bigger lorries caused the building to shake as they passed, giving an inkling of the activity on the outside. The port as a whole was a diesel-stained cacophony of noise and movement. Much of the movement now involved police vehicles. She longed to be part of it.

'Maddie.'

She spun to the coarse growl of Harry Blaker.

'Hey,' she said, then turned back to the window. 'If you came up here to rip into me or you want some sort of apology then you should wait around. The ACC's on his way from headquarters. You could take it in turns.'

'He's not going to make it today it seems. You have a stay of execution.'

Maddie turned back into the room. 'So I don't have to wait in here?'

'You do. You're released back to me and we need to talk. This is as good a place as any.'

Maddie huffed. 'It's all bollocks, this.'

'It's not a bad thing you're not seeing the ACC today. Maybe you can work on improving your attitude before you do.'

'My attitude? They would have shot her dead.' A silence hung over them for a minute or two. Maddie didn't care; she had nothing more to say anyway. It was Harry who broke it first.

'They got that car stopped — the car with Josh Haines. Only a few minutes ago. They reckon the kid had just been driving around. Seems he didn't know what to do once he'd given us the slip. He had his fifteen-year-old girlfriend in the passenger seat the whole time. You saved their lives, Maddie.'

'We know that for sure?'

'There's a device. Under the driver's seat. It's not confirmed as viable yet, but it will be. The MOD are doing this right so it'll take some time. The number registered in Grace's phone as *Dad* wasn't the number for Ian Hughes like she was told. She thought she would be saving her dad's life when she was actually going to take out those kids. But you had already worked out the lies she had been spun, hadn't you?'

'I had an idea.'

'So you saved their lives.'

'So would have shooting her dead.'

'Then you saved Grace. The ACC's furious. He still will be tomorrow. He's going to tear into you, but remember what you did today. Your job. Your whole purpose for carrying that badge is to protect the innocent. Following orders is a close second.'

Maddie turned back into the room. She hoped she was concealing her surprise at his apparent support. She moved a little closer to Harry, squatting on the edge of the table, close enough to see if he was being genuine.

'You have a warped sense of innocence, Harry. She killed Craig. She told me that. I think she had been planning to for a while.'

'She'll have her defence. Certainly she has quite a story.'

'She was played, Harry.'

'She was. He nearly got away with it, too. We won't struggle for evidence to link him now, but we might not have even looked.'

'I do worry that Grace is a big part of the evidence. It's not like it's going to be difficult to discredit her, is it? Once she's convicted of killing her partner, I mean. It won't matter why she did it, or how. Just that she did.'

Harry shrugged. 'Maybe she didn't?' he said. 'I mean what actual evidence is there linking Grace to Craig Dolton's death?'

'Apart from what I just said? About what she told me?'

'I heard her too. But, yes, apart from that.'

Maddie couldn't quite see where he was coming from but she played along. 'Her phone? She made the call from her phone that set off the bomb.'

Harry shrugged. 'We'll talk about it. A full debrief tomorrow. We'll work around your meeting with the ACC. You don't need to be telling the ACC or anyone else what she said just yet. We'll sit down and get it clear in our minds first.'

'What are you saying?'

'That we need to be consistent. This is a big job. We need to be sure we're clear. I have work to do tonight. You can go home. You should get some rest. And don't mention this conversation when you talk to the boss. I was told to send you home. He told me explicitly not to talk to you about what happened.'

'I'll try not to squeal you up!' Maddie managed a smile. It dropped away almost instantly. 'Oh, and, Harry!' He had started back for the stairs but turned in the doorway. 'I can't make tomorrow. I'm in London. Something I can't get out of.'

'It has to be tomorrow?' Harry's growl was deeper. She'd come to recognise that as a warning.

'Something I can't get out of,' she said again.

'And more important than your career? Because you don't turn up tomorrow and that's what's at stake.'

'Maybe, yeah. I'm not due in tomorrow. My duty sheet shows a rest day. Force policy . . . nobody can demand that I come in, not to write a statement.'

'You want to start quoting policy at the ACC while he's still clearing up a mess he thinks you're responsible for, you go right ahead, but I wouldn't be.'

'I'm not asking you to.'

Harry took a moment. 'I'll tell him. That you'll be available Monday. But I'll go on welfare issues. You've had a traumatic day.'

Maddie scowled, still confused at his level of support. 'Okay . . . You don't need to. I'm quite capable of calling him direct.'

'I wouldn't, if I were you. I need to call him anyway. Police discharged a firearm in a public area. They damned near shot you into the bargain. There's a lot of writing to do.'

'Why are you helping me, Harry? I know what I did.'

'So do I. You did your job. You saved lives. And when you get in front of the ACC, you remember that.'

Maddie smirked. That growl was there again, the sort he reserved for when he was upset, but now she didn't think it was for her. She would have to add this to the long list of times when she didn't fully understand Harry Blaker.

'I am beginning to realise though, Harry . . . saving people's lives doesn't seem to be working out so well for me!'

Harry smirked, too. 'Monday morning. Be in for seven a.m.' And then he was gone.

Chapter 39

Sunday

The woman's heels clicked and scraped on the polished floor as she approached. PC Ronnie Ward watched her all the way. She stood out: her walk had purpose; her arm was held out in front of her, a designer bag swinging from it and the rest of her following its lead. Her hips had a swing, too, like the whole world was her catwalk. She wore a pastel pink dress with cream stilettos. Her hair was tied up, the clips matching the dress and reflecting the hospital's harsh lighting.

Ronnie leant on a wall beside a set of double doors that led through to a segregated ward. His colleague, Jay Skinner, leant the other side. They made eye contact. There was no doubt that the woman was making for them. Ronnie pushed off and stepped forward. He made a slight move left too and shuffled the assault rifle that was angled across his chest. He hoped to be making it clear that there was to be no entry. He sighed. He had better things to be doing than guarding a door to a hospital ward. This was a favour: usually he worked in close protection and he much preferred the work. The armed response teams were stretched at the moment and they felt stitched up at having to provide officers to guard a door at King's Hospital in central London.

An armed guard was a requirement for assault victims where there was a genuine concern that someone might want to come back and finish the job. In this case, the job had been started by a number of men swinging baseball bats. Their victim was badly beaten, the damage mainly focused on his skull. His family were due in the next day; his condition was serious. No one was supposed to be visiting until then. Ronnie had been told of suspected links between their victim and a drug gang in the north of the country. At that point he had lost a lot of sympathy.

He spoke first. 'Can I help you, miss?'

The woman stopped short. She lifted her sunglasses just enough to look at him from the top down. 'I'm here to see my kid brother. I don't need the police.' Her accent had a northern drawl, the Manchester area. Their victim was from the same part of the country.

'Sorry, love. Visits are in for tomorrow.'

'I know . . . I had a call from my mum. The doctor's told her that he's serious. We've been told to come down as soon as we could. We've been told . . .' She gripped her nose and looked like she was holding her breath, fighting back tears. She sniffed. The tears didn't materialise and her voice came back level. 'We've been told that he might not recover, that we should be prepared for that. My mum . . . she won't deal with it well, my brother will just get angry . . .' She lifted her sunglasses and wiped at her eyes. She seemed to get a hold of herself quickly. 'I just want to see him. I can't be here when they are. If I can just see him on my own . . . I just want him to know that someone's here for him — from the family . . .' She stopped to wipe her eyes again. Ronnie cast a look back over to his mate. Jay had picked up a clipboard. It had a handwritten record of any movements on the top. There were some details on the family underneath.

'What's your name?' Jay said. He moved to stand next to Ronnie.

'Anita. Anita Yarwood.'

'You got a date of birth?'

'First of September 1981. Hang on . . .' She pulled open the bag and started a rummage. She pulled out a driver's licence. Jay took it off her and wrote something down.

'It don't matter, does it?' Jay said. Ronnie recognised he was talking to him. He shrugged.

'We were supposed to call it in.'

'We will. No need to hold her up, though. If you show her the way, I'll do it now.'

Ronnie nodded to the woman. 'Okay . . . I'll need to take you through.'

'Can I be alone, though? Just me and him. I just want to talk with him. She brushed away a loose strand of hair that had fallen over her face. 'These moments . . . they're private.'

'I'm supposed to stay with you, love. We might be able to arrange a minute or two.'

Ronnie led the way. The other side of the door was a long corridor with more doors coming off it. The second door on the right was labelled *ITU*. It had a buzzer on the wall. Ronnie pushed for attention. He shuffled from one foot to another. He didn't know what to say. Mercifully a nurse was quick to answer.

'Hey, a visitor for Adam Yarwood. His sister, she came down a day early.'

'Oh! Yes, we're not expecting anyone today.' The nurse looked unsure, a little apologetic even. She glanced at Anita and then over her shoulder. 'Hang on,' she said. The door fell closed. Ronnie shot an awkward smile that wasn't reciprocated. The nurse was quick to return.

'I can't give you long I'm afraid. We're appointment only here, really.'

Ronnie thanked her. The nurse led them through a ward of just eight beds, all of them on the right hand wall, with a long desk on the left side. Instruments bleeped next to each of the beds. They were all occupied. Two of the occupants were sitting up. Both were bare-chested, both looked pale and weak. They followed with their eyes but there was no other movement. Ronnie knew this ward: it was where treating serious illnesses and injuries often merged into managing pain and giving a peaceful end. He'd seen victims and even colleagues transferred here before. Very few of them had come back out again.

They kept walking. They passed more beds in another ward area and came to some private rooms. Adam Yarwood was in the first. The air was cooler in his room, less stuffy. There was more bleeping. The bed was a half turn to the right. A machine on the opposite side had moving parts that seemed to rise and fall in a breathing pattern.

'Fifteen minutes, okay?' the nurse said.

'S-sorry!' Anita called after the nurse, who stopped. 'Is there any update you can give me? I know our mum took the call but she isn't very good . . . at all this, I mean.'

'Oh . . . update.' She glanced over towards the bed. The machine rose and fell with a hiss another time. 'Mr Yarwood is very ill. He has a fractured skull and they found a bleed on the brain. Surgery was deemed a success as far as the doctor was able to stop the bleeding but it won't be possible to tell what damage has been done. Maybe not for some time.'

'He's going to recover though? In time?'

The nurse sighed. 'You have to be prepared that he may not recover. A full recovery is the least likely outcome here. If he does wake, Mr Yarwood's injuries are highly likely to have a lasting or permanent effect. For now, you should just be with him. Try not to worry about that, not today. Just be with him. Talk to him and tell him you're here. He may well be able to hear you.'

Ronnie hung his head, wishing he could disappear. He looked up to give the nurse a subtle nod as she stepped past him to walk away. It was just him now with the sister. He couldn't think of anything to say. He looked at her as she took off her sunglasses and hooked them by the arms onto her dress. She gazed at him and his discomfort increased. He was desperate to get out.

'I can give you a few minutes, but that's all. Rules, you see. I should stay with you all the time, really. Can I just . . .' he gestured at her bag. She held it open and he gave it the most cursory of searches. 'Sorry, thanks . . .'

She didn't reply and he stepped out of the room. He waited for the door to click shut before he exhaled.

* * *

Maddie kicked her shoes off first. They were digging into her heel and her toes and on both feet. The floor felt instantly cool. She looked back to the door. It was wooden with a slim, glass panel running vertically and off-centre. There was a blind rolled up. She pulled it down. She had seen the way the armed officer had acted. He was embarrassed even to be there and she was sure he wouldn't challenge her. She waited for a couple of moments, keeping her attention on the door. As expected, there was no sign of him bundling back through to demand the blind be rolled back up. She breathed out. She was going to have to turn around now.

She was going to have to look at Adam.

He was lying on his back, his head propped up by a couple of pillows. The top of his head was wrapped tightly in a white bandage. She was biting hard on her bottom lip, she bit harder still when her eyes ran over the dip in his head. The dent. The part where the blunt weapon had fractured his skull, damaging what was underneath, maybe beyond repair. His lips were contorted around a rubber pipe that trailed out of his mouth. It was taped so that it stayed in place. His eyes were only partially closed. The right one hung open enough for her to see his pupil underneath. She was still a few metres away, still stood next to her empty shoes. She wanted to be closer but something was holding her back.

'Hey!' she called out. She almost expected his eyes to snatch open, to flash with his usual mischief. There was no reaction. She finally moved forward. She walked around to the other side of the bed, reached out and took hold of his right hand. She was relieved when it felt warm. She felt for his pulse. It was slow and weak but it was there. She felt like she needed a sure sign of life. She gripped his fingers in hers, leant over to gather up his left hand, too. She massaged his ring finger. She managed a smile.

'What were you thinking, eh? Marriage! How the hell was that going to work? Sums you up, that does. Big gestures and never thinking past today.' She lifted his right hand, brushed her hair away from her face and rested his fingers on her cheek. Just like he used to do. His touch had always been so electric — it never mattered when, it never mattered why. No one had made her feel like that before. She wondered if anyone ever would again. 'I'm gonna miss that . . .'

She put his hand back down. She had already been here too long. This had been a stupid idea. But she had to see him.

'I'll be seeing you, Adam. You get better — you hear me?' she said. Maddie pushed her sunglasses back on. 'And my answer? You'll have to ask me properly to find that out! One thing I do know is that we're no good for each other, we never have been. But who wants to be good? Maybe it could work — somehow!' She fought her emotions and struggled to speak. 'I do love you.'

She leaned in and pressed her lips to his cheek, lingering with her eyes tightly shut. When she stood back up she moved away quickly. She picked up her heels rather than sliding them back on. She pulled the blind up roughly and pushed up close to the window. She couldn't see the officer. Quietly and carefully, she opened the door. She could hear the officer's voice — a murmur and then a stifled female giggle — it was to her right, back the way she had come. She pulled the door open further and moved into the corridor. She cast a quick glance to the right: the officer had his back to her and was talking to a slim nurse. Maddie turned quickly left. She didn't look back, her footsteps almost silent on the floor. She made it to a set of double doors and slipped through them.

'Hey! Miss!' The shout came from behind her; it was the officer. The closing door cut him off. Maddie couldn't answer, even if she had wanted to. The tears had come, her eyes were blurred and she broke into a run. She could just make out the lurid green of the fire exit signs hanging from the ceiling and she followed their direction through another set of doors. She came out into a busier corridor and ducked her head down as she ran, keeping to the green signs. Though the corridors seemed to go on forever, somehow she found her way out onto the streets of London, where the roads and pavements bustled with noise and movement.

Her senses were blurred, her head full of noise and confusion. She was still running when she felt an impact. Someone bundled over in front of her, and the shoes she had been clutching spilled onto the pavement. She held her hands towards the blur of colour now laid out on the pavement as a sort of apology. Someone was yelling at her and she broke back into a run. Her head still swirled, the world around her still distorted by her thick tears, her bare feet pounding on the damp concrete.

* * *

Maddie was still out of breath when she stumbled onto the train at Victoria Station. She felt hot too, despite the freezing weather, but overriding it all, she felt exhausted — entirely spent. She flopped into a seat. She felt like she had nothing more to give, as if just standing back up would be too much effort. She let her head lean against the window and dumped her bag on the table in front of her. The train was quiet. It was at the start of its route and it wouldn't be setting off for a few minutes yet. She stared out of the window. Foot traffic was still busy but she was only seeing blocks of colour rather than people. Her mouth hung open. She felt like she might cry again. She had lost her sunglasses at the same time she had lost her shoes. There would be nothing to conceal her tears, but she didn't care anymore. They didn't come anyway. She just felt empty.

'That was risky.'

Maddie flinched at the rumbling growl. A man had taken the seat next to her. She hadn't even noticed.

'Harry!' She wiped her face instinctively and sat up straight, now desperate to think of her story, her reason for being there. Years of conditioning. Normally she would have one ready to go.

'What do you think happens now?' Harry continued while she still floundered.

'What do you mean?'

'If those officers start making calls, asking questions. You might have got away with it today, but tomorrow, when his real sister turns up?'

Maddie fixed on him. She knew better than to try a pretence, even a well-practiced story wouldn't get her anywhere. Not with Harry. She relaxed. Conceded. Her body slumped, her apathy returned.

'You tell me? They might ask questions, sure. More likely those two officers will figure they've been duped and play the whole thing down. No harm done — assuming it's the same two on shift tomorrow.'

'Or they review the CCTV and send the stills up the line to your old force, just to see if anyone knows the mystery woman.'

'They might. Nothing I can do about that now. I was aware of the cameras on the way in . . .' Maddie pushed herself back into the headrest and peered forward. She heard a distant whistle then a fast beeping noise. The doors on the other side of the carriage slid shut and the train shuddered as if a forward gear had been engaged. She considered that she had kept her head down on the way into the hospital and, combined with the sunglasses it should be an effective disguise. She hadn't been so careful on the way out however. 'Nothing I can do about any of it.'

'The damage is done,' Harry said.

'It certainly is now. Do what you need to do, Harry. Tell whoever you need to tell. And you know what? I don't care. Maybe you'll be doing me a favour. I assume DCI Lowe knows you're here?'

'Of course he doesn't. You think telling him really does you a favour?'

Maddie didn't reply. She didn't know anything right now.

'I'm not here to get you in trouble.'

'Then what are you here for?'

'I wanted to talk to you.'

'Talk to me?' She let her head roll so she could look at him. He was facing forward. He looked pensive, not what she might expect from someone who had such an upper hand. 'You've got my number haven't you? You could have just called. Told me what you knew. You didn't have to make a grand gesture.'

'Grand gesture?'

'Coming here. Following me. Sitting next to me with my make-up running on the worst day of my life. Calling me into your office would have done the job. You didn't need to humiliate me in the process.'

'This wasn't what I had planned for a grand gesture.'

'You did have one planned then?'

She sensed movement. A cardboard box thumped onto the table in front of her. A shoebox. Harry knocked the lid off. He lifted out a pair of slip-on shoes. They were plain black and cheap looking.

'This was my grand gesture.' He swept the box away and put the shoes down. 'What are you? I reckoned on a size 5.'

Maddie snorted a laugh. It came from somewhere. It broke though the emptiness and the fatigue. She picked them up and pulled her legs up to try them on. They felt tight, but they fitted.

'Perfect fit,' she said.

'That's as grand as I get. And they were all I could get. I spent most of the time trying to keep up. Those were all they had here at the station. It was the only time you were still enough that I wouldn't lose you.'

'How did you know?'

'That you wouldn't go anywhere? I can read a train timetable.'

'That I was coming up here in the first place. And why.'

'I took a call from your superintendent up in Manchester after he spoke to you. He said he was worried about you. He said when he had spoken to you about the inspector's job you had surprised him a bit. He said you sounded *fragile*. I think he was worried he had put you under pressure from nowhere. He wanted me to keep an eye on you. I think he's worried you won't go back.'

'Pressure!' Maddie scoffed.

'You're a strong woman, Maddie. We all know it. If your mask slips, even for a moment, no one knows what to do. I asked him what you had talked about. He told me a bit about your history with this Yarwood guy — the brother at least. I couldn't see any reason why that call would have upset you. But it did. He doesn't have a clue, Maddie — your boss I mean — even when he was talking about this lad having a girlfriend down here. He was harsh when he talked about this Yarwood bloke. Derogatory. He certainly doesn't see him as a great loss. I reckon he spoke to you in the same way. I assumed that was why he got the reaction he did.'

'I understand his attitude. It's cops and robbers, right? All a game.'

'Except when it isn't.'

'Except when it isn't.' Maddie's attention was back outside. The world was now passing her window in a blur as they picked up speed.

'We got talking about the Yarwoods. Seems this Adam had some strange travel patterns when he was coming down south. He was losing his surveillance teams, not an easy thing to do unless he was taking advice from someone who might know how to do that. I had a hunch and I compared his travel against your rest days.' Maddie's attention stayed out the window. She didn't reply, Harry continued. 'The superintendent told me this Adam's in a bad way. We talked about his family coming down Monday, he wanted to see if I had any sway in getting some foot surveillance resources that might assist. He didn't realise that I don't cover the Met. Anyway, the family visit tomorrow gave you a very small window if you wanted to see him. It had to be today or nothing. That's the sort of thing you might consider worthy of upsetting the ACC for. It was the only theory that made sense.'

'Well done, Detective. So what? You came all the way up here to prove you were right? To prove to yourself that you've still got it?' Maddie felt a flash of anger as she turned back to him.

'Grace is getting off, Maddie.'

'What?'

'Grace Hughes. She was arrested and taken to hospital, but she'll be de-arrested and treated as a witness. Once she's out of surgery, that is. She'll walk free.'

'Walk free? What do you mean?'

'There's no actual evidence linking her to any of it. She'll give evidence to support Viktor's prosecution, but that will be all that is asked of her.'

'What do you mean no evidence? She made the call that killed Craig Dolton. And she knew it would. She had the phone on her that she used when she was arrested. And she told me there would be information on that phone linking her to everything else.'

'The phone was supplied by Viktor. We're working on proving that, but the important thing is, we can't disprove it. We'll be able to show that the call that killed Craig Dolton was made from that phone, but that doesn't mean Grace made it. Everything else we can now point towards Viktor, it won't be difficult to convince a jury that he made that call too. But he had done a good job of stitching her up. The only reason we knew to even look at him was because she scrawled his name up on that window and then you made sure she would be here to give her evidence.'

'She told me, though. We both heard it. She said she killed Craig. She made that call and she knew it would kill him.'

'On the way to hospital, I called Karen Wilson—'

'The defence solicitor? Why would you do that?'

'I told her I had someone under investigation for murder and I asked if she would come in and represent her when she made it to custody.'

'Karen Wilson, the queen of the no comment interview?'

Harry's face flickered a grin. 'I've since heard she has that reputation.'

Maddie was catching up. She could suddenly see where this was going. 'Grace was a mess. She was ready to blurt everything in interview, including how she made that call.'

'I sat next to her when they took her to hospital. I only left her to come back to speak with you. But I made it clear that she shouldn't be discussing the case. I spoke to Karen again too. I told her what we had. I also told her what we didn't have.'

'You mean any *actual* evidence?'

'Not with regard to her client. Not unless she wanted to make a full and frank confession in the interview that will follow.'

'She won't be doing that then?' Maddie was conscious that she was smirking.

Harry shrugged. 'Who knows what she'll do. But she thanked me.'

'I bet she did!'

'I've never had a defence solicitor thank me before. It was a little disconcerting.'

Despite everything, Maddie snorted a chuckle — but soon sobered up a little. 'This is serious stuff! She's a *murder* suspect, Harry. I had you pegged as Mr By-the-Book — black and white. She killed Craig and you know it. And why tell me? If you'd manipulated a situation to get someone off a murder case then you'd keep it to yourself, surely?'

'I'm telling you, so you know. So you know my truth. And I came here today so you would understand that I know yours. We already had trust, but that's not enough on its own. Not if we're going to be working together. We need more than that. Now we have it. Now we have this. What Grace said in the heat of the moment with guns pointed at her after seeing what she had seen . . . it could well have been argued that it wasn't admissible anyway. It would take a harsh judge and jury to convict her, but the whole experience of it . . . she would definitely have spent time in prison on remand. A good few months. Then have her life pulled apart in court. You can be sure her diary would be used as part of her cross-examination, including the images of that contraption. She's had enough.'

Maddie turned back to the window. They had moved out of the city and the world was now blocks of green and brown.

'That is something I cannot disagree with. And that's why you told me not to write a statement until we had talked about it? You didn't want me to put into the evidence that she told me she'd killed Craig Dolton.'

'I wanted you to know that you didn't have to.'

'It would be a lot tougher to do that now. It would put you in a difficult situation too.'

'I still need to put a statement in. You can write what you want. I just wanted you to know that there might be a way out. For Grace. And for you.'

'For me?'

'I read that diary, same as you. But I know you cared about her. I know you told her you would protect her. I know what it feels like when you let someone down. You didn't, Maddie, and you still get to keep her safe. She doesn't deserve prison. Not for doing what she did.' Harry's voice was becoming heavier with emotion, as much as she had ever heard from him. 'Grace will have had good legal advice by now — about what to say and what not to admit to. Right now she's a witness. I assumed you would want to keep her on that side of the courtroom.'

'Well, of course I do! That's what I don't understand. You could have just explained that you didn't pick up any verbals from Grace because of all the confusion and suggest that maybe I didn't either. I would have understood and it would have been unsaid — an understanding. That's how this works — I know that. You didn't have to come up here and show your position of power. I'm a little offended that you felt the need to strong-arm me. I guess I thought we trusted each other by now.'

'We do have trust already, but we need more if you and I are to work together. This is more.'

'We're working together now, are we?'

Harry hesitated. He pulled at his jacket to straighten it. 'I have a vacancy coming up in Major Crime. One of my sergeants wants to move on, for development reasons.'

'Really? Who's that?'

'Well, I'm not sure yet, whoever I choose to move out of your way.' Harry's lips curled into a more prominent grin this time.

Maddie couldn't help but mirror it. 'Thank you, Harry.'

'Don't thank me yet. You still have that job offer on the table back in Manchester — the next rank. You must be tempted?'

'I am.' Maddie fell silent. She let her head roll against the headrest with the movement of the train. 'Right now I can't be making decisions. I can't even think straight.'

A silence fell over them. Maddie's mind moved away from Grace. She was safe and she was free. Inevitably it moved onto Adam. She gazed out of her window where she now had an elevated view of a river with cattle grazing lazily either side.

'I love him, you know. But, however this plays out, today was the last time I'll ever see him.'

'How so?'

'He might die, Harry. The nurse said as much. She played it down with her words but I could tell what she was really thinking. But even if he doesn't, it will be a long recovery. I've seen people with head injuries. He will be laid up, his family buzzing around him back up in Manchester. There's no way I could get anywhere near him. It would be too dangerous for us both. I always knew it was going to end. I didn't think it would be like this. In a perverse way, this might all be for the best.'

'You don't know this is the end.'

'I do.' Suddenly Maddie couldn't speak, her lips quivered. She stifled her emotion, took a deep breath and swallowed. 'And you're the last person I wanted to see me like this. Stupid and weak.'

'No one ever fell in love and got weaker, Maddie. You didn't, I didn't. No one does. And when you lose someone, you get stronger still. Because you have to.'

The emotion in his voice was back and it was genuine, and suddenly she didn't feel so empty, so alone in her grief. She wasn't concerned that she didn't have her sunglasses to hide behind either. Maybe she didn't need to be hiding her emotions anymore. Not around Harry. Now they had more than trust.

She leaned a little to her right until her head found his shoulder. The train rocked gently. She closed her eyes. Her nostrils filled with the smell of his wax jacket. Adam had once worn one with a very similar scent. She listened to the train clack and bump as it whisked her away from London and towards her home. For a moment she could almost fool herself that she was sitting next to Adam Yarwood, that Grace Hughes's troubles might be over for good, that her own world hadn't been turned completely upside down and that she knew exactly what she should do next.

Almost.

THE END

Thank you for reading this book. If you enjoyed it please leave feedback on Amazon, and if there is anything we missed or you have a question about then please get in touch. The author and publishing team appreciate your feedback and time reading this book.

Our email is office@joffebooks.com

www.joffebooks.com

ALSO BY CHARLIE GALLAGHER

MADDIE IVES
Book 1: HE IS WATCHING YOU
Book 2: HE WILL KILL YOU

LANGTHORNE POLICE SERIES
Book 1: BODILY HARM
Book 2: PANIC BUTTON
Book 3: BLOOD MONEY
Book 4: END GAME

STANDALONES
MISSING
THEN SHE RAN
HER LAST BREATH

Made in the USA
Columbia, SC
06 May 2023